Penguin Education

Sociology of the Family

Edited by Michael Anderson

Penguin Modern Sociology Readings

General Editor

Tom Burns

Sociology of the Family

Selected Readings

Edited by Michael Anderson

Penguin Books

Penguin Books Ltd., Harmondsworth,
Middlesex, England
Penguin Books Inc., 7110 Ambassador Road,
Baltimore, Md 21207, U.S.A.
Penguin Books Australia Ltd,
Ringwood, Victoria, Australia

First published 1971
Reprinted 1971
This selection copyright © Michael Anderson, 1971
Introduction and notes copyright © Michael Anderson, 1971

Made and printed in Great Britain by
C. Nicholls & Company Ltd
Set in Monotype Times

Contents

Introduction

This volume presents a set of Readings on the sociology of the family. Its main emphasis is on family systems of the kind which occur in Western industrial society, and on the problems which any rigorous study of them inevitably involves. The geographical exclusiveness of this volume does not mean that I think we can fully understand the wide variations that are found in the family systems of Western societies by looking at them in isolation from the rest of the world. Rather, what is being suggested is that we must not merely try to place Western family types in certain broad theoretical boxes which they share with many other societies, but also must recognize that these societies have certain special characteristics and that, in consequence, hypotheses and methodological tools have to be somewhat more refined and more elaborate if we are to understand the variation in patterns of family relationships which obtain within the Western types themselves. This volume gives some idea of how far we have come along this road. A forthcoming volume in the Penguin series will set these Western systems in their broad cross-cultural setting.

The family in these societies remains a vitally important element in social structure. Its members bear prime responsibility for both the timing and number of conceptions of new members of the society, and for their nurture and early socialization. It is the normal unit in which resources are pooled and distributed for consumption, around which residence is organized and domestic tasks performed. Its members are for each other the principal source of affective and ascriptive relationships in an otherwise predominantly competitive society. To them falls also the main burden of meeting the many idiosyncratic needs of society's members which fall outside the scope of bureaucratically organized agencies. The family in these societies is, in sum, a collectivity which makes multiple and pressing demands on almost every individual, demands which inevitably influence his ability to participate in and meet the role demands of other collectivities of which he is a member. No social organization which is associated with such emotive issues as 'love', marriage and 'the home', and with such frequent matters of social concern as divorce, child rearing or sexual compatibility can be considered as unimportant in the layman's definition of his social world, nor in the sociologist's field of potential topics for research.

Yet, in spite of its apparent importance, and in spite of its many challenging unsolved problems, the reputation of the sociology of the family among professional sociologists is still rather low. Many see it as an academic deadend which contributes little or nothing of importance to the discipline as a whole; as concentrating on trivial and value-laden problems of more concern to journalism or social work than 'hard' sociology; as methodologically naïve and conceptually underdeveloped.

It is indeed certainly true that the sociology of the family took much longer than most other fields to escape from a past dominated by impressionistic ethnography and a concern with social problems shot through with preconceptions, into a new 'scientific' approach pushing towards explanatory theory-building and based on rigorous hypothesis testing. Only recently has it begun to break free into a theoretical and methodological style of its own adapted to the problems with which it must grapple. For, far more than most of its critics have realized, one reason for the slow development of a rigorous and challenging sociology of the family lies in problems largely unique to the very nature of its topic of study.

One source of difficulty lies in the special force in this field of the paradox with which every sociologist has to contend, namely, that he knows at the outset too much about what he is supposed to be studying. Normally he has been and still is a fully participating member, in the society he is studying, of a family unit of his own. He has been socialized from birth into certain beliefs about the family, and has internalized his society's rules. Thus he finds it difficult to stand back, view the family critically from without, and see beneath the manifest structures and functions of the system to the constraints which lie behind the traditional and normatively prescribed patterns he knows so well. Contrast, say, the industrial sociologist, who comes to an organization a stranger to many of its empirical features and must turn immediately to his sociologically trained perceptions for guides by which to order what he observes.

A second source of difficulty is closely related to the first. Because the family sociologist is so deeply involved in the system, and because family values have such strong, emotionally charged moral overtones, it is hard for him to view family behaviour in a value-free way. As a citizen he has learned to see certain forms of behaviour as social problems. He has thus found it very difficult to see behind these to the sociological problems, and too often has gone on to pose these problems in commonplace, man-in-the-street terms. He has tried to answer the question 'Why do divorces occur?' without asking the prior and more general question, why should couples want to stay married. He has asked whether industrialization is breaking up the kinship system, without asking first why actors should be committed to relationships with kin anyway. Societal pressures for quick solutions to problems that are themselves usually seen from the standpoint of a traditional consensus only present a further obstacle.

A third set of problems concerns respondents. The culture defines family relationships as intimate and personal matters, and many respondents are naturally reluctant to be interviewed about their family lives. It smacks of the worst kind of nosey-parkerism. The strong normative overtones which characterize family roles may also affect data reliability, with respondents tending to conceal serious tensions and to reply in terms of what they perceive as socially approved behaviour.

In addition to these problems of research method, there are major theoretical difficulties. Firstly, unlike most other social organizations, individual nuclear families have a life-cycle typically advancing from courtship, to marriage, to child rearing, to children leaving home, and then to dissolution. This poses many interesting research problems, but these in turn demand theoretical and conceptual frameworks capable of handling them; we are not often in sociology concerned with exploring the establishment, dissolution and orderly change in the organizations we study. The life-cycle also means that we usually cannot analyse *the* family, only the family at a particular point in the life-cycle, and the changes between these points. The impact of social change will vary with the family's life-cycle stage, as well as with the actor who is under consideration. Moreover, many of the variations in relational patterns that we must explain are not so much qualitative differences as variations in the *timing* of well-nigh universal increases or decreases in the intensity of an actor's involvement in a particular role.

Secondly, the family, unlike most other social organizations, largely lacks both clearly indentifiable boundaries and formal structure, and any one set of clearly specified functions; in other words, it lacks the conceptual benchmarks on which we usually base our analysis of difference and change. Instead, the kinship system is best seen as a recruitment base, organized around blood and marriage ties, with its theoretically almost infinite expansion limited only by intermarriage. It is a base from which, in different societies and different sub-groups within societies, different individuals at different periods of their lives, as a response to varying needs and constraints, come to interact with each other with varying degrees of frequency and affective content. It provides, to a widely diverse extent, almost any conceivable function, while sharing most functions with other organizations or primary groups. As a result of this variation, any one set of descriptive categories – which may be ideally suited for the analysis of one family system at one stage of the life-cycle in one place at one time – may be totally unsuited for the analysis in anything like its full subtlety of the same system at another time, and of adequately exploring the intervening changes. The only possible solution for this is to take each dyadic relationship separately, and to explore it over its normal life-cycle.

Finally, families are made up of small groups, and some of these groups in some cultures and sub-cultures perform important affective functions for their members. In many cultures, including most traditional societies, this fact need concern the sociologist but little, since role performance is fairly rigorously controlled by normative sanctions from without, and by internalization of a relatively homogeneous and traditional culture. In addition, because the family in these societies usually lays relatively greater stress on instrumental rather than affective functions, interpersonal compatibility of an affective kind is less important. But modern Western societies are rather different. Because they are heterogeneous and changing societies, there is considerable normative uncertainty. Nuclear family units are relatively insulated from all but very vague supervision and control of their behaviour by outsiders. The adequate performance of emotional functions is a primary criterion by which the nuclear family's success is judged. All these differences obviously vary in incidence from sub-culture to sub-culture even within Western societies, and the reasons for this are obviously a research issue. But the consequence is a much greater degree of variability in family patterns even within socio-economic and life-cycle sub-aggregates than is the case in traditional societies. Even where normative controls and reference groups are important in influencing behaviour, one still has to ask how and why their influence is being maintained. The differing role demands that are made on different individuals from outside the family, and the different resources that each can muster for the implicit or explicit bargaining process by which the precise pattern of any individual family relationship is increasingly determined, are among the other major sources of the variations that must be explained. Because these role demands and resources are largely socially determined, their mode of operation becomes a major focus of the sociological study of the family. Under certain circumstances, too, some social-psychological variables come to play a much greater part in determining the precise patterns of relationships observed, and these, or at least the situations under which they operate in any particular way, also become a topic of concern.

These would have been formidable problems for any area of sociology to overcome. That they were only really tackled so recently can, I think, be related to at least two sets of factors. Firstly, it was only from the later 1950s, when social action and interpersonal attraction theories, and role bargaining and exchange perspectives began to reach a more advanced degree of formalization, that many of the necessary theoretical tools became available. Further advances in some areas still await further development of one or other of these approaches.

One might, however, have expected that the sociology of the family would have pioneered some of these new or revamped perspectives, rather than, with notable exceptions, waiting for their development elsewhere. That this did not happen can probably be attributed to the two dominant focuses of those engaged in research in this field until comparatively recently. On the one hand were those whose research was oriented with at least one eye to social improvement or moral guidance. The disadvantages of this approach I have already discussed, but this concern with problems did make its contribution, because it encouraged quantitative empirical research, though usually on samples limited to one class or group. It also encouraged a focus on processes of interaction within nuclear family units.

On the other hand were those who were primarily influenced by social anthropological perspectives and techniques. The best of this group (though they are still perhaps a minority, given the continuing emphasis in social anthropology on the study of a culture rather than on the study of a theoretically interesting problem) did aim at developing theoretical propositions to explain what they found. But their focus was usually, and perhaps necessarily, broadly cross-cultural and thus tended to stress the similarities rather than the differences between the family patterns found within Western industrial societies. The rest, when they studied Western societies, focused mainly on a descriptive community-study approach which, while it provided a mass of data, was seldom integrated into any wider theoretical framework, and often totally unrelated in coverage or indices to any other piece of research. In addition, their perspectives and research methods, developed for very different societies, were not easily adaptable to a heterogeneous and changing society where the main focus of theoretical interest was the variation between and within social groups and sub-cultures. In a society where normative pressures were only of a very generalized kind, where no two actors had even similar role sets and expectations, and where the pattern of relationships which emerged in any family was as much the result of the almost naked use of bargaining power as of long hallowed tradition, theories based on structural functionalist principles and on implicit assumptions of consensus were obviously inadequate on their own.

Equally inadequate taken alone, for a scientifically oriented discipline in a heterogeneous society, were research methods based almost wholly on impressionistic observation supplemented by largely unstructured interviews and chats with 'key informants'. Such techniques make it difficult for anyone except the researcher to probe assumptions and preconceptions, to criticize indicators, or to assess the viability of possible alternative interpretations. All of which is not to say, however, that such methods will not continue to have a role, particularly for exploratory purposes.

The Readings in this volume show many traces of this diverse methodological and theoretical past. There are representatives of both the holistic structural and normative anthropological tradition, and of the newer approaches based on actor-focused, life-cycle/exchange/social psychological perspectives. Their different points of emphasis and contributions are often instructive, with the former typically pointing to the broad framework of constraints, normative and otherwise, within which the latter can explore the considerable variations. The methodological range is as large, from the almost purely impressionistic to the rigorously mathematical. Most of the writings I have selected have in common, however, some attempt to be cumulatively theory-building, to seek explanation within a broader conceptual framework than that of the situation under discussion. Those that do not, seem important because they provide valuable data or insights or point to difficulties or inconsistencies that have still to be overcome.

Too often in sets of Readings, it seems to me, the student is presented with only one position over a wide range of issues. These positions then appear as the unique truth handed down from above. Unfortunately, at least in the sociology of the family, the true situation is not like this. There are controversies and unsolved problems. Here, then, I have limited the coverage to a smaller number of what I see as important issues at the present time. Where divergent views exist, I have tried to produce a challenge to the reader by showing him these controversies either by including at least brief observations from both sides of an argument, or by presenting criticisms which seem to point to the need for future research, or by producing papers whose authors point clearly to such a need.

After an opening section which attempts to show at least something of the diversity of family patterns and of changes which we have to explain, the volume is organized around the patterns and content of dyadic family relationships at points in the life-cycle, looking in turn at relationships of adults with parents, siblings and wider kin, at the married couple in courtship, on-going marriage and dissolution, and at their relationships with their small children.

Part One
Change and Diversity in Family Systems

The Introduction pointed out that the Western industrial family has a number of characteristics which differentiate it sharply from family systems of the type usually found in pre-industrial societies. The excerpts from Arensberg and Kimball's classic study when contrasted with the rest of the volume clearly show many of these differences. Here we have in Ireland a family system where each role is precisely defined by long tradition, where the family and economic systems are intimately related, and where economic and community sanctions of the greatest severity are imposed on those who deviate from the normatively sanctioned patterns.

Parsons (Reading 2) is implicitly contrasting the family patterns of Western industrial employees with those of something like the Irish type. He argues that industrialization removes many functions from the family. But, in contrast to earlier views which tended to see this as part of a general decline in the family (Ogburn, 1938; Zimmerman, 1947), he proposes that an industrial society still logically requires a stable family system to maintain balanced personalities in the men who are subject to its competitive demands, and to ensure the successful socialization of new members of the society. However, Parsons argues, the demands of the occupational system that the individual be totally committed to it and be prepared therefore to be both geographically and socially mobile do imply that adults' involvement in their wider kinship system be at a low level. It is for these reasons that urban-industrial societies are typified by relatively stable but isolated nuclear family units (and see the discussion in Part Two).

Linton (Reading 3) agrees with Parsons that the isolated

nuclear family is becoming dominant, but, approaching the problem from an individual rather than a functionalist, system-based standpoint, he argues that these changes follow from the fact that industrialization allows both men and women greater freedom from the normative and direct economic control of others. In consequence, the individual is able, within limits, to vary his family relationships at his own instigation. This leads Linton to stress much more than Parsons the potential fragility of, and tensions involved in, family relationships in modern industrial societies.

Reading 4 from Kerr's study of a Liverpool dock area, and Reading 5 from Klein's commentary on Dennis, Henriques and Slaughter's comprehensive and insightful study of a mining town, remind us that even within industrial societies not all families conform to Parsons's isolated companionate type. In these areas, social and geographical mobility are rare, there is a long history of economic uncertainty, and both men and women are unwilling or unable to break away on marriage from their pre-existing close relationships with friends and kin (compare for one explanation Reading 16).

Parsons's writings, and those of earlier authors, set off a mass of research into the impact of industrialization on family systems (excellently summarized in Goode, 1963a) which suggested, in general, that modernization has tended to break up traditional kinship systems, and that it is indeed followed by some convergence onto a family system of a more nuclear type. Just what processes are involved remains, however, obscure (but see Goode, 1963b, and the intelligent discussion in Harris, 1969, pp. 97–148).

Most of the research on this topic falls outside the geographical scope of this volume, and the impact of industrialization on Western family systems has been little explored. Anderson (Reading 6) compares patterns of co-residence in pre-industrial and industrializing England with those of the present day. Pre-industrial patterns were predominantly nuclear (and compare for traditional societies, for example, Nimkoff and Middleton, 1960). The problems and potentialities offered by industrialization seem here to have actually strengthened bonds between parents and their married children. Of course, co-residence is not necessarily a valid indicator of the affective or even of the functional significance of kinship (see Part Two), but in this case there is reason to believe that it does tell us something of theoretical interest, at least for the poorer section of the population.

References

GOODE, W. J. (1963a), *World Revolution and Family Patterns*, Free Press.

GOODE, W. J. (1963b4), 'The process of role bargaining in the impact of urbanization and industrialization on family systems', *Current Sociology*, vol. 12, pp. 1–13.

HARRIS, C. C. (1969), *The Family*, Allen & Unwin.

NIMKOFF, M. F., and MIDDLETON, R. (1960), 'Types of family and types of economy', *American Sociological Review*, vol. 25, pp. 215–25.

OGBURN, W. F. (1938), 'The changing family', *Family*, vol. 19, pp. 139–43.

ZIMMERMAN, C. C. (1947), *Family and Civilization*, Harper & Row.

1 C. M. Arensberg and S. T. Kimball

The Small Farm Family in Rural Ireland

Excerpts from C. M. Arensberg and S. T. Kimball,
Family and Community in Ireland, Harvard University Press, 2nd edn,
1968, pp. 59–60, 45–56, 63–147. (1st edn, 1940.)

The relations of the members of the farm family are best described in terms of the patterns which uniformity of habit and
association build up. They are built up within the life of the
farm household and its daily and yearly work. The relations of
the fathers to sons and mothers to sons fall repeatedly into regular and expectable patterns of this kind that differ very little
from farm to farm.

If we are to understand them, then, we must trace them out
of this setting and see in what manner they offer us explanation
of Irish rural behavior. In terms of a formal sociology, such as
Simmel might give us, the position of the parents is one of extreme
superordination, that of the children of extreme subordination.
The retention of the names 'boy' and 'girl' reflects the latter
position. Sociological adulthood has little to do with physiological
adulthood. Age brings little change of modes of address and ways
of treating and regarding one another in the relationships within
the farm family. The relative positions of the parties must be
stated in terms of the events taking place between them. These
events run over the years and redefine relationships in their course.
This kind of development characterizes and gives form to family
relations and to the farm family itself.

The long years of intimate association in the acts and events of
a common life build up very complete adaptations and very close
emotional bonds among all those who share the life together.
The bonds must be compatible; adjustment is made all round,
again through gradual habituation. Otherwise conflict is ready
to set off young against old, men against women, persons against
one another. There is reciprocity of obligation and expectancy.

But the point of interest here is that it is the bonds that must be dealt with for understanding, not anything within them or the activities associated with them. Here there is an absolute co-incidence of 'social' and 'economic' factors within single relationships. In the case of a small farmer and his son, there is only one relationship; to separate their social from their economic activities is meaningless. They are one in fact, and, as far as the peasants are concerned, they are one in name.

Thus any of the words designating status in the relationship, such as father, son, owner, employee, heir, etc., might well be used, but in actual practice the first two of them are sufficient to cover all the activities of the relationship. Only the statuses of father and son are distinguished by the country people. These words are the only designations of status that are to be heard among them. All others are unnecessary. They are not part of the experience of the small farmers except as they become so when the outside world breaks in. Consequently, terms designating status are not to be understood or interpreted on a basis of *a priori* or philological meaning, but as references to the events in connexion with which they were used. [. . .]

At crucial points in the annual round we have sketched out, the whole family lends its labor. Particularly at the turf making, the hay saving and the potato planting, all members work together in bog, garden or meadow. Though tasks vary according to age, sex and relative status, the group works in a unison of effort in which a definite rhythm can be observed. Under the direction of the father, the husband and farm-owner, the variously divided tasks are correlated to the end in view. The periods of common effort in which all the family members, even to the children, are working in unison are also those in which the greatest speed is needed. At such times the pattern of daily household activity suffers; the regularities belonging to it are transferred to the field. Tea and bread, and perhaps sometimes heavier fare, make their appearance at the regular times, no longer within the house but on the edge of bog or meadow.

Within this concerted effort, a division of labor between the sexes and upon the basis of age appears. The division, however, is not confined entirely to farm work. It covers the whole field of the behavior of the individual. It divides obligations, duties, sentiments and values of the group, and is enforced by the group. It pertains both among the members of the family groups and in the community at large. It controls individual action and attitudes and gives a standard of comparison between one's own farm work and that of one's fellows. The interests and the desires of the individual concur in large measure with the norm, and he finds reward and pleasure in it. He can rely upon similar obligations and duties toward himself on the part of others.

The greatest scope and variation in activity which we have seen to fall to the lot of the male takes its form in part from his relationship to the others of the household. On the normal farm there is an adult male farmer who is husband, father and owner of the farm. Within the group he has the controlling role, subject to conventional restrictions of his authority. In farm work, as we have seen, he directs the activity of the family as it works in concert. In his special province he looks after and cares for the cattle, has full control over them, and takes complete charge of buying and selling them. He disposes of the income they bring in. But all this he is obliged to do in the interests of his wife and children. Should he fail to get a good price or prove a bad judge of cattle or handle them badly, his wife and children are entitled to a just anger against him.

As we have seen, all the work requiring heavy effort in garden and field falls to his lot. He makes and tends the drains, fences, barns and shelters, which protect both cattle and garden produce. He works the fields and gardens with plough, mower, harrow and spade. All the agricultural implements and the heavy work involved in their use and in the use of the horse are his province.

The produce which such work assures is his to be disposed of, as is all income derived from it. He may order it as he sees fit; yet his first charge is to the family he heads. The division of income between household needs and the demands of farm and livestock springs from his decisions; yet it is a matter of nice adjustment between himself and his wife in favor of the group as a whole. Custom and his own desire demand that he provide for his household to the best of his ability. Though he can make what disposal he will of the funds earned by the labor of the group, his wife and children can expect as of right that he shall make it for the family as a whole in which each member receives his share. For the work of his wife is complementary to his, and in its own sphere of as great importance to the livelihood and the organization of the family unit. While he may demand and expect of his wife that she fulfill her household duties, so may she demand and expect that he fulfill his in the management and working of the farm and in providing for herself and the children.

As regards income, all money derived from the sale of eggs and butter, the chief concern of the woman beyond the house itself, belongs to her to dispose of as she sees fit. Yet the fruits of her labors are also subject to the needs of the family unit, husband and children.

The division of labor between the sexes arises within a field of larger interests and obligations. It is part of the behavior expected reciprocally of husband and wife. It is a functional element of their relationship within the family.

The training each sex receives from childhood in farm work reflects this fact. Each learns his or her part in farm economy, not as a vocational preparation but as a making ready for marriage. The boy acquires his man's skills and techniques for the farm and farm family he may head himself some day; the girl learns the woman's role as an integral part of her future state of wife and mother. Each learns to expect of the other not only the loving consideration of husband or wife but the proper skills in farm economy.

Among the small farmers this dichotomy of tasks assigned to the sexes in the economy of the farm family is even more than the reciprocal duties of husband and wife, father and mother. It is also an integral part of the personalities of all men and women of the peasant's own kind. One can get many expressions of attitude of this sort. They show that the division of labor between males and females is regarded as corresponding to the natural propensities of the two sexes. That a man should concern himself with a woman's work, such as the sale of eggs or the making of butter, is the subject of derisive laughter, while a woman's smaller hands make it 'natural' for her to be a better hand at milking the cows.

Even when the communal labor of the family is demanded

and women take their place in bog, garden and meadow, a definite role is assigned them. Usually it is the lighter tasks which are known as women's work. There is no formal taboo confining a woman to women's work. Heavy work is merely felt to be a hardship upon her. At the potato planting the women do the arduous work of planting the sprouts which they have prepared, bending over to put them into the ridges prepared by the men. They do their share, if necessary, of cultivating, but they are not generally accustomed to the spade, which like the plough, the harrow, the mower, scythe and turf 'slan' is regarded as a masculine implement. At the potato lifting they go along behind the man who turns the potatoes out of the ridge with spade and plough, and pick them up. At the haymaking, the pitching, raking and some of the building of the haycocks are left to them. But the mowing, especially where it involves the horse-drawn mowing machine, and the building of the rick in the haggard, are masculine skills. In all cases of field work of this sort the role of the woman is usually auxiliary. The same holds in turf cutting. The men do the actual cutting in the bog trenches, while the women knead the peat into briquets and pile it for drying.

The many attitudes and beliefs which surround this type of division of labor illustrate again the socially determined character of the distinctions and their genesis in the intersexual relationship. Just as the man's work is the harder, the more various, and the wider in scope, so the attitudes express a greater valuation of the men's work within the limits of the restriction. Thus on several occasions the authors have heard men admonish a woman for interrupting with such phrases as: 'Woman, be silent while we [men] are talking about ploughing.' Ridicule and laughter greet suggestions that either sex busy itself with the work of the other, though in the case of a woman doing a man's work some of the praise bestowed upon surprising successes meets her if she does it well. There is also an entire body of popular belief and superstition surrounding the dichotomy in farm labor.

These beliefs and attitudes serve to uphold the conventional division and to evaluate the necessary behavioral specialization which is basic to the interrelationships within the farm family. The connexion between family status and labor performed brings about an identification between them. Ridicule and graver charges of unmanliness and unwomanliness can be brought to reaffirm the conventions against the offender in either sphere. Just as in the non-economic life of the family, behavior is enjoined upon members on the basis of sex, so, when the group acts in economic enterprise, different but complementary roles become conventional for each sex. The interesting point is the identification. For the farm family, farm work is as much a family matter as is sharing the same table.

Within the framework of the division of labor on the basis of sex, there is another just as great division on the basis of age differences. Though all the males of the farm family share the work which is regarded as the masculine province, there can be immediately observed great differences in the practice of the masculine technique by the male family members; the same can be observed in the feminine province.

These further divisions of tasks likewise reflect family status. They are part of the behavior expected of the farmer as a family member, and take their form in the complex of his relationship to his fellows within the group. The controls exercised among members in work and in the life of the family in general show themselves a constant pattern to be observed from farm to farm wherever one elects to examine the daily and annual rounds of activity.

Thus in any of the tasks which the group must perform in its economy, the division of labor between the adult farmer-father and his sons may be observed. The father is owner and director of the enterprise; in him the farm and its income are vested; in the community it is known as his and the sons are spoken of as his 'boys'. Thus in the draining of a field or the sale of cattle in a fair, the sons, even though fully adult, work under their father's eye and refer necessary decisions to him.

Perhaps the best method of illustrating this relationship is to present it from the point of view of the growing individual who takes his place in the farm family. He forms part of the productive unit which is his own family. The techniques of farming are passed on to him, and he learns them under the direction of his father, uncles and brothers. At their hands he acquires the conditioning which will fit him to form a farm family of his own, thus to continue the traditional pattern. Naturally, his conditioning is more than merely technological; he gets on the farm the full training which makes him a member of his class and time.

The growing child ordinarily sees his father as owner and principal worker of the farm. When the whole family group of father, mother, children, and whatever other relatives may be living with them, works in concert, as at the potato planting, the turf cutting and the haymaking, it is the father who directs the group's activities, himself doing the heavy tasks. The father looks after and takes care of the cattle, delegating minor tasks connected with them to his sons. Even though the cattle may be generally discussed by the household, he has full control of them, disposes of them, drives them to the fair, handles and uses the money got for them. If he fails to get a good price, handles the beasts badly, or proves himself a bad judge of them, the criticism of his wife and neighbors soon establishes the value of careful husbandry in the son's mind.

The father does all the constant heavy work necessary to keep the land in condition in so rainy and treeless a country. He makes drains, ditches, fences, walls, shelters and barns, as we have seen. As the son grows older, he learns to help at these tasks, finally taking them over. The father prepares the garden, ploughs, plants and harrows, does all the spade work of cultivation and everything involving the use of horses and agricultural implements. The son soon learns that these are men's tasks, and he gradually assumes his share of them. The adult men of the neighborhood rival one another at these tasks; they chaff and boast back and forth over their prowess. The son cannot fail to hear and value the techniques which he acquires.

He learns those techniques in a narrow school. Where tradition is still so strong and the incursions of trained agriculturalists still relatively infrequent, as among the small farmers, there is little variation from the tried and true way. Each operation and each tool demand a technique of their own. The father makes sure that the son learns it well. Command, rivalry, ridicule and many an adage and bit of folklore all conspire to the same result.

The father must make sure that the son has learned the right and traditional technique. For he must be ready to stand his ground with anyone in the community in farm skills. Every operation becomes the intimate concern of his neighbors; a man must hold his head high. More important, many skills are plied in cooperative activities, in turf cutting, haymaking and much of the work of the garden. In such cases, a definite rhythm is necessary for greater effectiveness among the cooperating workers, and any deviation from the accepted technique destroys such unison. This, too, the son learns at this father's hands.

At home the son learns that building and repairing the houses, sheds and other structures of the farm is men's work and that the duty of performing it devolves on the father. He watches his father buy and use all the feeding stuffs needed for farm animals and learns something of the nice adjustment which must be made between the expenditures of this kind and those demanded by the women of the household for food, clothing and household needs. He finds himself included in the family deliberations which impress upon him the economic interdependence of the family and the division of labor between men and women.

The process is a gradual one. It is an integral part of daily experience protracted over many years. In his earliest childhood, of course, the mother looms larger in the child's consciousness than the father. The child's first duties, as soon as he can speak and walk, are to run on petty errands to neighbors and nearby 'friends'. Soon he is taking his father's meals to him in the fields or going on errands to the nearest shop. Until he is seven and has gone through First Communion, his place is in the house with the women, and his labor is of very little importance. After First Communion, at six or seven, he begins to be thrown more with his elder brothers, and comes to do small chores which bring him more and more into contact with his father and with the other men of the neighborhood. By the time he is ten or eleven he will be brought home from school, if needed, to take his part in the important agricultural work of the year, particularly at spring sowing and hay harvest. But not till he passes Confirmation and leaves school (generally at the same time) does he take on full men's work. Even then, as he becomes adult and takes on more and more of the heavy tasks of the farm work, he never escapes his father's direction until his father dies or makes over the farm to him at his marriage.

If economic apprenticeship is also a process of conditioning within the family, so likewise the direction of economic enterprise coincides with the dominant and controlling role of the parent within the family. The son is subordinated in both spheres to his parents, particularly the father. Rather, the spheres are one.

For the child grows up within the full complex of life within the family. The petty errands which constitute his first steps in farm work are a mere incident in the conditioning he receives and the relationships he builds up with his fellows. He develops the sentiments of affection and dependence upon his mother and the other family members in those years in the care and attention he receives at their hands. He learns the code of conduct which constitutes the folkways of his group and the reciprocal relations within his family in a gradual process of training over years. This conduct ranges from the errands he runs for family members superordinate to him, to the learning of his prayers and the development of the sentiments which make of sexual behavior of any kind an offense and of that within the family, incest.

Thus the same landmark in his life which marks his beginning to do the minor chores of farm work after six or seven marks a change of his life within the household, for thereafter he sleeps with his brothers and the separation which begins to take him from his sisters in work and play now separates them within the household.

Later his sharing of chores with his brothers in farm work is again merely incidental to his long years of life with them. By the same token the commanding position which the father (and the mother) exercise over him in farm work is but one aspect of their control. We shall have occasion to see in a later section how this dominance expresses itself in household arrangement and in the grouping of individuals in other spheres than farm work.

This parental dominance continues as long as the father lives. Even though the major work of the farm devolves upon the sons, they have no control of the direction of farm activities nor of the disposal of farm income. They go to market and fair from the time they are twelve years old, but they buy or sell little, if anything, for themselves. Thus the small farmer and his sons are often seen at the fairs and markets together, but it is the farmer-father who does the bargaining. Once when one of the authors asked a countryman about this at a potato market, he explained that he could not leave his post for long because his full-grown son 'isn't well-known yet and isn't a good hand at selling'. If the son wants a half crown to go to a hurley match or to take a drink on market day with friends, he must get it from his father. The authors have seen many sons, fully adult, come into shops to buy some farm requirement, such as a bag of meal, and say that the 'old fellow' will pay for it. And a few days later the old fellow arrives to pay for the goods 'my young fellow got'. The son may, of course, earn money in employment off the farm, as many do at work on the roads in occasional employment with governmental bodies or large farmers. But in this case he is expected to contribute the larger part of the money to the general household expenses as long as he remains on the farm.

The procedure of the Land Commission, a government body, in providing additions to small holdings from the break-up of large estates illustrates well this retention of parental authority. It is the policy of the Commission to employ local men as much as possible in the reclamation and fencing work necessary at the division of an estate; the owners of the holdings to be enlarged are entitled to the work. Consequently, when the work is given, the farmer-owners are assigned it. But it is the sons who do the work, and at the pay-off the 'old fellows' walk sometimes many miles to be paid the wages their sons have earned. In one case of land division which the authors witnessed, a Land Commission official walked about the estate pointing out the plots which the selected farmers were to get. The farmers followed in a body at a respectful distance, each ready to step forward when his name was called. Behind them came all the young men of the neighborhood, the farmers' sons. When it was necessary to send someone back to a farmhouse or to cut up stakes to mark boundaries, the orders were transmitted from the official to the farmer and from the farmer to his sons, though these were in the majority of cases adult men. Likewise in country post offices, even after the farm has been made over to the son and the 'old people' have the old-age pension, it is the son who comes to collect it for them.

Even at forty-five and fifty, if the old couple have not yet made over the farm, the countryman remains a 'boy' in respect to farm work and in the rural vocabulary. A deputy to the *Dáil* (the Irish parliament) raised a considerable laugh in 1933, which echoed into the daily newspapers, when he inadvertently dropped into the country idiom and pleaded for special treatment in land division for 'boys of forty-five and older' who have nothing in prospect but to wait for their fathers' farms. Likewise, a countryman, complaining to one of the authors about his position, said: 'You can be a boy here forever as long as the old fellow is still alive.'

It goes without saying that the father exercises his control over the whole activity of the 'boy'. It is by no means confined to their work together. Indeed, the father is the court of last resort, which dispenses punishment for deviations from the norm of conduct in all spheres. Within the bounds of custom and law he has full power to exercise discipline. Corporal punishment is not a thing of the past in Ireland, and, especially in the intermediate stages of the child's development, from seven to puberty, it gets full play.

It is during those years that the characteristic relationship between father and son is developed in rural communities. The son has suffered a remove from the previous almost exclusive control of his mother, in which an affective content of sympathy and indulgence was predominant, and is brought into contact for the first time with the father and older men. But the transfer is not completed. There is a hiatus in his development through the years of school when his participation in men's work and his relationship with his father has little chance of developing into an effective partnership. A real union of interests does not take place until after Confirmation and school-leaving, when for the first time his exclusive contacts and his entire day-to-day activity, particularly in farm work, will be with his father and the older men.

This fact colors greatly the relationship of father and son, as far as affective content goes. There is none of the close companionship and intimate sympathy which characterizes, at least ideally, the relationship in other groups. Where such exists, it is a matter for surprised comment to the small farmers. In its place there is developed, necessarily perhaps, a marked respect, expressing itself in the tabooing of many actions, such as smoking, drinking and physical contact of any sort, which can be readily observed in any small farm family. Coupled with this is the lifelong subordination the retention of the name 'boy' implies, which is never relaxed even in the one sphere in which farmer-father and son can develop an intense community of interest – farm work. Nothing prevents the development of great mutual pride, the boy in his experienced and skillful mentor, tutor and captain in work, and the man in a worthy and skillful successor and fellow workman, but on the other hand everything within the behavior developed in the relationship militates against the growth of close mutual sympathy. As a result, the antagonisms inherent in such a situation often break through very strongly when conflicts arise.

The division of labor in the masculine sphere between father and sons, then, is more than an arrangement in farm management. It is very directly part of the systems of controls, duties and sentiments which make up the whole family life. The apprenticeship and the long subordination of the sons in farm work are reflections of the entirety of their relationship to parents; it is impossible to treat the two spheres of behavior separately. [...]

The work of the woman is as important in farm economy as the men's. The coincidence between family status and economic role holds for them as well. Women's work on the small farm is complementary to that of the men, as we have seen, though, of course, it is quite distinct. The young girl growing up on the small farm learns this, just as the young man acquires the masculine techniques. The girl is thrown constantly with the mother and the older women of the household. After she is seven, her pursuits differ completely from those of her brother and, except as she is in very close constant association within the household, she has no working contact with her father.

Many minor tasks fall to the girl as she grows up, particularly driving and milking the cows. Her conditioning prepares her to fill the role her mother occupies in the household. All the interior of the house, the immediate vicinity of courts and haggard where the fuel is stacked, the well, the poultry yard and sheds are her concern. She learns to milk cows, feed the pig, tend the chickens and look after all the young animals through helping the older women. She learns the lore of disposing of eggs, butter and occasionally of some of the vegetable produce of the garden, potatoes and cabbage, and occasionally goes to market with her mother.

In the chief business of the women, the house itself, the preparation and serving of food and the repair and upkeep of clothing, she serves a never-ending daily apprenticeship. A young girl may often be delegated to look after the hearth, make and keep the fires going, etc. Only the mother makes small purchases of food and household goods. Only the mother bakes the great variety of breads. But by the time she leaves school, the girl may be proficient in these tasks too. So also with the butter making. Income derived from this and from poultry belongs to the older woman; the girl has no share until she herself has married.

In the past century (and in isolated regions still) most of the clothing of the small farmers was made at home by the women. Now, however, it is nearly all shop-bought. Certain vestiges of the former practice remain, however, in knitting sweaters, gloves, socks and scarfs; and in the country districts, at least of West and North Clare, there is a custom which demands that some woman of the house be always at work. If there is no other task on hand, they must occupy themselves with knitting. In former days, the daughters of the community might gather in a *meitheal*, or cooperative work group, under the supervision of older women for carding and spinning flax and wool. In any event, the younger woman, the girl, is at the older woman's command. [. . .]

The mothers and fathers who order farm life are themselves sons and daughters. They have or have had (before their creation of a family of their own upon the farm) much the same relationships with their parents as their children have with them. Indeed in many cases households comprise three generations. Grandfathers and grandmothers of the children live in the house. Family structure is not confined to the immediate present family group, but descends with each generation as the boys and girls reach social maturity at marriage and the creation of their own families. [. . .]

The nearly universal form of marriage in the Irish countryside unites transfer of economic control, land ownership, reformation of family ties, advance in family and community status, and entrance into adult procreative sex life. It is a central focus of rural life, a universal turning-point in individual histories. This form of marriage is known as matchmaking. It is the usual, in fact until recently the only respectable, method of marriage and usually too of inheritance.

In Figure 1 the reader will find a graphic representation of the description of the movement of the family and the reformation of relations which the match involves and which is the burden of this section. It explains itself, and it gives a very good illustration of the generalities. Organicists should take heart at its resemblance to an amoeba expanding and budding. But the resemblance is accidental. The examples we cite come nearly all from County Clare, but literary references and interviewing in other places have been made to show that matchmaking prevails almost universally among small farmers with very little local modification. It is furthermore embedded in the Irish (Gaelic) tongue and very old in Irish history.

A match (Gaelic, *cleamhnas*, marriage, and *spré*, a dowry) is a contractual marriage made by the parents or families of the marrying parties and involving the disposal of properties. Generally it begins with a farmer's casting round for a suitable girl for one of his sons who is to inherit his farm. The choice of the heir from among the sons rests in the father's hands. Historically, all the sons and daughters were provided for on the land, and, where possible, this is still the ideal situation, but the closer identification of family with one particular plot of land and the difficulty of land division fostered through three generations of agrarian agitation and land reform have prevented this. One son, then, is ordinarily to be 'settled on the land'. Typically today only one son remains, and he gets the farm.

In the words of one countryman, the procedure would be:

If I wanted to give my farm over to my son and I would be worth, say, two hundred pounds, I would know a fellow up the hill, for instance, that would be worth three hundred pounds. I would send up a

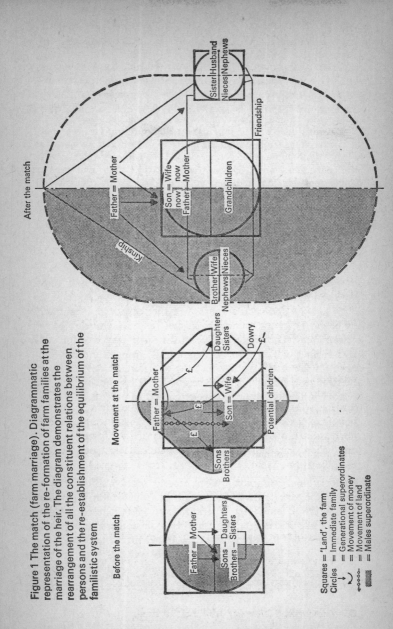

Figure 1 The match (farm marriage). Diagrammatic representation of the re-formation of farm families at the marriage of the heir. The diagram demonstrates the rearrangement of all the constituent relations between persons and the re-establishment of the equilibrium of the familistic system

Before the match

Father = Mother
Sons – Daughters
Brothers – Sisters

Movement at the match

Father = Mother
Sons
Brothers
Daughters
Sisters
Son = Wife
Potential children
Dowry
£
£
£

After the match

kinship

Father = Mother

Son = Wife
now
now Father—Mother
Grandchildren

Brother|Wife
Nephews|Nieces

Sister|Husband
Nieces|Nephews

Friendship

Squares = 'Land', the farm
Circles = Immediate family
= Generational superordinates
= Movement of money
= Movement of land
= Males superordinate

neighbour fellow to him and ask him if he would like to join my family in marriage. If the fellow would send back word he would and the girl would say she was willing [and the usual courtesies were exchanged], then on a day they agreed on I and the fellow would meet in Ennistymon [the local market town] and talk over the whole thing as to terms, maybe sitting on it the whole day. Then, before, if it was land I didn't know or the fellow came from afar off, I would walk his land and look at it and the cattle there were on it to make sure of the farm. Then we would go to a solicitor that day and make up the writings in Ennistymon. The money, say three hundred pounds, would be paid over in cash or in promissory notes, and it is usual here to divide it into two parts or sometimes more. One half is paid at the wedding, and the other is paid a year after.

This statement contains in essence nearly the whole of matchmaking. As the old fellow indicates, the initiative in the matter lies with the owner of the farm, usually the father of the boy. When the time comes for him to relinquish the farm, he lets it be known in the district to those who have daughters ready to be dowered. On the other hand, the father of the girl may often take the initiative, letting it be known that his daughter has a dowry at such and such a figure. In either case, when a suitable boy or girl has been found, the farmer sends an emissary to his or her parent. The relative value of the farms and the 'fortune' that a farmer will give for his daughter are generally pretty well known in the district, but where the two families are comparative strangers, or belong to different localities, the role of the emissary in laying the proposals of one set of parents before the other is more important. The emissary is not a relative of either party ordinarily. Certain individuals become well known locally as successful negotiators. In former days there was once a fully developed 'matchmaker' or marriage broker. The office is said to exist still in Connemara, but it has died out in Clare.

Quite often a well-known shopkeeper or local politician comes to play the role. One in particular in Ennistymon (a market town of 1200) came under the author's notice. The back room of his public house reserved for special customers became one of the centers of local matchmaking. It was there that the fathers of both boy and girl would meet and 'sit on the match'. Their deliberation, to the accompaniment of many bottles of stout, threshes out the whole matter of the disposal of the properties involved, the relative status of the families, and any possible barriers to the union, such as consanguinity, insanity or notorious crime in past ancestry.

The bargaining is a matter of nice adjustment between the 'fortune' and the farm. The custom known as 'walking the land', referred to above, ensures that the farm is roughly equivalent to the fortune, though each party strives for a higher valuation of its own claims. Thus, where a fortune of five hundred pounds has finally been agreed upon, the girl's father will have offered only four hundred and the boy's will have held out for six hundred, instancing all the prospects and advantages of his farm in support of his figure. Finally, through the offices of the intermediary and after concessions on each side, the two will 'split the difference' and thus reach an agreement. The decision rests with the fathers, but they will have had the quite vocal assistance of friends and older members of the kindred.

Perhaps the words of a countryman best describe the matching of values and prospects the bargaining entails. Farm and spouse are inextricably interwoven in his mind:

When a young man is once on the lookout for a lady, it is put through his friends for to get a suitable woman for his wife. It all goes by friendship and friends and meeting at public houses. The young man sends a speaker to the young lady and the speaker will sound a note to know what fortune she has, will she suit, and will she marry this Shrove? She and her friends will inquire what kind of a man is he, is he nice and steady? If he suits, they tell the speaker to go ahead and draw it down. So then he goes back to the young man's house and arranges for them to meet in such a place on such a night and we will see about it. The speaker goes with the young man and his father that night, and they meet the father of the girl and his friends or maybe his son and son-in-law. The first drink is called by the young man, the second by the young lady's father. The young lady's father asks the speaker what fortune do he want. He asks him the place of how many cows, sheep and horses it is. He asks what makings of a garden are in it; is there plenty of water or spring wells? Is it far from the road or on it? What kind of house is in it, slate or thatch? Are cabins good, are they slate or thatch? If it is too far in from the road, he won't take it. Backward places don't grow big fortunes. And he asks too is it near a chapel and the school or near town? If it is a nice place, near the road, and the place of eight cows, they are sure to ask three hundred and fifty pounds fortune. Then the young lady's father offers two hundred and fifty pounds. Then maybe the boy's father throws off fifty pounds. If the young lady's father still has two hundred and fifty pounds on it, the speaker divides the fifty pounds between them, so now it's two hundred and seventy-five. Then the young male says he is not willing to marry without three hundred pounds – but if she's a nice girl and a good housekeeper, he'll think of it. So there's another drink by the young man, and then another by the young lady's father, and so on with every second drink till they're near drunk. The speaker gets plenty and has a good day. After this, they appoint a place for the young people to see one another and be introduced. The young lady takes along her friends, and maybe another girl, and her brother and father and mother. The young man takes along his friends and the speaker. If they suit one another, they will then appoint a day to come and see the land. If they don't, no one will reflect on anybody, but they will say he or she doesn't suit. They do not say plainly what is wrong. The day before the girl's people come to see the land, geese are killed, the house is white-washed, whiskey and porter bought. The cows get a feed early so as to look good; and maybe they get an extra cow in, if they want one. Then next day comes the walking of the land. The young man stays outside in the street, but he sends his best friend in to show the girl's father round, but sure the friend won't show him the bad points. If the girl's father likes the land, he returns, and there will be eating and drinking until night comes on them. Then they go to an attorney until the next day and get the writings between the two parties and get the father [boy's] to sign over the land. Then there comes another day to fit her for a ring. The girl and boy meet in town some day. He buys her some present. They walk the town that day and all admire the pair and gander after them. [. . .]

After the 'walking of the land' and the making of the bargain, the two parties to marry go to a solicitor. There the agreements reached are cast into proper legal form. The 'writings' is a legal instrument conveying the ownership of the holding to the son. It is usually both marriage settlement and will. On the event of the stipulated marriage, the father conveys the farm and all appurtenances to his son in return for the portion brought in by the girl. The father makes also definite provisions for his own maintenance and that of his wife. Generally, these include the right to the 'grass of a cow', to food and the use of the hearth, perhaps the yield of one patch of potatoes, and the use of a room in the house. The room is nearly always, at least in West and North Clare, the one known as the 'west room'. To take care of possible disputes arising out of the failure of these provisions to work smoothly, certain very hard-headed stipulations are often included, allowing for the conversion of these rights into cash support or a lump sum.

In return for the farm, the father receives the fortune brought in by the girl and paid to him by her father. Furthermore, the provisions which must be made for other children are often transferred with the land. The father is now expected to give (if he has not given them already) portions to those of his children who are not to be settled at home on the land. Where the will and marriage settlement are one and the same document, these obligations are passed on to the inheriting son.

The following description of several 'writings' (which we examined) given by an Ennis solicitor specializing in this lucrative practice illustrates the type and the possibilities of variation. The solicitor is describing certain marriage settlements, the originals of which he held in his hand:

In this settlement John F — of C — had one son and two daughters at home. He left the farm, you see, all that goes with it, to his son on condition of his marrying the girl named here in the deed. He also made the transfer subject to the son's providing for the two daughters by giving them rights of residence and keep in the house as long as they remain unmarried, and by making them special money gifts when they should marry. He then reserved a right for his wife, leaving her a small sum, and the right to the potato patch and her bedroom free of all charge as long as she lived. In the event of her not liking the new arrangements, she was to get a monthly stipend in lieu of her keep and room until she died.

We shall go on to give this interview in some detail to illustrate the full character of the arrangements made. The solicitor continues:

If there are two sons ... one of them gets the farm, and when the old people find a girl with a suitable fortune, and the son marries her, they give the money over to the next son, or they provide with it for the other children who haven't yet gone off. It's a pernicious system. [An upper-class person is speaking, not a farmer.] You'll go out to a small holding and see several able-bodied men and women waiting around doing nothing. They are waiting for the eldest son to get married and for their share of the fortune the wife brings in. [...]

With the transfer of land at the marriage of the son who remains to work the farm, the relations of the members of the farm family to each other and to the farm they work undergo a drastic change. In the first place, the headship of the old couple under whom the family group worked undergoes change. The old couple relinquish the farm, they enter the age grade of the dying, and direction of the enterprise of the group passes from their hands to those of the young people. Something of the change has already been indicated in the 'writings'. From the point of view of the father, it means the abandonment of the ownership he has long enjoyed; from the point of view of the old woman it means she is no longer the 'woman of the house'. Her place is taken by the incoming daughter-in-law. Naturally, this change is accomplished in effect only with difficulty and with considerable reluctance upon the part of the old couple. Where the transition goes smoothly, father and son continue to work the farm together, but more often as the father grows older he retires to his seat by the hearth. For example, the authors know one family, consisting of a young man and his wife, their two children, and the old couple, which was regarded as a model of family harmony in the neighborhood. The young man did all the heavy work of the farm, but his father worked by his side. Yet the initiative in agricultural matters was clearly the young man's. The man, almost eighty, did not want to remain idle. 'Time enough to sit by the fire in the winter,' he would say. The greatest compliment the neighbors had for them was: 'Look at the C—s. Old Johnny gives his boy a hand with everything. You wouldn't know which one has the farm.'

The coming-in of the daughter-in-law is sometimes not so harmonious. Disputes arise, as the provisions made in the 'writings' indicate. The following quotation from an official with years of experience in dealing with country people illustrates this:

As years go on, either the parents die or, if they live sufficiently long, they receive the old-age pension. Before they are qualified for this, the farms have to be made over to a son or daughter. This is done on the occasion of the son's marriage. The father reserves to himself and his wife the use of a room and the freedom of the kitchen, and they are entitled to all their food. The points were carefully discussed at length in the process of matchmaking, and the family of the future wife had no hesitation in agreeing, realizing that such points formed the final phase of a cycle of life on the farm. If the daughter-in-law has been well and properly advised by her mother, she immediately on her arrival in the new house submits tactfully to all proposals of her mother-in-law and lets the old lady feel that she is still the master mariner. If she didn't, it would cause a lot of trouble, as sometimes happens. [...]

It is in the feminine province of farm work and household control that the transition is most difficult. Under the patrilocal type of marriage here described, the bride is a stranger and of necessity cannot rely upon the experience of an association of years in order to meet the new conditions, as can father and son. In the graphic phrase of the people, she is the 'new woman'.

For her the transition brings a violent uprooting from prior attachments. Unlike her urban sister, she has little of the ideal of romantic love to help her over the crisis. Consequently her introduction into the new household is gradual, and her assumption of her new duties takes place over a moderately lengthy period. Two considerations, of course, are her primary inspiration in moments of stress: first, that she is now a fully adult woman with a household of her own although she must still share its control with her mother-in-law; and second, that the customary usage of the countryside provides her with an occasional escape back to her own people still on the farm at home. [...]

The internal reorganization of the family consequent on the marriage of one of their number produces a marked change in the situation of the as yet unprovided-for brother and sisters. [...] The sons and daughters who are not to be portioned at home, in the words of the Luogh residents, 'must travel'. To that end both the savings of the family, created through their united efforts under the headship of father and mother, and the incoming dowry, are devoted. In Luogh there had been only four marriages in ten years; two of them were the usual farm-transferring matches, one a returned emigrant who married a boyhood sweetheart and bought a farm, and one a widower who took a second wife and a second fortune. An old woman described the situation: 'There aren't any matches nowadays. Nobody has a fortune to give his daughter and the young men must travel.' Yet the woman who lamented this state of affairs was carefully husbanding half-crowns for her baby granddaughter's fortune.

Nevertheless this necessary dispersal of the members of the family at its reorganization does not ordinarily destroy the family ties. The bonds of affection and family obligation still hold. If they have emigrated, the family members send back remittances and passage money for nephews and nieces and brothers and sisters left at home. A great many farms, especially in West and North Clare, are partially supported by Christmas gifts sent from children living abroad. It is unfortunate that the authors have not statements of the amount of these annual remittances for local districts. The total for Ireland, however, is enormous. There is a marked tendency for emigration from a local region to perpetuate itself, sons and daughters of each generation going out to join the members of the last. One district round Cross to the west of Carrigaholt, a little settlement on the Loop Head peninsula which juts out from Clare into the Atlantic at the Shannon's mouth, is said locally to be supported by sons in the Shanghai police force. The first to go became chief of police in the International Settlement there and many places in the force have gone to men of Cross. [. . .]

The role played by emigrated relatives in providing for the children upon the home farm and the role of the dispersed children in helping the old couple and the brother or sister at home is part of the general 'friendliness' by which the Irish countryman sums up the family obligations. The two roles are felt to be the same, and they are described in the same terms, as the obligations of actual charity between country families, agricultural cooperation, and ceremonial assistance at marriages, wakes and funerals. Brother and sister send back gifts to the home farm, especially when the old couple are still alive. Gifts of money, clothing and presents of all descriptions are sent back. Geese, farm delicacies and such mementos as shamrocks go from the farm to those relatives that keep in touch.

At family crises, such as death, marriage and birth, the new bonds come strongly into play and, where possible, the dispersed relatives come back to the farm at that time. The emigrant returns, if he does so at all, to the very townland of his birth, either to buy the old place or to settle nearby. In fact, there are many instances of countrymen, returned Americans, Australians, South Africans and British soldiers, who have roamed over the world but have never seen more of Ireland than their route to and from their port of embarkation and the nearest market towns.

The sentiments of place, farm and family become so inextricably intermingled as to be almost one. Perhaps the peculiarly Irish type of song and music owes its character as well as its popularity to that fact. The laments for a dear one, especially a mother, and the pangs of exile are the major motives. They are sung to the same tunes and call forth the same tears.

The break-up of the family at the transfer of land has changed the relation between the dispersed children and the old couple, just as it has changed that between the new farm family and their parents. Control of expenditure, in fact all vestiges of the strict parental control, is perforce destroyed. The best example of this fact is the change which comes over the attitudes of the old people towards their children's personal expenditures. The economic corporation which they directed is destroyed with their headship of the group. Consequently, they no longer can demand the services of their children as before. Thus the authors saw several old couples doing their best to learn how much a returned emigrant had earned but, because of the change in position, not daring to ask outright. If the son had remained on the farm, they would not have hesitated to demand a strict accounting. Likewise, in such important matters as marriage, over which the parents would have had great authority as long as the son or daughter remained at home, the parents lose their control. More than one old couple remarked, on hearing from a distant exiled son of his marriage, that they wished him well but that he must please himself now that he was on his own.

A word more might be said to clarify the position of the dispersed relatives. They equally share the new attenuated bonds which take the place of the old closely integrated family group. But, as might be expected in the structure of a family, which, as we have seen, is based, not upon the principle of rigidity in classification as in many primitive kinship systems, but upon the principle of extensions of relationship outward from the nucleus of the immediate family, the bonds are stronger as the original relationship is closer. The children of each generation growing up on the home farm can look far oftener to a father's or mother's emigrant brother for aid when their own time comes to emigrate than to father's and mother's emigrant cousins. The closer relatives are the ones who most often step forward, though the obligation theoretically binds them all. [. . .]

In summary, the dispersal of the family is part of a general movement arising out of the re-formation of the family group. Forces within the relations of the members of the group bring it into being. Yet the dispersal is carried out very often in ways which depend also upon familial ties. The whole movement is carried on in the midst of an orderly and organic transformation which comes over the family regularly at marriage and death. Old and new meet at marriage in Ireland. Between them social organization is passed on though a prior group is partially destroyed.

2 T. Parsons

The Family in Urban-Industrial America: 1

Excerpt from T. Parsons, 'The American family: its relations to personality and the social structure', in T. Parsons and R. F. Bales, *Family, Socialisation and Interaction Process*, Free Press, 1955, Routledge & Kegan Paul, 1956, pp. 3–21.

The American family has, in the past generation or more, been undergoing a profound process of change. There has been much difference of opinion among social scientists, as well as among others concerned, as to the interpretation of these changes. Some have cited facts such as the very high rates of divorce, the changes in the older sex morality, and until fairly recently, the decline in birth rates, as evidence of a trend to disorganization in an absolute sense. Such considerations as these have in turn often been linked with what has sometimes been called the 'loss of function' of the family.[1] This refers to the fact that so many needs, for example as for clothing, which formerly were met by family members working in the home, are now met by outside agencies. Thus clothing is now usually bought ready made; there is much less food-processing in the household, there is a great deal of commercial recreation outside the home, etc.

That changes of a major character have been going on seems to be beyond doubt. That some of them have involved disorganization of a serious character is clear. But we know that major structural changes in social systems always involve strain and disorganization, so the question of evaluating symptoms of disorganization, of which we can regard the high divorce rates as one, involves the question of how much is a general trend to disorganization as such, how much is what may be called the 'disorganization of transition'.

Certain facts about the most recent phases of development seem to us to throw doubt on the thesis of general disorganization. First, after the post-war peak, the upward trend of divorce

1. Emphasized particularly by W. F. Ogburn. See, for instance, *Recent Social Trends in the U.S.*, chapter 13, 'The family and its functions'.

rates has been checked, though it is too early to judge what the longer run trend is likely to be.[2] To judge the impact of the instability of marriages, also the distribution of divorces by duration of marriage and by relations to children is just as important as the absolute numbers. As the figures show, by and large divorces are, and continue to be, concentrated in the early periods of marriage and in childless couples. Even though married before and divorced, once people settle down to having children there is a relatively high probability that they will stay together.[3]

Second, divorce certainly has not led to a general disillusionment with marriage, so that people prefer to stay single or not to try again. In spite of a situation where it has become economically easier than ever before for single women to support themselves independently, the proportion of the population married and living with their spouses is the highest that it has ever been in

2.
Trends of Marriage and Divorce Rates in U.S. – 1920–51
Rates per 1000 population

Year	Marriage rate	Divorce rate
1920	12·0	1·6
1925	10·3	1·5
1930	9·2	1·6
1935	10·4	1·7
1940	12·1	2·0
1945	12·2	3·5
1950	11·1	2·6

The divorce rate dipped a little lower to 1·3 at the depth of the depression and its high point was 4·3 in 1946. Every year since has shown a drop. The marriage rate reached its peak of 16·4 in 1946 reflecting demobilization but has remained consistently above 10 since.

Source: National Office of Vital Statistics, 'Summary of marriage and divorce statistics, United States, 1951', *Vital Statistics – Special Reports, National Summaries*, vol. 38, no. 5, 30 April 1954.

3. '. . . two-thirds of those couples obtaining divorce are childless; one-fifth have only one child. In fact, there seems to be a definite relationship between childless marriages and divorce. That a relatively small number of children in the United States have divorced parents may be owing, in part, to the fact that many couples do not stay married long enough to have a large family. Over 35 per cent of those divorced in 1940 had been married less than four years. The average length of marriages ending in divorce is less than six years' (Barnes and Ruedi, 1951, pp. 652–3).

the history of the census and has risen perceptibly within the recent period.[4]

Third, though down until the mid-thirties there had been a progressive decline in birth rates until on a long-run basis the population was for a time no longer fully reproducing itself, by now it has become clear that the revival of the birth rate which began in the early forties has not been only a matter of catching up the deficit of war-time, but has reached a new plateau on what appears to be a relatively stable basis.[5] This is certainly suggestive of a process of readjustment rather than of a continuous trend of disorganization.

In this connexion is should be remembered that the immense increase in the expectancy of life since about the turn of the

4. See footnote 2.
5.

Crude Birth Rates, 1915–50, United States
Rates per 1000 population

Year	Rate	Year	Rate
1915	29·5	1945	20·4
1920	27·7	1946	24·1
1925	25·1	1947	26·6
1930	21·3	1948	24·9
1935	18·7	1949	24·5
1940	19·4	1950	24·1
1941	20·3	1951	24·5
1942	22·2	1952*	24·6
1943	22·7	1953*	24·7
1944	21·2		

It will be noted that a consistent rise started in 1940. Even the lowest war year was only down to 20·4 (1945) and the rate has remained substantially above the level of the thirties since.

Source: National Office of Vital Statistics, 'Summary of natality statistics, United States, 1950', *Vital Statistics – Special Reports, National Summaries*, vol. 37, no. 7, 19 May 1953.

Note: The national office estimates that the slight drop from the 1947 boom (itself caused by demobilization) is accountable by the following: drop in first children because of lowered marriage rates, 1946–9; but rise in births of second, third and fourth children during 1946–9.

Last three years, source: Office of Population Research, Princeton University, and Population Association of America, Inc., *Population Index*, July 1954.

*Provisional

century[6] has meant that continuance of the birth rates of that time would have led to a rate of population increase which few could contemplate with equanimity. The transition from a high birth-rate/high death-rate population economy of most of history to one where low death-rates have to be balanced by substantially lower birth-rates than before is one of the profoundest adjustments human societies have ever had to make, going as it does to the deepest roots of motivation. In processes of such magnitude it is not unusual for there to be swings of great amplitude to levels which are incompatible with longer-run stability. There

6.
Estimated Average Length of Life in Years
All races, both sexes, United States

1900	47·3
1910	50·0
1920	54·1
1930	59·7
1940	62·7
1950	68·4

Source: National Office of Vital Statistics, 'Abridged life tables, United States, 1951', *Vital Statistics – Special Reports, National Summaries*, vol. 38, no. 5, 30 April 1954.

The way birth and death rates have balanced out can be better seen from the following estimates of the net reproduction rate for the United States. It will be seen that during the 1930s the population was not quite reproducing itself but that at present rates a substantial, perhaps indeed an excessive, rate of increase is being maintained.

Net reproduction rates for U.S.A.

1930–35	0·98
1935–40	0·98
1940	1·03
1941	1·08
1942	1·20
1943	1·25
1944	1·18
1945	1·15
1946	1·37
1947	1·53
1948	1·45
1949	1·45
1950	1·44

Source: Office of Population Research, Princeton University, and Population Association of America, Inc., *Population Index*, April 1954.

is at least a good case for the view that the low birth-rates of the 1930s – not of course confined to the United States – constituted the extreme point of such a swing, and that extrapolating the trend up to that point simply failed to take account of adjustive processes already at work. At any rate, the recent facts have shifted the burden of proof to him who argues that the disorganization of the family is bringing imminent race suicide in its wake.

There is a further bit of evidence which may be of significance. The family after all is a residential unit in our society. If the family were breaking up, one would think that this would be associated with a decline of the importance of the 'family home' as the preferred place to live of the population. Recent trends of development seem to indicate that far from family homes being 'on their way out' there has, in recent years, been an impressive confirmation that even more than before this is the preferred residential pattern. The end of the Second World War left us with a large deficit of housing facilities. Since then, once the shortages of materials were overcome, there has been an enormous amount of residential building. In this building, as is

7.
Total New Construction Value, 1937–51, Corrected 1947–9 Values

In millions		In millions	
1937	$13,714	1947	17,795
1940	16,873	1948	20,759
1943	12,841	1949	22,180
1945	8,439	1950	26,852
1946	15,546	1951	26,650

Percentage of value of total new construction of residential building, 1937–51

Type of construction	37	38	39	40	41	42	43	44	45	46	47	48	49	50	51
Private, residential, non-farm*	21	23	28	29	25	10	9	11	13	28	33	35	32	40	32
Operators' dwellings, farm	1	1	1	2	2	1	1	2	2	3	4	3	3	3	3
Total percentage for new private residential construction†	22	24	29	31	27	11	10	13	15	31	37	38	35	43	35

*Does not include hotels, dormitories, clubhouses, tourist courts and cabins.

†Does not include new public residential construction, which averages 1 to 3 per cent during peacetime years, and includes barracks, officers' quarters, etc.

indicated by the figures, the single family house occupies an extraordinarily prominent place.[7] It seems that the added mobility given our population by modern means of transportation, especially in making possible a considerable geographical distance between place of residence and place of work, has led to a strengthening of the predilection to have a 'home of our own'. In the face particularly of a level of geographical and occupational mobility which makes permanence of tenure of a residential location highly problematical, this is a most impressive phenomenon.

The situation with which we are concerned may be summed up by noting again that, in spite of divorces and related phenomena, Americans recently have been marrying on an unprecedented scale. They have been having children, not on an unprecedented scale, but on one which by contrast with somewhat earlier trends is unlikely to be without significance and, third, they have been establishing homes for themselves as family units on a very large scale. Since the bulk of home-provision has been on the financial responsibility of the couples concerned, it seems unlikely that the having of children is a simple index of irresponsibility, that we have, as Professor Carver used to put it, produced a generation of 'spawners' as contrasted with 'family-builders' (Carver, 1915).

At various later points in this volume we are going to argue both that there are certain very important elements of constancy in the structure and in the functional significance of the family on a human cultural level, and that these elements of constancy are by no means wholly or even mainly a reflection of its biological composition. But this view is, in our opinion, by no means incompatible with an emphasis, in other respects, on certain important elements of variation in the family. The set of these latter elements on which we wish now to focus attention is that concerned with the level of structural differentiation in the society.

It is a striking fact of sociological discussion that there has been

It is not possible to find figures which exclude private multiple-family units, but the general evidence is that the proportion of these has decreased, not increased.

Source: Bureau of Labor Statistics, *New Construction, Expenditures 1915–51, Labor Requirements, 1939–51*, 1953.

no settled agreement on either of two fundamental problems. One is the problem of the structural and functional relations between the nuclear family on the one hand, and the other elements of the kinship complex in the same society. Structural analysis of kinship is, we feel, just reaching a point where the importance of clear discriminations in this field is coming to be appreciated. Second, there has been no clear conception of what are the important 'functions of the family'. Procreation and child care are always included, as is some reference to sexual relations, but in addition there are frequent references to 'economic' functions, religious functions and various others.

There has been little attempt to work out the implications of the suggestion that there are certain 'root functions' which must be found wherever there is a family or kinship system at all, while other functions may be present or not according to the *kind* of family or kinship system under consideration, and its place in the structure of the rest of the society.

The aspect of this problem in which we are particularly interested concerns its relations to the problem of structural differentiation in societies. It is well known that in many 'primitive' societies there is a sense in which kinship 'dominates' the social structure; there are few concrete structures in which participation is independent of kinship status. In comparative perspective it is clear that in the more 'advanced' societies a far greater part is played by non-kinship structures. States, churches, the larger business firms, universities and professional associations cannot be treated as mere 'extensions' of the kinship system.

The process by which non-kinship units become of prime importance in a social structure inevitably entails 'loss of function' on the part of some or even all of the kinship units. In the processes of social evolution there have been many stages by which this process has gone on, and many different directions in which it has worked out.

Our suggestion is, in this perspective, that what has recently been happening to the American family constitutes part of one of these stages of a process of differentiation. This process has involved a further step in the reduction of the importance in our society of kinship units other than the nuclear family. It has also resulted in the transfer of a variety of functions from the nuclear family to other structures of the society, notably the occupationally organized sectors of it. This means that the family has become *a more specialized agency than before*, probably more specialized than it has been in any previously known society. This represents a decline of *certain* features which traditionally have been associated with families; but whether it represents a 'decline of the family' in a more general sense is another matter; we think not. We think the trend of the evidence points to the beginning of the relative stabilization of a *new* type of family structure in a new relation to a general social structure, one in which the family is more specialized than before, but not in any general sense less important, because the society is dependent *more* exclusively on it for the performance of *certain* of its vital functions.

We further think that this new situation presents a particularly favorable opportunity to the social scientist. Because we are dealing with a more highly differentiated and specialized agency, it is easier to identify clearly the features of it which are essential on the most general level of cross-cultural significance. The situation is methodologically comparable to the relation between the emergence of the modern type of industrial economy and the problems of economic theory. The high level of differentiation of economic from non-economic processes under modern conditions, has made possible a kind of natural experimental situation which has been crucial to the development of modern economic theory.

The American family in the total society

From this perspective, then, let us review some of the most essential features of the structure of the American family-kinship system in its relation to the rest of the society.

The first feature to be noted is on the level of kinship organization as anthropologists ordinarily treat this; namely the 'isolation' of the nuclear family and its relation to 'bilaterality' with respect to the lines of descent. This 'isolation' is manifested in the fact that the members of the nuclear family, consisting of parents and their still dependent children, ordinarily occupy a separate dwelling not shared with members of the family of orientation of either spouse, and that this household is in the typical case economically independent, subsisting in the first instance from the occupational earnings of the husband–father (cf. Williams, 1951, chapter 4; also Parsons, 1954). It is of course not uncommon to find a surviving parent of one or the other spouse, or even a sibling or cousin of one of them residing with the family, but this is both statistically secondary, and it is clearly not felt to be the 'normal' arrangement.[8]

Of course with the independence, particularly the marriage, of children, relations to the family of orientation are by no means broken. But separate residence, very often in a different geographical community, and separate economic support, attenuate these relations. Furthermore, there is a strong presumption that relations to one family of orientation will not be markedly closer than to the other (though there is a certain tendency for the mother–married daughter relation to be particularly close). This bilaterality is further strongly reinforced by our patterns of inheritance. In the first place the presumption is that a newly married couple will 'stand on their own feet', supporting themselves from their own earnings. But so far as property is inherited the pattern calls for equal division between children regardless of birth order or sex, so that the fact or expectation of inheritance does not typically bind certain children to their families of orientation more closely than others. Furthermore, though it is not uncommon for sons to work in their fathers' businesses – almost certainly much less common that it was fifty years ago – this tendency is at least partially matched by the phenomenon of 'marrying the boss's daughter', so that no clear unilateral structure can be derived from this fact.

It has been noted that the primary source of family income lies in occupational earnings. It is above all the presence of the

8. 'Sixty-four per cent of husband and wife families in 1940 had no adult relatives eighteen years old and over living in the home. Very few, about one-eighth, of the families in which the husband was under thirty-five years of age contained any of these additional adults. . . . Nearly three-fifths of these (adult relatives) were single sons or daughters of the couple who had not left home, of whom most were between eighteen and thirty-four years old. . . . About one-eighth of the adult relatives were married, widowed or divorced parents of the husband or his wife. . . . Thus, all but one-fifth of the adult relatives were children or parents (own or in-law) of the family head and his wife' (Glick, 1947).

modern occupational system and its mode of articulation with the family which accounts for the difference between the modern, especially American, kinship system and *any* found in non-literate or even peasant societies. The family household is a solidary unit where, once formed, membership and status are ascribed, and the communalistic principle of 'to each according to his needs' prevails. In the occupational world, status is achieved by the individual and is contingent on his continuing performance. Though of course this is modified in varying respects, there is a high premium on mobility and equality of opportunity according to individual capacity to perform. Over much of the world and of history a very large proportion of the world's ordinary work is and has been performed in the context of kinship units. Occupational organization in the modern sense is the sociological antithesis of this.

This means essentially that, as the occupational system develops and absorbs functions in the society, it *must* be at the expense of the relative prominence of kinship organization as a structural component in one sense, and must also be at the expense of many of what previously have been *functions* of the kinship unit. The double consequence is that the same people, who are members of kinship units, perform economic, political, religious and cultural functions outside the kinship context in occupational roles and otherwise in a variety of other types of organization. But conversely, the members of kinship units must meet many of their needs, which formerly were met in the processes of interaction within the kinship unit, through other channels. This of course includes meeting the need for income with which to purchase the goods and services necessary for family functioning itself.

In this type of society the basic mode of articulation between family and the occupational world lies in the fact that the *same* adults are both members of nuclear families and incumbents of occupational roles, the holders of 'jobs'. The individual's job and not the products of the cooperative activities of the family as a unit is of course the primary source of income for the family.

Next it is important to remember that the *primary* responsibility for this support rests on the one adult male member of the nuclear family. It is clearly the exceptional 'normal' adult male who can occupy a respected place in our society without having a regular 'job', though he may of course be 'independent' as a professional practitioner or some kind of a 'free lance' and not be employed by an organization, or he may be the proprietor of one. That at the bottom of the scale the 'hobo' and the sick and disabled are deviants scarcely needs mentioning, while at the other end, among the relatively few who are in a position to 'live on their money' there is a notable reluctance to do so. The 'playboy' is not a highly respected type and there is no real American equivalent of the older European type of 'gentleman' who did not 'work' unless he had to.

The occupational role is of course, in the first instance, part of the 'occupational system' but it is not only that. It is an example of the phenomenon of 'interpenetration' which will be extensively analysed below. In this connexion it is both a role in the occupational system, *and* in the family; it is a 'boundary-role' between them. The husband–father, in holding an acceptable job and earning an income from it, is performing an essential function or set of functions for his family (which of course includes himself in one set of roles) as a system. The status of the family in the community is determined probably more by the 'level' of job he holds than by any other single factor, and the income he earns is usually the most important basis of the family's standard of living and hence 'style of life'. Of course, as we shall see, he has other very important functions in relation both to wife and to children, but it is fundamentally by virtue of the importance of his occupational role *as a component of his familial role* that in our society we can unequivocally designate the husband–father as the 'instrumental leader' of the family as a system.[9]

9. Comparative data confirm this interpretation. We now have a good deal of evidence about social situations where there is neither a strong 'lineage' structure in the kinship field nor a developed 'industrial' type of occupational structure. One of the first perceptive studies of this type was made by Frazier (1939). This has more recently been supplemented and refined by studies of kinship in the British West Indies. See Henriques (1953); Lloyd Braithwaite (1953); and especially the as yet unpublished study by Smith (1954). Dr Smith shows very clearly the connexion between the 'mother-centered' character of the lower-class rural Negro family in the West Indies (his study deals with British Guiana) and the 'casual' character of most of the available employment and income-earning opportunities. This is a sharp modification of the typical American pattern, but must not be interpreted to mean that the husband–father has, at the critical periods of

The membership of large numbers of women in the American labor force must not be overlooked. Nevertheless there can be no question of symmetry between the sexes in this respect, and, we argue, there is no serious tendency in this direction. In the first place a large proportion of gainfully employed women are single, widowed or divorced, and thus cannot be said to be either taking the place of a husband as breadwinner of the family, or competing with him. A second large contingent are women who either do not yet have children (some of course never will) or whose children are grown up and independent. The number in the labor force who have small children is still quite small and has not shown a marked tendency to increase. The role of housewife is still the overwhelmingly predominant one for the married woman with small children.[10]

the family cycle, altogether lost the role of instrumental leader. Dr Smith shows that this is not the case, and that the impression to the contrary (which might for instance be inferred from Henriques' discussion) arises from failure to consider the development of the particular family over a full cycle from the first sexual relations to complete 'emancipation' of the children from their family of orientation.

10.
Population and Labor Force, by Age and Sex, December 1950
*In thousands**

Age–sex group	Population	In labor force†	Not in labor force		
			Keeping house	In school	§ Other
Total U.S.	112,610	64,670	32,950	7570	7420
Total males 14 and over	55,420	45,640	120	2930	5740
14–24	12,360	8230	—	2670	450
25–34	11,660	11,090	—	240	310
35–44	10,370	9980	—	—	370
45–54	8680	8180	—	—	480
55–64	6810	5800	—	—	990
65 and over	5550	2360	—	—	3130
Total females 14 and over	57,180	19,030	32,830	3640	1680
14–24	12,150	4780	3580	3600	180
25–34	12,170	4160	7870	—	110
35–44	10,800	4240	6430	—	130
45–54	8910	3420	5340	—	140
55–64	6940	1840	4900	—	200
65 and over	6230	600	4720	—	910

*Figures under 100,000 are not included.
†Including armed forces.
§Including persons in institutions, disabled and retired, etc.
Source: U.S. Bureau of Labor Statistics, *Fact Book on Manpower*, 31 January 1951.

The following table shows the status of women in the labor force by marital status. It will be noted that the percentage of married women living with their husbands who were in the labor force increased over the nine-year period from 14·7 per cent to 22·5 per cent.

Labor Force Status of Women by Marital Status, April 1949 and April 1940
In thousands

Year and marital status	Population	In labor force	
		Number	Percentage of population
1949			
Total over 14	56,001	17,167	30·7
Single	11,174	5682	50·9
Married, husband present	35,323	7959	22·5
Other marital status (separated, widowed, divorced)	9505	3526	37·1
1940			
Total over 14	50,549	13,840	27·4
Single	13,936	6710	48·1
Married, husband present	28,517	4200	14·7
Other marital status	8096	2930	36·2

Source: U.S. Bureau of Labor Statistics, *Fact Book on Manpower*, 31 January 1951.

The concentration of women without children under five in the labor force is shown clearly in the following table.

Comparison of Labor Force Status of Married Women, with and without Children under Five, April, 1949

In thousands

Presence of children under 5	Married women – Husband present		
	Population	In labor force Number	Percentage of population
Total, ages 15–49	26,204	6758	25·8
Without children under 5	15,499	5637	36·4
With children under 5	10,705	1121	10·5

Source: U.S. Bureau of Labor Statistics, *Fact Book on Manpower*, 31 January 1951.

But even where this type does have a job, as is also true of those who are married but do not have dependent children, above the lowest occupational levels it is quite clear that in general the woman's job tends to be of a qualitatively different type and not of a status which seriously competes with that of her husband as the primary status-giver or income-earner.

It seems quite safe in general to say that the adult feminine role has not ceased to be anchored primarily in the internal affairs of the family, as wife, mother and manager of the household, while the role of the adult male is primarily anchored in the occupational world, in his job and through it by his status-giving and income-earning functions for the family. Even if, as seems possible, it should come about that the average married woman had some kind of job, it seems most unlikely that this relative balance would be upset; that either the roles would be reversed, or their qualitative differentiation in these respects completely erased.[11]

The principal functions of the nuclear family

Within this broad setting of the structure of the society, what can we say about the functions of the family, that is, the isolated nuclear family? There are, we think, two main types of considerations. The first is that the 'loss of function', both in our own recent history and as seen in broader comparative perspective, means that the family has become, on the 'macroscopic' levels, almost completely functionless. It does not itself, except here and there, engage in much economic production; it is not a significant unit in the political power system; it is not a major direct agency of integration of the larger society. Its individual

11. The distribution of women in the labor force clearly confirms this general view of the balance of the sex roles. Thus, on higher levels typical feminine occupations are those of teacher, social worker, nurse, private secretary and entertainer. Such roles tend to have a prominent expressive component, and often to be 'supportive' to masculine roles. Within the occupational organization they are analogous to the wife–mother role in the family. It is much less common to find women in the 'top executive' roles and the more specialized and 'impersonal' technical roles. Even within professions we find comparable differentiations, e.g. in medicine women are heavily concentrated in the two branches of pediatrics and psychiatry, while there are few women surgeons.

members participate in all these functions, but they do so 'as individuals' not in their roles as family members.

The most important implication of this view is that the functions of the family in a highly differentiated society are not to be interpreted as functions directly on behalf of the society, but on behalf of personality. If, as some psychologists seem to assume, the essentials of human personality were determined biologically, independently of involvement in social systems, there would be no need for families, since reproduction as such does not require family organization. It is because the *human* personality is not 'born' but must be 'made' through the socialization process that in the first instance families are necessary. They are 'factories' which produce human personalities. But at the same time, even once produced, it cannot be assumed that the human personality would remain stable in the respects which are vital to social functioning, if there were not mechanisms of stabilization which were organically integrated with the socialization process. We therefore suggest that the basic and irreducible functions of the family are two: first, the primary socialization of children so that they can truly become members of the society into which they have been born; second, the stabilization of the adult personalities of the population of the society. It is the combination of these two functional imperatives, which explains why, in the 'normal' case it is both true that *every adult* is a member of a nuclear family and that every child must begin his process of socialization in a nuclear family. It will be one of the most important theses of our subsequent analysis that these two circumstances are most intimately interconnected. Their connexion goes back to the fact that it is control of the residua of the process of socialization which constitutes the primary focus of the problem of stabilization of the adult personality.

In subsequent chapters we shall develop, in a variety of applications and ramifications, the view that the central focus of the process of socialization lies in the internalization of the culture of the society into which the child is born. The most important part of this culture from this focal point consists in the patterns of value which in another aspect constitute the institutionalized patterns of the society. The conditions under which effective socialization can take place then will include being placed in a social situation where the more powerful and responsible persons are themselves integrated in the cultural value system in question, both in that they constitute with the children an *institutionalized* social system, and that the patterns have previously been internalized in the relevant ways in their own personalities. The family is clearly in all societies, and no less in our own, in this sense an institutionalized system.

But it is not enough to place the child in any institutionalized system of social relationships. He must be placed in one of a special type which fulfills the necessary psychological conditions of successful completion of the process we call socialization, over a succession of stages starting with earliest infancy. One of the principal tasks of the subsequent discussion is to explore some of these conditions. A few of them may, however, be noted here, while the reasons for their importance will be discussed as we go along. In the first place, we feel that for the earlier stages of socialization, at least, the socialization system must be a *small* group. Furthermore, it must be differentiated into sub-systems so the child need not have an equal level of participation with all members at the same time in the earlier stages of the process. We will show that it is particularly important that in the earliest stage he tends to have a special relation to one other member of the family, his mother.

In this connexion a certain importance may well attach to the biological fact that, except for the relatively rare plural births, it is unusual for human births to the same mother to follow each other at intervals of less than a year with any regularity. It is, we feel, broadly in the first year of life that a critical phase of the socialization process, which requires the most exclusive attention of a certain sort from the mother, takes place. Furthermore, it is probably significant that in our type of society the family typically no longer has what by other standards may be considered to be large numbers of children. Partly, in earlier times, the effects of higher rates of birth have been cancelled by infant mortality. But partly, we feel, the large family – say over five or six children – is a different *type* of social system with different effects on the children in it. We will not try to analyse these differences carefully here.

Another very important range of problems in the larger setting concerns the impact for the outcome of the socialization process of the role of relatives other than members of the nuclear family. Particularly important cross-culturally are siblings of the parents, the role of whom varies with the type of kinship structure. [. . .]

We should like to suggest here only that what we have called the 'isolation of the nuclear family' for the contemporary American scene, may, along with reduction in the average size of family, have considerable significance for the character of the contemporary socialization process. This significance would, we think, have something to do with the greater sharpness of the *difference* in status, from the point of view of the child, between members of the family and non-members. It will be our general thesis that in certain respects the modern child has 'farther to go' in his socialization than his predecessors. There seem to be certain reasons why the number of fundamental steps of a certain type is restricted. If this is true, each step has to be 'longer' and it is important that the 'landmarks' along the way, the 'cues' presented to the child, should involve extremely clear discriminations.

A primary function and characteristic of the family is that it should be a social group in which in the earliest stages the child can 'invest' *all* of his emotional resources, to which he can become overwhelmingly 'committed' or on which he can become fully 'dependent'. But, at the same time, in the nature of the socialization process, this dependency must be temporary rather than permanent. Therefore, it is very important that the socializing agents should not themselves be *too* completely immersed in their family ties. It is a condition equally important with facilitating dependency that a family should, in due course, help in emancipating the child from his dependency on the family. *Hence the family must be a differentiated sub-system of a society, not itself a 'little society' or anything too closely approaching it*. More specifically this means that the adult members must have roles other than their familial roles which occupy strategically important places in their own personalities. In our own society the most important of these other roles, though by no means the only one, is the occupational role of the father.

The second primary function of the family, along with socialization of children, concerns regulation of balances in the personalities of the adult members of both sexes. It is clear that this function is concentrated on the marriage relation as such. From this point of view a particularly significant aspect of the isolation of the nuclear family in our society is again the sharp discrimination in status which it emphasizes between family members and non-members. In particular, then, spouses are thrown upon each other, and their ties with members of their own families of orientation, notably parents and adult siblings, are correspondingly weakened. In its negative aspect as a source of strain, the consequence of this may be stated as the fact that the family of procreation, and in particular the marriage pair, are in a 'structurally unsupported' situation. Neither party has any other adult kin on whom they have a right to 'lean for support' in a sense closely comparable to the position of the spouse.

The marriage relation is then placed in a far more strategic position in this respect than is the case in kinship systems where solidarity with 'extended' kin categories is more pronounced. But for the functional context we are discussing, the marriage relationship is by no means alone in its importance. Parenthood acquires, it may be said, an enhanced significance for the emotional balance of the parents themselves, as well as for the socialization of their children. The two generations are, by virtue of the isolation of the nuclear family, thrown more closely on each other.

The main basis of the importance of children to their parents derives, we think, from the implications of problems which psychoanalytic theory has immensely illuminated but which also, we think, need to be understood in their relation to the family as a social system, and the conditions of its functional effectiveness and stability. The most general consideration is that the principal stages in the development of personality, particularly on its affective or 'emotional' side, leave certain 'residua' which constitute a stratification (in the geological sense) of the structure of the personality itself with reference to its own developmental history. Partly these residua of earlier experience can constitute threats to effective functioning on adult levels, the more so the more 'abnormal' that history and its consequences for the individual have been. But partly, also, they have important positive functions for the adult personality. To express and in certain ways and contexts 'act out', motivational systems and complexes which are primarily 'infantile' or 'regressive' in their meaning, is, in our view, by no means always undesirable, but on the contrary necessary to a healthy balance of the adult personality. At the same time the dangers are very real and regulation of context, manner and occasion of expression is very important.

We shall attempt later to mobilize evidence that a particularly important role in this situation is played by the erotic elements of the personality constitution, because of the great importance of eroticism in the developmental process.

We suggest then that children are important to adults because it is important to the latter to express what are essentially the 'childish' elements of their own personalities. There can be no better way of doing this than living with and interacting on their own level with *real* children. But at the same time it is essential that this should not be an unregulated acting out, a mere opportunity for regressive indulgence. The fact that it takes place in the parental role, with all its responsibilities, not least of which is the necessity to renounce earlier modes of indulgence as the child grows older, is, as seen in this connexion, of the first importance. The circumstantially detailed analysis which alone can substantiate such a set of statements will be presented in the subsequent chapters. The general thesis, however, is that the family and, in a particularly visible and trenchant way, the modern isolated family, incorporates an intricate set of interactive mechanisms whereby these two essential functions for personality are interlocked and interwoven. By and large a 'good' marriage from the point of view of the personality of the participants, is likely to be one with children; the functions as parents reinforce the functions in relation to each other as spouses.

References

BARNES, H. E., and RUEDI, O. M. (1951), *The American Way of Life*, Prentice-Hall.

BRAITHWAITE, L. (1953), 'Social stratification in Trinidad', *Social and Economic Studies*, October.

CARVER, T. N. (1915), *Essays in Social Justice*, Harvard University Press.

FRAZIER, E. F. (1939), *Negro Family in the United States*, University of Chicago Press.

GLICK, P. C. (1947), 'The family cycle', *American Sociological Review*, vol. 12, pp. 167-74.

HENRIQUES, F. (1953), *Family and Colour in Jamaica*, Eyre & Spottiswoode.

PARSONS, T. (1954), 'The kinship system of the contemporary United States', *Essays in Sociological Theory*, Free Press.

Recent Social Trends in the U.S., Report of the President's Research Committee on Social Trends, 1933.

SMITH, R. T. (1954), 'The rural Negro family in British Guiana', Ph.D. thesis, University of Cambridge.

WILLIAMS, R. M. (1951), *American Society*, Knopf.

3 R. Linton

The Family in Urban-Industrial America: 2

Excerpt from R. Linton, 'The natural history of the family', in
R. N. Anshen (ed.), *The Family: Its Function and Destiny*, Harper & Row,
1959, pp. 45–8.

The outstanding feature of the present situation is the almost complete breakdown of the consanguine family as a functional unit. Although the Western European consanguine grouping has never dominated the conjugal one, its potentialities for function and its claims on the individual were much stronger even a hundred years ago than they are today. This breakdown seems to be directly correlated with the increased opportunities for both spatial and social mobility which have been created by the current technological revolution. A strong consanguine family organization provides its members with a high degree of economic security, but it also imposes many obligations. When the value of this security becomes less than the handicap imposed on the individual by the associated obligations, he is willing to sacrifice the former in order to avoid the latter. Colloquially speaking, when a man can do better without relatives than with them he will tend to ignore the ties of kinship.

The unparalleled expansion of Western European and American economy in the past century, with the wealth of individual opportunity which it has produced, has struck at the very roots of consanguine family organization. Moreover, the increase in spatial mobility which came with the opening of new areas to settlement and the development of modern methods of transportation made it easy for the ambitious individual to sever his kin ties by the simple process of moving away. At present the consanguine family retains its functions only in long-settled rural districts and in the case of a few capitalist dynasties. In both instances the advantages of membership outweigh the disadvantages. The average city dweller recognizes his extended ties of relationship only in the sending of Christmas cards and in the occasional practice of hospitality to visiting kin.

In spite of this extreme degeneration, it is possible that certain factors quite external to family structure may reverse the present trends. If the social crystallization which now appears to be under way continues, the next few generations will see a marked decrease in individual opportunity. Extended family membership may again become economically valuable, although the value is likely to lie less in joint claims on property than in access to jobs. There is already a strong tendency to make membership in many craft unions hereditary, and the same trend can be observed with respect to the more remunerative executive positions in organizations which are shielded from the threat of active competition. It is also conceivable that the growth of bureaucracy will be accompanied by a growth of nepotism, this trend being most probable in the case of one-party rule of the fascist sort. The consanguine type of family organization, therefore, may simply be in abeyance at present and may play a more important role in the not too remote future.

Whatever the future possibilities may be, the current breakdown of consanguine organization has had significant repercussions on the conjugal family. Historically, the presence of the consanguine group has tended to reinforce rather than to weaken marriage ties. European mores have stressed the continuity of matings, and the separation of partners has been felt as a disgrace by their kindred. As long as kin ties were strong and associations close, the consanguine group could bring heavy pressure to bear on its members. With the weakening of these ties the pressure has been correspondingly reduced. Partners can now separate without fear of effective punishment by their kin and without loss of the already almost non-existent advantages of consanguine family membership.

Another factor, closely comparable in its results, is the increasing anonymity of individuals and conjugal family groups in modern urban society. The disapproval with which other members of a small, closely knit community viewed separation was a deterrent almost as strong as the disapproval of kin. Although it might not entail the same economic penalties, the prospect of social ostracism was enough to daunt all but the bravest. In the modern urban community, with its diffuse and casual social relationships, community pressure toward maintenance of the marriage tie has almost ceased to exist. The former friend who disapproves of such conduct can be avoided, and most of the individuals with whom the offender comes in contact will not even know that the offense has been committed.

Breakdowns of kin ties and of the close social integration of individuals and conjugal family groups are no new thing in history. They were an accompaniment of urbanization and suddenly increased spatial mobility in ancient as well as modern civilization. Nevertheless, there is another factor in the present situation which, if it is not altogether new, is at least of unprecedented importance. This is the progressive diminution of the economic dependence of spouses upon each other. Although in the ancient urban civilizations women of the aristocratic group, inheriting and owning property in their own right, could live in comfort without husbands, the ordinary family still depended upon a rigid division of labor. Spouses living in a Roman slum were almost as dependent upon each other for their creature comforts as spouses living on an isolated farm. Extrafamilial substitutes for what were ordinarily domestic services were available only to the wealthy, and opportunities for a single woman to support herself by her own labor were so limited and so unremunerative that they would be turned to only as a last resort.

In the modern urban community the delicatessen, the steam laundry, ready-made clothes, and above all the opening to women of attractive and well-paid occupations have done more to undermine the sanctity of marriage than has any conceivable loss of faith in its religious sanctions. Under present conditions, adult men and women are at last in a position to satisfy their basic needs in the absence of any sort of familial association, either conjugal or consanguine. In the anonymity of city life and with the development of effective techniques for contraception even the sexual needs of both can be met without entering into permanent unions or entailing serious penalties. The revolutionary effect of these developments upon the family as an institution can scarcely be overrated.

4 M. Kerr

The Family in 'Traditional' Working-Class England: 1

Excerpts from M. Kerr, *The People of Ship Street*, Routledge & Kegan Paul, 1958, pp. 40–45.

'I couldn't get on without me mother. I could get on without me husband. I don't notice him.'

This rather surprising statement made by a married woman of thirty-nine with five children epitomizes what the Mums in this area feel about the relative values of mothers and husbands.

In the same way this account of beatings by a child of eleven epitomizes what children feel about the relative values of mothers and fathers.

'When me father beats us we hide behind our Mum: when me mother beats us I run out on the street.' I deliberately misinterpreted and suggested, 'So your mother must beat you much harder, Vi?' 'Oh no,' came the spontaneous reply, 'me mother will protect us but me father won't.'

This feeling of the power of the Mum is often instilled into children at an early age by the mother herself. A child of thirteen said:

'Me mother says, "You can get another father but you can't get another mother": and that's true, isn't it? You can't get another mother.' Ruth went on to say, that should her mother die and her father remarry she would run away from home and persuade her siblings to do the same. 'I would not have a stepmother.'

Two children of fifteen said: 'Me mother always says, "If you steal from your mother you're no good to anyone."' – 'Me mother always says, "If you steal from your mother your hands will wither off you."'

In adult life the general pattern seems to be for a woman to take her husband home to live with her mother. The following quotations from the field-notes illustrate this more vividly than any formalized account could do. When Mrs R. married she asked her mother if she could bring her husband home. Her mother replied, 'You can please yourself but I don't want him.' After a fortnight's honeymoon Mrs R. was back home with her husband and there they have remained ever since. She has never had nor wanted a home of her own. She has now been married twenty-five years and her husband and three surviving children are all members of her mother's home.

Mrs B. said that when she married, 'I went straight back to me mother's home with me husband.' I asked if her husband hadn't wanted to take her away and start a home of their own. I asked what would have happened if he had forced a choice on her. She looked at me in amazement and said, 'My husband loved my mother. He said I couldn't have a better mother in the world.' Mrs B. said she never would have left her mother as long as she lived. 'When she died I thought I would have died.' Other siblings, although married and with families, also remained in their parents' home. I asked Mrs B. if she felt the same towards her father as she did towards her mother. She replied her father was all right: 'I mean to say he worked hard and kept us clean, but he drank. There is only one mother.' (A woman aged fifty-three who says of her marriage, 'My marriage is happy, my husband is good.')

Here is a husband's experience who tried to break this general pattern, who wanted a home of his own. When Billy and Maureen first married, Billy got her a lovely home. One day he returned from work to find a removal van driving away from what looked like his house. He stopped the van and asked the men whose things they were moving. He learnt from them they were moving his own. His wife had ordered the van and given instructions. Billy went in and questioned his wife. She said, 'I'm going back to me mother. You can please yourself.' Billy returned with her. It's been like this throughout his married life. More than once he has attempted to set up a home with his wife and son alone; it's always ended in the same way. Either his wife has returned to her mother and he has eventually followed or else her mother has come and parked on them. On one occasion he tried to hold out. He refused to go to her mother's to live. He took their son and placed him with his married sister who had a daughter about the same age, while he himself returned to his own mother. He hoped his wife would come back to their home. She did not. In the end he fetched his son and joined his wife in her mother's home and there they are still.

This is what a married woman of forty with two children, whose mother is a member of her husband's household, says of the strength of the tie:

'I always tell her when she goes [dies], I will not be long after.'

In the section on 'The Tie to the Locality'[1] the generalized feeling of attachment to the place only was stressed. In the cases mentioned this appeared to be the main motivation. However, in some cases there is the fear of leaving the mother. In the following instance the woman's mother was tied to the locality and would not move even with her daughter to another place. Here is what the daughter's husband had to say. Mr Y. told me that he doesn't really like this neighbourhood or house and wants to move. Twice it was nearly achieved but on both occasions Mrs Y. ratted at the last moment. The first time he was offered a very nice house on a housing estate. His wife said she wanted to move and they went over the house. She liked it very much. As they were leaving the house 'she burst into tears and said she could never leave her mother'. Later he was offered a house somewhere else. His wife said she would like to see it. Again they went over it together and she was absolutely delighted with it. It was a lovely house, nicer than the other one and would have been very easy to run. His wife would have been saved a great deal of her present chores. When he returned from work a few days after, he could see that his wife had been crying. He asked her what was the matter. She replied, 'nothing'. He told her to come off it, he could see she had been crying. She told him she really liked the house at X but she didn't want to move because she would have no friends there. Mr Y. said he knew the truth was that she would not leave her mother. (A woman of forty-four with six children, married twenty-six years. In spite of her tie to her mother, the husband said of his marriage, 'If I had me life again, I'd do the same thing again. I'd marry the same partner – mind you the same partner – at the same early age.') [. . .]

Married daughters who do not live in the same house as their

1. Not reproduced here. [Ed.]

Mums either move as near as possible or pay frequent visits. In many cases these women come to see their Mums every day. One takes a bus each night to say 'goodnight' if she has been prevented from seeing her Mum in the day. This daughter, aged twenty-five, has since moved back into her mother's household taking her husband and three children with her.

5 J. Klein

The Family in 'Traditional' Working-Class England: 2 [1]

Excerpts from J. Klein, *Samples from English Cultures*,
Routledge & Kegan Paul, 1965, vol. 1, pp. 103–13.

In adolescence the young man starts work, and the pattern of
manliness which is so important in this community takes on its
adult form. The strong interdependence of the men at work is
reflected in their out-of-work and social relations. If the woman's
place is in the home, the man's place is as definitely outside it.
After work, the men go home for a wash and a meal, and then go
out again to meet their friends at the club, the pub, the corner, the
sports-ground. The bond between the men who are accustomed
to meet in this way is so strong and deep that Dennis, Henriques
and Slaughter (1956) liken these groups at one point to 'secret
societies'. It is here that the men experience most fully the emotional satisfactions which social life affords; it is with other men
that they are at their most relaxed, at ease and emotionally
expansive. A man's centre of activity is outside the home. He
works and plays and makes contact with others outside his home.
It is outside his home that the criteria of success and social
acceptance are located.

Mining is an occupation which encourages the formation of
peer-groups. 'The finest lot in the country,' Zweig (1948) often
heard ex-miners say about their former comrades. 'I agree,' said
Zweig. 'But tell me why you think so.' To this came the reply: 'If
a man is willing to die for his comrades, is that not proof enough
for you? And a miner would never spare himself or hesitate
for a moment to rush with help into the most dangerous spot.'[2]
[...]

1. Part of a commentary on N. Dennis, F. Henriques and C. Slaughter
(1956). [Ed.]
2. Zweig, like other authors, relates this characteristic also to the miners'
generosity, solidarity and sense of justice.

The youths in Ashton spend most of their leisure time in groups of about half a dozen. Such a group will grow naturally out of schoolday friendships, perhaps with additions from workmates or from those with whom sporting interests are shared. After his evening meal, the youth of between fifteen or eighteen will walk down to the street corner or the cricket field or the youth club, wherever it is that his particular group is accustomed to gather. Together, they will go to Calderford to the billiard saloon, go to watch a football match or play themselves, and at the weekend visit a dance together. Round about the age of eighteen most of them will begin to drink beer, though very few of them are heavy drinkers yet. It is usual for them to spend an hour or two in the public house before a dance. On occasion one of them will become involved in a scuffle and his mates will come to his aid. Often this results in a full-scale fight.

Fighting is only the extreme of solidarity which is found in these groups of young men. The group is a community group of the most exclusive and possessive kind. For years on end the members will continue to share their leisure time. They do not take kindly to part-time members who have interests elsewhere. It is soon remarked upon if one of the members begins to mix more with another group.

The strongest competition for the attention and time of the group's members is, of course, sex-interest. When a young man begins 'courting strong', the group reacts with strongly discouraging sanctions to the possible diversion of attention. He is teased and threatened with social isolation. 'Well we'd ask thee to come for a pint,' the others say, 'but we expect tha's off to get thy feet under t'table.' To stay with a girl and enjoy her company would be a form of unmanliness. Tenderness is not thought of as part of a man's psychological equipment. The young man has to insist that he is 'getting something out of it'. He will play down his emotional involvement with the girl, justifying to the group the time he spends with her by claiming that she allows him sexual intercourse. The justification is not in terms of giving but in terms of taking. In the group's behaviour and the youth's relation to it at this stage, we see the beginning of what will be a continuing conflict between home ties and peer ties.

The strength of the peer tie does not noticeably diminish with age. In adult life the group of men with whom the miner shares his activities will often still be the one within which he has grown up. When arrangements are made to visit a certain sporting event or when the group goes on a drinking spree, he does not like to be left out; he likes it to be thought that he is still 'one of the lads'.

The male group, over the years, develops a set of attitudes and ideas which very deliberately exclude women, children and strangers. It is at this point in the discussion that the authors refer to the resemblance to a 'secret society'. One of the exclusive mechanisms which define the limits of the group is the use of swear-words; these are directed familiarly to members of the group and offensively to those outside. Women are not supposed to hear these words from men, though they may use them in their own women's circle. Thus for instance the bookie's office is part of the men's world, where women have no place. A woman going into the office is subjected to jokes and language which in a more neutral locality would lead to a fight. The pub is somewhat less a male preserve than it was. A man in a pub swore in the hearing of a girl, was stopped and apologized. A minute or so later he repeated the offence. Her escort bristled. 'I'm sorry, old lad, but she must expect to hear what comes out if she comes into the place at all.' Nevertheless, the offender had to leave. This swearing is known as 'pit-talk', characteristically used in the pit and left behind there except in so far as the conditions are reproduced in other typically male assemblies. 'Pit-talk' not only demarcates the boundary between the women's world and the men's. It also preserves the gap between the generations.

I'm like any other miner; I can swear as well as anybody, and, of course, my son as well – after all, he's twenty-seven and he's working at the face. But we've never sworn in front of each other. In fact I don't think he's ever heard me swear. But one day I was sitting waiting to go out to the pit and a group of colliers came and sat nearby and he was one of them. They started talking and they swore just like any other lot. My lad didn't know I was there and so he swore as merrily as anybody else. Well, I've never felt so awkward in my life before. I could feel myself blushing and managed to creep away without him seeing me. I'm glad I did because we'd both have felt very awkward.

The distinction between men's conversation and women's conversation is determined not only by 'pit-talk'. Just as the men in the clubs talk mainly about their work and secondly about sport and *never* about their homes and families, so do their wives talk first of all about *their* work, i.e. their homes and families, and secondly within the range of things with which they are all immediately familiar. The men discourage any transgressions over the line of this division of interests. When a woman does express any interest in politics or other general topic, she speaks rather apologetically, and can be prepared for her husband to tell her not to interrupt intelligent conversation: 'What the hell do you know about it?'

Except at the weekend, when the men's clubs and the Miners' Welfare Institute allow women in, the women keep together much as the men do. For women as for men, the enjoyment of the company of others is a major source of leisure-time satisfaction. (The other leisure interests of the women are also as few and uncreative as those of the men.) At one or other house in the street, the women will be 'callin'', taking a cup of tea, with family, neighbours or both, spending some time in the morning or the afternoon regularly in this way. At these women's gatherings there is endless gossip about the neighbours, about their own husbands and children, about the past. [...]

The recurrence of strictly contractual attitudes within the domestic sphere, and the way the bargain operates on the whole to the women's disadvantage, makes striking reading for those from another culture. Strictness of role-definition is of course not necessarily related to male dominance, but it happens to be so in Ashton. In extreme cases, the management–worker catch-as-catch-can is repeated by husband and wife, he up to cunning dodges admired by his mates to avoid giving her housekeeping money – she after him to get the money off him before he has spent it all. Dennis, Henriques and Slaughter tell a remarkable story illustrating a possibly legendary extreme in the reproduction of man–management relations within the family sphere. A young panner married a girl from neighbouring Norwood and went to share the house of her parents. His wife's father was an old collier and before the marriage he confided in him:

'Now lad, tha knows we used to have to pay at t' pit if we broke a shovel or a pick. Well, I've never told Mary's mother any different, and every fortnight or so I knock a few shillings off her wages for a shovel or a pick, even though we get 'em supplied now. Mary knows I claim [*sic*] for these things so don't let on I've told thee t' secret; anyway, tha might as well do t' same thesen because she knows no different.'

The young panner maintains he still does this, and his workmates joke with him about his wages every week, making suggestions for deductions. He says that all his brothers-in-law carry on the practice, and one of them, while still living at home, once took no wages to his mother for a month after his pony had been killed in the pit.

Just as industrial conflict is endemic, so is conflict in the home. Our authors note that the many disagreeements between husband and wife are essentially concerned with the question: in which sector of the community shall the money be spent – in the family and the home, or in the club? A girl of eighteen, who had been married two months, replied, when surprise had been expressed at her having a row with her husband: 'Oh, that's nowt. We have a row regularly every Saturday when I ask him for my wage and he doesn't want to take me out with him.' It is not an exaggeration to say that the row is an institution for the present-day family in Ashton. Conditions external to each individual family are responsible for tension within; those same conditions make it impossible for harmony to be achieved by revolt against the whole structure of relations in the family. Nor does friendly and rational discussion of differences seem available as a technique for smoothing out the disagreements. Instead, there will be 'a row'. The row is the conventional way of expressing the conflict. At the same time it is a release.

The wife's role is defined in terms of the husband's convenience much as the husband's role of employee is defined in terms of management's convenience. (The children, similarly, are firmly kept in their place and from an early age made conscious of the social difference between the sexes.) The husband pays his wife an agreed weekly sum, called 'her wages'. She may not know how much he earns or what proportion of his earnings is given her. Indeed, the authors cite an instance in which a woman, asked whether her husband worked in town or nearer home, had to call a neighbour to ask if she knew. With her wage, the woman rules the household and makes all expenditure decisions, except for big items, such as a new cooker, for which her husband will pay out a further share from his wages. This practice is a great help to the wife, for ordinary hire-purchase items are paid out of her wages.

The pattern is established before marriage. The young single men are earning well and very generous in buying each other drinks. Once married, who is going to get the free money? The men's custom of paying the wife a regular wage ensures fairness at home (fairness here referring to the men's feeling that they have fulfilled their contractual obligations) and yet enables them to pay their proper share when drinking with the boys. The club, the pub, the bookie, have first claim on the free money. Leisure may also be bought with it, and the wife is conventionally prevented from putting pressure on the man to go to work. If money is plentiful, why not knock off work for a day? It isn't as though the work were so attractive.

The increased prosperity of the miner has not added in fair proportion to the wife's wages. Rather, because his pleasures are centred in the male group outside the home, it has added to the free spending money. By spending his money with his friends in the way which is conventional in Ashton, the Ashton way of life is perpetuated: the miner maintains his own standing while that of the women is as low as ever.

It is by reason of processes like this that the authors are led to the conclusion that in Ashton the family as a unit is weakened by the existence of a series of institutions and practices which are the domain of the adult miners in the town and which are fundamentally opposed to the families of these men. From the age of courtship, the attraction of the 'secret society' is a challenge to the growth of a full relationship between the miner and his girl or his wife. When he marries, the group's attraction competes with the amount of time, interest and money which he is willing to devote to his family. The authors have no doubt that the conflict between married couples springs from the antagonism between family interests on the one hand and the husband's group on the other.

Unlike the husband, the wives spend little on themselves without the approval of their spouse. The husband will query expenditure on items outside the normal household budget. This budget includes little for her clothes, less for her leisure, nothing for self-improvement. In this way the wife's life is restricted to her family and her neighbours.

Restricted to the home as they are, wives do not appear actively to resent it. When pressed they will acknowledge jealousy of their husband's freedom, but many of them say that they find satisfaction in the care of their children. (Indeed the confinement of the wife to the internal affairs of the family brings her much closer to her children than the father.) The husband having fulfilled his obligations when he has paid over the wife's wage, it is part of the women's side of the bargain that the home must be a comfortable place to come back to after work, with a meal prepared, a room tidy and warm, and a wife ready to wait upon him. There must be no cold meals, late meals, washing lying about, or ironing to do while he is at home. These duties should be performed while he is at work; when he is at home, the wife should concentrate on his comfort. The wife agrees with these stipulations; both acknowledge that a miner's work is hard and that it is a 'poor do' if the wife cannot fulfill her part of the contract as long as the husband fulfills his. The authors cite an instance where a wife had gone to the pictures after asking her sister to prepare a meal and serve it when the husband came home. The husband so confronted threw the dinner 'to t'back of t' fire'. It was his wife's duty to look after him. He would accept no substitute.

In fairness, it must be said that the contractual relation shows in a better light when one considers what happens when the man is unable to fulfill his part of the bargain. If the man is out of work or paid very low wages, he may agree that the wife should go out to work. Then the bargain changes, a new contract is made: he may cook or make the beds if he comes home before she does. That this is a deviant pattern is shown by the embarrassment of the man in acknowledging that he does this. That it is a socially permitted alternative is shown later in the history of this very man who had thrown the food away. Because of deafness he was forced to change to a job with much lower pay. His wife now goes out to work at 7 a.m. and returns at 5.30 p.m. He helps her in all manner of ways in the house and has a meal ready for *her* when she returns home.

In view of all these considerations it is no surprise that the authors comment that no developing or deepening of the conjugal relationship takes place after the intensive sex-life of early marriage. Marriages in Ashton are a matter of 'carrying on' pure and simple. So long as the man works and gives his wife and family sufficient, and the woman uses the family's 'wage' wisely and gives her husband the few things he demands, the marriage will carry on.

Because of the division in activity and ideas between men and women, husband and wife tend to have little to talk about or do together. Here, in Ashton, the family is a system of relationships torn by a major contradiction at its heart; husband and wife live separate and in a sense secret lives. Many married couples seem to have no intimate understanding of one another; the only occasions on which they really approach each other is in bed, and sexual relations are apparently rarely satisfactory to both partners. The stress on manliness defined as absence of tenderness, and the connexion of sexual matters with pit-talk, are obvious components for an explanation of this. In addition, the lack of give-and-take, the contractual view of all relationships, and the unusually rigid division of labour must be taken into consideration.

References

DENNIS, N., HENRIQUES, F., and SLAUGHTER, C. (1956), *Coal is Our Life*, Eyre & Spottiswoode.
ZWEIG, F. (1948), *Men in the Pits*, Gollancz.

6 M. Anderson

Family, Household and the Industrial Revolution

Adapted from M. Anderson, 'Household structure and the industrial revolution: mid-nineteenth-century Preston in comparative perspective', in T. P. R. Laslett (ed.), *The Comparative History of Family and Household*, Cambridge University Press, 1971.

Aims of the paper

The Lancashire cotton towns in the middle of the nineteenth century were in many ways a half-way house between a predominantly rural pre-industrial England and the predominantly urban-industrial/commercial post-capitalist society of the present day. Communities like Preston, the town I shall be most concerned with here, had between a quarter and a third of their adult male population directly involved in factory industry. Because of the extensive use of child labour, however, a considerably higher proportion of the population were at one time or another of their lives employed in the dominant cotton textile industry. The domestic handloom sector still survived, but it was of ever-shrinking size. Of those not employed in industry, hardly any had agricultural occupations. The prosperity of the mass of the population of almost 70,000 was firmly linked to the cotton textile industry.

These communities were, then, firmly a part of the urban-industrial order, oases in the midst of a predominantly rural nation. In them were to be found all the problems which beset capitalist societies – cyclical unemployment, overcrowding, large families struggling on low wages, factory-working wives and mothers, and large inmigrant populations. But this was still an early stage in the transition to the more integrated advanced industrial society we know today. The problems had emerged with full force but the social changes which were to ameliorate or remove them had not yet appeared. Thus bureaucratically organized social security provision for the old, the sick, the unemployed, the pregnant mother and the large family was minimal and only given at great social and psychological cost to the recipient. Bureaucratically organized community social welfare services were almost non-existent. Fertility control was only just beginning, and mortality was as high or higher than ever. Wages were low, primary poverty widespread, housing appalling and relatively expensive.

Obviously, these communities have particular interest to the social historian and the sociologist. By investigating their family and household structure we can perhaps get clues which will help us resolve the many paradoxes which appear when we compare pre-industrial England with the present day. Here I want to concentrate particularly on one of these.

Why, contrary to all that one might be led to expect by the predictions of the cruder, and even of many of the more sophisticated, proponents of the thesis of convergence of family structures with industrialization towards a conjugal type, has there apparently been a massive *increase* over the past two centuries in co-residence of married couples and their parents, and precisely how and when did it come about?

The remainder of this paper falls into two parts. The first presents some (necessarily selective) data on various aspects of household and family structure in Preston in 1851, and contrasts it, on the one hand, with some of the figures which Laslett has at various times made public from his investigations on pre-industrial England (e.g. Laslett, 1969), and, on the other, with recent data on British family structure, notably from the 1966 sample census and from Rosser and Harris's study of Swansea.[1] I have also included for comparison some figures for 1851 from my own data on the Lancashire agricultural villages where many of the migrants to Preston had been born. This area was, however, unlike most of the rest of rural England where the agriculture was based on large farms and outdoor day labourers. In rural Lancashire there was much more of an almost peasant-type subsistence family farm system, where what employed labour there was was mainly the indoor farm servant, marriage was late,

1. General Register Office (1968); Rosser and Harris (1965). Neither of these sources present data in quite the form required for the purpose at hand, so some estimates have had to be made. The data based on these two sources are, therefore, only approximate. For a fuller discussion of this point see the original version of this paper.

many never married, and children remained at home into their twenties in the expectation of an inheritance of the farm or of a portion of the family estate (cf. Anderson, in press, a, chapter 7).

The second part offers an interpretation of the trends which the first reveals. Many of these interpretations are necessarily rather speculative. We still do not have nearly enough studies of the family structure of factory towns in the nineteenth, let alone in the early twentieth, century to be able to make firm generalizations about the impact of the various facets of urban-industrial life. Nor do we have adequate descriptive data for pre-industrial rural England to support our crude data on co-residence. What data we have, however, seem compatible with the interpretations offered here.

The Preston data are taken from a 10 per cent sample of houses from the enumerators' books of the 1851 census. The rural sample is not representative of any finite population. It was drawn with the object of comparing the family structure of those persons who had migrated to Preston from villages where more than half the 1831 population had been employed in agriculture, with the family types which were found in the villages from which they had come. A variable fraction stratified sample was therefore drawn so that the percentage of sample households taken from any one village was proportional to the percentage of all the migrants who had come from that village. Since, however, the family and household structure of these migrants turned out to be little different from that of the population as a whole, I shall here, for convenience, use it for comparisons with the whole Preston population.

Households are taken as 'census families'. Doubtful cases follow the rules outlined elsewhere (Anderson, in press, c).

Historical data

Table 1 shows the extent to which households were likely, at different points in the past, to contain persons outside the nuclear family of the head.[2]

2. The figures for England and Wales are from General Register Office (1968, pp. 1–2). Those for Swansea are derived from Rosser and Harris (1965, p. 148). The figures in the original are for household, not family

Table 1 Percentage of Households with Kin, Lodgers and Servants for Various Communities

	Kin	Lodgers	Servants*
England and Wales 1966 (approx.)	10	†	0
Swansea 1960 (approx.)	10–13	<3	<3
Preston 1851	23	23	10
Rural 1851	27	10	28
Laslett 1564–1821	10	<1	29

*Servants include apprentices in Preston and the rural samples
†Figures not available

The most marked differences which seem to emerge here are:

1. When compared with pre-industrial England, the larger proportion of households with kin in both 1851 samples, to a level well above the modern figure. This figure, indeed, approximates to that for pre-industrial England. The Lancashire rural sample is probably not typical of England as a whole, though Professor Williams's Ashworthy figure (between 31 per cent and 34 per cent) is actually higher (Williams, 1963, p. 218). Both Ashworthy and North Lancashire had a predominance of family farms and few farm labourers, and it was above all on these family farms that kin, particularly married children co-residing with parents, were to be found.[3]

2. The far larger number of households with lodgers in Preston, compared both with pre-industrial England and with Swansea. In Preston, lodgers made up 12 per cent of the sample and over 20 per cent of the twenty to twenty-four age group. The married couples in lodgings were largely young and with small families, and inmigrants were over-represented in their number (cf. Anderson, in press, a, chapter 5).

3. Servants in Preston in 1851 already show signs of the ultimate

composition, and contain a 4 per cent 'other' category, which includes both co-residing non-kin, and families with kin other than married children and their children, and siblings. The figures for pre-industrial England are from Laslett (1969), except for the lodger figure which is from Armstrong (1968, p. 72).

3. For a fuller discussion and explanation, see Anderson (in press, a) chapters 3 and 7.

decline to which this class was destined. Employment in the factories was, of course, not conditional on co-residence, and the opportunities it offered to the young made it difficult to recruit suitable children to service. Servants and apprentices made up 3 per cent of the population.

In the rural sample servants made up 16 per cent of the sample population aged over fifteen. By contrast with the towns, the number of men more or less equalled the number of women, and the 225 farm servants who were aged over fifteen made up 43 per cent of the paid agricultural labour force in these age groups.

Table 2 turns attention to the structure of the families of household heads.

Table 2 Structure of the Families of Household Heads[4]

Family Type	England & Wales 1966 (approx.)	Swansea 1960 (approx.)	Preston 1851	Rural 1851	Laslett 1564–1821
No related person	17	10+	4	5	
Married couple only	24	22+	10	12	90
Parent(s) and unmarried child(ren) only	49	54+	63	56	
Parent(s) and married child(ren) but no other kin	5	9+	9	6	10
Parent(s) and married child(ren) with other kin	0	<5*	1	0	
Other combinations of kin	4		13	21	
All (percentage)	99	100	100	100	100
N =	1,533,954	1958	1240	855	..

*Some of this group are here because they have co-residing non-kin, since the figures for Swansea are for household structure, not structure of the families of the household heads.

4. For comment on the Swansea figures see footnote 2. The pre-industrial figures are derived from Laslett (1969).

The markedly higher present-day figures for both Swansea and England and Wales as a whole are obviously the most striking features of this table.

Little difference appears in Table 2 in the proportion living without any relative in their household. The different distribution of childless couples compared with couples with unmarried children mainly reflects the fall in family size and the older age distribution of the Swansea population.

Other highly significant differences appear in the remaining rows. Laslett's communities have very few parent/married child households indeed (Laslett, 1969). By contrast, in Preston, 10 per cent of all families were of this type, and Rosser and Harris's modern figures are at about the Preston level, though the figures for England and Wales as a whole are lower. Foster also found a 10 per cent figure for Oldham (1967, p. 314). The urban-industrial revolution, then, seems, contrary surely to all expectations ten years ago, to have been associated with a considerable increase in co-residence of parents and married children. However, Foster's (1967) finding[5] that the comparable 1851 figures for Northampton and South Shields, both industrial towns, were only 5 per cent and 4 per cent respectively suggests that the issue is not as simple as it might at first appear. Further discussion of this issue appears below.

The other main point to emerge from Table 2 is the way in which 'other kin' family types maintained or even increased their proportion in the urban industrial society, and only fell away in the past 100 years. This issue too is best discussed below. Suffice to note here that Foster found these 'other kin' in 12 per cent of Northampton families, 16 per cent of Oldham families and 11 per cent of South Shields families (1967, p. 314). Certainly this family type was a widespread phenomenon.

Just who these co-residing kin were is explored further in Table 3.

By far the most remarkable thing to modern eyes about both columns of Table 3 is the immense number of 'parentless'

5. Firth (1964, p. 74) found that only 16 per cent of his Highgate sample (though 30 per cent of the middle class (Crozier, 1965, p. 17)) had co-residing kin, which suggests that in London, too, this family type was not as predominant as it was in Lancashire.

Table 3 Relationship of Kin to Household Head
(Percentage of All Kin)

	Preston 1851		Rural 1851	
Father or father-in-law	3·3*		3·2†	
Mother or mother-in-law	5·7*		4·0†	
Married/widowed son or son-in-law	11·1		6·9	
Married/widowed daughter or daughter-in-law	12·3		5·9	
Grandchild with parents	13·7		10·9	
'Stem' family members		46·1		30·9
Unmarried siblings (married head)	9·1		8·4	
Unmarried siblings (unmarried head)	5·0		8·6	
Unmarried members of family of orientation		14·1		17·0
Married or widowed siblings or siblings-in-law	5·1		4·0	
Nieces/nephews with parents	4·3		2·2	
Married siblings and family		9·4		6·2
Nieces/nephews without parents	15·0		11·9	
Grandchildren without parents	13·3		30·2	
'Parentless' children		28·3		42·1
Uncles, aunts and cousins	1·4	1·4	2·0	2·0
Others	0·8‡	0·8	1·7§	1·7
All (percentage)	100·1	100·1	99·9	99·9
N =	513	513	404	404

*All widowed.

†All but one widowed.

‡Son-in-law's father, son-in-law's brother, grandmother, great nephew.

§Five not specified (probably nieces/nephews, siblings-in-law, or cousins) great-niece and her illegitimate child.

children, 28 per cent of all kin in Preston, and 42 per cent in the rural sample. I have been unable to find any comparable tables for present-day communities, but a glance at the first column of Table 2 suggests that the figure is well under 5 per cent. By contrast the proportion for pre-industrial England may well have been higher still, and can certainly have been little lower.

Thus in Preston, while there were also still large numbers of this 'parentless' group so rare today, there was also a much larger number of the 'new', 'twentieth-century' group of one or two grandparents, one or two married children and their families, and married siblings and their families. We appear, therefore, to have in Preston something of a halfway stage in the transition, with both pre-industrial and modern types of kinship super-imposed.

Before trying to analyse just who these various groups were, and why they were co-residing, attention is perhaps usefully turned to Tables 4 and 5. Aggregate tables on family structure, such as Tables 2 and 3, can be rather misleading in a comparative perspective, because, given the typical English pattern where co-residence of married children and parents is mainly confined to the first years of marriage, and to the old age (particularly the widowhood) of the parents, such tables are highly sensitive to varying population age structures. Before proceeding further, then, it is instructive to look briefly at some tables where age or life-cycle stage are controlled.

Table 4 shows the co-residence patterns of the section of the community aged over sixty-five. The 'Britain' figures are from the old people in a three industrial societies study (Stehouwer, 1965, p. 146).

The marked pattern of co-residence with children in Preston is particularly to be noted. Rather few old people there lived apart from a relative. Indeed, when the proportion of old people who could have had a child alive at all is estimated (and this figure is considerably below that for modern Britain and probably below the rural figure), it is obvious that well over 80 per cent of those old people who had a child alive were, in Preston in 1851, in fact living with one or other of their children.[6]

Table 5 shows the residence patterns of the young childless couples.[7]

In Preston, as in Swansea, only just over half of all childless younger couples lived in households of their own and apart from their parents. In contrast to Swansea, however, where most of the rest lived with parents, over half of this group in Preston lived as

6. For details of the estimate, see Anderson (in press, c).
7. For Swansea, from Rosser and Harris (1965, p. 167).

Table 4 Household Composition of the Over Sixty-Fives (Percentage) Listing in Priority Order

	Married			Widowed, single and separated		
	Britain 1962	Preston 1851	Rural 1851	Britain 1962	Preston 1851	Rural 1851
Living with:						
Married child(ren)	6	16	13	27	41	26
Unmarried child(ren)	26	47	36	27	29	21
Spouse only	68	37	50	–	–	–
Other kin only	–	–	–	4	8	18
No related person	–	–	–	42	22	35
All (percentage)	100	100	99	100	100	100
N =	1022	70	143	889	124	106

lodgers in another household. (None in Preston co-resided in a household headed by a kinsman other than a parent.) Part of this difference may be due to the rather different criteria by which households are distinguished in the two studies, but there is no doubt that many of these lodger couples did, in fact, share a common table and would therefore have been classified as lodgers even by Rosser and Harris. Compared with Laslett's figures, in contrast, even the 16 per cent who lived with parents are probably a very numerous body indeed.

Table 5 Residence Patterns of Childless Couples where the Wife was Aged under Forty-Five (Percentage)

	Swansea 1960	Preston 1851	Rural 1851
Percentage living:			
In own household	57	58	80
Co-residing with parents	40	16	13
Other	3	26	7
All (percentage)	100	100	100
N =	97	158	46

Thus it seems likely that urban-industrial life of the cotton-town type markedly increased the proportion of wage-earner families in which parents and married children co-resided. It also markedly increased the alternative form of residence for the young married couple, living as lodgers with another family. Compared with pre-industrial England, however, the proportion of 'parentless' children did not decline, and may even have increased somewhat. Twentieth-century urban life saw a marked reduction in this latter group but some considerable further increase in the co-residence of young married children and their parents, probably to some extent at the expense of the lodger group. But, in spite of this increase, more old people live alone today than in nineteenth-century Preston; possibly more do so than did in pre-industrial England.

Interpretation of data

I have argued elsewhere (Anderson, in press, a, especially chapter 2) that, if we are to understand variations and changes in patterns of kinship relationships, the only worthwhile approach is consciously and explicitly to investigate the manifold advantages and disadvantages that any actor can obtain from maintaining one relational pattern rather than another, and I have outlined what I see as the main considerations which must be taken into account in any such approach. Here I want to go further and suggest, that, in the case of *co-residence*, a very special set of hypotheses, which consider only economic advantages and disadvantages, may be appropriate. In short, I am suggesting that any significant proportion of one group of actors in a society (say young married men) will generally only be found *co-residing* with another given class of kin (say widowed parents) if:

1. The time discounted, average life-span, economic advantages to most of them of doing so (bearing in mind that co-residence will normally imply some sharing of resources and support if necessary) outweigh or at least are not greatly exceeded by the economic disadvantages which they would suffer either directly from the kinsman, or from third parties, if they did not do so: and

2. If most of the other party would also receive net advantages calculated in the same way.

Conscious calculation of these advantages is seen in this approach as only occurring under rather special conditions;[8] generally norms develop to set a seal on conduct which is in line with these economic pressures. In highly stable and fairly prosperous societies (which the societies we are concerned with here were not), where the future is reasonably predictable, it can be shown, on the premises used, that norms would logically develop as a kind of insurance policy to provide at least for all who have relatives, some minimum standard of living provided by kin, except if assistance at this minimal level were seen as obtainable from some other outside agency.

There is no space to go further into this matter in this paper. Here I am mainly concerned with the principle as a conceptual framework which may help us to understand changes and differences in patterns of co-residence. To this detailed problem I now return.

'Parentless' children

Firstly, then, who were these parentless children who seem to have been present in a sizeable proportion of households over most of rural and urban England?

Some of the odd grandchildren were undoubtedly illegitimate sons and daughters of co-residing daughters, or, indeed, of daughters who had left home to marry or for other reasons.[9] It is now impossible except by reconstitution techniques to ascertain what this proportion might have been, but it does seem as if this was a fairly standard behaviour pattern. A second group were children of orphaned parents, children who had lost one parent (particularly the mother), and also children of mothers who had remarried. In all these cases it seems to have been normal for relatives to take over the children, assisted often by a small parish allowance in return (Anderson, in press, a, chapter 10). Children in this class undoubtedly make up a not inconsiderable proportion of the group as a whole. A third, and probably small,

8. These problems, together with those raised by the next sentence, and such problems as the determinants of rates of time discount, are discussed at some length in Anderson (in press, a).

9. For the detailed references in support of this statement see Anderson (in press, a, chapter 10).

group are those who, though they had parents alive and living in the community, lived with aunts, uncles or grandparents to relieve the overcrowding in their own households or, possibly, to provide aged grandparents with some company and help around the house or in a small shop. Several cases which look very like this cropped up during the work on enumerators' books, and the phenomenon of 'lending a child' is not unknown in modern working-class communities (cf. e.g. Young and Willmott, 1957, p. 38).

Certainly, for one reason or another, widows and single women were more than twice as likely to have such 'parentless' kin in their households as were the rest of the population. Most of these young men and women were already earning and would thus be already keeping themselves and, indeed, probably making some useful contribution towards the family finances (about 80 per cent were over ten years of age). Many more would soon be doing so in a society where child labour was the norm (and many of those who were sent out to work very young do indeed seem to have been being cared for by kin; cf. e.g. Parliamentary Papers, PP 1833 XX, DI, 34, and see also Anderson, in press, a, chapter 11). Many of the rest would have been the children of co-residing daughters who more than paid for their keep.

To this social welfare function, however, one must also add an important economic function of kinship which both overlapped with the first and also made its own independent contribution to the figures. In the nineteenth century it was above all through the agency of kin that one got a job.[10] Where one had a kinsman who had his own business or farm he might frequently offer a job directly, particularly to the sons of siblings who had fallen on hard times, and this would frequently involve co-residence (Anderson, in press, a, chapters 9 and 10). Some of these kin are described in the occupation columns of the schedules as servants, while many so-called servants were almost certainly kin. Their status in the household was probably often little different from that of the non-relative who would otherwise have been given the place. The net cost, therefore, was probably minimal, the system meant that orphans and the children of destitute kin were provided for,

10. For a detail discussion see Anderson (in press, a, chapter 9).

and kin were probably easier to sanction, less likely to leave their jobs, and probably, therefore, more reliable.

In the towns, of course, most of the population were employees, but recruitment to jobs in the factories or in the labouring gangs was similarly influenced by kinship considerations. 'Asking for' a job for kin was normal in the factory towns, and the employers used the kinship system to recruit labour from the country (Anderson, in press, a, chapter 9). This process of drawing in kin from rural areas continued in London to the end of the nineteenth century at least.[11] Most of these kin were single, being especially siblings, and nieces and nephews. When they got to the town to the job their kinsman found for them, they had nowhere to live, so they normally lodged with him. This, then, is the second major source of 'parentless' kin. It is also, surely, the reason why inmigrant couples (except significantly those from other factory towns) had almost as many siblings, nieces and nephews, and cousins in their households as did the Preston born (for details, see Anderson, in press, a, chapter 10), and also, surely, the reason why it was above all the better paid factory workers – overseers and spinners and the like – who had these relatives in their homes (Anderson, in press, a, chapter 10). These were the men with the greatest influence over factory recruitment.

In sum, then, in industrializing England, men continued to be able, and indeed possibly became more able, to perform functions for their kin which were to these kin a considerable economic advantage. They could, moreover, do this at minimum cost to themselves except sometimes in the rather short run. The twentieth century, by contrast, reduced the control of kin over jobs, and reduced the scale of migration of young single persons. At the same time orphanage decreased and the Welfare State cushioned the poor from the worst ravages of crises. In consequence this class of kin largely disappeared from British homes.

Parents and married children

To explain the co-residence of parents and married children in larger proportions in Preston and Oldham than in both pre-industrial England, and other nineteenth-century towns so far

11. Perhaps the classic discussion of this kin-based migration and occupational recruitment service is in Booth (1892, pp. 132–5).

studied is a considerably more difficult problem. By contrast with the situation among the better-off farmers in rural Lancashire, a fairly simple economic explanation based on economic co-operation in a family enterprise and the promise of future rewards from it is clearly unsuitable (Anderson, in press, a, chapter 7); by far the larger proportion of the population of Preston were employees, and, anyway, there was there no clear association between socio-economic group, and parent/married child co-residence.

Rather, as I have argued at greater length elsewhere (Anderson, in press, a, especially chapters 10–12), my interpretation requires that attention be turned to other aspects of urban-social life. In most working-class communities before the coming of the Welfare State, if someone survived to old age (and many did not), then he could look forward to a life of poverty. This was particularly true, perhaps, in the towns, where the cost of living, and also rents were higher. It seems probable then that old people, particularly widows, would in general have been best off if they could co-reside with married children. They would thus save on rent, and participate in the economies of scale of the common table. Young married couples, too, might benefit from sharing, because they, too, would save on rent. But, and this is the crucial point, nineteenth-century society and the society which preceded it were, in general, poor societies, societies where after one had done one's best for one's own nuclear family, there was little left for anyone else, unless that someone else could contribute to the family's resources in return. And, if one was young and newly married, to take an old person into one's household or to join the household of that old person meant that this person could not but be given some of these scarce resources now, and also in the future when one's family was larger and poverty loomed at the door; the old persons would probably need some help even if they were receiving a parish pittance. If one refused to take them in, the Guardians would usually make sure they did not die of want; indeed their standard of living would probably be little if at all lower. Usually, moreover, this person could not give much of use in return. This, I would argue, explains the reluctance of the population of most nineteenth-century towns, and probably also of nineteenth-century and indeed pre-industrial rural areas, to share with old people even when soon after marriage they could for a while afford to do so. It is much more difficult to eject someone than never to take them in.

In the cotton towns, however, the situation was different. Here, though poverty was widespread, it was a little less biting than elsewhere and it lasted for a shorter part of the life cycle (cf. Foster, 1967). The drain of a non-productive relative was thus anyway somewhat less severe. But, and this may have been the crucial issue, the relative could also substantially *increase the family income*, not usually by seeking employment in the labour market, but by caring for the children and home while the mother worked in the factory. In this way the mother could have child and home looked after better, and probably more cheaply, than by hiring someone to do so, and the income she brought in kept the relative and gave a considerable surplus to the family budget.

Thus, in these communities, the old person could be valuable, not a drain on family resources. Even if the wife did not work, the old person could frequently earn her keep by performing similar services for a neighbour who did. It is, then, perhaps not surprising that few old people lived alone.

By contrast, however, not all young married couples had parents alive, and many were inmigrants whose parents lived elsewhere. It was migrants in particular who lived in lodgings rather than with kin, though some actually brought their parents in to join them. Some others had many siblings still living at home, so here considerations of overcrowding prevented their co-residing, though many lived near by. It would thus seem that only a minority of young married couples, even in Preston, were physically able to co-reside.

One may then perhaps suggest more speculatively that in the later nineteenth and early twentieth centuries these advantages of co-residence continued in Lancashire and gradually spread elsewhere. The advantages to young married couples of co-residence if anthing increased as housing continued to be in short supply. At the same time the decline in family poverty meant that, proportionally, the cash disadvantages to them of taking in dependent kin declined. At the same time family size began to fall. More space thus became available at home, and fewer other married siblings were competing for the right to co-reside. More people had parents available too, because inmigrants came to be a smaller proportion of the total population, and some decline in adult mortality set in.

On the other hand, this very stabilization of communities, together with the old-age pension, changed the situation for the old. They could live near their children, not with them,[12] and more and more could afford to pay rent for a home of their own. Their children anyway were younger and most had left home for a while before widowhood struck.

Thus, while more and more couples came to co-reside for a few years after marriage, the proportion of old people who wished to co-reside probably began to fall. Some detailed investigations of household structure in the early twentieth century are necessary before we can understand the full situation here. The changes brought about by the introduction of the old-age pension in 1908 may well have been particularly significant.

What evidence is there in support of this interpretation?

Firstly, it is possible to show that in Preston it was only those in more affluent states who took in kin who could not support themselves. In Preston, of all households whose family standard of living was estimated as being within 4s. of the primary poverty line, only 2 per cent contained kin none of whom had a recorded means of support; of those with a standard of living 20s. and more above, the figure was 11 per cent. By contrast 9 per cent of the first group and 12 per cent of the second contained kin at least one of whom was self-supporting.[13]

There is also considerable contemporary comment by members of the working class that the possibility of assistance to kin was severely circumscribed by the costs which it incurred, unless such kin could either bring in some income through employment, or unless the Poor Law authorities were prepared to pay them some relief (see Anderson, in press, a, chapters 10 and 11). The Poor Law Commissioners of 1834 found a similar attitude to support of parents to be prevalent in many parts of rural England (e.g.

12. For a similar observation on modern communities, cf. Willmott and Young (1960, p. 43).

13. Cf. Anderson (in press, a, especially chapter 11). The method of calculating the standard of living is set out in Anderson (in press, b).

PP 1834 XXVII, especially 54). In addition, calculating reactions of this kind to assistance to kin in situations of extreme poverty have been pointed out by my own research on pre-famine rural Ireland (Anderson, in press, a, chapter 7), by Banfield in Italy (1958, especially p. 121), and by Sahlins as typical of primitive societies (1965, especially p. 165).

Secondly, there is also supporting evidence for the special interpretation which has been offered for the cotton towns. Just such an explanation was offered for the low Lancashire poor rates by the special commissioner sent to inquire into the state of Stockport in 1842 (PP 1842 XXXV, 7 and 77). Households with children under ten where the wife worked were three times as likely to have had a co-residing grandmother (Anderson, in press, a). Some married couples actually took unrelated old people into their households rent free and all found to provide just such a service (cf. e.g. Waugh, 1881, p. 85; cited in Anderson, in press, a, chapter 11), and others brought their parents in from the country (PP 1836 XXXIV, 25, 69; PP 1859 Ses 2, VII, 116; PP 1837–8 XIX, 309; and sample data). Booth's (1894) data on poor relief for the elderly, compiled at the end of the century, show markedly fewer old people in receipt of relief in areas where married women habitually worked.

Obviously, at this stage, such an interpretation remains speculative, but it does seem to offer considerable scope for future research. The problem is a complex one, and many factors are obviously involved which we are only gradually coming to understand.

References

ANDERSON, M. (in press, a), *Family Structure in Nineteenth-Century Lancashire*, Cambridge University Press.
ANDERSON, M. (in press, b), 'Sources and techniques for the study of family structure in nineteenth-century Britain', in E. A. Wrigley (ed.), *The Study of Nineteenth-Century Society*, Weidenfeld & Nicolson.
ANDERSON, M. (in press, c), 'Standard tabulation procedures for houses, households and other groups of residents, in the enumeration books of the censuses of 1851 to 1891', in E. A. Wrigley (ed.), *The Study of Nineteenth-Century Society*, Weidenfeld & Nicolson.

ARMSTRONG, W. A. (1968), 'The interpretation of the census enumerators' books for Victorian towns', in H. J. Dyos (ed.), *The Study of Urban History*, Edward Arnold.

BANFIELD, E. C. (1958), *The Moral Basis of a Backward Society*, Free Press.

BOOTH, C. (ed.) (1892), *Life and Labour of the People in London*, vol. 3, Macmillan.

BOOTH, C. (1894), *The Aged Poor in England and Wales*, Macmillan.

CROZIER, D. (1965), 'Kinship and occupational succession', *Sociological Review*, new series, vol. 13, pp. 15–43.

FIRTH, R. (1964), 'Family and kinship in industrial society', in P. Halmos (ed.), 'The development of industrial societies', *Sociological Review Monograph*, no. 8, Keele.

FOSTER, J. O. (1967), 'Capitalism and class consciousness in earlier nineteenth-century Oldham', Ph.D. thesis, University of Cambridge.

GENERAL REGISTER OFFICE (1968), *Sample Census, 1966, Household Composition Tables*, H.M.S.O.

LASLETT, T. P. R. (1969), 'Size and structure of the household in England over three centuries: mean household size in England since the sixteenth century', *Population Studies*, vol. 23, pp. 199–223.

ROSSER, C., and HARRIS, C. C. (1965), *The Family and Social Change*, Routledge & Kegan Paul.

SAHLINS, M. D. (1965), 'On the sociology of primitive exchange', in M. Banton (ed.), *The Relevance of Models for Social Anthropology*, Tavistock.

STEHOUWER, J. (1965), 'Relations between generations and the three generation household in Denmark', in E. Shanas and G. F. Streib (eds.), *Social Structure and the Family: Generational Relations*, Prentice-Hall.

WAUGH, E. (1881), *Factory Folk During the Cotton Famine*, in *Works*, Haywood, vol. 2.

WILLIAMS, W. M. (1963), *A West Country Village: Family Kinship and Land*, Routledge & Kegan Paul.

WILLMOTT, P., and YOUNG, M. (1960), *Family and Class in a London Suburb*, Routledge & Kegan Paul.

YOUNG, M., and WILLMOTT, P. (1957), *Family and Kinship in East London*, Routledge & Kegan Paul; Penguin Books, 1962.

Parliamentary papers

1833 XX *First report of the ... Commissioners ... [on] ... the employment of children in factories ... with minutes of evidence ...*

1834 XXVII *Report from His Majesty's Commissioners for inquiring into the administration and practical operation of the Poor Laws.*

1836 XXXIV *Poor inquiry, Ireland; Appendix G. Report on the state of the Irish poor in Great Britain.*

1837–8 XIX *Report by the Select Committee of the House of Lords ...*
[on]... *several cases* ... [arising from] ... *the operation of the Poor
Law Amendment Act* ..., *with minutes of evidence* ....

1842 XXXV ... *Evidence taken, and report made, by the Assistant Poor
Law Commissioner sent to inquire into the state of the population of
Stockport.*

1859 Ses 2 VII *Minutes of evidence taken before the Select Committee
on irremoveable poor.* ...

Part Two
Relationships of Adults with Parents and Wider Kin

Parsons's assertion (Reading 2 and Parsons, 1959) that 'the isolated nuclear family' typified the American kinship system set off a major controversy among family sociologists (cf., for example, Litwak, 1960a and b; Rodman 1965). Sussman and Burchinal (Reading 7) were among Parsons's most vehement critics, producing in support of their case a mass of evidence on exchange of services, cash and valuable gifts, on visiting patterns, and on the extent of the desire to interact with kin.

Parsons (Reading 8), replying to his critics, argues that he has been misunderstood. He was seeking to demonstrate that, by comparison with many pre-industrial societies, there is a much greater differentiation of the kinship system from the other major sub-systems of society. There is a much greater degree of *choice* over the extent to which one interacts with kin, and therefore of variation in patterns of kinship relationships, of a kind largely unknown in other societies. Readers may like to contrast Reading 1, and also to refer to the useful discussion in Harris (1969).

More recent writers have sought to explore more deeply the extent and the sources of these variations, and have shown up something of the complexity of the problem. Readings 9, 10 and 11 are three good examples of attempts to elucidate the patterns and social significance of kinship relationships in modern societies on the basis of empirical research. Note particularly Adams's stress (Reading 10) on the need to differentiate clearly between different categories of kin. A major problem, however, has been to agree on just what one is trying to measure and why, and each of these authors approaches the problem from a different standpoint. Note, also, the range of variables reviewed by Sussman and Burchinal (Reading 7).

Thus, Turner (Reading 9) treats as his dependent variable the extent to which kinship directly influences the patterning of social relationships in other social organizations. Adams (Reading 10) stresses feelings of obligation and affect, and contact rates. Bell (Reading 11) concentrates particularly on the extent to which kinship relationships provide resources which the nuclear family can use to attain its goals, particularly its goal of maintaining status in the local community. Obviously, these different approaches to the subject lead to different conclusions and to problems of comparability. It is at least arguable that much of the difference between Bell's and Adams's conclusions on the effect of social mobility on kinship is the result of their different concepts rather than of differences in attitudes towards social mobility in the two societies. There is obviously some scope for conceptual clarification in this area.

Another issue that has attracted much recent attention is the relationship between kinship, friendship and neighbours in mobile industrial societies. Litwak and Szelenyi (Reading 12) offer an interesting theoretical discussion of this problem, but there have been a number of other lines of approach (cf. particularly Adams, 1967). The setting of kinship in a wider primary group setting is obviously a fruitful line for future research.

References

ADAMS, B. N. (1967), 'Interaction theory and the social network', *Sociometry*, vol. 30, pp. 64–78.
HARRIS, C. C. (1969), *The Family*, Allen & Unwin.
LITWAK, E. (1960a), 'Occupational mobility and extended family cohesion', *American Sociological Review*, vol. 25, pp. 9–21.
LITWAK, E. (1960b), 'Geographic mobility and extended family cohesion', *American Sociological Review*, vol. 25, pp. 385–94.
PARSONS, T. (1959), 'The social structure of the family', in R. N. Anshen (ed.), *The Family, its Function and Destiny*, Harper & Row, pp. 241–74.
RODMAN, H. (1965), 'Talcott Parsons' view of the changing American family', in H. Rodman (ed.), *Marriage, Family and Society: A Reader*, Random House.

7 M. B. Sussman and L. G. Burchinal

The Kin Family Network in Urban-Industrial America

M. B. Sussman and L. G. Burchinal, 'Kin family network:
unheralded structure in current conceptualization of family functioning',
Marriage and Family Living, vol. 24, 1962, pp. 231–40.

Introduction

Most Americans reject the notion that receiving aid from their
kin is a good thing. The proper ideological stance is that the
individual and his family should fend for themselves. The family
in this instance is nuclear in structure and consists of husband and
wife and children. Further investigation would probably reveal
that most of these rejectors are receiving or have received financial
and other types of aid from their kin long after the time they were
supposed to be on their own. After marriage many are involved
within a network of mutual assistance with kin, especially with
parents. Moreover, one would find that independence of the
nuclear family of procreation is being maintained. Where independence is threatened, it is probably due to other causes. The
rejection of the idea of receiving aid from kin and actually being
helped by them is another case of discrepancy between belief and
practice.

Discrepancies between belief and practice of 'ideal' and 'real'
behavior are common in our society. In family sociology the
reason is 'academic cultural lag', the lag between apparently
antiquated family theory and empirical reality. The theory
stresses the social isolation and social mobility of the nuclear
family while findings from empirical studies reveal an existing and
functioning extended-kin family system closely integrated within
a network of relationships and mutual assistance along bilateral
kinship lines and encompassing several generations.[1]

The major purpose of this paper is to reduce the lag between

1. The authors adopt Eugene Litwak's interpretation of the modified
extended family. It is one that 'does not require geographical propinquity,
occupational nepotism, or integration, and there are no strict authority
relations, but equalitarian ones.' (see Litwak, 1960b). The components of

family theory and research in so far as it concerns the functioning of the American kin family network and its matrix of help and service among kin members. The procedure is to review relevant theory and conclusions derived from research on kin family networks completed by sociologists and anthropologists. Appropriate modifications of existing theory which posits the notion of the isolated nuclear family are then suggested.[2]

Nuclear family theory

Durkheim, Simmel, Tönnies and Mannheim have stressed that the family in urban society is a relatively isolated unit. Social differentiation in complex societies requires of its members a readiness to move, to move where there are needs for workers and where there are opportunities for better jobs.

American social theorists such as Linton (1959), Wirth (1938) and Parsons (1943, 1953, 1959; Parsons and Bales, 1955, pp. 3–33), support this position. Parsons suggests that the isolated nuclear family system consisting of husband and wife and offspring living independent from their families of orientation is ideally suited to the demands of occupational and geographical mobility which are inherent in modern industrial society. Major obligations, interactions and nurturance behavior occur within the nuclear family. While bonds exist between the nuclear family and other consanguineous relatives and affinals of the kin group, these lack significance for the maintenance of the individual conjugal family.

Family sociologists generally accept the isolated nuclear theory as promulgated above. They report the changes in the structure and functions of the American family system which have occurred as the system has adapted to the demands of a developing industrial society. There is general agreement that the basic functions reserved for the family are procreation, status placement, biological and emotional maintenance and socialization (cf. Winch, 1952; Goode, 1959). However, these functions are

the system are neolocal nuclear families in a bilateral or generational relationship. This system is referred to as the 'kin family network'.

2. The implications of parental support to the married child's family for the functioning of the American family system is discussed in another paper. The major question is whether parental aid affects the independence of the married child's family (Sussman and Burchinal, 1962).

generally analysed in the context of the 'isolated' nuclear family. The functions of intergenerational and bilateral kin family networks regarding the processes of biological and emotional maintenance or socialization are given little attention by theorists or analysts. The conclusion reached is that demands associated with occupational and geographical mobility have brought about a family pattern in urban areas consisting of relatively isolated nuclear family units which operate without much support from the kinship system.

The textbooks are written by family sociologists. Few among them, either texts on the sociology of the family or those written for marriage and family preparation courses, give theoretical or empirical treatment to the maintenance of the family system by the mutual assistance activities of the kin group. Among the texts examined, only one considers in any detail financial arrangements among kin members (Duvall, 1957, pp. 129–33, 206–10). One result of the review of basic family and preparation for marriage texts regarding current knowledge of the functioning of the kin network and its matrix of help and service is that the theory of the isolated nuclear family prevails.

Discussion of the theoretical argument

The lack of research until the 1950s and the almost complete omission of the topic, kin family network and its matrix of help and services, in family texts are closely related. If the generalized description of the American family system as atomistic and nuclear were valid, there would be very little exchange of financial help or services within the kin family network. Parental support of married children or exchange of services and other forms of help among kin members would be comparatively rare and hence, unimportant (see Hill, 1949). Research would be unnecessary and discussion of the subject, except in crisis situations, could be safely omitted from textbook discussions. However, accepting this theory as essentially valid without considerable empirical substantiation has contributed to errors in descriptions of kin family networks and aid patterns among families. A new empiricism emerging in the late 1940s questioned the persistence of the isolated nuclear family notion and presented evidence to support the viability of kin family network in industrial society.

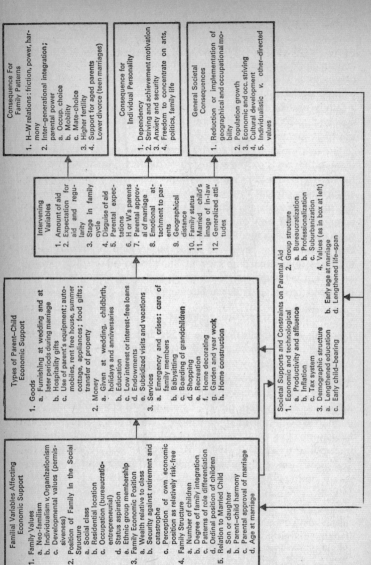

Family Variables Affecting Economic Support

1. Family Values
   a. Neo-familism
   b. Individualism v. Organizationism
   c. Developmental values (permissiveness)
2. Position of Family in the Social Structure
   a. Social class
   b. Residential location
   c. Occupation (bureaucratic-entrepreneurial)
   d. Status aspiration
   e. Ethnic group membership
3. Family Economic Position
   a. Wealth relative to class
   b. Security against retirement and catastrophe
   c. Perception of own economic position as relatively risk-free
4. Family Structure
   a. Number of children
   b. Degree of family integration
   c. Patterns of role differentiation
   d. Ordinal position of children
5. Relation to Married Child
   a. Son or daughter
   b. Parent-child harmony
   c. Parental approval of marriage
   d. Age at marriage

Types of Parent-Child Economic Support

1. Goods
   a. Furnishing at wedding and at later periods during marriage
   b. Hospitality gifts
   c. Use of parent's equipment; automobiles, rent free house, summer cottage, appliances; food gifts; transfer of property
2. Money
   a. Given at wedding, childbirth, holidays and anniversaries
   b. Education
   c. Low interest or interest-free loans
   d. Endowments
   e. Subsidized visits and vacations
3. Services
   a. Emergency and crises: care of family members
   b. Babysitting
   c. Boarding of grandchildren
   d. Shopping
   e. Recreation
   f. Home decorating
   g. Garden and year work
   h. Home construction

Societal Supports and Constraints on Parental Aid

1. Economic and technological
   a. Productivity and affluence
   b. Inflation
   c. Tax system
2. Group structure
   a. Bureaucratization
   b. Professionalization
   c. Suburbanization
3. Demographic structure
   a. Lengthened education   b. Early age at marriage
   c. Early child-bearing   d. Lengthened life-span
4. Values (as in box at left)

Intervening Variables

1. Amount of aid
2. Expectation for aid and regularity
3. Stage in family cycle
4. Disguise of aid
5. Parental expectations
6. H or W's parents
7. Parental approval of marriage
8. Emotional attachment to parents
9. Geographical distance
10. Family status
11. Married child's image of in-law
12. Generalized attitudes

Consequence For Family Patterns

1. H-W relations: friction, power, harmony
2. Inter-generational integration; parental power
   a. Occup. choice
   b. Mobility
   c. Mate-choice
3. Higher fertility
4. Support for aged parents
5. Lower divorce (teen marriages)

Consequence for Individual Personality

1. Dependency
2. Striving and achievement motivation
3. Anxiety and security
4. Freedom to concentrate on arts, politics, family life

General Societal Consequences

1. Reduction or implementation of geographical and occupational mobility
2. Population growth
3. Economic and occ. striving
4. Cultural development
5. Individualistic v. other-directed values

Figure 1 Functional analysis of parental aid to married children

The ideal description of the isolated nuclear character of the American family system cannot be applied equally to all segments of American society. Regional, racial, ethnic, and rural and urban, as well as socio-economic status differences in modified extended relations and family continuity patterns are known to exist. Family continuity and inheritance patterns of families in several social strata have been described (Warner and Lunt, 1941).[3] Among upper-class families direct, substantial and continuous financial support flows from the parents, uncles, aunts and grandparents to the children both before and after marriage. Only by receiving substantial kin support can the young high-status groom and his bride begin and sustain their family life at the financial and social level which is shared by their parents, other relatives and their friends. This support frequently includes obtaining a position for the husband in his or his in-law family's economic enterprise.

Members of lower class kin groups generally have few financial resources with which to assist married children. Among certain European ethnic groups some effort is made to assist the young couple at marriage; the notion of a dowry still persists. Generally, however, there is little knowledge, tradition or tangible form of assistance transmitted to children which directly aids children in establishing or enhancing their socio-economic status (Faris, 1947). Kin support in this class most frequently takes the form of providing services and sharing what financial resources are available at the time of crises or of exchanging non-monetary forms of aid. Marginal financial resources and the impact of unemployment hits all kin members alike (Cavan, 1959).

The description of the isolated, nuclear American family system, if valid, is most suited to the white, urban, middle-class segment of American society.[4] Presumably, the leisure time of the members of these families is absorbed in the activities of secon-

3. See also Cavan (1963, pp. 119–87), for a review of other studies of social status differentials in family behavior.

4. Someone has facetiously suggested the samples of white, urban, middle-class Protestant respondents be labeled as WUMP samples. If family sociologists continue to draw samples principally from this segment of our social structure or wish to limit generalizations to this segment, there would be more than a facetious basis for arguing for the merit of the convenient shorthand expression represented by WUMP.

dary, special interest social groups. Since urban, lower-class family members participate less than middle-class family members in voluntary organizations, it is believed that social activities of adult lower-class family members are restricted to informal visiting patterns. Visiting with relatives would be a significant proportion of all their social relations. However, prevailing sociological theory suggests that the disparities between an extended kin family system and the requirements of a mobile labor force and intergenerational family discontinuities generated by social nobility should be reflected in the lack of continuity among lower-middle-class families as well as among middle-class families.

The degree to which urban lower- or middle-class families function as relatively isolated from their extended kin family systems is critical for all subsequent discussions of the question of kinship network and its matrix of help and service. Unless there is a reasonably frequent occurrence of primary group interaction among kin members very likely there will be an insignificant help pattern.

The emphasis on the atomistic character of urban families has contributed to incorrect assumptions concerning interaction within the kinship matrix. It has led family sociologists to incorrectly assume that assistance among kin members was comparatively rarely sought or offered. A reconsideration of these assumptions is necessary. The bases of reconsideration are logical constructs and empirical realities set forth in the following data.

Family networks and mutual aid: conceptualization and research

A theory is here considered to be composed of logically interrelated propositions which explain phenomena. Concepts are elements of a theory, defining what is to be observed. Concepts by themselves cannot be construed as a theory. They require integration into a logical scheme to become a theory.

The existence of a modified extended family with its intricate network of mutual aid in lieu of the isolated nuclear family notion is probably more of a conceptualization than a theory. However, it approaches the state of being a theory since it is not an isolated concept but is integrated with other propositions concerned with the maintenance over time of the family and other social systems of the society.

Family networks and their patterns of mutual aid are organized into a structure identified as a 'modified extended family' adapted to contemporary urban and industrial society (Litwak, 1960b, p. 335; see also Litwak 1960a, p. 10). This structure is composed of nuclear families bound together by affectional ties and by choice. Geographical propinquity, involvement of the family in the occupational placement and advancement of its members, direct intervention into the process of achieving social status by members of nuclear family units, and a rigid hierarchical authority structure are unrequired and largely absent. The modified extended family functions indirectly rather than directly to facilitate the achievement and mobility drives of component families and individual members. Its tasks complement those of other social systems. By achieving integration with other social systems, concerned with the general goals of maintenance and accomplishment of these systems, the extended family network cannot be considered as an isolated or idiosyncratic concept. Its elements require organization as logically interrelated propositions and whereupon it should emerge as a theory replacing the prevalent one of the isolated nuclear family.

Our concepts die hard and one way to speed their demise is to examine the evidence supporting the new ones. Evidence and measurement are difficult terms to define. When do you have evidence and when have you achieved a measurement? The reader will have to judge. The approach here is to examine the writings and research emerging from several disciplines. In some cases the work is focused on testing hypotheses or describing relationships relevant to the new conceptualization. In others, the discussions and findings emerge incidentally to the major purpose of the study. There are cases of serendipity. They occur more frequently than one would expect and add to the uncertainty of the notion of the isolated nuclear family.

One assumption of the isolated nuclear family conceptualization is that the small nuclear family came into existence in Western Europe and the United States as a consequence of the urban-industrial revolution. Furthermore its small size is ideally suited for meeting requirements of an industrial society for a mobile workforce. The effect of the urban-industrial revolution is to produce a small sized family unit to replace the large rural one.

This assumption can be challenged. A study of different societies reveals that industrialization and urbanization can occur with or without the small nuclear family (Greenfield, 1961).

If household size reflects in any way the structure and characteristics of the joint extended family in India, then few changes have occurred in this system during the period of industrialization in India from 1911 to 1951 (Orenstein, 1961).

The uprooting of the rural family, the weakening of family ties, and the reshaping of the rural family form into a nuclear type as a consequence of the industrial revolution are disclaimed for one Swiss town in a recent investigation. On the contrary, many fringe rural families were stabilized and further strengthened in their kin ties from earning supplementary income in nearby factories. Able-bodied members obtained work near by and no longer had to leave the family unit in search of work. Families which moved closer to their place of employment were accommodated in row houses; these units facilitated the living together of large family groups (Braun, 1960). These findings question the impact of industrialization upon the structure and functioning of the pre-industrial family.

It is difficult to determine if the conditions of living during the transition from a rural to an industrial society ended the dominance of the classical extended family and replaced it with a modified kin form, or if it was replaced by the nuclear one. The question is whether the modified extended family has existed since industrialization occurred; is it a recent pheonomenon or an emergent urban familism, a departure from the traditional nuclear form; or is it non-existent? The evidence to support either of these positions is inconclusive. It remains however that the family network described variously as 'an emergent urban familism' or 'modified extended family' exists and functions in the modern community.

The family network and its functions of mutual aid has implications for the functioning of other social systems. With the growth of large metropolitan areas and concomitant occupational specialization, there is less need for the individual to leave the village, town, city or suburb of the urban complex in order to find work according to his training. Large urban areas supply all kinds of specialized educational and occupational training. The individual can remain in the midst of his kin group, work at his speciality and be the recipient of the advantages or disadvantages preferred by the kin family network. If individuals are intricately involved within a kin family network, will they be influenced by kin leaders and be less amenable to influence by outsiders; will they seek basic gratifications in kin relationships in lieu of the work place or the neighborhood; will they modify drastically current patterns of spending leisure time thus affecting current leisure forms and social systems?[5]

Empirical evidence from studies by investigations in a variety of disciplines substantiate the notion that the extended kin family carries on multitudinous activities that have implications for the functioning of other social systems of the society. The major activities linking the network are mutual aid and social activities among kin related families. Significant data have been accumulated on the mutual aid network between parents and their married child's family in a number of separate and independent investigations (Sussman, 1953a;[6] Sharp and Axelrod, 1956; Burchinal, 1959a and b). The conclusions are:

1. Help patterns take many forms, including the exchange of services, gifts, advice and financial assistance. Financial aid patterns may be direct as in the case of the young married couples Burchinal interviewed; or indirect and subtle, such as the wide range of help patterns observed by Sussman, Sharp and Axelrod.

2. Such help patterns are probably more widespread in the middle- and working-class families and are more integral a feature of family relationships than has been appreciated by students of family behavior. Very few families included in available studies reported neither giving nor receiving aid from relatives. However, these relationships until recently have not been the subject of extensive research.

3. The exchange of aid among families flows in several directions, from parents to children and vice versa, among siblings, and less frequently, from more distant relatives. However, financial assistance generally appears to flow from parents to children.

4. While there may be a difference in the absolute amount of

5. Haller (1961) raises interesting questions on the significance of an emerging urban familism.

6. For related analyses see Sussman (1953b, 1954, 1955, 1959, 1960).

Table 1 Direction of Service Network of Respondent's Family and Related Kin by Major Forms of Help (Sussman, 1959, p. 338)

Major forms of help and service	Direction of service network				
	Between respondent's family and related kin* %	From respondents to parents* %	From respondents to siblings* %	From parents to respondents* %	From siblings to respondents* %
Any form of help	93·3	56·3	47·6	79·6	44·8
Help during illness	76·0	47·0	42·0	46·4	39·0
Financial aid	53·0	14·6	10·3	46·8	6·4
Care of children	46·8	4·0	29·5	20·5	10·8
Advice (personal and business)	31·0	2·0	3·0	26·5	4·5
Valuable gifts	22·0	3·4	2·3	17·6	3·4

*Totals do not add up to 100 per cent because many families received more than one form of help or service.

financial aid received by families of middle- and working-class status, there are insignificant differences in the proportion of families in these two strata who report receiving, giving or exchanging economic assistance in some form.

5. Financial aid is received most commonly during the early years of married life. Parents are probably more likely to support financially 'approved' than 'disapproved' ones, such as elopements, inter-faith and inter-racial marriages. Support can be disguised in the form of substantial sums of money or valuable gifts given at the time of marriage, at the time of the birth of children, and continuing gifts at Christmas, anniversaries or birthdays. High rates of parental support are probably associated with marriages of children while they are still in a dependency status; those among high school or college students are examples.

6. Research data are inadequate for assessing the effects of parental aid on family continuity and the marital relations of the couple receiving aid. Few studies report associations between the form and amount of aid given with the parents' motivations for providing aid. Additional studies on these points are necessary before the implications of aid to married children can be better known.[7]

Social activities are principal functions of the kin family network. The major forms are inter-family visitation, participation together in recreational activities, and ceremonial behavior significant to family unity. Major research findings are:

1. Disintegration of the extended family in urban areas because of lack of contact is unsupported and often the contrary situation is found. The difficulty in developing satisfactory primary relationships outside of the family in urban areas make the extended family *more important* to the individual (Key, 1961).

2. Extended family get-togethers and joint recreational activities with kin dominate the leisure-time pursuits of urban working-class members (Dotson, 1951).

3. Kinship visiting is a primary activity of urban dwelling and outranks visitation patterns found for friends, neighbors or co-workers (Axelrod, 1956; Greer, 1956; Bell and Boat, 1957; Sussman and White, 1959; Reiss, 1959).

7. Further analyses on the implications of parental aid to married children are found in Sussman and Burchinal (1962).

4. Among urban middle classes there is an almost universal desire to have interaction with extended kin, but distance among independent nuclear related units is a limiting factor (Frazier, 1957).

5. The family network extends between generational ties of conjugal units. Some structures are identified as sibling bonds (Cumming and Schneider, 1961), 'occasional kin groups',[8] family circles and cousin clubs (Mitchell, 1961a and b; Mitchell and Leichter, unpublished paper). These structures perform important recreational, ceremonial, mutual aid, and often economic, functions.

Services performed regularly throughout the year or on occasions are additional functions of the family network. The findings from empirical studies are:

1. Shopping, escorting, care of children, advice giving and counselling, cooperating with social agencies on counselling and welfare problems of family members, are types of day-to-day activities performed by members of the kin network (Sussman, 1953a; Leichter, 1958, 1959a and b).

2. Service to old persons such as physical care, providing shelter, escorting, shopping, performing household tasks, sharing of leisure time, etc., are expected and practised roles of children and other kin members. These acts of filial and kin responsibility are performed voluntarily without law or compulsion (Kosa, Rachiele and Schommer, 1960; Schorr, 1960, pp. 11–18; Townsend, 1957; Young and Willmott, 1957; Bott, 1957; Streib and Thompson, 1958;[9] Shanas, 1961[10]).[11]

8. Millicent Ayoub, 'American child and his relatives: kindred in South-West Ohio', project supported by the Public Health Service, 1961. Dr Ayoub is continuing her studies under the subtitle, 'The nature of sibling bond'. She examines the solidarity or lack of it between siblings in four focal subsystems and at different stages of the life cycle.

9. Streib and Thompson have done the most creative thinking and analysis of data on these points. Streib's (1962) paper is most pertinent.

10. A more complete report is in *Family Relationships of Older People*, Health Information Foundation, 1961.

11. The best treatment of uses of leisure during the later years of life is found in Kleemeier (1961). See particularly the chapters by Wilensky, Streib and Thompson.

3. Families or individual members on the move are serviced by units of the family network. Services range from supplying motel-type accommodation for vacationing kin passing through town, to scouting for homes and jobs for kin, and in providing supportive functions during the period of inmigration and transition from the rural to the urban pattern of living (Sussman and White, 1959; Mills, Senior and Goldsen, 1950, pp. 51–5; Brown, Schwarzweller and Mangalam, 1961; Rossi, 1955, pp. 37–8; Koos, 1946).

4. Services on occasions would include those performed at weddings or during periods of crisis, death, accident, disaster and personal trouble of family members. A sense of moral obligation to give service or acknowledgement of one's kin appropriate to the occasion is found among kin members. The turning to kin when in trouble before using other agencies established for such purposes is the mode rather than the exception (Sussman, 1954; Bellin, 1960; Sharp and Axelrod, 1956; Quarantelli, 1960).

5. General supportive behavior from members of the kin family network facilitates achievement and maintenance of family and community status (Barber, 1961).[12] Supportive behavior of kin appears to be instrumental in affecting fertility rates among component family members (Goldberg, 1960).[13]

A convergence of many of these findings occurs in the work of

12. In this paper Barber challenges the current conceptualization of social class for designating an individual's position, and power within a community. He differentiates social class position, family status and local-community statuses into three types of social ranking. Each one has its own structure and functions; each allocates position, power and prestige; and each has its own range of variation. The family kin network and support received from it determines family status. President Kennedy's family and its extended family relations illustrates the point of this thesis.

13. Recent fertility research has focused upon the relationship of family organization to differential fertility since variations in family planning and family size cannot be explained by differences in socio-economic status. One variable of family organization is the family kin network. Goldberg observes, ... and incidentally one which may ultimately prove fruitful in cross-cultural studies, is a consideration of the relative benevolence of the environment in defraying the economic and social costs of having children. Here it is hypothesized that the greater the amount of help available from one's community or kinship system the weaker the desire to prevent or postpone pregnancy' (1960, p. 9).

Eugene Litwak. In an extensive study of a middle-class population Litwak tests several hypotheses on the functional properties of the isolated nuclear family for an industrial society: (a) occupational mobility is antithetical to extended family relations; (b) extended family relations are impossible because of geographical mobility. His findings summarized briefly are: (a) the extended kin family as a structure exists in modern urban society at least among middle-class families; (b) extended family relations are possible in urban industrial society; (c) geographical propinquity is an unnecessary condition for these relationships; (d) occupational mobility is unhindered by the activities of the extended family, such activities as advice, financial assistance, temporary housing, and the like provide aid during such movement; and (e) the classical extended family of rural society or its ethnic counterpart are unsuited for modern society, the isolated nuclear family is not the most functional type, the most functional being a modified extended kin family (Litwak, 1959–1960a and b).

Conclusions

There exists an American kin family system with complicated matrices of aid and service activities which link together the component units into a functioning network. The network identified by Litwak as extended family relations is composed of nuclear units related by blood and affinal ties. Relations extend along generational lines and bilaterally where structures take the form of sibling bonds and ambilineages, i.e. the family circle or cousin club.

As a consequence of limited historical work and particularistic developments in theory and research in sociology there is uncertainty concerning the impact of industrialization upon the structure and function of the pre-industrial family. Was the extended classical type found in rural society replaced by a nuclear one, or did it evolve into the modified kin form described in this paper? It is suggested that the notion of the isolated nuclear family stems from theories and research on immigrant groups coming into the city to work during the period of urbanization in Western society (Key, 1961, p. 56; Sussman, 1959, p. 340). Anomie in family behavior resulted from individual and institutional failure to make appropriate adjustments required by this migration. The coldness and indifference of the workplace and the city as a steel and concrete bastion contributed to a feeling of aloneness and isolation. The basic concern of the inmigrant was survival in an unknown man-made jungle. Survival was related to dependence upon small family units. These could make quicker and more complex adjustments to the new ways of urban life. The ethos of a competitive and expanding industrial society supported the flexibility of movement now possible by an atomistic unit. Every man is for himself, every man should be unencumbered by ties that will hinder his economic or social progress, and every man should seize opportunities to better himself. One assumption of this position is that early urban man had little time for concern or activity with kinsmen. A more logical assumption is that isolation, a depressive workplace and uncertainty produced greater reliance upon kin. Once new immigrants became established in the city they served as informants, innkeepers and providers for later kin arrivals.[14] Once these followers arrived the kin family network then functioned most effectively to protect and acculturate their members into urban ways.

Major activities of this network are that members give to each other financial aid and good of value, and a wide range of services at specific times and under certain conditions. The aid and service provided within the network supplement rather than displace the basic activities of nuclear family units. Kinship behavior assists more than negates the achievement of status and occupational advance of component families and their members.

The main flow of financial aid is along generational lines, from parents to young married children and from middle-aged parents to aged parents. Such aid is not restricted to emergencies, but may be given at various occasions such as support for education, to start a family, at time of marriage, to begin a career, and the like.

The network is used among middle-class families as a principal source of aid and service when member families or individuals

14. Key discusses this point in his (1961) paper. From studies on immigration to the United States and geographical movement of families within the country one concludes that family members perform invasion or scout roles and then attract other kin, into their communities and neighborhoods.

are in personal difficulty, in times of disaster and crisis, and on ceremonial occasions. There are some indications that established working-class families are following the same pattern. Some situations cannot be handled by the nuclear unit alone, e.g. destruction of the family home by a tornado; while other situations involve more than one nuclear family or individual member, e.g. the death of an ageing parent. In such situations there are mutual expectations of going to the aid of kin. Aid is sought from the most immediate kin chiefly along sibling or generational lines. Then it is followed by help from more distant kin.

In many instances everyday or weekly activities link together the members of the kin family network. Joint participation in leisure time activities are possible because of reduction of the work week. Visiting among kin is facilitiated by high-speed highways and other conveyances of a modern transportation system. Constant communication among kin members is possible by the widespread adoption on all class levels of the telephone as a household necessity.[15,16]

The feasibility of the kin network in modern society is due to the existence of modern communication and transportation systems which facilitate interaction among members; a bureaucratic industrial structure suited to modern society which removes the responsibility for job placement from the network will still permit the network to concentrate on activities intended to

15. Several empirical studies are currently in progress on the extensity of kin family network functions in metropolitan areas. Robert W. Habenstein and Alan D. Coult are conducting one in Kansas City on 'The functions of extended kinship in an urban milieu'. 'The purpose of this research is to discover, describe and analyse the social correlates and functions of extended kinship in representative samples of blue collar and white collar socio-economic classes in Kansas City' (p. 1, research proposal, 1 July 1961).

16. A second study is being undertaken by Marvin B. Sussman and Sherwood B. Slater in Cleveland, Ohio. 'The objectives of the Cleveland Study are to investigate the working- and middle-class families; to compare the kinship networks of "illness" and "non-illness" families; to estimate the normative form of kinship networks for social class and family life cycle stages to variations in normative patterns' (p. 1, research plan, 27 September 1961).

aid the social and economic achievement of network members;[17,18] and expansion of metropolitan areas in which individuals can obtain educational, occupational and status objectives without leaving their kin area. Kin members can live some distance from each other within the metropolitan area and still have relationships within the network. Nuclear units function autonomously. Decisions on what and when to act are responsibilities of the nuclear family. Influence may be exerted by the kin group upon the nuclear units so that the latter may make the 'right' decision. However the kin group seldom directs the decision or action of the nuclear family in a given situation. Immunity from such control is guaranteed by legal and cultural norms which reaffirm the right and accountability of the nuclear family in such situations. The role of the family kin network is supportive rather than coercive in its relationship with the nuclear family.

Understanding of the family as a functioning social system interrelated with other social systems in society is possible *only by rejection of the isolated nuclear family concept*. Accepting the isolated nuclear family as the most functional type today has led to erroneous conclusions concerning the goals and functions of these other social systems. In social service fields, for instance, institutions establish goals and programs concerned with caring for individuals and families who are unable to fend for themselves. Institutions assume that the family unit is a small and isolated unit easily injured and upset by the many problems it faces in contemporary society. The therapeutic approach is to treat the individual or at best the members of the nuclear family. The kin network is overlooked. Often nuclear families respond hesitantly to the overtures of these institutions; the nuclear unit prefers to find solutions to its problems within the family kin network. When

17. One investigation being conducted by John Bennett is concerned with the variations in business operations due to kinship behavior. Business organization practice according to current theory operates with bureaucratic, universalistic and impartial norms. Bennett is investigating the compatibility and conflict between these bureaucratic norms and those which characterize the kinship network, particularistic behavior for idiosyncratic situations. 'Kinship in American business organization', meeting of the Central States Anthropological Society, May, 1961.

18. Mitchell (1961b) finds some integration of kinship and business activity. There is a tendency to 'throw business to kin members'.

such solutions are impossible then the specialized service institution may be used. How the operations of the kin family network effect the functioning of other social systems is yet to be established. Their positive or negative effects are unknown. Some beginning research on this problem is now under way (Leichter, 1959a).

References

AXELROD, M. (1956), 'Urban structure and social participation', *American Sociological Review*, vol. 21, pp. 13–18.

BARBER, B. (1961), 'Family status, local-community status and social stratification: three types of social ranking', *Pacific Sociological Review*, vol. 4, pp. 3–10.

BELL, W., and BOAT, M. D. (1957), 'Urban neighborhoods and informal social relations', *American Journal of Sociology*, vol. 43, pp. 381–98.

BELLIN, S. S. (1960), *Family and Kinship in Later Years*, N.Y. State Dept of Mental Hygiene, Mental Health Research Unit Publication.

BOTT, E. (1957), *Family and Social Network*, Tavistock.

BRAUN, R. (1960), *Industrialisierung Volksleben*, Reutsch, Erbenback-Zierrich.

BROWN, J. S., SCHWARZWELLER, H. K., and MANGALAM, J. J. (1961), 'Kentucky mountain migration and the stem family: an American variation on a theme by LePlay', paper given at the meeting of the American Sociological Association, 1 September.

BURCHINAL, L. G. (1959a), 'Comparisons of factors related to adjustment in pregnancy-provoked and non-pregnancy-provoked youthful marriages', *Midwest Sociologist*, vol. 21, pp. 92–6.

BURCHINAL, L. G. (1959b), 'How successful are school-age marriages?', *Iowa Farm Science*, vol. 13, pp. 7–10.

CAVAN, R. S. (1959), 'Unemployment – crisis of the common man', *Marriage and Family Living*, vol. 21, pp. 139–46.

CAVAN, R. S. (1963), *The American Family*, 3rd edn, Crowell.

CUMMING, E., and SCHNEIDER, D. M. (1961), 'Sibling solidarity: a property of American kinship', *American Anthropologist*, vol. 63, pp. 498–507.

DOTSON, F. (1951), 'Patterns of voluntary association among urban working-class families', *American Sociological Review*, vol. 16, pp. 689–93.

DUVALL, E. M. (1957), *Family Development*, Lippincott.

FARIS, R. E. L. (1947), 'Interactions of generations and family stability', *American Sociological Review*, vol. 12, pp. 159–64.

FRAZIER, E. F. (1957), 'The impact of urban civilization upon negro family life', in P. K. Hatt and H. S. Reiss, Jr (eds.), *Cities and Society*, rev. edn, Free Press.

GOLDBERG, D. (1960), 'Some recent developments in fertility research', reprint no. 7, *Demographic and Economic Change in Developed Countries*, Princeton University Press.

GOODE, W. J. (1959), 'The sociology of the family', in R. K. Merton, L. Broom and L. S. Cottrell, Jr (eds.), *Sociology Today*, Basic Books.

GREENFIELD, S. M. (1961), 'Industrialization and the family in sociological theory', *American Journal of Sociology*, vol. 67, pp. 312–22.

GREER, S. (1956), 'Urbanism reconsidered', *American Sociological Review*, vol. 21, pp. 22–5.

HALLER, A. O. (1961), 'The urban family', *American Journal of Sociology*, vol. 66.

HILL, R. (1949), *Families under Stress*, Harper & Row.

KEY, W. H. (1961), 'Rural–urban differences and the family', *Sociological Quarterly*, vol. 2, pp. 49–56.

KLEEMEIER, R. W. (1961), *Aging and Leisure*, Oxford University Press.

KOOS, E. L. (1946), *Families in Trouble*, Columbia University Press.

KOSA, J., RACHIELE, L. D., and SCHOMMER, C. O., S. J. (1960), 'Sharing the home with relatives', *Marriage and Family Living*, vol. 22, pp. 129–31.

LEICHTER, H. J. (1958), 'Life cycle changes and temporal sequence in a bilateral kinship system', paper read at the annual meeting of the American Anthropological Association, Washington, D.C.

LEICHTER, H. J. (1959a), 'Kinship and casework', paper read at the meeting of the Groves Conference, Chapel Hill, North Carolina.

LEICHTER, H. J. (1959b), 'Normative intervention in an urban bilateral kinship system', paper read at the meeting of the American Anthropological Association.

LINTON, R. (1959), 'The natural history of the family', in R. N. Anshen (ed.), *The Family: Its Function and Destiny*, Harper & Row.

LITWAK, E. (1959), 'The use of extended family groups in the achievement of social goals: some policy implications', *Social Problems*, vol. 7, pp. 177–87.

LITWAK, E. (1960a), 'Occupational mobility and extended family cohesion', *American Sociological Review*, vol. 25, pp. 9–21.

LITWAK, E. (1960b), 'Geographic mobility and extended family cohesion', *American Sociological Review*, vol. 25, p. 385–94.

MILLS, C. W., SENIOR, C., and GOLDSEN, R. K. (1950), *Puerto Rican Journey*, Harper & Row.

MITCHELL, W. E. (1961a), 'Descent groups among New York City Jews', *Jewish Journal of Sociology*, vol. 3, pp. 121–8.

MITCHELL, W. E. (1961b), 'Lineality and laterability in urban Jewish ambilineages', paper read at the 60th annual meeting of the American Anthropological Association, Philadelphia, Pa.

MITCHELL, W. E., and LEICHTER, H. J. (n. d.), 'Urban ambilineages and social mobility', unpublished report on research from the project 'Studies in family interaction', sponsored by the Jewish Family Service of New York City and the Russell Sage Foundation.

ORENSTEIN, H. (1961), 'The recent history of the extended family in India', *Social Problems*, vol. 8, pp. 341–50.

PARSONS, T. (1943), 'The kinship system of the contemporary United States', *American Anthropologist*, vol. 45, pp. 22–38.

PARSONS, T. (1953), 'Revised analytical approach to the theory of social stratification', in R. Bendix and S. M. Lipset (eds.), *Class, Status and Power*, Free Press.

PARSONS, T. (1959), 'The social structure of the family', in R. N. Anshen (ed.), *The Family: Its Function and Destiny*, Harper & Row.

PARSONS, T., and BALES, R. F. (1955), *Family, Socialization and Interaction Process*, Free Press.

QUARANTELLI, E. L. (1960), 'A note on the protective function of the family in disasters', *Marriage and Family Living*, vol. 22, pp. 263–4.

REISS, P. J. (1959), 'The extended kinship system of the urban middle class', Ph.D. thesis, Harvard University.

ROSSI, P. H. (1955), *Why Families Move*, Free Press.

SCHORR, A. L. (1960), *Filial Responsibility in a Modern American Family*, Social Security Administration, U.S. Department of Health, Education and Welfare.

SHANAS, E. (1961), 'Older people and their families', paper given at the meeting of the American Sociological Association, September.

SHARP, H., and AXELROD, M. (1956), 'Mutual aid among relatives in an urban population', in R. Freedman *et al.* (eds.), *Principles of Sociology*, Holt, Rinehart & Winston.

STREIB, G. F. (1962), 'Family patterns in retirement', *Marriage and Family Living*, vol. 24, pp. 46–60.

STREIB, G. F., and THOMPSON, W. E. (1958), 'Adjustment in retirement', *Journal of Social Issues*, vol. 14, pp. 18–34.

SUSSMAN, M. B. (1953a), 'The help pattern in the middle-class family', *American Sociological Review*, vol. 18, pp. 22–8.

SUSSMAN, M. B. (1953b), 'Parental participation in mate selection and its effect upon family continuity', *Social Forces*, vol. 32, pp. 76–81.

SUSSMAN, M. B. (1954), 'Family continuity: selective factors which affect relationships between families at generational levels', *Marriage and Family Living*, vol. 16, pp. 112–20.

SUSSMAN, M. B. (1955), 'Activity patterns of post-parental couples and their relationship to family continuity', *Marriage and Family Living*, vol. 17, pp. 338–41.

SUSSMAN, M. B. (1959), 'The isolated nuclear family: fact or fiction?', *Social Problems*, vol. 6, pp. 333–41.

SUSSMAN, M. B. (1960), 'Intergenerational family relationships and social role changes in middle age', *Journal of Gerontology*, vol. 15, pp. 71–5.

SUSSMAN, M. B., and BURCHINAL, L. G. (1962), 'Parental aid to married children: implications for family functioning', *Marriage and Family Living*, vol. 24, pp. 320–32.

SUSSMAN, M. B., and WHITE, R. C. (1959), *Hough: A Study of Social Life and Change*, Western Reserve University Press.

TOWNSEND, P. (1957), *The Family Life of Old People: An Inquiry in East London*, Routledge & Kegan Paul; Penguin Books (abridged edn), 1963.

WARNER, W. L., and LUNT, P. S. (1941), *The Social Life of a Modern Community*, Yale University Press.

WINCH, R. F. (1952), *The Modern Family*, Holt, Rinehart & Winston.

WIRTH, L. (1938), 'Urbanism as a way of life', *American Journal of Sociology*, vol. 44, pp. 1–24.

YOUNG, M., and WILMOTT, P. (1957), *Family and Kinship in East London*, Free Press; Penguin Books, 1962.

8 T. Parsons

Reply to His Critics

Excerpt from T. Parsons, 'The normal American family', in
S. M. Farber (ed.), *Man and Civilization: The Family's Search for
Survival*, McGraw-Hill, 1965, pp. 34–6.

The author has, perhaps more than anyone else, been responsible
for diffusing the phrase 'isolated nuclear family' to describe one
aspect of this unit.[1] This concept has recently been challenged
notably by two groups of sociologists, Eugene Litwak and Mel-
vin Seeman and their associates, in the name of the importance
of the network of extended kinship relations beyond the nuclear
family. To my mind the two views are not contradictory but complementary. The concept of isolation applies in the first instance
to kinship structure as seen in the perspective of anthropological
studies in that field. In this context our system represents an
extreme type, which is well described by that term. It does not,
however, follow that all relations to kin outside the nuclear
family are broken. Indeed the very psychological importance for
the individual of the nuclear family in which he was born and
brought up would make any such conception impossible.

By and large, however, as our population elements are further
removed from peasant or other similar backgrounds, these extended kinship elements do not form firmly structured units of the
social system. They are not residential or economic units – in the
consuming, to say nothing of the producing, sense – nor are they
'corporate groups' in the sense that clans and lineages in so many
societies have been. There are above all two significant features of
their relations to the nuclear family. First, in the maintenance of
going relations, though there seems to be clear precedence of
members of the families of orientation of both spouses – parents
so long as they live, and siblings, even among siblings as between
the two families, and much more so beyond that – there is a
marked optional quality of the expectation system. There cer-

1. The modern American family. [Ed.]

tainly are some structured preferences on kinship bases, and others on those of geographical propinquity, but still there is a strong tendency for kinship to shade into friendship in the sense of absence from the latter of ascriptive components of membership. Hence, the amount of visiting, of common activity, of telephone and written communication, etc., is highly variable within formal categories of relationship. This suggests that extended kin constitute a resource which may be selectively taken advantage of within considerable limits.

This supposition is greatly strengthened by the second consideration. This is the extent to which extended kin, especially members of the family of orientation but not only they, serve as a 'reserve' of expectations of solidarity and willingness to implement them which can be mobilized in case of need. To take one primary context there is a clear expectation that adult siblings, children and, increasingly, parents of adults will be economically independent and should not need to be the recipients of direct financial aid from relatives. The extended family is, in this sense, normally not a solitary-operating economic unit. In case of special need, however, the first obligation to help, if there is no organized community provision and sometimes when there is, falls on close relatives who are financially able to bear the burden. Such obligations are not likely to be unlimited, but they are none the less real – in cases of sickness, of the dependency of old age and similar cases.

9 C. Turner

The Social Significance of Kinship: 1

Excerpt from C. Turner, *Family and Kinship in Modern Britain*,
Routledge & Kegan Paul, 1969, pp. 85–90.

A kinship system provides one basis upon which an individual may build up his social network. In small-scale societies with comparatively simple material cultures, kinship can easily supply the dominant organizing principle for social life. Allocation of social positions can be made on the basis of an individual's position in the kinship system. But the likelihood of a reasonable 'fit' between the patterning of kinship, and economic, political, religious or leisure activities decreases with the development of a more complex society. The major spheres of social life tend to become more insulated from each other, and specialization of activities leads to proliferation and differentiation of social positions, and hence to an increasingly complex structure of social relationships within a society. When highly complex and differentiated social structures have developed, kinship is only likely to provide the basic structural principle underpinning social relationships for members of certain special groups such as the British Royal Family, or a large 'family firm'.

The social significance of kinship depends upon the extent to which it provides a basis for social relationships. In Britain, the kinship system is structured and operated in such a way that all of an individual's recognized kin rarely, if ever, come together as an exclusive group. Rites of passage – christenings, initiation, marriage and funeral ceremonies – are sometimes referred to as events which bring together an individual's kin as a corporate group, but it should be noted that in the majority of instances the guests on such occasions constitute a group of selected or self-selected kinfolk and unrelated friends. Nevertheless, rites of passage do provide a basis for reaffirming the existence of kin ties, and to a lesser extent they help to introduce the young person's present to genealogical complexities.

Generally speaking, however, relationships within the wider kin group tend to be diffuse and selective. Some differentiation of kinship positions from economic, educational, political, recreational and religious positions has clearly occurred, and the net result appears to be that there are very few, if any, rights, duties and obligations which are generally associated with relationships between distant kin. In fact, unless common political, economic, educational, religious or leisure interests cement ties of kinship between second degree or peripheral kin, the product of common social descent or affinity is likely to be mere social recognition, rather than a close social relationship. In so far as the more distant bonds of kinship are becoming less important, in industry, politics, education, religion and leisure activities, such ties are increasingly unlikely to give rise to effective social relationships. It must be noted, however, that, although it appears possible to infer an over-all trend towards the decreasing importance of second degree or more distant kinship links, it is hardly possible to make a serious attempt at *measuring* the trend because of the inadequacies of the data.

There are some difficulties in assessing the significance of kinship linkages in the fields of political, economic, educational, recreational and religious activities. An analysis of the kinship connexions between certain 'top decision makers' in the fields of banking, insurance, politics and public administration provides a good example of the sort of problems involved (Lupton and Wilson, 1959). The initial focus of the study was upon persons involved in the Parker Tribunal (i.e. Bank Rate Tribunal, 1957), but the research was extended to cover six categories of 'top decision makers'. At least 18 per cent of these 'top decision makers' proved to be related by blood or affinity. The actual ties linking any 'top decision maker' to any other undoubtedly constituted only a small proportion of the ties in his kinship universe, and his kin ties probably coincided with only a small proportion of his total links with other decision makers. This immediately raises the problem of how to assess the significance of the kin ties that were demonstrated. Were kinship linkages an important factor, either in helping an individual to become a 'top decision maker', or in the actual decision making process? A provisional answer can be suggested to the first part of this question, but at the present it would be mere speculation to attempt to answer to the second part.

Many studies demonstrate that family background and kinship connexions are two sets of variables influencing an individual's position in economic, educational, political and leisure institutions. But they also firmly indicate that family and kinship variables are merely a few amongst many, which need to be considered. In *The British Political Élite*, for example, it is suggested that family influence and connexions are more likely to be important in helping cabinet ministers to their first steps on the political ladder, than during subsequent phases of their careers (Guttsman, 1963, p. 217). It is also evident that 'influential kinship connexions' are not a prerequisite for holding Cabinet office in contemporary Britain.

The implications, which may be restated in a more general form, are that in non-kinship institutions, kinship ties may or may not be of importance. When they do assume a special significance it is quite likely to be because kinship provided the basis of initial personal contact, and the ensuing social relationship developed within a kinship frame of reference. There is little evidence to suggest that the existence of kinship ties provides a basis for determining the content of non-kinship activities. The possibility remains, however, that in a particular social situation an individual will act in the interests of his kin, in what can be socially defined as a non-kinship context.

The distinction between kinship activity *per se*, and non-kinship activity which involves kinsmen, presents considerable analytical problems. It is theoretically possible to distinguish between (a) the rights and obligations which are generally accepted as part of particular kinship roles, (b) mutual expectations which develop from an initial basis of kin roles – these can be termed quasi-kinship expectations, and (c) rights, obligations and expectations which accidentally or incidentally involve kin. In practice, it is more difficult to apply these categories. Rights and obligations involved in specific kin relationships may be defined differently according to such variables as social class, proximity of residence, age, personality, etc. This is a matter for empirical investigation. It is somewhat more difficult to analyse the way in which kinship and non-kinship activities and interests interlock in complex social situations. Even in cases where kinship linkages are superimposed upon existing relationships, as for example, when the 'up and coming young executive' marries his managing director's daughter, there are considerable problems involved in attempting to assess the significance of kin ties. Nevertheless it is arguable that if kinship ties are specifically recognized they are potentially of significance in any social context.

The general impact of increasing specialization of activity and differentiation of social positions, therefore, appears to have led to a decline in the significance of linkages between second degree or peripheral kin. The degree of selectivity permitted in the establishment and perpetuation of social relationships with these categories of recognized kin is of interest in this context. On the one hand, it suggests that kinship ties constitute somewhat less of a basic organizing principle in economic, political, educational and recreational activity than they did, for example, in Victorian times. On the other hand, there is fairly strong evidence to indicate that shared economic, political and recreational interests coincide with the existence of social relationships between recognized kin, which suggests that the sentiments of kinship are not in themselves sufficient basis for the continuance of social relationships between kin. There is so little systematic evidence available, however, that it remains for future research to explore and modify these ideas.

References

GUTTSMAN, W. L. (1963) *The British Political Élite*, MacGibbon & Kee.
LUPTON, T., and WILSON, C. S. (1959), 'The social background and connections of top decision makers', *Manchester School of Economic and Social Studies*, vol. 27, pp. 30–51.

10 B. N. Adams

The Social Significance of Kinship: 2

Excerpt from B. N. Adams, *Kinship in an Urban Setting*, Markham, 1968, pp. 163–78.

Economic structures and motivations dominate urban, industrial society, being basic to many of its central characteristics. The a personal nature of many social contacts, the relative ease of residential movement and the mass educational system are all geared to serve the needs of the economy. At many points these same structures and values are seen to be consistent with the variety and style of kinship relations found in the city. The scatter of kin networks, the use of the means of communication for keeping in touch with close kin, and the weak and preferential or volitional nature of secondary kinship (i.e. 'my secondary kin contacts are with whom and as frequent or infrequent as I want them'): all these characteristics and more 'make sense' in the urban, industrial setting.

In this work we have set ourselves the task of characterizing the kin involvements of residents of one urban place. The attempt has been made to answer many of the open questions regarding urban kinship, including the kinds of and occasions for contact which occur, the subjective attributes of kin relations, differences in relations according to degree of kinship, the dimensions of the network, and the problem of occupational mobility effects upon kin relations. The summary which follows should make it possible to perceive the extent to which we have achieved at least provisional answers to any or all of these questions.

Parents, siblings and secondary kin

Relations between young adults and their kin are dominated by involvement with their parents. The parents are objects of extremely frequent contact among our Greensboro respondents. These intergenerational kin of orientation perform several functions on each other's behalf. Foremost is the provision of primary relations, including intimate communication and relationship for its own sake, in the midst of the segmental and often economically motivated social contacts of the urban setting. Contact patterns indicate that a mutual affection and obligation dominate the relation of parents and their adult offspring, the relationship focusing in a basic *concern* for each other's welfare. This concern finds a tangible and intangible outlet in the various forms of mutual aid, either financial or services, which are shared periodically as well as when a specific need is perceived, and also in the aforementioned frequent contact. The underlying obligation to keep in touch with parents is so pervasive, though not always overt, that the result is little association between one's expressed feelings toward his parents – be they close or distant – and frequency of contact with them. For even when affectional ties are weak, general obligation results in the maintenance of regular contact with parents by whatever means are available.

Adult sibling relations may be best characterized by the terms *interest* and *comparison*. The term 'interest' signifies less of the positive, active element of concern than was apparent in relations with parents. Thus, the sharing of mutual aid is infrequent, being virtually idiosyncratic to a specific situation. Nevertheless, fairly frequent contact is maintained, demonstrating the interest which siblings ordinarily have in how the other is getting along. Sibling contact among a majority of our sample does not manifest the characteristics of social companionship; rather, it consists of home visiting, communication and family ritual occasions. The primary subjective factor in sibling relations is a result of comparison and/or identification. The question 'How am I doing?' can be quickly and readily answered by comparing oneself with his sibling or siblings. Such rivalry or comparison appears crucial, particularly in brother relations, even in adulthood. Due to a less intense feeling of obligation to keep in touch with siblings than with parents, contact tends to be somewhat more frequent if the young adult is affectionally close to his sibling than if he is not. *In toto*, the relations between young adult siblings seem constrained to some extent by divergent values and interests, but there is a concurrent tendency, especially among females, to reaffirm ties when both siblings are married and have children.

Whether the later stages of the life cycle see an increased development of the friendship aspects of sibling relations, as Cummings and Schneider (1961, p. 502 *et passim*) hypothesize, remains for other research to determine.

When attention turns from parents and siblings, the kin of orientation, to cousins and other secondary relatives, one is hard pressed to find great significance in such relationships among young adult Greensborites. A small minority, just slightly over 10 per cent of the respondents, state that both objectively and subjectively their relations with certain secondary kin are valued. However, on the whole the young adults consider these relationships – to aunts, uncles, cousins, and so on – to be functionally irrelevant. Thus, we may characterize secondary kin ties in Greensboro as for the most part circumstantial or *incidental*. Incidental relations are thus contrasted with intentional, in which perpetuation would be for the sake of the relationship itself, either as a result of common interests or of concern for the other's welfare. Kin obligation, at least in so far as it demands frequent or diverse types of contact, is seldom a part of the relationship of these young married persons and their secondary kin.

The contrasts between relations with parents, siblings and secondary kin which we have just summarized are elucidated in Table 1. Here we observe that frequency of contact, feelings of affection and a sense of obligation are congruent. Affection for one or both parents tends to be strong, feelings of obligation are present and often important, and contact is modally – in fact almost universally – monthly or more. Siblings are less likely to be objects of close affectional ties, only about one in three of the age-near siblings are the focal point of a strong overt sense of obligation, and contact frequency ranges from two or three up to a dozen times a year ordinarily. Cousins are seldom recipients of either strong affectional or obligational sentiments, and the frequency of contact is modally once or twice a year. Of course, the respondents are in some cases more involved with another sibling or other secondary kin than with the age-near sibling or best-known cousin. However, the increases in total involvement with these two categories are relatively minor. For, in fact, there is a great amount of overlap in secondary kin involvement, so that the same respondents who are subjectively and objectively close

Table 1 Expression of Affection, Obligation, Frequency of the Most Frequent Form of Contact – Face-to-Face, Telephone or Letter – and Contact Patterns with Parent or Parents, Age-Near Sibling and Best-Known Cousin

Kin category	Number of respondents	% Affectionally close	% Obligation important	% Contact monthly or more	% Contact several times a year or more	Mean number of contact patterns
Parent(s)	(724)	75	50	94	98	3·8
Age-near sibling	(697)	48	32	61	90	2·1
Best-known cousin	(682)	18	10	27	63	1·0

to their best-known cousin are likely to be concerned about aunts or grandparents as well. Contact patterns, i.e. contacts of a specific type at least several times a year, typically include home visits, communication, mutual aid, and either rituals, organizations or recreational contact with parents. With the age-near siblings, contact patterns, as stated above, are usually restricted to home visits and communication, with a minority engaging in social activities or ritual interaction, or some other contact type. Some cousins visit and/or communicate in a patterned fashion; many do neither.

One qualification and two extensions are pertinent to the foregoing general conclusions. A brief comment by Haller and the inferences of other authors have been noted to the effect that in the large metropolis there are now being reborn – or may still be found – the meaningful secondary kin networks of earlier rural-agricultural days. The ghetto, the ethnic mutual-aid kin association, and other megalopolitan kin groups – these may be important, if not emerging, phenomena. However, while the present author would grant the existence and importance of a few such networks in urban settings, he is not prepared to accept the generalizability to urban places of the functionally significant *wider* kin network, i.e. secondary kin as well as the kin of orientation, much beyond the 10 to 15 per cent of urbanites found in the Greensboro study. Of course, further evidence to the contrary would be both of interest and theoretically significant.[1]

Two extensions of the categorical conclusions presented above may help to explicate further the characteristics of urban kin networks, especially the interrelations between degrees of kinship. First, we recall the important position which the ageing apparently occupy in the kin network. Ageing parents play a particularly central role both in perpetuating their nuclear families of procreation, i.e. in linking siblings together after they leave the parental home, and in maintaining their family of orientation, or ties with their own ageing siblings and their children. They further serve to relate their families of procreation and orientation to each other, so that young adults at least keep posted on the activities of, if they don't keep in touch with, aunts, uncles and cousins, as well as their siblings. After the death of the older generation there is likely to be loss of interest on the part of young adults in their secondary kin, i.e. their parents' family of orientation. They, in turn, are apt to begin to focus upon *their* nuclear families of orientation and procreation, and extensions of these in children, as they grow older. The effective kin network is thus continually expanding by birth and contracting by death and loss of contact on the part of the ageing. One important hub of such kin involvement in urban society is the aged or grandparental generation, and the other is the females in the network.

A second extension of our findings by means of comparisons of categories of kin concerns one's orientation toward them. Everett Rogers and Hans Sebald (1962), in a study of Iowa and Ohio farm families, demonstrate that familism, or strong family concern and involvement, while a useful concept, is basically ambiguous unless a distinction is drawn between the nuclear family and the 'extended kinship group'. We would now propose that the results of this present study indicate that instead of a

1. Personal conferences with Jewish students from New York, Detroit and other megalopolitan centers indicate that an exception to our generalization regarding the incidental nature of secondary kinship may very well be found in the Jewish kin networks of these urban complexes. One pattern seems to be for the successful individual to help nephews and sometimes nieces, and not just his own children, in their attempts to achieve in society. Leichter and Mitchell (1967) should increase our understanding of kinship in such settings.

dichotomy between family and kin a trichotomy is necessary in order to comprehend the empirical family–kinship actualities. Many, if not a majority, of our respondents state that their parents, brothers and sisters are important to them, while none or a small number of secondary kin are considered significant. Among the familistic should therefore be distinguished three types: (a) the *nuclear familistic*, whose dominant values and interests include concern for their spouse and children but little concern for other kin; (b) the '*kin of orientation' familistic*, who are actively engaged in perpetuating ties with parents and siblings, their kin of orientation, as well as with their families of procreation; and (c) the *wider kin oriented*, who are involved in a complex network of contact with and concern for kin of various degrees of relationship. These ideal types would, of course, contrast with non-familistically oriented individuals who either have no family ties or little family concern, e.g. the man who is 'lost in his work'. It seems quite possible, in view of the data on kin importance, that in our urban society the majority of married females could be characterized as kin of orientation familistic, while the males would be divided between kin of orientation and nuclear familistic. These latter husbands are likely to assert that 'what matters to me is my work, my wife and my children'. As is true of many other findings of this study, the predominance of these orientations toward family and kin is open for further testing in various social settings, such as rural areas and other cities. Nevertheless the fourfold typology may be helpful in reconciling some of the divergent opinions found in the literature on kinship in urban society. What occurs is that some researchers have generalized a great amount of kin involvement from the observation of young adult/parent relations, and others, viewing the *total* network, have concluded that urban kin ties are weak. Each approach, we are implying, is apt to be only partially correct in its results.

Distance, sex, occupational position and kinship

Residential distance is stated by Reiss and others to be unquestionably the prime determinant of, or limiting condition upon, frequent interaction between kin. Our findings are relatively consistent with this conclusion, but qualifications must be added to the influence of distance upon kin affairs. Not only does distance limit interaction frequency, but it also determines the kinds of interaction and the occasions upon which face-to-face contact occurs. The greater the residential separation, the more likely is interaction to be restricted to vacation or holiday reunions. We have, in addition to noting the restrictive effects of distance upon interaction, discovered unmistakably that, as Litwak asserted, distance does not necessarily limit or determine total contact, due to the availability of the telephone and postal service. Nor does distance prevent the exchange of tangible aid, or emotional involvement or primary relations between kin, or the perception of kin as important to the individual. However, here again the degree of kin relationship is associated with distance effects: the closer the kin relationship, the less likely is increasing distance to affect adversely total contact frequency, exchange of aid and emotional ties. Thus, it is primarily for parents, and secondarily for siblings, that the concept of the 'isolated nuclear family' fails to hold among the residentially mobile.[2] Degree of relationship alters distance effects in another way also. Face-to-face contact with parents living within one hundred miles of Greensboro but outside the city is more frequent than with secondary kin living in Greensboro, and the same comparison holds for other distance categories. Our conclusion is that if kin desire to maintain contact and keep concern active, as is true of the majority of young adults and their parents, distance is but a qualifier, not a deterrent.

Kin affairs according to the sex of the young urban adult may be summarized rather briefly. The strength of the mother–daughter bond, so central to Young and Willmott's studies in England, is likewise observable in Greensboro, North Carolina. However, differences between males and females in relations with parents are discernible primarily in the subjective sphere; contact frequencies are quite similar. The close mother–daughter bond may be extended further to indicate that females play a more dominant role in the kin network than do males. Young wives

2. This concept, i.e. the isolated nuclear family, can be looked upon, we have said, as a construct of the lag between migration and communication theories, the former simply pre-dating the latter. Distance does not imply isolation in urban-industrial society.

tend to express a closer affectional relation to all degrees of kin, are in slightly more frequent contact with siblings and secondary kin, and are more likely to feel that kin are an important part of their lives. Females and the ageing, we have said, are the foci of urban kin affairs.

A variable which has been of much concern in the present study is occupational status and mobility. One reason for this is the divergence of viewpoints in the literature regarding the effects of social mobility upon kin relations. As is true of other studies, the blue-collar kin networks are characterized by less residential dispersion, the result being that more frequent blue-collar interaction with various kin occurs. When there is residential separation it is the middle classes who make the most use of the means of communication to sustain kin contact. We recall that Parsons's paper, which referred to the middle classes, asserted that the chances of residential separation from kin are great, and intimated that separation really means isolation (Parsons, 1943, pp. 27, 35). This should be altered to read that the chances of middle-class separation from kin are moderately great, but that this eventuality does not result in isolation from kin of orientation. On the other hand, working-class migration and separation from kin, though less frequent, is apt to result in virtual isolation from all kin except parents when it does occur.

There is a basic working-class division by sex in secondary kin affairs which does not appear in the middle classes. Blue-collar male kin are ordinarily more involved with each other, and females with each other. Even in the case of parents such sex divisions occur among the working classes. This is apparent in correspondence between young married adults and their parents. Regardless of occupational stratum the female tends to serve as family correspondent; the result is that the middle-class wife writes both sets of parents, while the working-class wife concentrates upon her own. The close female relations in blue-collar kin networks are also apparent in the great amount of mutual aid shared between mothers and daughters, and even in some cases between blue-collar sisters.

The divergent opinions on occupational mobility and kinship relations are exemplified in articles by Schneider and Homans (1955) and by Litwak (1960). The former authors comment, in their discussion of kin terminology, that 'upward mobile persons keep only shallow ties with members of their kindred, if they keep them at all; downward mobile persons may be neglected by their kindred' (p. 1207). Litwak, on the other hand, states that in his sample even a movement from manual to business or professional, or vice versa, does not distinguish with regard to frequency of interaction (p. 16). The first result of our study concerns interaction. Frequency of interaction is intimately associated with residential distance, which is, in turn, related to one's occupational position. The occupationally mobile person is an individual of one stratum whose kin network is likely to be characterized by the majority being of the other stratum. Therefore, the mobile tend to form a middle category between white-collar offspring of white-collar parents and blue-collar offspring of blue-collar parents with respect to both distance from and frequency of interaction with various kin. Whether the occupationally mobile are perceived as having strong or weak kin ties is thus likely to be a function of the group with whom they are compared. Comparing the upwardly mobile with the stable blue-collar in interaction frequency with kin, our conclusion would resemble that of Schneider and Homans, i.e. the mobile have weaker or shallower kin ties. But if the comparison is made between the upward mobile and the occupationally stable members of their new stratum, it can only be concluded that the interactional ties of the mobile to their kin are as strong, if not stronger, than those of the stable middle class.

This finding provides an introduction to the dominant theme which pervades the investigation of occupational mobility and kinship: individual movement or non-movement in the economic-occupational system is not the key factor in determining kin relations in adulthood. Rather, the middle-class success values of the society, and the *current* occupational positions and concomitant value systems of the parties involved appear more determinative of present relationships. Upward mobility is not a 'boot-strap' phenomenon; it requires social support from parents and often from other kin, particularly for the male. Thus, the influence of both parents upon the upwardly mobile male and of the mother upon the upwardly mobile female result in close adult relations with parents, rather than the rejection which is inherent in Schneider and Homans's comment. Sibling relations are likewise affected by differential achievement, so that occupational or status disparity between brothers usually means an affectional distance and non-identification, and between cross-sex siblings and sisters often means a non-reciprocated identification of the lower-status sibling with the 'family success'. In contrast, mutually upward or downward mobile siblings are drawn together, not apart. Similarity of life circumstances, whether successful or deprived, and mutual support result in strengthened bonds, especially between the downward mobile who have, in effect, been failed by their parents.

Looked at as a network, the foregoing parent and sibling relations illustrate the importance of middle-class success values and present status in relations between the kin of orientation. Parsons asserts, concerning our occupational and kinship systems, that the open, isolated, nuclear or conjugal family system seems most functional for our mobile occupational system and urban living (1943, p. 37). The results of the Greensboro investigation imply that the economic values of urban, industrial society do influence considerably the integration of the family of orientation when the children reach adulthood. Cleavages and solidarities occur which are most readily accountable in terms of such societal values. This may be demonstrated by Figure 1. Mutually downward mobile siblings (Diagram 1) are affectionally close while manifesting affectional distance from their parents, particularly their mothers. When only one of the children is downwardly mobile (Diagram 2) he or she is affectionally distant from parents and the sibling. Although the numbers are too small to be definitive, these young adults appear most likely to have attenuated kin networks, including a shallow relation with their kin of orientation.

The stable blue-collar adult whose sibling is upwardly mobile tends to identify with his sibling's achievement, but may blame his parents for the fact that he was not also mobile (Diagram 3). However, occupational salience and open competition prevent even such one-way identification and affection between occupationally disparate brothers (Diagram 3a).

The upwardly mobile devise different solutions to the problem of integration with the kin of orientation. Mutually upward

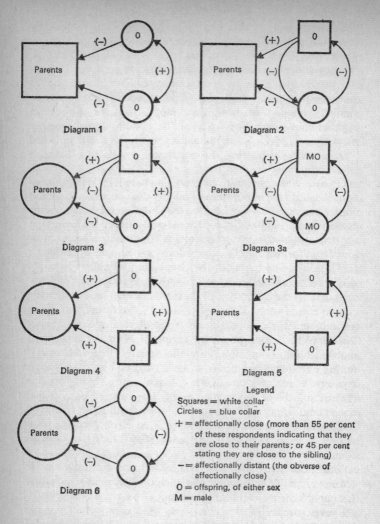

Legend

Squares = white collar
Circles = blue collar
+ = affectionally close (more than 55 per cent
of these respondents indicating that they
are close to their parents ; or 45 per cent
stating they are close to the sibling)
− = affectionally distant (the obverse of
affectionally close)
O = offspring, of either sex
M = male

Figure 1 Affectional relations with the kin of reorientation, according
to comparative occupational positions (reprinted with permission
from Adams, 1967, p. 375)

mobile siblings are relatively close to each other in their mutual achievement, and in addition respond positively to their parents' efforts on their behalf (Diagram 4). The upward mobility of one offspring (Diagram 3) results in this young adult tending to be affectionally close to his parents, but feeling little emotional attachment to his lower status, or less successful, sibling. Diagrams 5 and 6 present the typical mutual affectional closeness of stable white-collar kin of orientation and distance of stable blue-collar kin of orientation.

There are variations according to the sex of the individual, either young adult or parent, especially in the role convergence and close relation of working-class daughters and their working-class mothers. Yet these diagrams reveal and summarize the effect of economic-occupational values upon kin solidarity in adulthood. Such values characteristically override kin familistic values in altering subjective relations between the kin of orientation. Nevertheless, the general obligation to, and often circumstantial contact of, these immediate kin causes the quantity of contact to be maintained despite variation in both its quality and types.

Secondary kin affairs are likewise not affected negatively by the upward mobility of the individual. The upward mobile are able to find kin with whom to perpetuate a modicum of involvement – frequently persons of their current stratum – and their total numbers of kin acquaintances are no smaller, and are often larger, than are the networks of the occupationally stable. Either through kin rejection or feelings of inadequacy, the downwardly mobile tend to relinquish ties with many of their secondary kin. Once again, the incidental or circumstantial nature of secondary kinship in general results in few observable differences, either subjective or objective, which might be accounted for by occupational stability or movement.

An attempt to summarize occupational mobility and kin relations confronts us with a multiplicity of complicating factors. The guiding hypothesis drawn from the literature and based upon degree of relationship and the sex of the individual is much too simplistic. Rather, the primary factors include migratory history and the resulting residential distances, society's economic-occupational success values, the role of parents in their children's achievement or non-achievement, present occupational and value similarity or divergence between siblings, and the basically incidental nature of secondary kinship.

Future research and functional centrality: a postscript

The primary purposes of the present study have been two-fold. First and foremost, the endeavor has been made to piece together the scattered and often fragmentary materials on urban kinship into a generally unified picture, including both its subjective and objective attributes. A second purpose coincides with the exploratory nature of much of the analysis, especially of adult sibling and secondary kin relations. That is, besides the general characterization there are numerous hypotheses and areas of study which merit further, more detailed, investigation. The depth of our findings could be increased in several directions.

1. What are the values upon which perceived consensus or dissensus in the kin network is based? Political attitudes, optimism or pessimism, success orientation, religious outlook, reactions to minorities or children – these are some of the ideas that respondents may be thinking about when they say that they and a relative have the same opinions or different opinions on things that matter. On the basis of extemporaneous comments, it seems likely that the two crucial sets of values which are salient to kin relations are *economic* and *moral*. By economic we mean feelings that 'he works hard', or 'he is a good provider', or 'she doesn't care if she goes down'. Some of the ways in which such economic values impinge on the kin network have already become apparent. By moral values we mean feelings that 'he is a good man', or 'he drinks a lot', or 'she is religious and tries to live the right kind of life for her children'. Other attitudes, such as political among upper-middle-class males, are apt to be less universally salient to kin relations in urban-industrial society than these.

2. A second direction for increased depth would be to attempt a full investigation of downward mobility. The either–or choice between husband and family of orientation is apt to be greater for the downwardly mobile female than for the male. The downwardly mobile male has made his own choice, due perhaps to school difficulties, and involvement with lower status friends,

while the female has simply chosen a husband. But downward mobility is far from a settled issue as regards its relation to kin affairs.

3. The extent of knowledge of urban kinship could be expanded in many directions. Further breakdown in status categories, marital relations and kinship, kin and other societal systems, and change – all these are of interest and importance. Do upper-class persons still have the strong kin networks that are attributed to them in the literature? I would hypothesize that the old upper classes would have such networks – non-localized – but that the *nouveau riche* and upper-middle classes would come closest to epitomizing the 'nuclear familistic' described above. Also, the lower-blue-collar are likely to have looser-knit kin networks than the true urban working classes, i.e. the industrial or semi-skilled workers. In any case, further occupational and status breakdown is needed.

4. What is the relation of marital power relations to involvement with one or both kin networks? It is quite possible that the agreement of both spouses that they should be close to both sets of kin, or neither, or one and not the other, is enough to keep peace within the couple and with kin and in-laws. However, a struggle for power may be manifested in those cases where a choice must be made regarding settling near one set of kin or the other. Much needs to be done on marital interaction and kin involvement.

5. It seems to this author that the two most fruitful aspects of urban kinship for future concern are change and interrelations with other systems. How does kinship affect and adapt to the urban-industrial environment? One way to study this would be to follow longitudinally the characteristics of urban inmigrants, such as those from Eastern Kentucky into Southern Ohio, as they change over a period of years. It would be well to parallel this with an investigation of a minority group of urban migrants, to note whether minority status results in more emphasis being put on the maintenance of kin ties for the sake of mutual survival and a greater chance of societal success.

6. The question of interrelations and the societal role of kin requires somewhat more extended comment before leaving the sub-

ject of urban kinship. Litwak and Sussman, as well as our study, have rather convincingly demonstrated that being part of an urban society signifies neither uniformly great distance from one's kin; nor does remoteness, when it does occur, necessarily signal isolation in terms of lack of contact. But isolation from kin is not the principle issue of either Parsons's or Wirth's discussions of urban kinship. These authors are saying that, in historical and societal perspective, our kinship system does not appear to be as functionally central, or as crucial an element, in the total society as it has been in many other times and places. Parsons, for example, makes this explicit when he states that at marriage the individual is drastically segregated, in comparison with other societies, from his parents and siblings (1943, p. 30). Parsons's concern here is with kinship in the 'contemporary United States' in a comparative way. His critics, on the other hand, have collected data which are significant in their own right, and have replied to Parsons in the following vein: 'See, the kinship system does "function" in urban settings. Relatives interact, keep in touch, celebrate happy occasions, and parents and their adult children even help each other from time to time.' Parsons and his critics, in their conceptions of functionality, are in fact talking past each other. The major concern of Parsons and the Chicago school is with the relation of the part to the whole, of the kin network to the society. Sussman, Litwak, Greer, Axelrod and the present study have largely dealt with the functioning of the part. We have generally agreed with these latter studies regarding the function of parents in providing primary relations and aid to their adult offspring, and have noted the comparative function performed by siblings. But to generalize from such findings to the functional role of kin in the total society would be presumptuous. Were we to infer societal functionality from our findings regarding nepotism, total aid exchanged between kin, mutual involvement in voluntary organizations, or the few instances of parents or other kin residing with a respondent, we would be inclined to agree with Parsons. Adult kin relations do appear, in comparison to other societies historically and to other institutional spheres in modern urban society, to be functionally peripheral to the ongoing of the total structure. But our study has not probed very far into the functional comparisons or interrelations between institutional spheres, nor have we sought to resolve cross-cultural or historical issues – these remain to be removed from the literature and investigated in the empirical arena.

Ours has been primarily a characterization of kin relations in one urban place, and that task is at an end. Relations with kin, we have found, should be generalized with reference to a specific kin category, not to the total network. Parents are objects of positive concern, which includes frequent contact, readiness to help, and strong feelings of affection and obligation. Siblings are objects of continuing interest and comparison in urban society. Finally, secondary kin are commonly objects of but little concern and incidental contact.

References

ADAMS, B. N. (1967), 'Occupational position, mobility and the kin of orientation', *American Sociological Review*, vol. 32.

CUMMINGS, E., and SCHNEIDER, D. M. (1961), 'Sibling solidarity: a property of American kinship', *American Anthropologist*, vol. 63.

LEICHTER, H. J., and MITCHELL, W. E. (1967), *Kinship and Casework*, Russell Sage Foundation.

LITWAK, E. (1960), 'Occupational mobility and extended family cohesion', *American Sociological Review*, vol. 25.

PARSONS, T. (1943), 'The kinship system of the contemporary United States', *American Anthropologist*, vol. 45.

ROGERS, E. M., and SEBALD, H. (1962), 'A distinction between familism, family integration and kinship orientation', *Marriage and Family Living*, vol. 24.

SCHNEIDER, D. M., and HOMANS, G. C. (1955), 'Kinship terminology and the American kinship system', *American Anthropologist*, vol. 57.

11 C. Bell

The Social Significance of Kinship: 3

Excerpts from C. Bell, *Middle-Class Families*, Routledge & Kegan Paul, 1968, pp. 88–95.

On the basis of the American evidence it has been argued that the middle-class extended family is used as 'a principal source of aid and service when member families are in personal difficulties or in times of disaster and crisis and on ceremonial occasions' (Sussman and Burchinal, 1962, p. 234). Although I collected data about crisis situations and ceremonial occasions I do not want to present it here. I aimed to describe ordinary families and I want to emphasize the ordinary rather than the unusual. It is central to my argument that middle-class extended family aid is not dependent upon crisis and ceremonial; and that it is not only on these occasions that the middle-class extended family is a functioning social entity but that it works continually, if not day to day then month to month, to maintain and/or advance the status of its members.

Mutual aid between members of an extended family flows in several directions depending upon stages in the family cycle. Most of the families that I have been studying are in the first two stages of the family cycle:[1] that of 'home-making' and 'child-rearing'. These two stages are the time of greatest expenditure and, because of the nature of the middle-class career pattern, the time of lowest income. Whereas the large literature of gerontology (see Townsend, 1964) has added to our knowledge of the structure and function of the family, through the study of support and aid flowing towards the final stage of the family cycle, I know

1. Definitions of stages in the family cycle:
(i)   Home-making: from marriage to the birth of first child.
(ii) Child-rearing: from birth of first child until marriage of first child.
(iii) Dispersal: from marriage of first child until marriage of last child.
(iv) Final: from marriage of last child until death of original partners.

of no systematic study of support and aid flowing towards the first two stages of the family cycle. [. . .]

The kind of aid that I am discussing is not exceptional aid in exceptional times. Shaw, writing about a predominantly working-class London suburb, gives a very fine example of what I mean. One of the very few professional families she studied reported that the husband's mother and father had bought a new winter outfit for the first child when the expense of the second left them short of money (1954, p. 185). This is an example of the middle-class extended family providing important and significant increments of aid for the idiosyncratic needs of the elementary family. There was no need for geographical proximity.

The ability, although not the desire, to provide this type of aid will vary with social class. As Fletcher has written:

The kinds and degrees of mutual aid, and the reasons for it, may differ between social classes. For example, young middle-class parents may desire, and obtain, help from elder relatives in order to send their children to public school; or they may want their *father's* [my emphasis] influence in prevailing upon a friendly solicitor so that they can purchase their house with minimum legal costs; and beyond such financial aid and influence there may be little sentimental attachment and little desire for closer interdependence. Young working-class parents, on the other hand, will not and cannot expect or require these degrees of financial aid of their elder relatives their desires; and their problems will be different, and they may experience deeper sentimental feelings of attachment (1966, p. 169).

This last point I feel can be doubted. Middle-class kin networks may have fewer day-to-day demands but I think that there is little evidence to suggest that they necessarily show any different affective quality. [. . .]

Before I go into a more detailed discussion of some of my field material may I suggest that all the data I have gathered are likely to be underestimations. These topics are considered private and most of it was gleaned indirectly. Most of the remainder of this section is therefore qualitative rather than quantitative.

It became apparent that in certain spheres of social activity aid from kin was more important than in others. So I pursued these topics, together with collecting more general kin information. The topics I concentrated on were careers, housing and their children. In examining these subjects – which in many cases are the dominant interests of the families I studied – I found that over and over again where there had been aid from the extended family the important structural link between members of the extended family was the father-in-law/father–son/son-in-law link. This led me to reanalyse a great deal of my field material.

In doing so I felt very similar to Aberle and Naegele who in a paper on the socialization of middle-class children in the United States wrote that 'One reason we are stressing the father is that he is forgotten or recedes into the background in the face of the overwhelming focus on the mother in recent work' (1952, p. 367). Or in my case the overwhelming focus on the mother–married daughter link in recent work. The father–son link is structurally important in the middle-class extended family because through it flows aid to the elementary family.

Here I would like to take an 'apt illustration' from my field notes. (The speaker is a thirty-seven-year-old geographically mobile but socially immobile architect.)

'I wanted to leave the firm I was working for and buy into a practice as a partner. I had had a very attractive offer. But I wanted a couple of hundred more than I had. When we went home [to a town in the Midlands which both husband and wife came from and returned to visit parents about four times a year] I went to the local with my father-in-law [his father is dead] and told him I was considering changing my job like I said. I didn't ask but to tell the truth I hoped. He said 'How much?' and I told him and he said that he would see. Eventually he gave it to me, called it a loan but said I needn't pay it back. But I am though – £5 a month so I don't feel obligated to him. I didn't ask my bank because they were also the firm's bank and you know Rotary and that. It was easier to ask him.'

He told me that he would have approached his father had he been alive. As Rosser and Harris have pointed out in their paper on relationships through marriage one function of affinal relationships under certain circumstances is for them to be utilized as substitutes for missing consanguineal kin (1961, p. 318). This is well documented by Young and Willmott, and Townsend for the working-class mother–daughter link. It would seem that substitution (in the sense of role adoption) can also be found in the middle-class father–son link. In a bilateral system such as ours there is always the possibility of alternatives within the structure.

This illustration also shows that the recipient felt less obligation for accepting aid since he did not ask for it; also it illustrates a recurrent mechanism. The money was not asked for, the case was stated and the action was left up to the parent. In this way there seems to be at least a partial resolve of the conflict between the stress on independence and actual dependence. Physical distance allows the recipients to maintain an appearance of independence and the ubiquity of financial institutions means that distance is irrelevant to aid of this kind. Jane Hubert wrote: 'It is not the "done thing" to be on the receiving end of kin help and influence, but to use one's influence is quite acceptable. Though they do not necessarily see it in these terms, status is conferred by giving, not receiving' (1965, p. 68). As the majority of the 120 families studied are in the first two stages of the family cycle and at the beginning of a middle-class career, they are disproportionately on the receiving end of extended family aid.

In contrast to the first example let me quote an example of a thirty-five-year-old geographically mobile but socially immobile insurance man.

'My father was hurt I think when he knew I went to the bank rather than him for a down payment on a new car but if I'd gone to him for it, the money I mean, we would have had to go there for our holidays. We did anyway, but we didn't have to.'

By going to an institution rather than his father he thought he avoided obligations and kept his independence.

In another case I found that the need could be stated to siblings, but the parents were not told directly. The siblings however were quite expected to tell their parents who were expected to act on this information.

Another mechanism was secrecy or quasi-secrecy. (Speaking is a thirty-four-year-old geographically mobile but socially immobile engineer.)

'When we had the last baby my father said we should have a home help regularly – very practical man, my dad. He said he would leave the knitting to mum and my sisters but he would pay for the woman and he said not to tell mum as she thought we should be independent. I told Jane [his wife] of course.'

The 'independence' here clearly refers to monetary independence. This case-study is also interesting in that it illustrates the invasion of the sphere usually dominated by the mother–daughter relationship by that of the father and son.

Another mechanism frequently utilized by the families I studied is the giving of aid on socially approved occasions: this is acceptable and can be received without any loss of independence. This begins at the wedding: I recorded one case of the house being given outright and two cases of a substantial deposit being put down on the house. In these cases naturally arrangements were made through the bank but it was the father or father-in-law that made them. This mechanism continues at Christmas and at birthdays – I noted a case of central heating being given as a Christmas present from the husband's parents.

Indirect aid may be given through the children, i.e. from grandparents to grandchildren. When as in one case a lump sum of £100 was given to 'buy things for the baby' it was grandfather who signed the cheque.

This is of course an indirect way of raising the standard of living of the recipients, because it releases money to be spent on other things. In the words of one informant extended family aid 'makes things that much easier'. Extended family aid often is used to provide important status props and helps in the purchase of status signs. I have already mentioned central heating: an important indicator of status amongst the families that I studied was having regular help in the home. Another case from my field notes: speaking is the wife of a geographically mobile but socially immobile chemist.

'Dad gave me £20 to buy Jim [her fourteen-year-old son] a bike for his birthday – he knew that we were going to buy him one anyway. So we got a new carpet as well. [And then very quickly and somewhat guiltily.] Aren't I awful! But without little bits like that I don't know how we would live here.'

The giving of status props to children: the expensive 'toys' like the bicycle mentioned above or a trampoline was not uncommon. Whilst I was doing the fieldwork great pressure was being put on several parents by their young daughters to be allowed to have riding lessons. This expensive and status-conferring pastime was initiated by one girl whose grandfather was paying for them. Another example I have is the paying for ballet lessons by an uncle (husband's father's brother).

It is not coincidence that all my examples are taken from informants who have not been socially mobile, i.e. have middle-class parents. Working-class parents would very rarely be in a position to give aid of the proportions described above. If no geographical mobility had been experienced mothers could still give aid to their daughters of the kind described by Willmott and Young and others for the working class. But none of the families studied had been socially mobile *and* geographically immobile. Consequently there seems to have been a readjustment in emphasis in the structure of the extended family away from the mother–daughter relationship towards the father–son relationship.

The exact effects of extended family aid flowing between father and son is very difficult to determine especially as it was impossible to collect this information systematically and uniformly. But as a rough guide I compared the ages of husbands who had been socially mobile, i.e. had come from manual homes, with those who had come from middle-class backgrounds. The hypothesis being that the estates could be seen as a certain status level and that those who were in the theoretical position to receive extended family aid would reach this status level sooner than those who were not in a position to receive extended family aid. For example this was very noticeable in the case of a twenty-five-year-old bank clerk, who could only have been classified as 'junior non-manual', living on the estate who was the recipient of a great deal of financial assistance from both his father and father-in-law. It turned out that the thirty-one socially mobile husbands were on average 2·1 years older than those from middle-class backgrounds. It would not be correct to put this 2·1 years advantage down completely to extended family aid but as a socially mobile informant told me 'there's a lot of what I call real money here, you know family money, we lived in a two-roomed flat when we started, but look at them'. She was referring to a family who had moved to the estate on marriage.

The variable of social mobility was far more important to the function of the middle-class extended family than was geographical mobility. Osterreich (1965) compared forty-five English-speaking middle-class Canadians who were homogeneous in all other respects and compared those who had been geographically mobile with those who had not. She found that the greatest difference between the mobile and the non-mobile was in caring for children, help during illness, taking care of the house and advice on personal matters. In other words the greatest differences were in those actions that depended on availability at short notice and/or physical presence. She found that she could support Litwak's hypothesis.[2] But she quite ignores the factor of social mobility which seriously detracts from her findings. The amount of aid is likely to be very different for those from middle-class backgrounds when compared with those from working-class backgrounds.

2. That other kinds of activity are not seriously impeded by geographical mobility. [Ed.]

References

ABERLE, D. F., and NAEGELE, K. O. (1952), 'Middle-class fathers' occupational role and attitudes towards children', *American Journal of Orthopsychiatry and Psychology*, vol. 22, pp. 366–78.

FLETCHER, R. (1966), *Family and Marriage*, rev. edn, Penguin Books.

HUBERT, J. (1965), 'Kinship and geographical mobility in a sample from a London middle-class area', *International Journal of Comparative Sociology*, vol. 6, pp. 61–80.

OSTERREICH, H. (1965), 'Geographic mobility and kinship: a Canadian example'. *International Journal of Comparative Sociology*, vol. 6, pp. 131–44.

ROSSER, C., and HARRIS, C. C. (1961), 'Relationships through marriage in a Welsh urban area', *Sociological Review*, vol. 9, pp. 293–321.

SHAW, L. A. (1954), 'Impressions of family life in a London suburb', *Sociological Review*, vol. 2, pp. 179–94.

SUSSMAN, M. B., and BURCHINAL, L. (1962), 'Kin family network: unheralded structure in current conceptualization of family functioning', *Marriage and Family Living*, vol. 24, pp. 231–40.

TOWNSEND, P. (1964), Discussant to Firth, R., 'Family and kinship in industrial society', in P. Halmos (ed.) 'The development of industrial societies', *Sociological Review Monograph*, no. 8.

12 E. Litwak and I. Szelenyi

Kinship and Other Primary Groups

Excerpt from E. Litwak and I. Szelenyi, 'Primary group structures and their functions: kin, neighbors and friends', *American Sociological Review*, vol. 34, 1969, pp. 465–81.

Introduction

Until recently, little attention has been given in sociology to a theoretical statement on the variety of 'primary' group structures and their differential function in an industrial society. We would like to suggest that under the impact of modern industrial society primary group structures tend to assume a variety of structural forms.[1] Furthermore, these different structures can handle different types of tasks more effectively. We shall confine our discussion to three types of primary groups – kinship ties, neighbors and friends – and use Cooley's (1955) terminology (viz. face-to-face, permanent, affective, non-instrumental and diffused) for primary groups, rather than Parsons's equally useful pattern variables (particularistic, collective, diffused, affective and ascribed).

Until the late 1940s many sociologists had adopted the point of view that there was little need to study primary groups in modern industrial society because primary groups were doomed (Tönnies, 1940; Wirth, 1957; Simmel, 1957). The theoretical bases for this orientation were (a) industrial bureaucratic organizations were more effective than primary groups in achieving most goals, and (b) they required social conditions which were antithetical to primary groups. One of the major conditions so required was the need for primary group members to engage in differential

1. Goode (1963, pp. 1–86) points out that because of the many diverse kinds of pre-industrial societies and common pressures for industrialization, the historical trends may look quite different for each of them. Japan had a decreasing rate of divorce with industrialization while the United States had an increasing one because pre-industrial Japan had high rates of divorce and the U.S. didn't. The analysis in this paper assumes 'Western' type societies.

geographical and occupational mobility. In the late 1940s, Parsons suggested the 'isolated nuclear family' as a very special kind of primary group that could meet the conditions of urban society and avoid the problems of differential mobility. It did this by having one member in the labor force and restricting itself to a two-adult family unit. In the 1950s, a series of studies emerged which suggested that the extended kin relations could also survive in modern urban society but, unlike the Parsons solutions, these studies argued that primary groups could maintain cohesion despite differential mobility (Sussman and Burchinal, 1968; Litwak, 1960a and b). Continuing work in the field has further suggested that friendship groups, neighborhood groups and work groups may also be viable in current society. But little, if anything, has been done to demonstrate in theory that these various forms of primary group relationship can deal with problems of differential mobility. Do these forms represent vestigial remains which will soon disappear; do they represent ineffectiveness in the operation of industrial society; or do they (as we hypothesize) represent groups consistent with industrial society? Most important, if these different types of primary groups are all viable, are they structurally the same and can they handle the same type of problems?

To clarify this point, we are advancing the following propositions: in order for extended kin to remain viable, they must learn to communicate and exchange services in other than face-to-face situations; in order for neighbors to remain viable, they must learn to exchange services and communicate despite short membership turnover; and for friendships to remain viable, friends must learn to do both, in addition to learning how to deal with the most idiosyncratic aspects of life. In terms of 'small group theory', we are asking what mechanisms permit group cohesion under conditions of limited face to face contact or rapid membership turnover. In terms of stratification theory, we are asking under what conditions do people identify with primary groups across class lines. Most generally, we are asking, in terms of theories of urban society, what are the differential structures and functions which are performed by 'primary type' groups in an urban society. Though at first blush this may seem a bit ambitious, many of these problems are so intertwined that solutions to one lead to solutions to others. Within this general framework, we will undertake the analysis of specific primary groups.

Structure of neighborhoods

Neighborhoods are characterized by geographical proximity of members. Consequently, neighbors tend to be in face-to-face contact with one another. At the same time, industrialization demands that people in a given neighborhood have short tenure. If a neighborhood requires geographical proximity and industrialization requires short tenure, it follows that if neighborhoods are to survive in current industry they must stress face-to-face contact without one of the dimensions of a classical primary group, i.e. permanent membership.

To clarify this point, two thoughts will be elaborated, viz. to what extent does industrial society demand high neighborhood membership turnover, and to what extent does it provide mechanisms for primary group survival despite lack of permanence.

Technological pressure forces high neighborhood turnover. There are several ways in which technological developments in an industrial society force high membership turnover in neighborhoods. First, rational allocation of labor demanded by modern industry frequently means the labor force has to be shifted to where the work is. Jobs are mechanized or automated, causing shifts in geographical demands for labor (e.g. agriculture to industrial). Technology might create new industries as well as produce innovations which make previously undesirable areas habitable.

Technology also forces membership turnover, because land and housing, like labor, are subject to 'rational' redefinition. Large residential areas have been turned into super-highways even as commercial areas have been redeveloped for residential use. Technology brings about rapid shifts in housing standards. Housing put up ten to twenty years ago may be viewed as currently obsolete. Technology makes it economical to shift houses and neighborhoods with family life cycle. It also leads to continuous rises in standard of living, giving people a continuous option to move to better housing. Finally, because technology leads to occupational specialization, members of a neighborhood are often differentially effected by automation and pressure to move.

Technological support for neighborhood cohesion despite high membership turnover. If, indeed, technology tends to force high membership turnover in neighborhoods, can neighborhoods survive as meaningful primary groups? Several recent works suggest that in principle neighborhoods can survive despite short membership tenure (Litwak, 1960c; Festinger, 1951; Whyte, 1956; Fellin and Litwak, 1963; Wilensky, 1961). The basic point is that short tenure can be partially compensated for by rapid means of group indoctrination. If an individual is rapidly accepted into the group (from the moment of his appearance), the group might survive considerable membership turnover (Fellin and Litwak, 1963). What are some of the mechanisms which permit groups to indoctrinate members rapidly? The movement between groups can be made without loss of cohesion where the movement is ordered, i.e. expected and planned (Wilensky, 1961; Fellin and Litwak, 1963). Thus, where the group norms state newcomers are to be welcomed and newcomers have norms that long-term residents are friends, speedy indoctrination is encouraged (Fellin and Litwak, 1963). Other devices for rapid indoctrination are: groups with special subunits formally designated to seek out newcomers and introduce them to their neighbors, e.g. welcome wagons, ministers, P.T.A. members, etc. (Fellin and Litwak, 1963); neighborhood voluntary organizations (i.e. consisting of neighbors) where group norms can be publicly stated and re-enforced, e.g. P.T.A. block clubs, church related clubs, etc. (Litwak, 1961); extra economic resources which permit use of professional movers, freeing the newcomer to socialize. The fact that newcomers and long-term residents already share many basic values, languages and roles can speed up group socialization.

The question arises, how systematically are such mechanisms encouraged in a technological society? It has been suggested that the occupational milieu which is prototypical of the advanced technological society is that of the professional in large-scale bureaucratic organizations. In addition, the argument has been made that such occupations systematically require the development of ordered change while encouraging integration into primary-group-type work situations (Litwak and Fellin, 1963). As such, the occupational experience provides training for the development of norms welcoming strangers, as well as norms in which ordered change is accepted as good in itself. Furthermore, technological society encourages the development of nationally based industry, mass media, nationally based educational norms which in turn mean that individuals in such a society share a common language and a common culture even though they may have occupational specialties which differ. Technological societies, through their rising standards of living, permit more and more people to use professional movers. Finally, technological society encourages the development of education. This in turn enables the individual to take into account longer time spans (e.g. plan for ordered change) and to equip people interpersonally to run neighborhood voluntary associations with success.

To summarize, high membership turnover can be overcome where groups can evolve rapid modes of indoctrination, and this tends to be systematically the case in technological societies. However, to say it can survive does not mean that its structure will be the same as the 'traditional' neighborhood primary group. For the fact remains that it is a group which does have a high membership turnover, and this key structural fact will, we hypothesize, limit the kinds of tasks it can best handle.

Structure of kin groups

If the kinship structure (i.e. the relations between nuclear families) is examined, we find that central to its traditional historical meaning is the idea that people are related in semi-permanent biological or legal ways (e.g. mother–son relationship). At the same time, it is suggested that the kinship system, like the neighborhood, is faced with pressures for differential mobility in a technological society. If these two considerations, viz. permanent membership and differential mobility, are taken into account, then the kinship system can survive only by dropping the traditional primary group demand for face-to-face relations. It is hypothesized that this is possible in modern society because technological developments permit kinship exchanges over large distances. Before developing this point, a brief review will suggest that differential kinship mobility is intrinsic to modern technological development.

Differential kinship mobility. If we examine those pre-industrial societies which stressed kinship cohesion, we see, generally, three factors which prevented differential kinship mobility: (a) the kin controlled the occupational system; (b) a norm that any movement of kin must involve the total kinship structure; and (c) a strongly centralized authority system within the kin structure. It is our view that all three of these have been undermined by modern technological development. Thus, technology has encouraged the development of bureaucracies and professions. These in turn have loosened the hold of the kin on the occupational structure.[2] Technological pressure for change means that father and son may have different jobs and be subject to differential pressures for mobility (e.g. father's job automated to a point where few opportunities are left for sons, or better educational opportunities for young lead to different occupational choices). The child may not be offered the same job, may not want it, or may not be trained for it. Furthermore, where labor was unskilled, it was easily interchangeable and large kinship groups could move together. With specialization, introduced by modern technology, kinship members who move together might find it more difficult to find a job at a common locality.[3]

Finally, it would be argued that the modern technological

2. The various studies which show considerable social class inheritance in American societies do not contradict the assertions made herein. All such studies demonstrate is that the family can affect one's chances of entering the occupational world at a given level. But they do not assert that the family can control the child's being hired or fired. Nor can the family control the geographical re-location of the child, his rate of promotion, or whether he will be automated out of a job, etc. except as these processes are indirectly related to education. Since many of these attributes are inversely related to education, the families' control of a specific occupation for purposes of controlling the movement of their offspring is very limited.

3. Gutkind (1962, pp. 93–112) provides some limited support for one aspect of our argument. He points out that in certain African states the extended family will move as a totality even when there are no jobs; i.e. they work against the rational distribution of labor.

system undermines a highly centralized power structure within the kinship system. It is suggested that this erosion is brought about in the long run by the fact that the kinship system is no longer able to control completely the occupational market.

To summarize, a modern industrial society tends to offer maximal economic rewards to those willing to engage in differential mobility. It prevents the kin from using traditional means for halting mobility, and, as we shall point out, it lessens the cost of differential mobility to the kinship system.

Mechanisms for maintaining kinship ties. The question arises as to whether a kinship system can survive the loss of face-to-face contact (i.e. differential mobility) in any meaningful way. It has been suggested elsewhere that kinship systems can maintain their viability despite breaks in face-to-face contact (Adams, 1967; Lansing and Muller, 1967; Litwak, 1960b). The general point is that modern means of communication – the telephone, car and airplane – have made it increasingly easy for families and individuals to communicate with each other, even though not living within immediate geographical proximity of each other. Furthermore, our monetary economy (essential to a technologically advanced society) requires the use of money as a generalized means to most goals. Money can be easily and quickly transmitted, making it possible for kinship units to exchange aid over great distances.

Some have argued that estrangement between kin might arise, since differential economic success leads to a different cultural milieu. Without denying this point, it is only necessary to suggest that such differences take place within a larger context where society provides much in the way of common elements. The mass media, the large-scale mass education, etc. all lead to the evolvement of a common cultural and language base (Dahl, 1966, pp. 35–59; Adams, 1967; Streib, 1968, pp. 408–9; Litwak, 1960a). People have overlapping group memberships and so differences take place within a context of communality as contrasted to situations of complete group polarization (Dahl, 1966, pp. 367–86; Williams, 1964, pp. 352–91). It is suggested that the communality will increasingly become a sufficient base for maintaining kinship identity across class lines (Streib, 1968, pp. 408–9; Adams, 1967).

To argue that kinship structures can exist despite breaks in face-to-face contact does not mean that such structures are the same as the traditional kinship structures. This difference is hypothesized to affect significantly the kind of tasks they can best perform.

Structure of friendship peer groups

With these thoughts on kin and neighbors in mind, let us now examine friendship relationships. In some ways, these are structurally the weakest ties of all. They do not have the permanence of the kinship link or the face-to-face contact characterizing the neighborhood. Nevertheless, they are confronted with the very same social pressure that both of these groups are faced with – differential mobility. One would hypothesize that the major factor holding friendship ties together is affectivity. Unlike the other two groups, the individual has more options in choosing his friends. We suggest that because of this greater choice, friendship ties have affectivity as their major base of strength. The question arises as to how such affectivity can survive breaks in face-to-face relationships. To some extent, the answer would be the same as for the kinship group, e.g. modern modes of communication. However, friendship ties may be much more vulnerable to breaks in face-to-face contact than kin groups because there are no institutional pressures for permanence.

In any case, what we are suggesting is that friendship ties tend to rest on free choice and affectivity; neighborhood ties, face-to-face contact; and kinship structures, permanent relations. There is no reason at any moment in time why all these primary groups could not overlap – friends may be neighbors and family members at the same time. However, the main point of our discussion is that there are pressures in an industrial society for each of these groups to separate.

Structure of the nuclear family group

Although we will not present empirical evidence on the isolated nuclear family, it is necessary to make a few remarks about it to highlight the role of the other primary groups. The isolated nuclear family is the husband, wife and young children. Married children and relatives are excluded. The nuclear family comes closest to meeting the traditional demands of the primary group, e.g. face-to-face, permanent, affective, non-instrumental and diffused. However, a key structural feature of the isolated nuclear family is its lack of human resources. By definition, it has only two adult members. Because of this limitation in size, the nuclear family often cannot handle crucial problems even though they fall within the province of primary group structures. Thus they find it difficult to deal with tension management problems where the source of trouble is disputes between themselves – husband and wife (e.g. neither adult is able to provide succor to the other). In addition, because of the intense affectivity, family members may not be able to diagnose objectively incipient states of mental illness (Landy, 1960). Finally, because of technological innovation, family members often cannot use their personal history as a base for handling all problems (e.g. newest techniques for handling children, how to deal with new norms on dating, etc.). In a rapidly changing society, it is not enough for two adults to have only each other to draw upon.

We feel that the chief virtue of the kin and neighborhood and friendship primary groups is their ability to provide supplemental resources to the isolated nuclear family. They are able to do this because structurally they are close enough in form to the traditional primary group to minimize problems of communication.

Functions of neighborhood peer groups

With these ideas as background, the analysis will focus on the unique capacities of the neighborhood, the kinship group and the friendship group which might emerge because of their structural differentiation. We pointed out that the neighborhood has face-to-face contact as its distinguishing factor. The question now arises: what are the advantages of face-to-face contact? We suggest here three important advantages without claiming these are exhausted.

Perhaps the first advantage of face-to-face contact is speed of reaction. However, this would be true only if all other things were equal – knowledge, equipment, etc. We are talking about actions which are, on the one hand, simple enough for the ordinary person to handle and, on the other hand, so idiosyncratic that they cannot be programmed efficiently for large-scale equipment (Litwak and Figueira, 1968). For instance, the need to borrow a cup of sugar in the midst of preparing a meal, or having someone watch the baby for five minutes while one runs out unexpectedly to the store are both simple, widespread, yet idiosyncratic events. Such emergency situations range from the trivial matters to catastrophes. According to Form and Nosow (1958, pp. 54–82), as high as 75 per cent of the people connected with major natural disasters may be rescued in the first few hours by neighbors or kin living nearby.

The second advantage involves all those services which are technologically based on people living in the same territory. For instance, all people living on the same street have common problems if the water supply, police protection, street pavement, schools, etc. are inadequate. Most certainly, the chance of improving these services are immeasurably increased if the neighbors act cooperatively (Davies, 1966).

Third, neighbors' face-to-face contact may play a role in situations where continuous observation is necessary for learning. It is possible that much in the way of socialization – how to be a good mother, whether children's peer groups encourage delinquent attitudes or low school achievement – takes place in the neighborhood because it depends so heavily on everyday personal observation (Whyte, 1956, pp. 296 ff; Deutsch and Collins, 1951, pp. 78–103; Coleman, Campbell and Hobson, 1966, pp. 217–333).

To summarize, there are three tasks which are thought to be the special province of the neighborhood – time emergencies, services based on territoriality and activities which require everyday observation to be learned.

Function of family kin groups

As noted, the kin structure is distinguished by its permanence. It would seem, therefore, (all other things being equal) such a structure would do best where the task involved long-term ties. It is frequently true that parents with young children will draw up wills making kin, rather than good friends, responsible for rearing their children. The kin, in addition to providing long-term medical help, may play a decisive role in shaping the long-term career and attitudes of the individual.

Function of friendship peer groups

We have suggested that modern society is characterized by overlapping memberships; this means that there are certain things that group members hold in common and others on which they differ (Dahl, 1966, pp. 260–84, 367–86; Williams, 1964, pp. 352–91).

What also characterizes modern society is continuous uncorrelated change; technology may introduce changes in the educational world with no matching change in the work world or leisure-time one. If the preceding speculations are correct, then it should also be true that the number of elements which can be shared with a fixed group is definitely limited. To illustrate, an offspring who goes to college will be confronted by a series of problems which are outside the knowledge and interest of the parents, e.g. studying for examinations, dealing with peers, dating, etc. Even in the cases where the parents had also attended college before, it is quite likely that many of the norms will have changed so radically since the parents' stay in college that their knowledge base is limited.

The reader will recall that the family, because of its long-term biological and legal criteria, and the neighborhood, by virtue of its geographical definition, both provided a somewhat fixed and arbitrary definition of group. From all of the above, we concluded that the friendship groups can best handle matters involving continuous fluctuation while the others can handle the general communalities. It is not just because friendship groups provide the greatest options to choose matching group members but also because people with only ties of mutual affectivity may be more motivated to adjust to each other. Illustrative of some areas where friends would predominate would be the following: clothing fashions are continuously changing within some common value set; a liberal or conservative political tradition still permits variations in choice of candidate, e.g. Goldwater, Reagan, Nixon, Rockefeller, etc.

Summary of structure and function of types of primary groups

The structure and function of different types of primary groups have been summarized in Table 1. Reading across the top line of the table, we see that the nuclear family has all of the classical

Table 1 Level of Task Performance by Primary-Group Structure

	Nuclear family	Extended kin	Friends	Neighbors	Non-primary group
Face-to-face	High	Low	Low	High	Very low – significant amount of behavior ordered by rules
Permanent (ascribed)	High	High	Moderate	Low	Very low – achieved
Diffused	High	Moderate	Moderate	Moderate	Very low – specific or specialized
Affective	High	Moderate	High	Moderate	Very low – affectively neutral or impersonal
Non-instrumental (particularistic)	High	Moderate	Moderate	Moderate	Very low – universalistic or contractual

Human resources	Low	High	High	High	Very high – any number more than 20*.
Type of task optimally done.	All primary group tasks which require only two or fewer adults.	All primary group tasks which require low face-to-face contact, long-term commitments, and more than two people.	Those primary group tasks which require the closest manifest agreement to be accomplished but involve relatively long-term involvement.	Those primary group tasks which require everyday contact and more than two adults, e.g. time-urgent tasks, everyday socialization tasks, etc. However, no task which requires long-term commitment.	All tasks requiring specialized training, large capital goods investments, or groupings of very large numbers of people.

*This is, at best, only a rough guess. It can be as high as 1000 or 100,000.

dimensions of the primary group but is so limited in human resources that it frequently cannot perform all of the primary-group functions. The extended kin tends to be quite high on permanence and human resources but very low on face-to-face relations, but only moderately so on other dimensions of organization. The other lines may be read similarly. There are many logically possible types as well as concrete ones which we have not discussed, e.g. friendship groups which take place at the job site and are intimately bound to the job itself.

In sharp contrast to any of these primary-group types of organizations are the non-primary groups, e.g. bureaucratic relations. Table 1 shows these groups as very low on all dimensions. This line is introduced to the reader to highlight explicitly the danger of dichotomizing social relations. To say that a group does not have all of the dimensions of the classical primary group does not automatically make it a secondary or bureaucratic one. Between these poles is much distance, and one way of describing the analysis is to say that we are attempting to specify the structure of some of these intervening groups which, though they differ from the classical primary group, are much closer in structure to it than to any other type of group.

References

ADAMS, B. N. (1967), *Kinship in an Urban Setting*, Markham.

COLEMAN, J. S., CAMPBELL, E. Q., and HOBSON, C. J. (1966), *Equality of Educational Opportunity*, United States Department of Health, Education and Welfare, Government Printing Office.

COOLEY, C. H. (1955), 'Primary groups', in A. P. Hare *et al.* (eds.), *Small Groups*, Knopf.

DAHL, R. A. (1966), 'The American oppositions: affirmation and denial', in R. A. Dahl (ed.), *Political Oppositions in Western Democracies*, Yale University Press.

DAVIES, J. C. (1966), *Neighborhood Groups and Urban Renewal*, Columbia University Press.

DEUTSCH, M., and COLLINS, M. E. (1951), *Inter-Racial Housing*, University of Minnesota Press.

FELLIN, P., and LITWAK, E. (1963), 'Neighborhood cohesion under conditions of mobility', *American Sociological Review*, vol. 28, pp. 364–76.

FESTINGER, L. (1951), 'Architecture and group membership', *Journal of Social Issues*, no. 7, pp. 152–63.

FORM, W. H., and NOSOW, S. (1958), *Community in Disaster*, Harper & Row.

GOODE, W. J. (1963), *World Revolution and Family Patterns*, Free Press.

GUTKIND, P. (1962), *La famile africaine et son adaptation à la vie urbaine*, Diogène.

LANDY, D. (1960), 'Problems of the person seeking help in our culture', *Social Welfare Forum*, Columbia University Press.

LANSING, J. B., and MULLER, E. (1967), *The Geographic Mobility of Labor*, University of Michigan Survey Research Center.

LITWAK, E. (1960a), 'Occupational mobility and extended family cohesion', *American Sociological Review*, vol. 25, pp. 9–21.

LITWAK, E. (1960b), 'Geographic mobility and extended family cohesion', *American Sociological Review*, vol. 25, pp. 385–94.

LITWAK, E. (1960c), 'Reference group theory, bureaucratic career and neighborhood primary group cohesion', *Sociometry*, vol. 23, pp. 72–84.

LITWAK, E. (1961), 'Voluntary associations and neighborhood cohesion', *American Sociology Review*, vol. 26, pp. 258–71.

LITWAK, E., and FIGUEIRA, J. (1968), 'Technological innovation and theoretical functions of primary groups and bureaucratic structures', *American Journal of Sociology*, vol. 73, pp. 468–81.

SIMMEL, G. (1957), 'The metropolis and mental life', in P. K. Hatt and A. J. Reiss, Jr (eds.), *Cities and Society: The Revised Reader in Urban Sociology*, Free Press.

STREIB, G. F. (1968), 'Family patterns in retirement', in M. B. Sussman (ed.), *Sourcebook in Marriage and the Family*, 3rd edn, Houghton Mifflin.

SUSSMAN, M. B., and BURCHINAL, L. (1968), 'Kin family network: unheralded structure in current conceptualizations of family functioning', in M. B. Sussman (ed.), *Sourcebook in Marriage and the Family*, 3rd edn, Houghton Mifflin.

TÖNNIES, F. (1940), *Fundamental Concepts of Sociology*, trans. C. P. Loomis, American Book Co.

WHYTE, W. H., Jr (1956), *The Organization Man*, Simon & Schuster; Penguin Books, 1960.

WILENSKY, H. L. (1961), 'Orderly careers and social participation', *American Sociological Review*, vol. 26, pp. 521–39.

WILLIAMS, R. M., Jr (1964), *Strangers Next Door*, Prentice-Hall.

WIRTH, L. (1957), 'Urbanism as a way of life', in P. K. Hatt and A. J. Reiss, Jr (eds.), *Cities and Society: The Revised Reader in Urban Sociology*, vol. 272, pp. 39–46.

Part Three The Choice of a Spouse

Until the early 1960s research on mate selection was dominated
by a search for correlations rather than explanations. Four main
correlations emerged. A mass of studies established that mate
selection was most likely to occur homogamously (like married
like) with respect to individual background variables like race,
ethnic group, religion, education, age, and parental social class
(cf. especially Hollingshead, 1950b, and the useful review in
Zelditch, 1964). This was most commonly attributed to the strong
normative element which was believed to operate in this area.
Secondly, marriages were usually propinquitous (marked
tendency to marry someone living near by), and this too was partly
attributed to normative factors (Katz and Hill, 1958). Thirdly,
marriages were found usually to be homogamous with respect to
values (e.g. Kerckhoff and Davis, 1962). Finally, some evidence
emerged that within a normatively prescribed so-called field-of-
eligibles, complementarity of personality needs was important,
at least under certain circumstances (Winch, 1958; Kerckhoff
and Davis, 1962).

In the 1960s it was increasingly realized that the conditions
under which and the reasons why such variables as homogamy or
complementarity arise are themselves variable, and should be
key focuses of research.

As Kerckhoff (Reading 13) points out, homogamy can be the
result of at least three sets of factors, personal preference,
external pressures and restricted opportunities for interaction,
and these, as he demonstrates, undoubtedly vary from item to
item and from group to group for reasons we do not yet by any
means fully understand. Recently, the normative field-of-eligibles
hypothesis has been under considerable attack, and while it

undoubtedly plays a role, particularly in higher socio-economic groups (Sussman, 1953; Hollingshead, 1950a), and in many traditional areas (cf. Reading 1 and Goode, 1959; Zelditch 1964) the conditions under which it can be maintained to any given degree are not yet fully understood. Catton and Smircich (Reading 14) demonstrate that in Seattle at least propinquity seems simply to reflect a quest for economy of time and effort on the part of suitors. They suggest that rather than norms determining propinquity, normative homogamy can perhaps only be maintained because interaction (through residential segregation by class) is most likely to be easiest with those of similar background. In doing so, Catton and Smircich show the benefits that can be derived from mathematical formulations both in terms of conceptual precision and for the investigation of competing hypotheses. A similar conclusion with regard to the primary influence of interaction in educational homogamy emerges from an equally sophisticated analysis, this time using partial correlation techniques, reported by Blau and Duncan (1967, pp. 346–60).

Research into other aspects of this topic has also recently pointed to the need to explore *the conditions under which* any particular correlation occurs. Winch (Reading 15), reviewing the literature on complementarity of needs, hypothesizes that the role played by complementarity of needs will vary with the marital role expectations of the couple concerned. A similar conclusion has been tentatively suggested with respect to value homogamy by the empirical research of Kerckhoff and Bean (1967).

References

BLAU, P. M., and DUNCAN, O. D. (1967), *The American Occupational Structure*, Wiley.
GOODE, W. J. (1959), 'The theoretical importance of love', *American Sociological Review*, vol. 24, pp. 38–47.
HOLLINGSHEAD, A. D. (1950a), 'Class differences in family stability', *Annals of the American Academy of Political and Social Science*, vol. 272, pp. 39–46.
HOLLINGSHEAD, A. D. (1950b), 'Cultural factors in the selection of marriage mates', *American Sociological Review*, vol. 16, pp. 619–27.
KATZ, A. M., and HILL, R. (1958), 'Residential propinquity and

marital selection: a review of theory, method and fact', *Marriage and Family Living*, vol. 20, pp, 27–35.

KERCKHOFF, A. C., and BEAN, F. D. (1967), 'Role-related factors in person perception among engaged couples', *Sociometry*, vol. 30, pp. 176–86.

KERCKHOFF, A. C., and DAVIS, K. E. (1962), 'Value consensus and need complementarity in mate selection', *American Sociological Review*, vol. 27, pp. 295–303.

SUSSMAN, M. B. (1953), 'Parental participation in mate selection and its effect upon family continuity', *Social Forces*, vol. 32, pp. 76–81.

WINCH, R. F. (1958), *Mate-Selection: A Study of Complementary Needs*, Harper & Row.

ZELDITCH, M. (1964), 'Family marriage and kinship', in R. E. L. Faris (ed.), *Handbook of Modern Sociology*, Rand McNally.

13 A. C. Kerckhoff

Patterns of Homogamy in Mate Selection

A. C. Kerckhoff, 'Patterns of homogamy and the field of eligibles', *Social Forces*, vol. 42, 1963–4, pp. 289–97.

The principle of homogamy in the mate selection process is well established in the sociological literature. Numerous studies have supported the general proposition that the dominant pattern in our society, even within the framework of 'freedom of choice', is for marital partners to come from similar social categories. However, in spite of the wealth of empirical evidence of this kind, we have not yet gone much beyond the rather simple generalization that choices are usually made within broad social categories. We have stopped raising questions about the social bases of mate selection seemingly because we assume that the important sociological analysis has already been carried out by demonstrating homogamous patterns. In contrast, the major thesis of this paper is that studies of homogamy have only begun to examine the sociological aspects of mate selection. They have only posed the problem, not solved it.

There is nothing new in the idea that problems remain in this area of inquiry. At least a decade ago Burgess and Locke (1953, p. 370) suggested that 'the actual factors determining assortative mating have not been studied', and they proceeded to list six possible explanations of the empirical findings. Most of these explanations are of two types. The first type views the patterns of mate selection as a function of opportunities. It explains similarities of mates on the basis of residential segregation and differences in activity patterns of various social categories which limit the range of contacts of any person to encounters with persons like himself. The second explanation is a normative one. It views the patterns of similarity as the result of preferences on the part of the chooser for persons like himself and/or the enforcement of such homogamous choices through social sanctions.

A recent treatment of some of the issues by Katz and Hill (1958) attempts to combine the two under a general 'norm-interaction' theory.[1] Although such a combination may have theoretic value, it makes even more apparent the fact that the same behavior may be the result of very different antecedents. Conformity with the pattern of homogamy, when it occurs, may be due to *either* limited opportunities *or* adherence to a norm. Simple reporting of the pattern will not determine which is the case.[2]

One particular aspect of the normative explanation is also worthy of consideration. If we assume that there is a norm of homogamy which is realized to variable degrees by persons in our society, we might ask if it is thus reasonable to assume that there is a *general* norm which calls for 'like to marry like' or whether there is a whole set of *independent* norms which call for 'Negro to marry Negro', 'Protestant to marry Protestant', 'college graduate to marry college graduate', etc. The former view would call for some pattern in an individual's adherence to the general homogamy norm as manifested on the various dimensions of homogamy (race, religion, class, etc.), the latter view would not. That there is a general 'tendency to seek the near and similar' has been suggested in discussions of homogamy,[3] but evidence of such a tendency is not available.

One final issue is also relevant. Although discussions of 'the principle of homogamy' seldom raise the point, there seems to be

1. The first two assumptions of this theory are: '(a) that marriage is normative; (b) that, within normative fields of eligibles, the probability of marriage varies directly with the probability of interaction' (p. 33).

2. These two factors occupy different positions in the logic of explication of patterns of homogamy because adherence to a norm of homogamy is possible only if opportunities to meet potential spouses who are similar to the chooser are provided. Conversely, if no heterogamous opportunities are provided, there is no basis for testing the efficacy of the norm. However, since there are likely to be very few cases in which *no* opportunities are available for heterogamous contacts, behavior in keeping with the principle of homogamy will normally be subject to both of these interpretations unless other information is available.

3. This is seldom made as an explicit point, but is implied by the inclusion of all patterns of homogamy in the same textbook discussions (cf. Kirkpatrick, 1963, p. 416). The intent here is not so much to question the adequacy of previous formulations, but to examine the reasonable limits of future formulations.

a priori reason to expect that both opportunities and norms might vary in different segments of our population. If it is true, for instance, that middle-class people have a wider range of contacts (a broader 'life space') than working-class people,[4] one would expect differences in the degree of homogamy in the two classes. Within any one broad segment such as a class, one would also expect that differential life experiences would lead to varying degrees of homogamy. For instance, the person who has been more mobile, either socially or spatially, might logically be expected to have had a wider range of contacts than would others in his class, and this would lead to the expectation of a different level of homogamy. Whether in such cases a wider range of contacts would lead to a prediction of a lower or higher degree of homogamy, however, would still be in doubt, as has already been noted.

The discussion thus far leads us to suggest three researchable questions. They are:

1. Do the patterns of homogamy, as a function of the range of contacts, fit more nearly the normative or the opportunities explanation?

2. Is there evidence of a general norm of homogamy which finds expression in homogamous choices on the several dimensions usually reported, or are the several dimensions independent of each other?

3. Is there evidence that patterns of homogamy vary in different segments of the population?

In order to deal adequately with these questions, especially the first two, it will be necessary to deviate somewhat from the usual research design used in homogamy studies. Most of the data used in support of the principle of homogamy are statements about the degree of similarity between spouses. That is, the data deal with the *outcome* of mate selection, not with the *process*. They are usually interpreted, however, as indicating something about the process. Winch has presented this interpretation very explicitly

4. Some studies of propinquity present data which indicate that people with higher income and education are less propinquitous than others. Such data are consistent with the claim of a broader range of contacts of middle-class people. See Kerckhoff (1955) and Katz and Hill (1958).

in the following passage (in which he also uses an opportunities explanation):

In summary, I should like to interpret the studies on homogamy as follows. There is a set of variables upon which homogamy has been shown to function: race, religion, social class, broad occupational grouping, location of residence, income, age, level of education, intelligence, etc. It is my opinion that these variables function to select for each of us the sort of people with whom we shall be most likely to interact, to assure that the people with whom we work and with whom we play and with whom we otherwise associate are more or less like us with respect to that set of variables and also with respect to cultural interests and values. In the sense that these variables determine with whom we shall associate, I suggest that they define for each of us a 'field of eligible spouse-candidates' within which it is likely that we shall choose our spouses (Winch, 1958, p. 14).

Winch's concept of 'the field of eligibles' clearly expresses the notion that the search for a mate goes on within a restricted segment of the population, and the data on homogamy of spouses are interpreted as providing evidence of this. What remains unanswered, however, is the basis of definition of the dimensions of this field of eligibles, as well as the degree of variation of definition on the several dimensions and among different segments of the population. In order to deal with these questions, we must examine the process as well as the outcome. This clearly calls for a longitudinal perspective. We would expect, for instance, that if the opportunities explanation of homogamy is correct, one's field of eligibles is a very different field than if the normative explanation is correct. And if we should finally decide that *both* norms *and* opportunities play a part in the process of mate selection, the field of eligibles of an individual would tend to change during the process of selection in a way that could not be derived from an examination of the outcome data alone. Put another way, the field of eligibles can only be viewed as a static categorical definition if we use outcome data, but it can be seen as at least potentially a dynamic, changing, emerging definition if we use both process and outcome data.

It is possible to conceive of a research design which would permit us to clarify our conceptions of this process. This would necessarily be a longitudinal design covering the period of selection and including both normative measures and records of interpersonal contacts over the entire period. Ultimately, this is the kind of study which will be necessary.

Short of this, however, it may be that other types of studies can add to our knowledge of the process. Such studies would begin by deriving logically the kinds of outcomes that would be expected given the various suggested explanations of homogamy. For instance, the opportunities explanation would lead us to expect that persons who have a wide range of contacts ought to exhibit less homogamy than those with a more restricted range. The opposite expectation would follow from the normative explanation. That is, a normative explanation would lead to the prediction that persons with a wider range of contacts would be more likely to be homogamous since they would have a greater opportunity to find a person with the proper homogamous characteristics.

Such studies can also be strengthened by choosing subjects at the end of the selection period and asking them for information about the process itself. Such a method would, of course, include all of the sources of error in any retrospective data, and many of the crucial variables could not be included. For instance, it would not be reasonable to ask subjects if their normative definitions of the field of eligibles had changed, and data on range of contacts could at best be crude. It would be possible to get some indication of the dimensions of the field of eligibles in an earlier period, however, by asking about earlier pairings prior to the final choice on the logic that if there had been a serious relationship between the subject and a person other than the spouse, this other person must have been within the field of eligibles at that time.

Reported below are the findings of a study of this kind. Given the fact that we did not assume a constant rate and pattern of homogamy throughout the population and given a limited research budget, it was considered wise to restrict the sample to a very homogeneous segment and to focus on variations within this segment. Also, since we had an interest in the possibility of changes in the definitions of the field of eligibles, subjects who were known to have experienced a change in opportunities for interaction were considered desirable. For once the ubiquitous undergraduate was seen as not only convenient but ideally suited to these research needs. At the particular school used, undergraduate women are very homogeneous in many respects, and almost all of them have experienced a major shift in their life space by coming to college. Although the findings resulting from the use of such a sample cannot be seen as relevant to very different samples, these findings are clearly relevant to the questions which led to the study.

Method

One hundred and fourteen engaged coeds at Duke University were interviewed on the subject of their experiences in the period of mate selection. Specifically, they were asked about three young men in whom they had been 'seriously interested'. These three were defined as: the fiancé, the last serious beau before the fiancé, and the first beau in whom they were seriously interested. They were asked to answer a series of questions about each of these young men as well as a number of questions about themselves. In general, these questions dealt with the social characteristics of the girl and the three young men – age, education, religion, occupation of father, home town, and so on. Given these data, patterns of homogamy–heterogamy could be discerned for the girl with regard to each of the men, and any longitudinal trends could be noted.

The three points in the mate selection process which were examined in this way were, of course, arbitrarily chosen, and no claim can be made that they are the best for the purposes at hand. They were chosen to insure a considerable time period over which changes could have taken place in patterns of homogamy and/or the definition of the field of eligibles.

Of the 114 girls, sixteen denied having been serious about any man other than their fiancé, and twenty said there had been only one such previous beau. The data to be reported, therefore, will be from the seventy-eight girls who could report on all three types of men about whom we were inquiring.

Although the subjects were chosen solely on the basis of their being engaged, because of the nature of the population from which they were drawn, they formed a very homogeneous group with respect to age at the time of the interview. All were between eighteen and twenty-two with 80 per cent of them being either twenty or twenty-one. There was somewhat more variability in their ages at the time they were going with the 'last beau' (before the fiancé) and with the 'first beau'. The modal age at the time of the last beau was eighteen, and at the time of the first beau it was sixteen, but in each case less than 50 per cent fell in the modal class. Roughly, then, we are dealing with data from ages sixteen, eighteen and twenty-one. The men involved tend to be home-town boyfriends in the case of the first beau and college boy-friends in the case of the last beau and the fiancé.

The girls were also quite homogeneous in many respects besides age. They were all white, almost all Protestant (seventy-two of the seventy-eight), their parents were both native born in all but five cases, and their fathers were largely from the upper two Hollingshead occupational categories (sixty-eight out of seventy-eight). They are thus not representative of girls their age or even of college girls their age. This degree of homogeneity, however, does make it somewhat easier to make meaningful generalizations about the group.

Of the basic social characteristics normally referred to in dis-cussions of homogamy, the four characteristics which proved to be of interest were: education, class, religion and urbanity. The operational definitions of homogamy with respect to urbanity and religion were rather simple. All cases in which the boy and girl came from the same major religious category (Protestant, Catholic, Jew) were called homogamous (Hm), and others were called heterogamous (Ht). All girls and their three boyfriends were classified into the following urbanity categories: farm or town less than 2500; 2500 to 10,000; 10,001 to 50,000; 50,001 to 250,000; over 250,000 (including suburbs of large cities). Pairs in which both boy and girl came from the same category were classified Hm; others were classified Ht on urbanity.

For education and class, however, the operational definition was different, because the significance of a girl's coming from a higher educational or class category is very different from her coming from a lower one. Since men generally have higher levels of education than women and since the man's social position largely determines the position of the couple after marriage, cases in which the boy's educational or class category was higher were classified Hm along with cases in which the categories were the same. Only cases in which the girl was higher than the boy were classified Ht. The educational categories were: no college; college but no degree; a B.A. degree; work beyond a B.A. For class categorization, the girl was asked regarding each boy: 'Would you say he lives (lived) in a better or poorer neighborhood than you do (did at that time)?' Cases were then classified Ht only if the girl said 'poorer', all other cases being Hm.

Results

The proportion of pairs which were homogamous was computed on each dimension for each of the three pairings. These are reported in Table 1. There is a clear tendency for the proportions Hm to decrease on urbanity and generally to increase on the other three dimensions as we move from first beau to second beau to fiancé. If we assume that all of these girls have experienced an increase in opportunities for interaction by going to college, these data may be interpreted with reference to the basic question of the effect of increased opportunities on patterns of homogamy. Evidently the general pattern is one of increased homogamy in spite of increased opportunities, which supports the normative interpretation of homogamy. Given the fact that urbanity is an exception to this pattern, we would have to assume that urbanity is not a normatively prescribed dimension of homogamy. Thus, on this dimension, increased opportunities for interaction lead to decreased homogamy, which is in keeping with the opportunities interpretation of homogamy. We can only conclude from this initial examination of the data that the effect of increased opportunities on the level of homogamy will depend on the dimension of

Table 1 Proportion Homogamous by Dimension and Stage in Mate Selection Process*

Stage (Boyfriend)	Dimension Religion	Urbanity	Education	Class
First beau	0·787 (75)	0·705 (78)	0·645 (76)	0·533 (75)
Second beau	0·730 (74)	0·554 (74)	0·756 (78)	0·754 (57)
Fiancé	0·846 (78)	0·436 (78)	0·987 (78)	0·782 (78)

*The numbers in parentheses following each proportion are the sizes of the sub-groups on which the proportions were computed.

homogamy in question. Some will increase; others will decrease. We may interpret this as an indication of differential degrees of normative prescription of homogamy on the several dimensions.

The second question suggested above was: is there evidence of a *general* norm of homogamy which finds expression in homogamous choices on the several dimensions usually reported, or are the several dimensions independent of each other? The fact that level of homogamy increased on some dimensions and decreased on another evidently indicates a lack of generality of the tendency of 'like to choose like', but a more refined analysis is even more revealing.

One operational form of this question might be: is there a tendency for individuals to maintain their levels of Hm through the period of mate selection? It might be hypothesized, for instance, that the changes in proportions Hm shown in Table 1 are due to changes by a limited number of girls (who have not internalized the general tendency to make homogamous choices), whereas the modal pattern is to be stable in this regard. Of the fifty cases for which all twelve measures (four dimensions for three boyfriends) are available, only eight are Hm on the same *number* of dimensions for all three boyfriends, and only four of these are Hm on the same *specific* dimensions on all three. Less than one-half are Hm on the same number of dimensions for any two of the three boyfriends, and less than one-fourth are Hm on the same specific dimensions for any two of the three boyfriends. If the measure of homogamy on urbanity is dropped from the analysis because of its deviant general pattern, substantially the same results occur. Using just religion, education and class, only eleven of the fifty cases are Hm on the same number of dimensions for all three boyfriends, and less than 60 per cent of the cases are Hm on the same number of dimensions for any two boyfriends. There is, therefore, little evidence of general stability in the tendency to make homogamous choices during the mate-selection process.

A second operational form of the basic question might be: is there a tendency for individuals, whatever degree of homogamy they exhibit originally, to become more homogamous as they pass through the mate-selection period? This form of the question recognizes that the general pattern for at least three of the dimensions is to exhibit a greater degree of homogamy with the fiancé than with either of the earlier boyfriends. It thus suggests a convergence hypothesis rather than a stability hypothesis and implies that the tendency to make homogamous choices may be a constant for any individual, and yet a pattern of change may occur during the selection process due to the increasing seriousness of the search and/or a greater range of choices.

Perhaps the simplest way to examine the data with reference to this question is to note the changes in the number of dimensions on which the girls are Hm as we shift from first beau to second beau to fiancé. Although about one-third of the girls become Hm on more dimensions at each of these two points of comparison, about one-fourth become Hm on *fewer* dimensions at each point also. If we again drop the urbanity dimension from the analysis, we also find that about one-third of the girls become Hm on more dimensions at each of the two points of transition, and that again about one-fourth become Hm on fewer dimensions between the first and second beau. However, only one-tenth become Hm on fewer dimensions between the second beau and the fiancé. The inclusion of urbanity thus has an influence on the longitudinal pattern, but there is still no clear evidence of a pattern of increasing homogamy throughout the period.

Each dimension was also considered separately. Throughout the analysis the same general pattern was found: more than one-third as many change from Hm to Ht as change from Ht to Hm at each point of transition on each dimension. The only clear exception to this is the transition from last beau to fiancé on the education dimension, since all of the girls but one are Hm with the fiancé on this dimension. These data, therefore, do not seem to fit the convergence hypothesis. Although individuals begin the mate-selection process at different points on a continuum of homogamy, and many do become more homogamous, a sizeable number also become less homogamous during the process.[5]

5. A third operational form of the basic question regarding a general tendency to make homogamous choices might take a form such as: is there some systematic tendency for heterogamy, when it occurs, to occur on some dimensions before it occurs on others? Basically, this is simply the question of whether or not homogamy is a unidimensional variable. If the usual

The analysis thus far suggests that these dimensions are largely independent of each other and that, if there is a 'tendency to seek the near and similar', there is either considerable variation in the dimensions of similarity used in the search or there is considerable variation in the success the girls had in finding what they were looking for. It suggests also that the field of eligibles is not so neatly and stably defined as has been suggested and/or that it is defined in rather different ways by different girls. The fact that this sample is as homogeneous as it is makes the variations reported above particularly noteworthy as a basis for questioning the earlier simplistic conceptions of categorical definitions of the population within which choices are made.

Unless we are to accept a chaotic view of the choice process, however, the data and interpretations presented here provide additional challenge to find a basis for ordering the multiplicity of patterns we have noted. We thus turn to our third question: is there evidence that the patterns of homogamy vary in different segments of the population?

Four independent variables were used to investigate variations in degree of homogamy: geographic mobility, social mobility, size of home town and occupation of father. Each of these variables was dichotomized. The measure of geographic mobility was the number of home towns lived in during the previous ten years. A mobile girl is one who had lived in two or more home towns, and a non-mobile girl is one who had lived in only one. Social mobility was measured by asking the girl: 'Is the house you live in now in a better or poorer neighborhood than the one you lived in when you were in junior high school?' No one said 'poorer' and thus mobile girls are those who said they now live in better neighborhoods, and non-mobile girls are those who said they lived in the same level of neighborhood when in junior high school. A higher occupation was defined as one in the top category of the Hollingshead system, and any other occupation is a lower

---

Guttman scale criteria are used, only the data on first beaus are at all suitable for testing this hypothesis, because the proportions Hm are too high for the fiancé, and the proportions on the several dimensions are too similar for the second beau. Using the data on the first beau, the coefficient of reproducibility is only 0·881, and the coefficient of scalability is only 0·414. The data of this study are not an adequate basis for testing this hypothesis, however, and it should be considered further in future research.

Table 2 Proportion Homogamous by Dimension, Stage and Independent Variables†

Dimension	Stage (Boyfriend)	Independent variables							
		Not geographically mobile	Geographically mobile	Not socially mobile	Socially mobile	Small city	Large city	Higher occupation	Lower occupation
Religion	First beau	0·854 (48)*	0·667 (27)	0·804 (56)	0·750 (16)	0·743 (35)	0·825 (40)	0·864 (44)*	0·677 (31)
	Second beau	0·809 (47)*	0·577 (26)	0·796 (54)*	0·529 (17)	0·647 (34)	0·800 (40)	0·705 (44)	0·767 (30)
	Fiancé	0·900 (50)	0·778 (27)	0·897 (58)*	0·706 (17)	0·889 (36)	0·810 (42)	0·804 (46)	0·906 (32)
Urbanity	First beau	0·780 (50)*	0·571 (28)	0·759 (58)*	0·529 (17)	0·722 (36)	0·690 (42)	0·761 (46)	0·625 (32)
	Second beau	0·617 (47)	0·444 (27)	0·582 (55)	0·500 (16)	0·457 (35)	0·641 (39)	0·614 (44)	0·467 (30)
	Fiancé	0·500 (50)*	0·296 (27)	0·500 (58)*	0·235 (17)	0·444 (36)	0·429 (42)	0·435 (46)	0·438 (32)
Education	First beau	0·694 (49)	0·538 (26)	0·684 (57)*	0·438 (16)	0·639 (36)	0·650 (40)	0·773 (44)*	0·469 (32)
	Second beau	0·720 (50)	0·815 (27)	0·741 (58)	0·824 (17)	0·722 (36)	0·786 (42)	0·717 (46)	0·813 (32)
	Fiancé	1·000 (50)	0·963 (27)	0·983 (58)	1·000 (17)	1·000 (36)	0·976 (42)	1·000 (46)	0·969 (32)
Class	First beau	0·571 (49)	0·462 (26)	0·554 (56)	0·500 (16)	0·571 (35)	0·500 (40)	0·432 (44)*	0·677 (31)
	Second beau	0·757 (37)	0·700 (20)	0·727 (44)	0·900 (10)	0·821 (28)	0·690 (26)	0·706 (34)	0·826 (23)
	Fiancé	0·820 (50)	0·741 (27)	0·810 (58)	0·706 (17)	0·833 (36)	0·738 (42)	0·696 (46)*	0·906 (32)

† See text for explanation.
* The numbers in parentheses following each proportion are the sizes of the sub-groups on which the proportions were computed.

one. A small city is one with 50,000 or fewer persons, and a large city is one with more than 50,000 persons.

Since this was viewed as a purely exploratory analysis, no emphasis was given to the statement and testing of hypotheses. However, the four variables were used in the analysis because we expected on *a priori* grounds that they would probably be related to level of Hm at some stage in the mate selection process. In general, we expected big-city girls and mobile girls to have a higher probability of Ht at each of the three stages. We had fewer reasons for expecting occupation to be a relevant variable (especially given the limited range of occupational levels), but we originally guessed that girls whose fathers had higher occupations would have higher Hm levels.

The proportion of pairs which are Hm within each of these categories was computed for each dimension for each of the boy–girl pairs. These proportions are reported in Table 2. For each of the four independent variables, there are twelve possible comparisons – four dimensions each for three boy–girl pairs. For geographic mobility, all but one of these comparisons show non-mobile girls to be higher in proportion Hm. For social mobility, nine of twelve comparisons are in this same direction. Size of home town is not so clearly related to proportion Hm; only seven of the twelve comparisons show small-city girls higher in proportion Hm than big-city girls. Finally, the findings with regard to father's occupation proved to be almost the opposite of our expectations. In seven of twelve comparisons, girls whose fathers have higher occupations are *lower* in proportion Hm. In general then, girls who have been socially and geographically stable, who are from small cities, and who have fathers with lower occupations tend to be Hm in greater proportions than their opposites.

The size of the differences between sub-group proportions is quite variable, however. If we consider only those differences that are fairly large,[6] the picture is simplified. Thirteen of the forty-

6. In order to have a standard definition of 'large', t tests were run on the differences between proportions, and only those differences which produced a t value of 1·65 or greater were defined as 'large'. Although this is the standard t value for a 0·10 level of significance, a claim of statistical significance is not in order, since no judgements are being made about a population which this sample is presumed to represent.

eight comparisons show such large differences. These are indicated by asterisks in Table 2.[7] Five of these differences involve the measure of Hm on religion, four involve urbanity, and education and class exhibit two each.

Geographic mobility accounts for four of the thirteen large differences. It is fairly consistently related to proportion Hm on religion and urbanity, the only exceptions (Hm on religion for fiancé and Hm on urbanity for second beau) also exhibiting sizeable differences in the same direction. Social mobility, which accounts for five of the sizeable differences, is also most clearly related to proportion Hm on religion and urbanity. Father's occupation accounts for four of the thirteen large differences, three of them with reference to the first beau. The two most notable of the four are the very sizeable differences on class for the first beau and the fiancé, girls whose fathers have lower occupations having a greater proportion Hm in both cases. Size of city is not clearly related to any of the homogamy dimensions.

The most consistent correlates of Hm on religion are geographic and social mobility. These same two variables are also most consistently related to Hm on urbanity. For education, notable differences are found only with reference to first beau, social mobility and father's occupation being related at that point. With respect to class, only father's occupation is related to proportion Hm.

If we view these relationships longitudinally, the findings with respect to patterns of change are more difficult to generalize. In most cases, the patterns for the sub-groups parallel each other rather closely so that the sub-group which has a lower proportion Hm for the first beau also has a lower proportion Hm for the second beau and the fiancé.

Although there are a number of deviations from this modal pattern, only two which seem to be in keeping with expectations derived from the earlier discussion will be noted here: (a) With

7. Of these, five are found in measures involving the first beau, two involve the second beau, and four involve the fiancé. The variation in these numbers of large differences is at least in part due to the very small number of cases (fifty-seven) for whom class data are available for the second beau and the almost unanimous Hm on education with fiancés. Therefore, no significance is attributed to these differences.

regard to the patterns of Hm on religion, the two social mobility sub-groups exhibit different longitudinal shifts. The mobile sub-group takes a very sharp dip in proportion Hm from first to second beau and never returns to its original level, whereas the stable sub-group makes almost no dip between first and second beau and moves well above its original level for the fiancé. If we may view the move from home to college as a broadening of the opportunities for contact with diverse types of people, evidently this has a rather different effect on socially mobile and non-mobile girls. The latter move toward greater homogamy on religion, the former toward less homogamy. This may imply a differential degree of internalization of the norm calling for homogamy on religion by these two types of girl. (b) With regard to proportion Hm on education, the pattern of change between first and second beau is noteworthy. In each of the three cases in which there is a sizeable difference between sub-groups for the first beau (geographic mobility, social mobility and father's occupation), the group originally having the lower proportion Hm exhibits a dramatic increase from first to second beau and reaches a higher proportion than the sub-group which was originally higher. This is in spite of the fact that each of the three sub-groups which were originally higher also increases in proportion Hm. One might see this as an indication that these mobile, lower occupation girls had not had the opportunity to meet boys with high educational aspirations prior to meeting the second beau, or it could also be that the girls' definitions of criteria of a prospective spouse had changed.

The consideration of these few independent variables has succeeded in ordering the findings to a limited extent. The variables of social and geographic mobility are rather consistently related to proportion Hm on religion and urbanity, and father's occupation is consistently related to proportion Hm on class. This suggests that both position in the social structure and the experience of movement within the structure may be relevant to degree of homogamy in mate selection. Although the findings are much less clear, these same variables seem to be related to longitudinal patterns of homogamy–heterogamy. Mobile girls especially seem to exhibit much more variation in degree of homogamy longitudinally. Whether these are simply chance findings cannot be determined at the present time, but our knowledge of social structure and mobility leads us to believe that they are not.

Discussion

The data presented here provide evidence of a need to re-examine our ideas about patterns of homogamy and the process of mate selection within a field of eligibles. Not only does the postulation of a general 'tendency of like to seek like' seem unwarranted, one can even question the central importance of such a tendency at the dimension-specific level. The data reported here suggest that, if there is such a dimension-specific tendency, it either changes through time, or other factors intrude to influence the degree to which it will be manifest in behaviour.

With regard to the choice between a normative and an opportunities explanation of patterns of homogamy, no simple solution can be offered. Clearly, however, some dimensions (e.g. education) follow a longitudinal pattern more in keeping with a normative explanation while others (e.g. urbanity) follow a pattern more in keeping with an opportunities explanation. The fact that girls whose fathers have higher occupations are more likely to be Ht on class is also in keeping with the opportunities explanation. Although the analysis with regard to the mobility experiences of the girls more easily fits the opportunities explanation, some of the patterns of change also suggest that there are different degrees of normative adherence in mobile and non-mobile girls. We are left, however, with the need for actual longitudinal measures, especially measures of internalization of norms of homogamy.

The most important point to be made here, therefore, is that further investigation is both necessary and promising. We need to know more about patterns of choice along each of the individual dimensions. We need to know more about the social structural and the dynamic factors associated with patterns of choice. We need to explore the variations in such factors and their correlates in different segments of the population. In any future investigations we need particularly to differentiate clearly between the process of mate selection and the outcome of that process, and between interpretations based on structural opportunities on the one hand and those based on normative adherence on the other

In short, it is necessary to explore carefully the degree to which the field of eligibles is a 'field of availables' or a 'field of desirables'. Finally, and most generally, we must give more attention to the patterns of deviation from homogamy, now that we have established that homogamy is the mode.

References

BURGESS, E. W., and LOCKE, H. J. (1953), *The Family*, American Book Co.

KATZ, A. M., and HILL, R. (1958), 'Residential propinquity and marital selection: a review of theory, method and fact', *Marriage and Family Living*, vol. 20, pp. 27–35.

KERCKHOFF, A. C. (1955), 'Notes and comments on the meaning of residential propinquity as a factor in mate selection', *Social Forces*, vol. 34, pp. 207–13.

KIRKPATRICK, C. (1963), *The Family*, Ronald Press.

WINCH, R. F. (1958), *Mate-Selection*, Harper & Row.

14 W. R. Catton and R. J. Smircich

Propinquity in Mate Selection Reassessed

W. R. Catton and R. J. Smircich, 'A comparison of mathematical models for the effect of residential propinquity on mate selection', *American Sociological Review*, vol. 29, 1964, pp. 522–9.

The idea that mate selection involves a 'propinquity factor' is well established in the sociology of family behavior. Evidence to support this idea usually takes the form of a frequency distribution or cumulative percentages of marriages in some community, classified by the distance separating bride's residence from groom's residence just prior to marriage.[1] Almost no attempts have been made, however, to fit these distributions with a mathematical model.[2] Several hypothetical explanations for the regularity have been suggested, but not in precise quantitative terms (Katz and Hill, 1958).

These crude procedures understate the extent to which mate selection is limited by residential propinquity. This can be readily seen in a sample of Seattle marriages. In the first column of Table 1, the frequency distribution is similar to those obtained in previous studies elsewhere. When these figures are converted to cumulative percentages, as shown in the second column, it is clear that a majority of grooms were residing within three miles of their brides at the time they applied for marriage licenses. This is as far as most propinquity studies have carried the analysis and interpretation of their data. In what follows, we will show that the effects of propinquity are more dramatic than has been apparent from the usual *treatment of the data*, but less dramatic than the usual *interpretation* implies. Because the usual treatment doesn't carry the analysis far enough, some theoretical implications of the propinquity pattern have been overlooked.

1. The typical propinquity study has followed the pattern set by Bossard (1932).
2. For a summary of the various propinquity studies, see Katz and Hill (1958).

Table 1 Distribution of a One-Month Sample of Seattle Marriage License Applications by Distance between Groom's Residence and Bride's Residence*

Distance†	Number of couples	Cumulative percentage
Miles		
0·00 to 0·49	81	19·61
0·50 to 0·99	34	27·82
1·00 to 1·49	31	35·32
1·50 to 1·99	31	42·82
2·00 to 2·49	25	48·87
2·50 to 2·99	23	54·44
3·00 to 3·99	42	65·14
4·00 to 4·99	30	72·40
5·00 to 5·99	25	78·45
6·00 to 7·99	30	85·71
8·00 to 9·99	21	90·79
10·00 to 15·99	20	95·63
16·00 and over	20	100·00

*Seattle residents only.
†Zone widths vary so that no zone frequency is less than 20.

The prevalent normative interpretation

Sociological literature on marriage and the family contains abundant references to 'assortative mating', and to norms of endogamy and exogamy. A wealth of evidence supports the conclusion that marriages are predominantly homogamous with respect to the many dimensions of population heterogeneity. In keeping with a prevalent assumption,[3] sociologists are in the habit of explaining this homogamy as the result of norms. The

3. Probably most sociologists today would agree that 'norms help to make human behavior predictable'. See Merrill (1957, p. 94). Some go farther, however. For example. Hare says '. . . there is no basis for *organized* interaction in a group until some agreement is reached about [norms and goals]' (Hare, 1962, p. 24). In a similar vein, Landis has asserted, 'Without authority there can be no order in human society, in fact, no society. . . . Without it the whims and fancies of every person or group would have free reign, and group living would become impossible' (Landis, 1956, p. 14).

propinquity studies, however, may indicate that the norms arise from the fact of homogamy rather than vice versa.[4]

Propinquity is treated differently in different family textbooks. The variety of treatment suggests some uncertainty in sociological thought as to the true relations between norms and behavior. Fairly clear distinctions can be made among the following five types of response to the findings on propinquity in mate selection. Each type is represented in one or more currently used textbooks on the family.

Type I – propinquity not mentioned. Some texts give no information on propinquity as such, and describe mate selection in terms of such factors as Oedipal conflicts, the search for a parent substitute, cultural and legal influences, rules of endogamy and exogamy, family influences, an Ego ideal, neurosis and complementary personality needs (see, for example, Kenkel, 1960, and Cavan, 1963). In short, selective mating is explained voluntaristically, normatively or social-psychologically.

Type II – propinquity as merely reflecting homogamy. Some texts 'explain away' the propinquity findings as a mere artifact of residential segregation combined with normative pressures for like to marry like (see Truxal and Merrill, 1953, p. 181, and Martinson, 1960, pp. 115–30). In this view, physical distance has no independent effect on mate selection, either in terms of time and energy costs, or even in terms of intervening courtship opportunities.

Type III – propinquity as opportunity. Physical proximity is seen as simply a permissive factor, making interaction possible. Actual selection of a mate is more dependent on social nearness than on physical nearness, in this view (see Woods, 1959, p. 349). Emphasis is still on normative factors in mate selection, though their operation is seen as circumscribed by non-normative facts of life.

Type IV – propinquity as powerful but so obvious it requires apology. Though the exact mathematical characteristics of the distance gradient are by no means self-evident, some authors

4. It has been argued long ago that '. . . nations have always had that system of morals which justified their current rules of life. Moral theories no more make customs than do our ideas about the constitution of matter make the properties of bodies' (Rueff, 1929, p. 81).

appear apprehensive that the student may find unimpressive the proposition that A's probability of marrying B decreases as the distance between their homes increases.[5] Obviousness is somehow assumed to be inversely correlated with importance.

Type V – propinquity as accounting for homogamy. Few, if any, textbooks go quite this far, though some hint at this conclusion.[6]

Some texts mention the tendency to marry someone living near by as a special case of the tendency for like to marry like.[7] Example: 'Residential propinquity is an ecological form of homogamy' (Winch, McGinnis and Barringer, 1962, p. 471). To say that it is a 'form' of homogamy is not the same as saying either that it is a cause or that it is a result of homogamy. Kirkpatrick avoids the very term 'propinquity', and refers instead to 'locality homogamy', meaning 'similarity in location of residence prior to marriage'.[8] This seems almost a reversal of the usual drive to convert qualitative variables into quantitative ones.

Types I through V roughly constitute a scale of the causal importance attributed to propinquity, running from least to most. The notion of 'locality homogamy' is ambiguous with regard to this scale. Depending on interpretation, authors using such phrases might have intended something like either Type II or Type V, or they might even have in mind a legitimate combination of the two, where propinquity and homogamy are conceived as mutually interdependent.

5. Such apologies appear in Winch (1963, p. 322) and Burgess, Locke and Thomes (1963, p. 253).

6. For example, Kephart (1961, pp. 268–70) attempts to determine whether divorce is less likely among propinquitous marriages (as among homogamous marriages) than among others. See especially the reasoning on p. 269.

7. See, for example, Bell (1963, pp. 132–3). Though he says it is not strictly a category of endogamy, Bell includes propinquity in his discussion of endogamy because 'it refers to "like marrying like" '. He also notes that 'it states the obvious. . .'.

8. Kirkpatrick (1963, pp. 418–19). Kirkpatrick does not indicate that locality homogamy might account for other dimensions of homogamy, but he says: 'Katz and Hill are not content with the mere facts but attempt to find an explanation in terms of the probability of interaction in relation to opportunities of interaction at a given distance in turn related to intervening opportunities.' This suggests that locality homogamy needs to *be explained* rather than used *to explain* other aspects of homogamy.

The lack of consensus among sociologists as to the role of propinquity is interesting. Without proof that our interpretation is correct, it may nevertheless be instructive to suggest that this lack of consensus arises from the conflicting commitments incumbent upon all sociologists. Presumably committed to a concern for empirical fact, sociologists also happen to be committed to the prediction and explanation of behavior *in terms of norms*. Conflict between these two commitments is not apparent to most of us. But so far we have not fully reconciled the facts of propinquitous mate selection with theories attributing causal influence chiefly to folkways and mores. If we are unable to decide whether homogamy explains propinquity, or explains it away, or is explained by it, and if we are tempted by the conclusion that homogamy and propinquity are mutually reinforcing, we owe it to scientific clarity at least to take this position explicitly rather than adopt it inadvertently by resorting to ambiguous or vague terminology.

The distance gradient for marriage rates

The usual propinquity study overlooks the fact that for a given groom more potential brides generally reside at a greater distance from his residence than at a lesser distance – as a manifestation of a simple geometric principle. That is, for concentric zones of constant width, the area of the zone will increase in direct proportion with increases in the radius of the zone's inner boundary. If the population of potential brides were evenly distributed over the land, then the number of potential brides residing at a given distance from a given groom would vary directly with that distance. In such circumstances, even a rectangular distribution of actual marriages by distance would indicate a propinquity factor in mate selection, since this distribution would involve diminishing marriage *rates* with increasing distance. The observed decrease in the *number* of marriages as distance increases, then, implies an even more powerful effect of the propinquity factor than has been supposed. Since the number of potentially available brides would not remain constant but actually would increase with distance, marriage *rates* should show an even steeper distance gradient than is apparent in the usual frequency or percentage table.

In real communities, of course, brides are not evenly distributed in space, any more than are other categories of population. Moreover, cities have edges, which further limits the applicability of this simple geometric principle. For Seattle in particular, the shape of the city is quite irregular, and therefore it cannot be assumed that the number of potential brides available is a simple linear function of distance.

From marriage license data, however, it is possible to get an empirical estimate of the mean number of potential brides available at various distances from each groom. In our sample of Seattle marriages, the addresses given in the marriage license applications for August 1961 were plotted on a city map, and the frequency distribution given in Table 1 was compiled. Then the map was photographed. A transparent overlay was made, with concentric circles at one-half scale mile intervals. For each of the 413 grooms in turn, this overlay was centered on his residence (on the photograph) and a frequency distribution of brides by half-mile concentric zones was tabulated. These 413 frequency distributions were added together and the mean number of brides available at each distance was computed.

Table 2 (column 1) shows that up to a distance of about four miles the mean number of brides in the sample residing a given distance from a sample groom tends to increase with distance (as the simple geometric model implied). Beyond four miles this number begins to decline again, although this decline is partially concealed by our combining zones to maintain adequate marriage frequencies at the larger distances. The decline may be attributed to an 'edge effect' – the fact that our sample was limited to residents of Seattle.[9] This arbitrary limitation does not

9. A number of non-residents took out marriage licenses in Seattle during the sample period. There were fourteen couples in which one or both partners omitted the address and could not be included in our sample. There were 176 couples in which both bride and groom gave a non-Seattle address; in the majority of these the same town was listed by both bride and groom (in many instances it was some Seattle suburb), so only a minority represent clearly non-propinquitous marriages. In another 256 couples, one partner gave a Seattle address and the other a non-Seattle address. Of these, 167 involved Seattle brides and non-Seattle grooms, compared with eighty-nine involving Seattle grooms and non-Seattle brides. About half of the apparently non-Seattle grooms were servicemen, who might have been either

Table 2 Seattle Marriage Data, Observed and Expected, by Pre-Marital Residential Propinquity

	Data (1) Mean number of brides available per groom	(2) Observed number of marriages	(3) Marriage rate: Marriages per 1000 available brides	Stouffer model (4) Ratio of brides at a given distance to all brides at lesser distance	(5) Expected number of marriages (col. 4 × 51·23)	Zipf model (6) Median distances	(7) Ratio of col. 1 to col. 6	(8) Expected number of marriages (col. 7 × 3·08)
Distance								
Miles								
0·00 to 0·49	5·08	81	38·61			0·35	14·51	45
0·50 to 0·99	10·99	34	7·49	2·16	111	0·79	13·91	43
1·00 to 1·49	14·62	31	5·13	0·91	47	1·28	11·42	35
1·50 to 1·99	17·14	31	4·38	0·56	29	1·77	9·68	30
2·00 to 2·49	20·20	25	3·00	0·42	22	2·26	8·94	28
2·50 to 2·99	21·81	23	2·55	0·32	16	2·76	7·90	24
3·00 to 3·99	48·49	42	2·10	0·54	28	3·54	13·70	42
4·00 to 4·99	41·67	30	1·74	0·30	15	4·53	9·20	28
5·00 to 5·99	40·06	25	1·51	0·22	11	5·52	7·26	22
6·00 to 7·99	64·68	30	1·12	0·29	15	7·07	9·15	28
8·00 to 9·99	47·37	21	1·07	0·17	9	9·00	5·26	16
10·00 to 15·99	66·99	20	0·72	0·20	10	13·34	5·02	15
16·00 and over	13·90	20	3·48	0·03	2			

greatly distort reality, however, as the markedly lower population density of the open country outside the city would produce such an 'edge effect' anyway.

Comparison of the first and second columns of Table 2 shows that frequency of marriage by zones tends to decrease with increasing distance *in spite of* this pattern of distribution of available brides by distance. In the third column each zone's marriage *rate* is given. These rates decrease monotonically as distance increases. Moreover, they fall away sharply from the initial high figure for the innermost zone. Even if we were to regard as spurious every one of the forty-five cases in which the same address was given by both bride and groom, and exclude these from our sample, the rate in the first half mile would still be 17·16, which is over twice the rate for the second half mile.

Thus, the probability that a given groom will marry a given potential bride decreases as the distance between their premarital residences increases – the decrease being very rapid at first but diminishing as distance increases. The effect is stronger than might be supposed if analysis were carried no farther than calculation of cumulative percentages as in Table 1.

The intervening opportunities model

Years ago, Stouffer suggested that his hypothesis of intervening opportunities, which he proposed as a migration model, might 'illuminate' the relation between residential propinquity and mate selection (Stouffer, 1940, p. 867). His hypothesis states that 'the number of persons going a given distance is directly proportional to the number of opportunities at that distance and inversely proportional to the number of intervening opportunities' (p. 846). Rephrased to apply to mate selection, it might read as follows: the number of marriages to persons who resided a given distance away just prior to marriage is directly

---

of Seattle origin or 'residing' in Seattle under military auspices at the time. Thus, although as many couples were excluded from the sample by non-Seattle residence as were included within it, they hardly refute the principle of propinquitous mate selection. Neither the present study nor any previous propinquity study denies that occupational or educational propinquity, etc. may be as important as residential propinquity.

proportional to the number of potential spouses residing at that distance and inversely proportional to the number residing at shorter distances.[10]

The fourth column of Table 2 gives these *opportunity ratios*, computed from the data in the first column, and the fifth column gives marriage frequencies proportional to these ratios, as expected by the Stouffer model. (No opportunity ratio, and hence no expected frequency, can be calculated for the innermost zone.) The discrepancies between the observed data and the model are not random. When each observed frequency is divided by the corresponding expected frequency, there is a marked tendency for the quotient to increase with distance. In other words, the intervening opportunities hypothesis underestimates the number of marriages that occur at the greater distances. It exaggerates the steepness of the distance gradient.

The inverse distance model

Bassett has suggested that Stouffer's model could be improved by applying the intervening opportunities hypothesis to *perceived* rather than actual opportunities (Bassett, 1954, p. 246). It has also been suggested that the probability of marrying a given person varies with opportunities for intimate interaction, and those opportunities in turn vary inversely with distance (Katz and Hill, 1958, p. 31). Thus a potential bride may have less potential as her remoteness from a given groom increases, *regardless of intervening brides*. A simple modification of Zipf's $P_1 P_2 / D$ model describes this pattern. According to Zipf's (1946) model, the amount of interaction between two social entities is proportional to the product of their populations and inversely proportional to the intervening distance. That is, $I = kP_1 P_2 / D$. But this could be rewritten: $I/P_1 = kP_2/D$. Where P_1 is a sample of grooms and P_2 is the corresponding sample of brides, this equation would stipulate that the percentage of grooms marrying brides residing at a given distance is proportional to the number of brides at that distance and inversely proportional to the distance. This differs

10. A similar formulation in sociometric terms reads: 'The number of persons in a group, m, choosing another group, n, varies directly with the attraction of n and inversely with the sum of intervening attractions.' See Bassett (1954, p. 246).

from the Stouffer model only in substituting intervening distance for intervening opportunities.

The sixth column of Table 2 gives the median distance for each of the zones, i.e. the distance that bisects the zone into inner and outer halves of equal area and (approximately) equal population. The seventh column gives the ratios of the means in column one and these distances. Proportional to these ratios, the zone marriage frequencies expected by the Zipf model are in the eighth column. No expected frequency can be calculated for the open-ended outermost zone, since no exact median distance can be specified. Both the first and last zones were therefore ignored in computing coefficients of agreement between expected and observed marriage frequencies. For the Zipf model, the co-efficient of agreement is 0·93, compared with 0·60 for the Stouffer model, and the ratios of observed frequencies to expected frequencies are more nearly constant for the Zipf model.

Though not included in our computation of the agreement co-efficient, an expected frequency for the open-ended outermost zone was obtained from the Stouffer model. It is only one-tenth the observed frequency. Similarly, an expected frequency for the innermost zone (not used in computing the agreement coefficient) was obtained from the Zipf model. It is a little more than one-half the observed frequency. Moreover, had we excluded from our sample the forty-five couples who gave the same address for bride and groom, this disproportion for the first zone would have been negligible.[11]

11. These couples might reasonably be excluded on grounds that one member actually was not a resident of Seattle. The disproportion for the first zone would similarly disappear if we assumed that these forty-five couples had given their anticipated address rather than their actual pre-marital addresses, and that the latter were distributed among the various zones in proportion to the rest of the sample. Of course, some of them may actually have had the same street address because they were neighbors in the same apartment building. If we assumed that these forty-five couples were illicitly cohabiting prior to marriage, then the relevant distance data should have been derived from their pre-cohabitation addresses; these are not known but could be expected to have been distributed in proportion to the rest of the sample.

Exclusion of some or all of the forty-five couples as 'spurious' on any of the grounds mentioned above would have tended to enlarge the ratios in column four of Table 2, affecting the ratios for the inner zones most

These results tentatively suggest, then, that the effect of propinquity on mate selection can be quantitatively described by Zipf's $P_1 P_2/D$ model. In addition, Stouffer's attempt to provide a theoretical explanation for the occurrence of distance gradients in human interaction apparently requires further elucidation. Rephrased to apply to mate selection, his model took a very plausible form; yet it did not fit the data. Why not?

In this connexion, note that in the simple case where population is assumed to be evenly distributed over a plane, with no edges, the number of intervening opportunities would increase in proportion to the square of the distance. In the limiting case, then, the two models differ only in the exponent assigned to the distance factor: Zipf's model relates marriage frequencies to the inverse first power of intervening distance, while Stouffer's model would relate them to the inverse second power of distance. Neither of these models says anything about *normative* aspects of mate selection, though. The 'norm interaction' theory proposed by Katz and Hill suggests that normative selectivity in marrying is compounded with spatial (or opportunity) selectivity. To the extent that ethnic, religious, class and other social differences tend to be reflected in residential segregation, the Katz–Hill theory implies that mate selection should exhibit a distance gradient as a function of intervening opportunities *and* as a function of residential segregation. Thus, the Katz–Hill model requires a distance exponent *at least as high or higher than* that involved in the intervening opportunities model. But our data fit even the intervening opportunities model less closely than they fit the simple $P_1 P_2/D$ model, and would therefore depart still farther from the kind of pattern predicted by the Katz–Hill 'norm interaction' theory.

Implications and interpretations

Distance gradients in patterns of human interaction may be plausibly interpreted as representing economy of time and energy, rather than either competition between distant and inter-

---

strongly because the denominator would have been reduced proportionately more than for the more distant zones. Thus, exclusion of such couples from the sample would have further reduced the agreement between the Stouffer model and the observed marriage frequencies.

vening opportunities, or response to norms reflected in ecological segregation. This is not to say that human beings always economize with regard to time and energy in all their interactions. But since marriage rates seem to decline more nearly as a function of distance than as a function of intervening opportunities, we may infer than the number of *meaningful* 'opportunities' for a person seeking a mate may be quite small. As the array of potential spouses physically present in the environment increases beyond a small number, the additional ones do not really constitute additional 'degrees of freedom' in mate selection. The average person, no matter how many potential spouses may be 'available' to him in terms of physical location and normative considerations of exogamy and endogamy, can be intimately acquainted with only a few of them. The probability that a given person of the opposite sex will be included in that small number apparently depends on the time and energy costs of crossing the intervening distance to engage in interaction rather than on intervening opportunities to interact with other similar persons.

But what about normative pressures? These may be less important than sociologists have supposed, and cultural variability with respect to marriage mores may be less significant than it seems. American students, taking a course in marriage and the family, sometimes react ethnocentrically when they learn of such exotic mate selection practices as go-betweens, family-arranged marriages, etc. On the other hand, the sociologist may sometimes overemphasize the cultural relativity of marriage norms by exaggerating the extent of cultural variability. Taking arranged marriage as one extreme and the American image of unrestricted individualism and romantic love as the other extreme, the range of variation in degrees of freedom in mate selection *appears* to be from one to infinity. The propinquity studies suggest that the actual range from one cultural extreme to the other may be only from one to about half a dozen or so.

As to the five scaled types of textbook interpretation of propinquity in mate selection, our findings suggest that Type V merits more serious consideration than it has heretofore received. It is possible that propinquity produces a substantial degree of homogamy, and that the familiarity of homogamous marriages gives rise to homogamy norms. The inference that non-homogamous marriages are rare because they are taboo may be less accurate than the inference that the taboos are enforceable precisely because the non-homogamous marriages are rare. At a still higher level of abstraction, we might say that a norm (in any realm) is enforceable only to the extent that it prescribes behavior which is likely for other reasons and prohibits behavior which is unlikely for other reasons. We suggest that these are fundamental notions to which sociological research should be specifically addressed.

References

BASSETT, R. E. (1954), 'A note on Stouffer's theory', *American Sociological Review*, vol. 10, pp. 426–7.

BELL, R. R. (1963), *Marriage and Family Interaction*, Dorsey Press.

BOSSARD, J. H. S. (1932), 'Residential propinquity as a factor in marriage selection', *American Journal of Sociology*, vol. 38, pp. 219–22.

BURGESS, E. W., LOCKE, H. J., and THOMES, M. M. (1963), *The Family*, 3rd edn, American Book Co.

CAVAN, R. S. (1963), *The American Family*, Crowell.

HARE, A. P. (1962), *Handbook of Small Group Research*, Free Press.

KATZ, A. M., and HILL, R. (1958), 'Residential propinquity and marital selection: a review of theory, method and fact', *Marriage and Family Living*, vol. 20, pp. 27–35.

KENKEL, W. F. (1960), *The Family in Perspective*, Appleton-Century-Crofts.

KEPHART, W. M. (1961), *The Family, Society and the Individual*, Houghton Mifflin.

KIRKPATRICK, C. (1963), *The Family as Process and Institution*, 2nd edn, Ronald Press.

LANDIS, P. H. (1956), *Social Control*, rev. edn, Lippincott.

MARTINSON, F. M. (1960), *Marriage and the American Ideal*, Dodd, Mead.

MERRILL, F. E. (1957), *Society and Culture*, Prentice-Hall.

RUEFF, J. (1929), *From the Physical to the Social Sciences*, trans. Herman Green, Johns Hopkins Press.

STOUFFER, S. A. (1940), 'Intervening opportunities: a theory relating mobility and distance', *American Sociological Review*, vol. 5, pp. 845–67.

TRUXAL, A. G., and MERRILL, F. E. (1953), *Marriage and the Family in American Culture*, Prentice-Hall.

WINCH, R. F. (1963), *The Modern Family*, rev. edn, Holt, Rinehart & Winston.

WINCH, R. F., McGINNIS, R., and BARRINGER, H. R. (eds.) (1962), *Selected Studies in Marriage and the Family*, rev. edn, Holt, Rinehart & Winston.

WOODS, Sister F. J. (1959), *The American Family System*, Harper & Row.

ZIPF, G. K. (1946), 'The $P_1 P_2/D$ hypothesis: on the inter-city movement of persons', *American Sociological Review*, vol. 11, pp. 677–86.

15 R. F. Winch

Need Complementarity Reassessed

R. F. Winch, 'Another look at the theory of complementary needs in mate selection', *Journal of Marriage and Family*, vol. 29, 1967, pp. 756–62.

Introduction

The purpose of this paper is to review the theory of complementary needs in mate selection and to indicate the direction in which the theory has recently been developing.

From 1954 through 1958 the writer and his associates published several papers and a book on the theory of complementary needs in mate selection.[1] Very simply, the theory begins with the observation that in the United States mate selection has been shown to be largely homogamous with respect to age, race, religion, social class, education, location of previous residence and previous marital status. It has been proposed that these variables define for each individual a field of eligible spouse-candidates and that there remains the task of accounting for mate selection within the field of eligibles. Toward this objective the theory of complementary needs offers the following hypothesis: in mate selection each individual seeks within his or her field of eligibles for that person who gives the greatest promise of providing him or her with maximum need gratification.

The original test of the theory

In 1950, twenty-five young married couples served as test subjects for the theory. At the time of testing, one or both members of each couple were undergraduate students. In 1950 a considerable

1. The theory and the immediately relevant data were presented in a series of three articles in the *American Sociological Review*: Winch, Ktsanes and Ktsanes (1954) and Winch (1955a and b). Further consideration of the data by means of multivariate analysis appears in Ktsanes (1955) and Winch, Ktsanes and Ktsanes (1955). In addition there were two articles on methodological features of the study: Winch and More (1956a and b). The most general treatment of the theory appears in Winch (1958).

number of veterans of the Second World War were still completing their education, and a considerable number of the husbands in this study were veterans. An effort was made to obtain couples as soon after marriage as possible.[2] No couple had been married more than two years; the median couple had been married for one. At the time of being interviewed no couple had children.

The data-gathering procedure employed two interviews and a projective test. The main interview (called a 'need interview') was based on nearly fifty open-ended questions. Each question was designed to elicit information on the intensity of one of the needs or traits, i.e. to give an indication as to the strength of the need in the person being interviewed and the manner in which that person went about obtaining gratification for the need or expressing the trait. For example, to elicit information about the subject's hostile need (n Hos), he was asked the following:

Let us suppose that you have entered a crowded restaurant, have stepped in line, have waited your turn, and presently someone enters and steps in front of you in line. What would you do? Has this ever happened to you? When was the last time this happened? Tell me about it.

A second interview sought to uncover the subject's perceptions concerning the salient relationships in his life and how he saw these as being related to his psychic and social development. In particular, he was asked to recount from his earliest memories the history of his relationships with his parents and siblings, as well as those in school and peer group. The third procedure was an abridged (ten-card) version of the Thematic Apperception Test, wherein a person is presented with a somewhat ambiguous picture concerning which he is asked to tell a story.

2. That is, the decision was made (a) to study only those who had already selected mates and (b) those who had selected their mates as recently as possible. With respect to criterion (a), it was reasoned that among dating and even engaged couples there would be some who would not marry and at least some of these broken relationships would result from non-complementariness of needs. With respect to criterion (b), it was not assumed that a couple would necessarily remain complementary all their lives; changes in their roles, especially in their occupational and familial roles might modify their need-patterns with the consequence that they would become less complementary.

From each of these three sets of information a separate set of ratings was developed. For each instrument at least two raters were employed.

The theory was interpreted as predicting two types of complementariness:

Type I: The same need is gratified in both person A and person B but at very different levels of intensity. A negative interspousal correlation is hypothesized. For example, it is hypothesized that if one spouse is highly dominant, the other will be very low on that need.

Type II: Different needs are gratified in A and B. The interspousal correlation may be hypothesized to be either positive or negative, contingent upon the pair of needs involved. For example, it is hypothesized that if one spouse is highly nurturant, the other will be found to be high on the succorant (or dependent) need.

Statistical analysis of the results came out in the hypothesized direction, and the data were interpreted as providing adequate, though not overwhelming, support for the theory of complementary needs in mate selection.[3]

Qualitative analysis of the same fifty persons suggested that there were two principal psychological dimensions underlying the various needs: (a) nurturance–receptivity, or a disposition to give versus a disposition to receive, and (b) dominance–submissiveness. On the basis of these dimensions, the following types of complementariness were induced:

Dominant–submissive dimension	Nurturant–receptive dimension	
	Husband nurturant, wife receptive	Husband receptive, wife nurturant
Husband dominant, wife submissive	Ibsenian*	Master–servant-girl
Husband submissive, wife dominant	Thurberian†	Mother–son

*After *A Doll's House*.

†After James Thurber's conception of the relation (battle?) between the sexes.

3. See the first three papers listed in footnote 1.

Subsequent effort by others to test the theory

Unfortunately no one has ever replicated the original study. For a time the literature bristled with articles purporting to be tests of the theory, and it seemed that the more categorical the claims of the authors in this regard, the less directly their results actually bore on the theory.

There is one probably very significant difference between the original study and all subsequent studies of complementary needs in mate selection of which the author is aware. In the original study each test subject was interviewed about his need pattern and then his answers were assessed by two or more trained analysts, whereas all subsequent studies of which the author is aware used some paper-and-pencil test in which the subject assessed himself. Some critics of the original study have made the seemingly absurd observation that the analysts on the mate selection study were probably more subjective in their ratings (and hence less valid) than would have been the subjects themselves. How can it be reasoned that the analysts would be more concerned whether Subject 17, whom they did not know, was rated high or low on need dominance, say, than Subject 17 himself? It is this author's view that the frequently observed disposition of test subjects (like human beings generally) to portray themselves in a favorable light biases their responses.

In 1954 Allen Edwards published the Personal Preference Schedule (P.P.S.), a paper-and-pencil test designed to measure fifteen of the needs that had been postulated and nominally defined by Murray. By name ten of the fifteen needs in the P.P.S. were similar with or cognate to those used in the Winch study. Presumably this fact encouraged a considerable number of social scientists to think that an easy way to duplicate the Winch study was to use the P.P.S. The fact is that no evidence was presented to show that the Edwards test was valid either by means of a behavioral or a peer-rating criterion. Undaunted by this fact, a very considerable number of studies have purported to have tested the theory of complementary needs by means of the P.P.S.

Other ways in which subsequent studies have failed to be true replications include: extraneous variables (when all of the variables of the P.P.S. are used, more than half of the resulting matrix of correlations involves variables not even proposed by name in the original study), incomplete concept of complementariness (a good many studies have ignored what is designated above as Type II complementariness), and inappropriate subjects (instead of a sample of newly-married couples selected in order to have complementariness at its presumed maximum, various studies used dating couples, couples married ten to thirty years, couples belonging to one unspecified church, and couples selected in such a way that they could be called only a 'grab' sample).

Perhaps one should expect that if the theory were a really good one, then even with poor samples and even with a very questionable instrument the results should support the theory. In the original study, the support was visible though not overwhelmingly strong. In the subsequent studies, the general result was to show no correlation between members of couples and such correlation as did appear was more often in the direction of similarity than of complementarity.

Criticisms of the theory

Several thoughtful critiques of the theory have been published. Irving Rosow is the author of the first of these to come to this writer's attention (Rosow, 1957). Beginning with the observation that the theory had applicability to other social groups as well as to marital dyads,[4] Rosow went on to point out that Winch's statement of the theory did not make clear at what level the needs were hypothesized to be functioning, i.e. whether at the overt or behavioral level or at some covert or perhaps even unconscious level. The locus of gratification he saw as another problem; by this is meant the question of what happens to the expression of a need within the marriage if the person is obtaining gratification of that need outside the marriage, or if the gratification of that need is being frustrated outside the marriage. Perhaps Rosow's most important criticism of the theory is that it does not provide criteria for determining which needs are complementary; a further difficulty, he says, is that in many cases similarity of need may be as compatible and as functional as complementarity.

4. An example of such an application is Moos and Speisman (1962).

Levinger (1964) has proposed some remedies for the difficulties posed by Rosow. The former writer has suggested an operation that he believes removes the conceptual ambiguity between complementarity and similarity of needs. He advocates having the testing procedure concentrate on gratification derived from within the marital relationship in order to remove the problem about the locus of gratification, and he sees the formulation of needs by Schutz (1958) as clarifying the idea of complementarity by offering the more limited idea of compatibility. Another proposal, about which more will be said below, is that of Tharp (1964), who advocates substituting the sociological concept of role for the psychological concept of need.

Development bearing on a reformulation of the theory

Two studies have contributed to the development and refinement of the theory of complementary needs. Kerckhoff and Davis (1962) have studied a sample of undergraduates who were 'engaged, pinned or "seriously attached"', and concluded that there was a sequence of filtering factors such that first individuals sort out each other by characteristics of social background (social class, religion, etc.), later by consensus on familial values (place in the community, having healthy and happy children, etc.), and still later by need complementarity.[5] It is perhaps worth noting that this is the first time the theory of complementary needs received support from a study using a paper-and-pencil test; that test was not the Edwards P.P.S. but Schutz's F I R O-B, each scale of which deals with the desire of the respondent to act toward others with respect to inclusion, control and affection and also to have the others act towards him with respect to the same three variables.

A very interesting development comes from an application of the theory of complementary needs in a context other than that of mate selection. Bermann (1966) has been studying the stability of dyadic relationships among female students at the University of

5. The idea of a sequence of selective procedures is present in the earlier formulations of the field of eligibles and of homogamy with respect to interests and attitudes. Kerckhoff and Davis have provided empirical support for the proposition that such a sequence exists and have proposed the useful term 'filtering' to denote the process.

Michigan. He dealt with three categories of undergraduate women: student nurses, women residents of a cooperative house and residents of a sorority house. He determined that membership in each category involved a set of norms distinctive from each of the others. That is, his investigation revealed that a nursing student is expected to be friendly, gregarious, affiliative, abasing, to suppress concern about any bodily ailments she might experience, and to be low on dependent needs as well as needs for recognition. This set of norms may be regarded as defining part of the role of the student nurse. Normative traits contributing to a definition of the role of the resident of the cooperative house were that she should be politically progressive and active, rebellious, sorority-shunning, avoid the constraints of conventional dormitories, and be a member of a religious or ethic minority, of urban residence, highly intellectual, achieving, autonomous, non-deferent, aggressive, non-abasing and individualistic. The only norm Bermann lists as pertaining to the role of the sorority girl is that of emitting highly dominant behavior.

Bermann reports on a study of forty-four pairs of room mates in a dormitory for nursing students. Of these, twenty-two pairs were rated by themselves and by peers as highly stable pairs, whereas the other twenty-two were rated as being of low stability. As in Winch's study, interviews provided the basis for assessing the needs of the subjects; the questions designed to elicit data about needs were open ended. The protocols of the interviews were coded for nine needs: dominance, deference, exhibition, aggression, abasement, nurturance, succorance, achievement and affiliation.

Bermann sought to predict the stability of pairs of room mates on the basis of the relationship between the pattern of needs of one girl in each pair to the pattern of her room mate. To do this, he used role theory and the theory of complementary needs to generate competing hypotheses. Using role theory, he reasoned that if both room mates were close to the ideal specified by the appropriate set of norms – in the case of student nurses, if both were friendly, abasing, etc. – each would serve the other as an object of identification with a resulting solidarity that would bind the two room mates into a stable relationship. From this reasoning he inferred, e.g., that, if both should be low on the need to dominate, the pair should be stable (since low dominance was found to be an element in the definition of the role of student nurse). Using the theory of complementary needs, however, Bermann reasoned, as was done in Winch's study of mate selection, that a more solidary relationship should exist where one was high and the other low on dominance (Type I complementariness).[6] More formally, Bermann hypothesized (a) that compatibility with respect to role is predictive of stability, (b) that complementariness of needs is predictive of stability, and (c) that both of these predictors considered together predict stability better than either does when taken separately. Generally, Bermann's data supported all of these propositions. Need complementarity predicted stability, but role compatibility predicted it better. Bermann's index of total compatibility, which is a combination of need complementarity and role compatibility, was the most effective predictor of stability.

Some thoughts on a reformulation of the theory

The theory of complementary needs is a psychological theory in that it refers to the actor's personality, conceived as the organization of a set of needs and traits. Role theory is a sociological theory in that its referent is a role, which is the product of the consensus of some collectivity. What Bermann has done is to show that the psychological *plus* the sociological theory is better than either of these standing alone.[7]

Before attempting to integrate the significance of these findings and formulations, it may be useful to distinguish a bit more explicitly between role and personality. Very simply, the distinction is seen as follows. Role directs our attention to behaviors and attitudes that are appropriate to a situation, irrespective of the actor, whereas personality directs our attention

6. It may be recalled that Rosow had made the point that the theory of complementary needs might be generalizable beyond the marital dyad, a point made also by Winch (1958, pp. 305–9).

7. Students of social thought may note that this outcome seems pragmatically to give the lie to the stricture of Durkheim to the effect that the explanation of a 'social fact' must be another social fact, or in our language, that it is intellectually illegitimate and logically indefensible to combine the two levels of explanation (psychological and sociological) in a single problem. Cf. Durkheim (1938).

to behaviors and attitudes that are characteristic of the actor, irrespective of the situation. As Bermann has shown, both role and personality may be stated in terms of needs.

How can Bermann's results, obtained from studying pairs of girls rooming together, bear on the marital dyad? In the general statement of the theory of complementary needs, the sex of the actor is not significant; the gender of the actor became significant in Winch's study because he placed the test of the theory in the context of mate selection.

This writer would argue that the theoretically significant feature is not whether the members of the dyad are of the same or different sexes but whether their roles are or are not differentiated. The student nurses were enacting identical roles; there is always some difference between the familial roles of men and women because of the fact that women bear and nurse children. The degree to which roles of the sexes are differentiated beyond this inescapable consideration varies from one societal and cultural context to another. Elsewhere the present writer has argued that the degree of differentiation of sex roles varies inversely with the use of non-human power (Winch, 1963, pp. 399–401).

Beyond the point of initial attraction, at which differences between the sexes tend to be emphasized,[8] the Kerckhoff–Davis study shows that during the filtering process prospective mates are selecting each other as they find that they participate in the same subculture. After that, according to Kerckhoff and Davis, selection occurs on the basis of complementarity. But is this complementarity of personality or of role or of both?

Before trying to answer the foregoing question, the writer must pause for a slight detour. It has been noted above that the study of complementary needs concluded with the proposal that there were two underlying dimensions of complementariness: nurturance–receptivity and dominance–submissiveness. Subsequent reflection leads the writer to the view that those same data revealed a third dimension that was not quite as well determined as the other two but seems, nevertheless, to be conceptually distinct from them. This dimension may be called 'achievement–

8. The qualifying phrase 'tend to' seems warranted by the fad of self-presentation during the latter 1960s in a manner that seems to minimize such differences.

vicariousness'. In the theory of complementary needs, it will be recalled, it makes no difference which spouse is high on needs pertaining to which end of any of these three dimensions – if one spouse is high on one, e.g. nurturance, the other spouse is predicted to be low on that need and to be high on its complement, in this case, receptivity.[9]

As we try to incorporate role theory into the above formulation, the first question is whether or not any of these variables enters into the specification of the role of husband or of wife. If so, what bearing would this have? It seems justified to assert that the traditional public image of the husband-father in the American middle class represents him as the dominant member of the family and as being strongly oriented to achievement. The wife-mother is traditionally portrayed as nurturant but as having the children as the objects of her nurturance; also she is traditionally seen as deriving vicarious gratification from the achievements of her husband.

If these statements of role-specification are correct (or to the extent that they are correct), it does follow that the variables of Winch's study of mate selection can be related to roles that are familial, including marital. At this point it is useful to recall that roles, through what Gross, Mason and McEachern (1964) call the 'norm-senders', put a strain on personality to conform to the specifications of the roles. To the extent that one sees that one's need pattern (personality) is consistent with present and prospective roles, one can feel comfortable and adjusted. But where personality is inconsistent with role(s) – e.g. the succorant or submissive or non-achievement-oriented husband – there is room for regarding oneself a misfit and for developing intrapsychic

9. Actually, the name used to designate the need is 'succorance'. In Table 7 of Winch (1958, p. 125) evidence of Type I and Type II complementariness for these dimensions may be noted for the following pairs of variables: nurturance and succorance (the nurturance–receptivity dimension); dominance and abasement (the dominance–submissiveness dimension); and achievement and vicariousness (the achievement–vicariousness dimension). Of the 12 cells (3 dimensions × 2 variables in each dimension × 2 spouses) referred to in that table, there is only one cell that fails to support the theory: with respect to the interspousal correlation on the traits of vicariousness, the data show no relationship instead of the predicted negative correlation.

conflict. Placed in the present context, the Bermann study suggests a hypothesis:

A pair of spouses who are attracted to each other on the basis of complementary needs will be a less stable pair if the complementariness is counter to role-specification than if it is consistent with role-specification.

The point here is that, where personality and role are mutually consistent, this state of affairs should not generate intrapsychic conflict, while the pair of actors should find that their relationship is given normative support. On the other hand, where personality is in conflict with role, each actor is put in a situation to suffer intrapsychic conflict (unless each accepts a self-definition as a deviant) and the marital relationship is open to criticism on normative grounds.

Perhaps an example is in order. Let us assume there are two persons, A and B, in a dyadic relationship. A is high on dominance and low on submissiveness; B has the opposite need pattern. At this point we do not specify which is male, which is female. With respect to needs they are complementary on this dimension. Accordingly, the theory of complementary needs predicts they are more likely to select each other as mates than a pair in which both are dominant or both are submissive. (And of course the theory of complementary needs purports to predict only mate selection, not marital happiness nor marital stability.) With respect to role what is the situation? If we are given the information that they are members of a society wherein the male role is defined as dominant and the female role submissive, then we are part of the way home. If, in addition, we learn that A is the male and B the female, we conclude that their need-complementariness on the dominance–submissiveness dimension is consistent with their role-specifications. Then, on the basis of the hypothesis derived from the Bermann study, we might predict that this relationship would be a relatively stable one. Of course if we were told that B was the man and A the woman, the prediction about their being attracted to each other would still stand but the prediction about the stability of their marriage would be reversed. 10

10. In practice, such a prediction would have to be made contingent on the pair having an opportunity to get well acquainted. It appears that

This case has been over-simplified for heuristic purposes; one would not be justified in predicting either mate selection or marital stability on only this narrow view of the two parties.

The next step in the prediction of mate selection and marital stability would seem to be the further analysis of marital and other familial roles. It is not clear whether or not it is desirable to continue working with the needs and traits used by Winch and by Bermann. The latter has shown that, to a limited extent at least, such variables may be used as elements of both personality and of role and thus can be used to integrate the two kinds of theory. It is in contemplating further, even exhaustive, analysis of marital and other familial roles where there arises some uncertainty as to just how adequately such an analysis can be made in terms of, or translated into, needs and traits. Some idea of the task can be seen from the following examples taken from a list of components of marital roles derived from a middle-class sample by Hurvitz (1961): performer of domestic chores; companion of spouse; friend, teacher and guide of offspring; sexual partner; and model for offspring. The present author has previously published the following list of conceptually derived components or marital subroles (Winch, 1963, p. 664):

progenitor or progenitrix

father or mother (nurturer, disciplinarian, socializer, model)

position conferrer (provider of position in society for self, spouse, offspring)

emotional gratifier

sexual partner

The list of five subroles shown just above is intended to be universal, or culture-free, although precisely how they are defined is of course specified in each culture. For the specific setting of the American middle class, the following might be added:

initially men and women tend to create images of their ideal mates in terms of normative definitions. At this stage they are disposed to reject as spouse-candidates those who complement their need patterns if, at the same time, they deviate from the normative standards (i.e. from role-specifications). Later some discard normatively defined ideals after experience convinces them that a better fit results from one who complements their idiosyncratic need-patterns. Case materials supporting this point can be seen in chapters 7 to 13 of Winch (1958), and in Winch (1963). See also the discussion of the cultural ideal and the psychic ideal in Winch (1963).

host or hostess
home manager
companion in leisure

Presumably the task of translating such subroles into needs is to analyse (a) how the spouses complement each other with respect to these subroles and (b) the needs involved in such complementariness.

There are two further ideas to be taken into account in suggesting a possible direction for the analysis of marital roles. First, there will be variation from one society to another and from one segment to another within even moderately differentiated societies as to the number and nature of the subroles relating spouses to each other. In general, the more functional the nuclear family is, the greater will be the number of such subroles. Second, the importance of complementary needs as a mate selective criterion appears to vary inversely with the functionality of the extended family (Winch, 1963, pp. 41–3 and 318–20). It may be surmised that the relevance of complementary needs to marital stability is also inversely related to the functionality of both the nuclear and extended family forms. In other words, in societal contexts where the family – extended and/or nuclear – is highly functional, the resulting subroles are important; it should follow that the more important such subroles are, the less importance the culture will give to the idiosyncratic needs of the individual. In middle-class America, where the extended family appears to be relatively non-functional and where the functions of the nuclear family also tend toward the low end, love can exist as a criterion for mate selection and its absence as a criterion for marital dissolution. Hence it is reasoned that complementariness of needs, as a basis for such love, tends to assume importance with respect to both mate selection and marital stability in family systems of low functionality, whereas role compatibility tends to assume importance for both the selection and retention of mates in more functional family systems.

One final consideration not to be lost sight of is that with the passage of time very significant changes take place in roles and in gratifications and frustrations, and quite possibly in need patterns. As we follow a couple from their period of engagement into early marriage with its concomitants of occupational demands for the man and domestic demands for the wife-mother into middle and later years when their offspring have been launched and the breadwinner retires, it is obvious that the roles are modified, and energy levels changed and aspirations modified.

Summary

Twenty-five recently married young couples were examined by means of two lengthy interviews and a projective technique in order to provide a test of the theory of complementary needs in mate selection. The data were interpreted as providing some support of the theory. Originally two dimensions of complementariness were induced from the data: nurturance–receptiveness and dominance–submissiveness. Subsequently a third has been proposed: achievement–vicariousness. A spate of non-replicative tests based on the P.P.S. has provided no support for the theory; however, Kerckhoff and Davis's study based on Schutz's FIRO-B has shown a culturally homogenizing filtering process followed by mate selection on the basis of complementary needs. Whether or not replication of the study of mate selection would provide additional support of the theory remains an unanswered question.

In a study of room mates in a dormitory of nursing students, Bermann has strongly suggested the advisability of adding the concept of role compatibility to that of need complementarity; he showed that the stability of pairs of room mates could be predicted better by using both concepts together than by using either singly.

References

BERMANN, E. A. (1966), 'Compatibility and stability in the dyad', paper presented before the American Psychological Association, New York.

DURKHEIM, E. (1938), *The Rules of Sociological Method*, trans. S. Solovay and J. H. Mueller, University of Chicago Press.

GROSS, N., MASON, W. S., and McEACHERN, A. W. (1964), *Explorations in Role Analysis*, Wiley.

HURVITZ, N. (1961), 'The components of marital roles', *Sociology and Social Research*, vol. 45, pp. 301–9.

KERCKHOFF, A., and DAVIS, K. E. (1962), 'Value consensus and need complementarity in mate selection', *American Sociological Review*, vol. 27, pp. 295–303.

KTSANES, T. (1955), 'Mate selection on the basis of personality type:

a study utilizing an empirical typology of personality', *American Sociological Review*, vol. 20, pp. 547–51.

LEVINGER, G. (1964), 'Note on need complementarity in marriage', *Psychological Bulletin*, vol. 61, pp. 153–7.

MOOS, R. H., and SPEISMAN, J. C. (1962), 'Group compatibility and productivity', *Journal of Abnormal and Social Psychology*, vol. 65, pp. 190–96.

ROSOW, I. (1957), 'Issues in the concept of need-complementarity', *Sociometry*, vol. 20, pp. 216–33.

SCHUTZ, W. C. (1958), *FIRO: A Three-Dimensional Theory of Interpersonal Behavior*, Holt, Rinehart & Winston.

THARP, R. G. (1964), 'Reply to Levinger's note', *Psychological Bulletin*, vol. 61, pp. 158–60.

WINCH, R. F. (1955a), 'The theory of complementary needs in mate-selection: a test of one kind of complementariness', *American Sociological Review*, vol. 20, pp. 52–6.

WINCH, R. F. (1955b), 'The theory of complementary needs in mate-selection: final results on the test of the general hypothesis', *American Sociological Review*, vol. 20, pp. 552–5.

WINCH, R. F. (1958), *Mate-Selection: A Study of Complementary Needs*, Harper & Row.

WINCH, R. F. (1963), *The Modern Family*, Holt, Rinehart & Winston.

WINCH, R. F., KTSANES, T., and KTSANES, V. (1954), 'The theory of complementary needs in mate-selection: an analytic and descriptive study', *American Sociological Review*, vol. 19, pp. 241–9.

WINCH, R. F., KTSANES, T., and KTSANES, V. (1955), 'Empirical elaboration of the theory of complementary needs in mate-selection', *Journal of Abnormal and Social Psychology*, vol. 51, pp. 508–13.

WINCH, R. F., and MORE, D. M. (1956a), 'Quantitative analysis of qualitative data in the assessment of motivation: reliability, congruence and validity', *American Journal of Sociology*, vol. 61, pp. 445–52.

WINCH, R. F., and MORE, D. M. (1956b), 'Does TAT add information to interviews? Statistical analysis of the increment', *Journal of Clinical Psychology*, vol. 12, pp. 316–21.

Part Four
Patterns of Interaction between Spouses

The boldest attempt at theory building in this area is undoubtedly to be found in the work of Elizabeth Bott, first in Reading 16, and later in her book, *Family and Social Network* (Bott, 1957). Bott relates differences in couples' conjugal role expectations to the extent to which the spouses are closely attached to, and influenced by, a network of kin and friends within which contact is maintained independently of the couple. However, a number of studies claiming to test Bott's hypothesis have failed to verify it (e.g. Aldous and Strauss, 1966; Udry and Hall, 1965; note also the very useful critique of Bott's work in Harris, 1969, pp. 169–75). As Turner (Reading 17) indicates, however, there are considerable difficulties in rigorously defining and then operationalizing Bott's concepts. Turner does find some support for the hypothesis, and suggests a number of modifications of it, but it is obvious that a rather different, and probably more complex, approach is needed.

Bott found variations in expected conjugal role behaviour and sought an explanation. The correlation which she established was with primary group structure, though the mechanism which links the two variables (a mechanism which she derived intuitively from her material) is neither wholly clear, nor wholly consistent. Much recent work has approached the topic from a different standpoint. It has sought to explain differences in behaviour, not expectations. It has started from the individual spouses and their individual resources, expectations and role demands in other social organizations, and has posited that the final behaviour patterns adopted will result from the *interaction* between these interests of the two spouses. It has thus introduced many other variables than membership and reference groups; indeed, these have been largely ignored. Such an approach obviously raises great difficulties which have yet to be overcome but looks to be a fruitful supplement or partial substitute in the long run.

Dyer (Reading 18) elaborates a possible general conceptual perspective for dealing with this kind of problem, from a basis in role theory. Blood and Wolfe (Reading 19), starting from a similar though less articulated position, use an exchange perspective to suggest some of the factors influencing the task patterns that emerge. The Rapaports (Reading 20) also have much the same basic orientation, but they stress the *reciprocal interaction* between family and work roles, with family role demands influencing occupational performance as well as vice versa, and point to the period of transition to new role patterns as a crucial area for research. While the conceptualization of this paper is obviously particularly relevant for conjugal roles the reader should not miss its wider implications for research in the sociology of the family. The fact of reciprocal interplay between the family and its environment is often overlooked in both family and industrial sociology. The general perspective of the relationship patterns of individual families as resulting from the intermeshing of the idiosyncratic role demands, choices, resources and expectations of its members is also obviously of far wider relevance. So too is the notion that choices made at one stage in the life cycle affect the options open at subsequent stages.

References

ALDOUS, J., and STRAUS, M. A. (1966), 'Social networks and conjugal roles: a test of Bott's hypothesis', *Social Forces*, vol. 44, pp. 576–80.

BOTT, E. (1957), *Family and Social Network*, Tavistock.

HARRIS, C. C. (1969), *The Family*, Allen & Unwin.

UDRY, J. R., and HALL, M. (1965), 'Marital role segregation and social networks in middle-class, middle-aged couples', *Journal of Marriage and Family*, vol. 27, pp. 392–5.

16 E. Bott

Urban Families: Conjugal Roles and Social Networks

Excerpts from E. Bott, 'Urban families: conjugal roles and social networks', *Human Relations*, vol. 8, 1955, pp. 345–84.

In this paper I should like to report some of the results of an intensive study of twenty London families. The study was exploratory, the aim being to develop hypotheses that would further the sociological and psychological understanding of families rather than to describe facts about a random or representative sample of families. Ideally, research of this sort might best be divided into two phases: a first, exploratory phase in which the aim would be to develop hypotheses by studying the interrelation of various factors within each family considered as a social system, and a second phase consisting of a more extensive inquiry designed to test the hypotheses on a larger scale. In view of the time and resources at our disposal, the present research was restricted to the first phase.

The paper will be confined to one problem: how to interpret the variations that were found to occur in the way husbands and wives performed their conjugal roles. These variations were considerable. At one extreme was a family in which the husband and wife carried out as many tasks as possible separately and independently of each other. There was a strict division of labour in the household, in which she had her tasks and he had his. He gave her a set amount of housekeeping money, and she had little idea of how much he earned or how he spent the money he kept for himself. In their leisure time, he went to football matches with his friends, whereas she visited her relatives or went to a cinema with a neighbour. With the exception of festivities with relatives, this husband and wife spent very little of their leisure time together. They did not consider that they were unusual in this respect. On the contrary, they felt that their behaviour was typical of their social circle. At the other extreme was a family in which husband and wife shared as many activities and spent as much time together as possible. They stressed that husband and wife should be equals: all major decisions should be made together, and even in minor household matters they should help one another as much as possible. This norm was carried out in practice. In their division of labour, many tasks were shared or interchangeable. The husband often did the cooking and sometimes the washing and ironing. The wife did the gardening and often the household repairs as well. Much of their leisure time was spent together, and they shared similar interests in politics, music, literature, and in entertaining friends. Like the first couple, this husband and wife felt that their behaviour was typical of their social circle, except that they felt they carried the interchangeability of household tasks a little further than most people.

One may sum up the differences between these two extremes by saying that the first family showed considerable segregation between husband and wife in their role-relationship, whereas in the second family the conjugal role-relationship was as joint as possible. In between these two extremes there were many degrees of variation. These differences in degree of segregation of conjugal roles will form the central theme of this paper.

A *joint conjugal role-relationship* is one in which husband and wife carry out many activities together, with a minimum of task differentiation and separation of interests; in such cases husband and wife not only plan the affairs of the family together, but also exchange many household tasks and spend much of their leisure time together. A *segregated conjugal role-relationship* is one in which husband and wife have a clear differentiation of tasks and a considerable number of separate interests and activities; in such cases, husband and wife have a clearly defined division of labour into male tasks and female tasks; they expect to have different leisure pursuits; the husband has his friends outside the home and the wife has hers. It should be stressed, however, that these are only differences of degree. All families must have some division of labour between husband and wife; all families must have some joint activities.

Early in the research, it seemed likely that these differences in degree of segregation of conjugal roles were related somehow to forces in the social environment of the families. In first attempts to explore these forces, an effort was made to explain such segregation in terms of social class. This attempt was not very successful. The husbands who had the most segregated role-relationships with their wives had manual occupations, and the husbands who had the most joint role-relationships with their wives were professionals, but there were several working-class families that had relatively little segregation and there were several professional families in which segregation was considerable. An attempt was also made to relate degree of segregation to the type of local area in which the family lived, since the data suggested that the families with most segregation lived in homogeneous areas of low population turnover, whereas the families with predominantly joint role-relationships lived in heterogeneous areas of high population turnover. Once again, however, there were several exceptions. But there was a more important difficulty in these attempts to correlate segregation of conjugal roles with class position and type of local area. The research was not designed to produce valid statistical correlations, for which a very different method would have been necessary. Our aim was to make a study of the interrelation of various social and psychological factors within each family considered as a social system. Attempts at rudimentary statistical correlation did not make clear how one factor affected another; it seemed impossible to explain exactly how the criteria for class position or the criteria for different types of local area were actually producing an effect on the internal role structure of the family.

It therefore appeared that attempts to correlate segregation of conjugal roles with factors selected from the generalized social environment of the family would not yield a meaningful interpretation. Leaving social class neighbourhood composition to one side for the time being, I turned to look more closely at the immediate environment of the families, that is, at their actual external relationships with friends, neighbours, relatives, clubs, shops, places of work, and so forth. This approach proved to be more fruitful.

First, it appeared that the external social relationships of all families assumed the form of a *network* rather than the form of an organized group.[1] In an organized group, the component individuals make up a larger social whole with common aims, interdependent roles and a distinctive subculture. In network formation, on the other hand, only some but not all of the component individuals have social relationships with one another. For example, supposing that a family, X, maintains relationships with friends, neighbours and relatives who may be designated as A, B, C, D, E, F . . . N, one will find that some but not all of these external persons know one another. They do not form an organized group in the sense defined above. B might know A and C but none of the others; D might know F without knowing A, B, C or E. Furthermore, all of these persons will have friends, neighbours and relatives of their own who are not known by family X. In a network, the component external units do not make up a larger social whole; they are not surrounded by a common boundary.

Secondly, although all the research families belonged to networks rather than to groups, there was considerable variation in the *connectedness* of their networks. By connectedness I mean the extent to which the people known by a family know and meet one another independently of the family. I use the term *dispersed network* to describe a network in which there are few relationships amongst the component units, and the term *highly connected network* to describe a network in which there are many such relationships. The difference is represented very schematically in Figure 1. Each family has a network containing five external units, but the network of Family X is more connected than that of Y. There are nine relationships amongst the people of X's network whereas there are only three amongst the people of Y's network. X's network is highly connected, Y's is dispersed.

A detailed examination of the research data reveals that the

1. In sociological and anthropological literature, the term 'group' is commonly used in at least two senses. In the first sense it is a very broad term used to describe any collectivity whose members are alike in some way; this definition would include categories, logical classes and aggregates as well as more cohesive social units. The second usage is much more restricted in this sense, the units must have some distinctive interdependent social relationships with one another; categories, logical classes and aggregates are excluded. To avoid confusion I use the term 'organized group' when it becomes necessary to distinguish the second usage from the first.

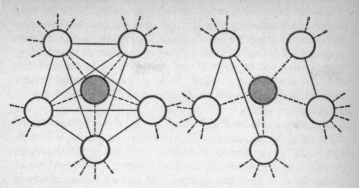

Family X
Highly connected network

Family Y
Dispersed network.

Figure 1 Schematic representation of the networks of two families. The grey circles represent the family, the white circles represent the units of the family's network. The broken lines leading off from the grey circles represent the relationships of the family with the external units; the solid lines represent the relationships of the members of the network with one another. The broken lines leading off from the white circles indicate that each member of the family's network maintains relationships with other people who are not included in the family's network. This representation is, of course, highly schematic; a real family would have many more than five units in its external network

degree of segregation of conjugal roles is related to the degree of network connectedness. Those families that had a high degree of segregation in the role-relationship of husband and wife had a highly connected network; many of their friends, neighbours and relatives knew one another. Families that had a relatively joint role-relationship between husband and wife had a dispersed network; few of their relatives, neighbours and friends knew one another. There were many degrees of variation in between these two extremes. On the basis of our data, I should therefore like to put forward the following hypothesis: *the degree of segregation in the role-relationship of husband and wife varies directly with the connectedness of the family's social network*. The more connected the network, the more segregation between the roles of husband and wife. The more dispersed the network, the less segregation between the roles of husband and wife. This relationship between network connectedness and segregation of conjugal roles will be more fully illustrated and discussed below.

No claim is made here that network connectedness is the only factor affecting segregation of conjugal roles. Among the other variables affecting the way conjugal roles are performed, the personalities of husband and wife are of crucial importance. Most of this paper will be devoted to a discussion of the effect of network connectedness, however, because the importance of this variable has been insufficiently stressed in previous studies of family role structure.

It thus appears that if one is to understand segregation of conjugal roles, one should examine the effect of the family's immediate social environment of friends, neighbours, relatives and institutions. The question remains, however, as to why some families should have highly connected networks whereas others have dispersed networks. In part, network connectedness depends on the family themselves. One family may choose to introduce their friends, neighbours and relatives to one another, whereas another may not. One family may move around a great deal so that its network becomes dispersed, whereas another family may stay put. But these choices are limited and shaped by a number of forces over which the family does not have direct control. It is at this point that the total social environment becomes relevant. The economic and occupational system, the structure of formal institutions, the ecology of cities, and many other factors affect the connectedness of networks, and limit and shape the decisions that families make. Among others, factors associated with social class and neighbourhood composition affect segregation of conjugal roles, not solely and not primarily through direct action on the internal structure of the family, but indirectly through their effect on its network. Conceptually, the network stands between the family and the total social environment. The connectedness of a family's network depends on the one hand on certain forces in the total environment and on the other hand on the personalities of the members of the family and on the way they react to these forces.

In this paper a first attempt will be made to carry out an analysis in terms of these concepts. Part I will be devoted to a discussion of conjugal role-segregation in relation to network connectedness.

In Part II the relation of networks to the total environment will be discussed.

Whether my central hypothesis, the direct relationship between network connectedness and segregation of conjugal roles, is valid for other families I do not know. At this stage I am not attempting to make generalizations about all families, and I am not concerned with whether or not the families we have studied are typical of others. What I am trying to do is to make a comparative study of the relationship between conjugal role-segregation and network connectedness for each of the twenty families considered as a social system. In so doing I have developed a hypothesis that, with further refinement of definition, preferably in quantifiable terms, might be tested on other families and might facilitate further and more systematic comparisons.

Conjugal role-segregation and network connectedness

[. . .] If families are classified according to the extremes of the two dimensions of conjugal role-segregation and network connectedness, four patterns are logically possible: (a) segregated conjugal role-relationship associated with a highly connected network; (b) segregated conjugal role-relationship associated with a dispersed network; (c) joint conjugal role-relationship associated with a highly connected network; and (d) joint conjugal role-relationship associated with a dispersed network. Empirically, two of these patterns, the second and third, did not occur. There were no families in which a highly segregated conjugal role-relationship was associated with a dispersed network; there were no families in which a joint conjugal role-relationship was associated with a highly connected network.

Six of the research families were clustered in the first and fourth patterns. There was one family that conformed to the first pattern, a high degree of conjugal role-segregation being combined with a highly connected network. There were five families that conformed to the fourth pattern, a joint conjugal role-relationship being associated with a dispersed network. These six families represent the extremes of the research set. There were nine families that were intermediate in degree of conjugal role-segregation and similarly intermediate in degree of network connectedness. Finally there were five families that appeared to be in a state of transition both with respect to their network formation and with respect to their conjugal role-relationship.

Among the twenty families, there was thus some clustering at certain points along a possible continuum from a highly segregated to a very joint conjugal role-relationship, and along a second continuum from a highly connected to a dispersed network. The families did not fall into sharply separated types, however, so that divisions are somewhat arbitrary, but for convenience of description, I shall divide the families into four groups: (a) highly segregated conjugal role-relationship associated with highly connected network; (b) joint conjugal role-relationship associated with dispersed network; (c) intermediate degrees of conjugal role-segregation and network connectedness and (d) transitional families. No claim is made here that these are the only patterns that can occur; further research would probably reveal others. [. . .][2]

The data having been described, the nature of the relationship between conjugal role-segregation and network connectedness may now be examined in more detail.

Connected networks are most likely to develop when husband and wife, together with their friends, neighbours and relatives, have all grown up in the same local area and have continued to live there after marriage. Husband and wife come to the marriage each with his own highly connected network. It is very likely that there will be some overlap of their networks; judging by the Ss' account of their genealogy, one of the common ways for husband and wife to meet each other is to be introduced by a person who is simultaneously a friend of one and a relative of the other.

Each partner makes a considerable emotional investment in relationships with the people in his network; each is engaged in reciprocal exchanges of material and emotional support with them; each is very sensitive to their opinions and values, not only because the relationships are intimate, but also because the people in his network know one another and share the same values

2. Dr Bott, in a section of her paper not included in this volume, then gives examples from her research data of these four types in order to illustrate her proposition. [Ed.]

so that they are able to apply consistent informal sanctions to one another.

The marriage is superimposed on these pre-existing relationships. As long as the couple continue to live in the same area, and as long as their friends, neighbours and relatives also continue to live within easy reach of the family and of one another, the segregated networks of husband and wife can be carried on after marriage. Some rearrangement is necessary; the husband is likely to stop seeing some of the friends of his youth, particularly those who work at a different place and go to different pubs and clubs; after children are born, the wife is likely to see less of her former girl friends and more of her mother and other female relatives. But apart from these readjustments, husband and wife can carry on their old external relationships, and they continue to be very sensitive to external social controls. In spite of the conjugal segregation in external relationships, the overlapping of the networks of husband and wife tends to ensure that each partner finds out about the other's activities. Although a wife may not know directly what a husband does with his friends away from home, one of the other men is likely to tell his wife or some other female relative who eventually passes the information on, either directly or through other women, to the wife of the man in question. Similarly any defection on the part of the wife is likely to be made known to her husband.

Because old relationships can be continued after marriage, both husband and wife can satisfy some of their personal needs outside the marriage, so that their emotional investment in the conjugal relationship need not be as intense as in other types of family. Both husband and wife, but particularly the wife, can get outside help with domestic tasks and with child care. A rigid division of labour between husband and wife is therefore possible, since each can get outside help. In other words, the segregation in external relationships can be carried over to activities within the family.

Networks become dispersed when people move around from one place to another, or when they make new relationships that have no connexion with their old ones. If both husband and wife have moved around a good deal before marriage, each will bring an already dispersed network to the marriage; many of the husband's friends will not know one another; many of the wife's friends will not know one another. After the marriage they will meet new people as well as some of the old ones, and these people will not necessarily know one another. In other words, their external relationships are relatively discontinuous both in space and in time. Such continuity as they possess lies in their relationship with each other rather than in their external relationships. In facing the external world, they draw on each other, for their strongest emotional investment is made where there is continuity. Hence their high standards of conjugal compatibility, their stress on shared interests, on joint organization, on equality between husband and wife. They must get along well together, they must help one another as much as possible in carrying out familial tasks, for there is no sure external source of material and emotional help. Since their friends and relatives are physically scattered and few of them know one another, the husband and wife are not stringently controlled by a solid body of public opinion, but they are also unable to rely on consistent external support. Through their joint external relationships they present a united front to the world and they reaffirm their joint relationship with each other. No external person must seriously menace the conjugal relationship; joint relationships with friends give both husband and wife a source of emotional satisfaction outside the family without threatening their own relationship with each other.

In between these two extremes are the intermediate and transitional families. In the intermediate type, husband and wife have moved around a certain amount so that they seek continuity with each other and make their strongest emotional investment in the conjugal relationship. At the same time, they are able to make some segregated relationships outside the family and they are able to rely on considerable casual help from people outside the family, so that a fairly clearly defined division of labour into male tasks and female tasks can be made.

The transitional families illustrate some of the factors involved in changing from one type of network to another. Husbands and wives who change from a connected to a dispersed network find themselves suddenly thrust into a more joint relationship without the experience or the attitudes appropriate to it. The eventual outcome depends partly on the family and partly on the extent to which their new neighbours build up relationships with one another. An intermediate form of network connectedness seems to be the most likely outcome. Similarly, in the case of families who change from a dispersed to a more highly connected network, their first reaction is one of mild indignation at losing their privacy, but in time it seems likely that they will tend to develop an intermediate degree of network connectedness and conjugal role-segregation.

Networks in relation to the total environment

Having discussed the relation of the family to its network, I should like now to consider the factors affecting the form of the network itself. First the general features characteristic of all familial networks in an urban industrialized society will be examined, then I shall turn to consider some of the factors affecting variations from one urban familial network to another.

As described above, all the research families maintained relationships with external people and institutions – with a place of work, with service institutions such as schools, church, doctor, clinic, shops, and so forth, with voluntary associations such as clubs, evening classes and recreational institutions; they also maintained more informal relationships with colleagues, friends, neighbours and relatives. It is therefore incorrect to describe urban families as 'isolated'; indeed, no urban family could survive without its network of external relationships.

It is correct, however, to say that urban families are not contained within organized groups, for although they have many external relationships, the institutions and persons with which they are related are not linked up with one another to form an organized group. Furthermore, although individual members of a family frequently belong to groups, the family as a whole does not. There are marginal cases, such as the situation arising when all the members of the family belong to the same church or go to the same general practitioner, but in these cases the external insitution or person controls only one aspect of the family's life, and can hardly be said to 'contain' the family in all its aspects.

In the literature on family sociology, there are frequent references to 'the family in the community', with the implication that the community is an organized group within which the family is contained. Our data suggest that the usage is misleading. Of course every family must live in some sort of local area, but very few urban local areas can be called communities in the sense that they form cohesive social groups. The immediate social environment of urban families is best considered not as the local area in which they live, but rather as the network of actual social relationships they maintain, regardless of whether these are confined to the local area or run beyond its boundaries.

Small-scale, more isolated, relatively 'closed' local groups provide a marked contrast. This type of community is frequently encountered in primitive societies, as well as in certain rural areas of industrialized societies. A family in such a local group knows no privacy; everyone knows everyone else. The situation of the urban family with a highly connected network is carried one step further in the relatively closed local group. The networks of the component families are so highly connected and the relationships within the local group are so clearly marked off from external relationships that the local population can properly be called an organized group. Families are encapsulated within this group; their activities are known to all, they cannot escape from the informal sanctions of gossip and public opinion, their external affairs are governed by the group to which they belong.

In many small-scale primitive societies, the elementary family is encapsulated not only within a local group, but also within a corporate kin group. In such cases, the conjugal role-segregation between husband and wife becomes even more marked than that described above for urban families with highly connected networks. Marriage becomes a linking of kin groups rather than preponderantly a union between individuals acting on their own initiative.

These differences between the immediate social environment of families in urban industrialized societies and that of families in some small-scale primitive and rural communities exist, ultimately, because of differences in the total economic and social structure. The division of labour in a small-scale society is relatively simple; the division of labour in an industrial society is exceedingly complex. In a small-scale, relatively closed society, most of the services required by a family can be provided by the other families in the local group and in the kin group. In an urban industrialized society, such tasks and services are divided up and assigned to specialized institutions. Whereas a family in a small-scale, relatively closed society belongs to a small number of groups each with many functions, an urban family exists in a network of many separate, unconnected institutions each with a specialized function. In a small-scale, relatively closed society the local group and the kin group mediate between the family and the total society; in an urban industrialized society there is no single encapsulating group or institution that mediates between the family and the total society.

One of the results of this difference in the form of external relationships is that urban families have more freedom to govern their own affairs. In a small-scale, relatively closed society, the encapsulating groups have a great deal of control over the family. In an urban industrialized society, the doctor looks after the health of individual members of the family, the clinic looks after the health of the mother and child, the school educates children, the boss cares about the individual as an employee rather than as a husband, and even friends, neighbours and relatives may disagree amongst themselves as to how the affairs of the family should be conducted. In brief, social control of the family is split up amongst so many agencies that no one of them has continuous, complete governing power, and within broad limits, a family can make its own decisions and regulate its own affairs.

The situation may be summed up by saying that urban families are *more highly individuated* than families in relatively closed communities. I feel that this term describes the situation of urban families more accurately than the more commonly used term 'isolated'. By 'individuation' I mean that the elementary family is separated off, differentiated out as a distinct, and to some extent autonomous, social group. Of course, in most societies the elementary family is individuated to some extent; one could not say that it existed as a distinct group if it were not. The difference in individuation between an urban family and a family in a relatively closed community is one of degree. It should be remembered, however, that urban families differ among themselves in degree of individuation; families with highly connected networks are less individuated than those with dispersed networks.

The individuation of urban families provides one source of

variation in role performance. Because families are not encapsulated within governing and controlling groups, other than the nation as a whole, husband and wife are able, within broad limits, to perform their roles in accordance with their own personal needs. These broad limits are laid down by the ideal norms of the nation as a whole, many of which exist as laws and are enforced by the courts. But informal social control by relatives and neighbours is much less stringent and less consistent than in many small-scale societies, and much variation is possible. [. . .][3]

Social class, network connectedness and segregation of conjugal roles

Because of the complexity of the situation it is not surprising that we could not find a simple correlation between class position and segregation of conjugal roles. In my view such segregation is more directly related to network connectedness than to class status as such, although there are probably some aspects of class position that affect conjugal role-segregation directly. For example, if both husband and wife are highly educated, they are likely to have a common background of shared interests and tastes, which makes a joint relationship easy to conduct. Although it is unlikely that teachers deliberately plan to teach children about joint conjugal relationships, higher education is probably a chief means of passing on the ethic appropriate to a joint relationship from one generation to another, and of teaching it to socially mobile individuals whose parents have had a more segregated relationship. It is doubtful, however, whether such education alone could produce joint conjugal relationships; it works in conjunction with other factors.

But for the most part factors associated with class – however one defines that complex construct – affect segregation of conjugal roles indirectly through having an effect on the connectedness of the family's network. To sum up the empirical resultant: families with highly connected networks are likely to be working

3. Dr Bott then discusses some of the sources of this variation. She considers economic ties between network members, types of neighbourhood, opportunities for alternative relationships, physical and social mobility, and personality characteristics. Finally, she turns to social class. [Ed.]

class. But not all working-class families will have highly connected networks.

It is only in the working class that one is likely to find a combination of factors all working together to produce a high degree of network connectedness: concentration of people of the same or similar occupations in the same local area; jobs and homes in the same local area; low population turnover and continuity of relationships; at least occasional opportunities for relatives and friends to help one another to get jobs; little demand for physical mobility; little opportunity for social mobility.

In contrast, the structure of professions is such that this pattern of forces almost never occurs. Homogeneous local areas of a single profession are very rare; a man's place of work and his home are usually in different local areas; professional training leads him to make relationships with people who do not know his family, school friends and neighbours; in most cases getting a job depends on skill and training rather than on the influence of friends and relatives; many professional careers require physical mobility. Almost the only factor associated with high-class status that tends to foster network connectedness is ownership of shares in common enterprises by relatives – and this is less likely to occur among professional people than among wealthy industrialists and commercial families.

But because a man has a manual occupation he will not automatically have a highly connected network. He may be living in a relatively heterogeneous area, for not all manual occupations are localized. He may live in one place and work in another. He may move from one area to another. Similarly his friends and relatives may move or make new relationships with people he does not know. A high degree of network connectedness *may* be found in association with manual occupations, but the association is not necessary and inevitable.

In brief, one cannot explain network connectedness as the result of the husband's occupational or class status considered as single determinants. Network connectedness depends on a whole complex of forces – economic ties among members of the network, type of local area, opportunities to make new social contacts, physical and social mobility, etc. – generated by the occupational and economic systems, but these forces do not always work in the same direction and they may affect different families in different ways.

Finally, network connectedness cannot be predicted from a knowledge of situational factors alone. It also depends on the family's personal response to the situations of choice with which they are confronted.

In a situation of such complexity, little is to be gained by trying to explain conjugal role-segregation in terms of single factors. In the approach to this problem, the most useful conceptual model has proved to be that of field theory: 'behaviour is a function of a person (in this case a family) in a situation'. Performance of conjugal roles is a function of the family in its social network. The form of the social network depends, in turn, partly on the members of the family and partly on a very complex combination of forces in the total social environment.

17 C. Turner

Conjugal Roles and Social Networks Re-Examined

C. Turner, 'Conjugal roles and social networks: a re-examination of an hypothesis', *Human Relations*, vol. 20, 1967, pp. 121–30.

Bott concentrated on two main aspects of family organization in an intensive study of twenty families in the Greater London area (Bott, 1955, 1956, 1957).[1] On the one hand she carried out a thorough analysis of the patterns of conjugal role-relationship, on the other she examined the network of kinfolk, friends and neighbours of each family. A major hypothesis advanced as a result of this exploratory study is that '*The degree of segregation in the role-relationship of husband and wife varies directly with the connectedness of the family's social network*' (Bott, 1957, p. 60). Two recent American studies by Udry and Hall (1965) and Aldous and Straus (1966) question the general validity of the hypothesis. Although both of these pieces of research purport to test Bott's hypothesis, it can be argued on methodological grounds that neither of them constitutes a reasonable test.

This paper is an attempt to re-examine Bott's hypothesis in the light of information from a somewhat different social setting. The data upon which this report is based was collected as part of a much wider study of the social structure of a Pennine parish, which will be referred to by the pseudonym of Leadgill. The study was not specifically oriented towards a test of the Bott hypothesis. Nevertheless an *ex post facto* analysis seems justifiable in this instance, since it sheds some light on the original hypothesis and suggests certain potentially fruitful ideas for future research.

Both Bott (1957) and Udry and Hall (1965) base their findings on married couples drawn from large urban areas. Aldous and

1. I am indebted to Professor R. Frankenberg for the initial suggestion that my data could be used to throw further light on this hypothesis, and for his subsequent encouragement and comments.

Straus (1966) drew approximately half of their married female informants from small-town backgrounds and half from rural-farm backgrounds. The Leadgill data is drawn from the married couples living in a small relatively isolated rural community, at a given point in time. Twenty couples formed the 'sample' for Bott's analysis, forty-three for the Udry and Hall study, and 115 for the Leadgill research. Aldous and Straus 'sampled' 391 people, but confined their attention to wives only, which may possibly have biased their results. A further distinction is provided by the fact that Bott concentrated on couples in the early child-rearing phase of the developmental cycle of the family as a domestic group, Udry and Hall upon middle-aged couples with at least one child at college, and Aldous and Straus upon married women with at least one child at home. The Leadgill data includes couples at all major phases of the developmental cycle.

Problems of operational definition

A recurrent problem in contemporary sociology is that of operational definition. Bott's work on degree of conjugal role-segregation and interconnectedness of social networks provides an interesting illustration of intuitive definition based on considerable empirical evidence (Bott, 1957, pp. 58–9 and 238–40). The use of this type of definition renders an accurate replication of the study almost impossible. In contrast, Udry and Hall (1965) and Aldous and Straus (1966) developed relatively simple, though differing, operational definitions of degree of network interconnectedness and type of conjugal role-segregation, and incorporate reference to them in their respective papers. A distinct advantage of the questionnaire method is that the study can easily be replicated, but an associated criticism is that their narrow operationalism hardly does justice to the ideas behind the concepts suggested by Bott.

The procedure adopted with the Leadgill data resembles that of Bott, rather than that of the other writers, although the data were not specifically collected in order to test the Bott hypothesis. The definitions used are unsatisfactory in two main respects. Firstly the data available set certain limits on the definitions. Secondly there is too much reliance on the judgement of the researcher.

Nevertheless it is hoped that the present discussion will help to clarify at least some of the issues and problems raised by Bott's initial insightful analysis.

The interconnectedness of social networks

The basic unit used by Bott in the analysis of the social network is somewhat ambiguously referred to as 'the family'. This term is used variably to denote: (a) the household groups comprising parents and their dependent children, which were the basic units studied; (b) the married couples in the household groups defined under the first heading; (c) the other household groups, or possibly just their adult members, with whom the married couples under examination regularly interacted. A social network as defined by Bott is a network of households rather than of individuals, but the criterion by which inter-household linkages are judged is the interaction of individuals (presumably adults). A particular household is conceptualized as the central focus of a social network, thus each network is 'closed', in the sense that the focal household is directly connected to a finite number of other households. Bott defined the 'interconnectedness' of each social network in terms of the extent to which households other than focal households are linked directly by regular interaction between members.

The maximum possible number of *interconnecting* linkages of this type is given by the formula: $[n(n-1)/2]-(n-1)$, where n equals the total number of households in the network (see Kephart, 1950, for further elaboration). These interconnecting linkages range from a fixed minimum of zero to a variable maximum, which is a function of n for any particular network. The point which should be noted is that the potential of interconnecting linkages increases at a much faster rate than the number of households in the group, as the following series indicate:

Number of households	3	4	5	6	7	8	9 ...
Maximum number of interconnecting linkages	1	3	6	10	15	21	28 ...

Thus the number of households in a particular network is an important factor to take into account when attempting to calculate degree of interconnectedness.

Both American studies set out to examine the interconnectedness of partial social networks. Udry and Hall (1965) defined the network of each husband and wife in terms of *the four persons with whom each spouse claimed to have had most frequent social contact* in the year prior to the interview. Aldous and Strauss (1966) defined the network of each married woman in terms of *the eight women whom she most often visited socially*. It seems quite possible that such predetermination of network closure might seriously bias the results, in so far as they purport to relate to Bott's original hypothesis. It is also necessary to note that the original hypothesis refers to interconnexions between households, not to networks of the individual spouse. This represents a further potential source of discrepancy.

An attempt has been made to analyse the Leadgill data in terms of the social networks of married couples both at the individual level and at the household level. The main focus, however, is upon inter-household connexions, following Bott. An important point which requires consideration is the method of identifying households or individuals, who are to be included in each closed social network. This problem was first approached in terms of individual rather than household networks. Members of a focal individual's network were defined as persons (a) to whom the focal individual was bound by positive affectional ties (i.e. kinfolk and friends), and (b) with whom the focal individual had regular social contact (in this instance 'regular' is defined as at least once per fortnight on average throughout the year). The same criteria were used for assessing interconnecting links between the non-focal individuals in each specific network. It must be admitted that these two indicators taken in combination provide a fairly arbitrary and subjective basis for the reckoning of network membership. The individual networks of each married couple were aggregated and expressed in terms of inter-household connexions. Similarly the data on non-focal individuals was aggregated and expressed in terms of inter-household connexions for each network. It should be noted that this method of calculating inter-household linkages only takes account of a selection of the possible universe of household connexions.

On the basis of these calculations three degrees of network connectedness can be distinguished at the inter-household level:

loose knit, medium knit and close knit. A *loose knit* network is characterized by the existence of interconnecting linkages between less than one-third of the non-focal households in a particular network. The equivalent proportions of interconnecting linkages for a *medium knit* network is between one-third and two-thirds, and for a *close knit* network more than two-thirds. A minimum number of five households, i.e. the focal household and four others, was arbitrarily set for inclusion in the analysis. As a result the networks of five couples in Leadgill were excluded. The maximum number of households in any network was twelve, and the median was seven.

Conjugal role-relationships

It is obvious from a reading of available literature on the husband–wife relationship that 'degree of conjugal role-segregation' is not an unidimensional concept (see, for example, Blood and Wolfe, 1960). Varying degrees and forms of cooperation and independence are found in each of the major spheres of marital organization. The time which a married couple have available to devote to their husband–wife relationship is partially controlled by many factors, including occupation, place of work, hours of work, the presence of children, relatives or unrelated persons in the home, and by the various extra-family commitments of each spouse. Even a crude classification of marital role-relationships, therefore, involves an extremely complex set of problems. The three areas of marital organization, for which there is adequate information on Leadgill couples, are leisure activities outside the home, domestic tasks and child rearing.

Leadgill couples were classified according to whether their activities in each of the first two spheres, and where applicable in the third sphere as well, were predominantly joint or predominantly segregated. As far as leisure activities outside the home are concerned, a couple was counted as having a joint relationship if they predominantly went out together, and as having a segregated relationship if they predominantly went out separately. (It is perhaps worth noting at this point that there was no significant correlation between amount of time spent in leisure activities outside the home and a given type of marital relationship.) As far as domestic tasks are concerned, the criteria used to distinguish a

couple with a joint role-relationship were, (a) the regular participation of the husband in domestic duties, and (b) the interchangeability of at least certain domestic tasks between husband
and wife. If a husband did not regularly carry out domestic
duties, or if there was a rigid division of labour in respect of
domestic work, the conjugal relationship was recorded as
segregated. As far as child rearing is concerned, a joint relationship was defined as one in which father and mother (a) usually
discussed methods of discipline and/or child rearing, and (b)
shared certain of the tasks of child rearing; a segregated relationship was defined as one in which they did not.

An over-all classification of the marital role-relationship was
derived from a combination of the classifications for the applicable sub-areas. A joint conjugal role-relationship was characterized by joint relationships in all applicable sub-areas.
Correspondingly a segregated conjugal role-relationship was one
in which segregated relationships were found in all applicable
sub-areas. If there was any discrepancy between sub-area
classifications, the conjugal role-relationship was counted as
intermediate. This gives a crude threefold classification of types
of conjugal role-relationship. Four couples have been excluded
from the analysis because of the difficulty of classifying them in
this manner.

Leadgill results

The Leadgill results are presented in Table 1, with Bott's figures
listed in brackets for purposes of comparison.

Table 1 Conjugal Roles and Social Networks in Leadgill*

Conjugal role-relationship	Interconnectedness of social networks		
	Close-knit	Medium-knit	Loose-knit
Segregated	42 (1)	10 (0)	4 (0)
Intermediate	13 (0)	0 (9)	7 (0)
Joint	8 (0)	8 (0)	14 (5)

Total number of married couples = 115 (20).
Not classified 9 (5)

*Bott's figures in brackets for comparative purposes.

An initial visual inspection of the data suggests that the Bott hypothesis is not fully supported, although a general statistical test does indicate that the observed values differ significantly from those expected by chance ($\chi^2 = 26 \cdot 92$, significant at the $0 \cdot 01$ level).

Leadgill can fairly accurately be described as a face-to-face community. It is not surprising, therefore, that the proportion of couples with close-knit networks is substantially higher than in the other studies. There tends to be a high degree of inter-connectedness in the role networks because the majority of individuals in most networks were drawn from within the community. This had the additional advantage of allowing for cross-checking on network membership, and on interconnecting linkages.

When the individual networks of Leadgill husbands and wives are analysed separately an interesting set of facts emerges. Firstly both husband and wife tend to include the same kinfolk in their respective social networks. Secondly, when kinfolk are excluded, thirty-two couples could be unambiguously identified for whom the husband's friends constituted a close-knit *male* network, and the wife's friends a close-knit *female* network. These thirty-two couples also demonstrated a high degree of conjugal role-segregation. In each instance a strict division of labour within the home was accompanied by a sharp division of leisure interests. Even when kinfolk and friends were entertained in the home, the males and females showed a marked proclivity for splitting into separate groups. It must be noted, however, that the husbands spent much of their leisure time outside the home with their male companions (cf. Dennis, Henriques and Slaughter, 1956). It is not altogether surprising that the segregation of the sexes within the total social network of a couple is accompanied by marital role-segregation, but it does appear to constitute something of a special case. When the networks of husband and wife show considerable overlap, no distinctive pattern of conjugal role-relationship appears to be associated with them.

The degree of network interconnectedness seems to provide only a partial prediction of the form of conjugal role-relationship developed between husband and wife. Therefore it is pertinent to investigate further factors which might be directly related either to network interconnectedness or to marital relationships, and possibly to both. Bott found type of neighbourhood to be an important factor underlying network connectedness. This variable is regarded as 'controlled' for the Leadgill data, since all the married couples from one single community have been used as the subjects. One other major variable which Bott investigated, personality characteristics, is not reported on here because it was beyond the scope of the Leadgill study. Five further factors seem to merit attention on both theoretical and empirical grounds: (1) occupation, (2) geographic mobility, (3) education level, (4) stage of developmental cycle, and (5) cosmopolitan or local orientations.

Occupation

Perhaps the most striking difference in the Leadgill data is between farm and non-farm families, as shown in Table 2. Membership of a farm family seems conducive to the development of both a close-knit social network, and a segregated conjugal role-relationship.

Leadgill farms are for the most part small. The farmer himself usually runs the farm, with the help of his family. In a few cases the 'farmer' has a second job in order to make a better living. The farmer works in and around the homestead most of the time. There is a strict division of labour between husband and wife concerning farm tasks and duties. A similar division of labour is also to be found in household activities – the farmer clearly does not expect to be asked to do 'women's work', such as cooking, sewing, mending, ironing or putting the baby to bed. Most farmers like to spend at least some of their leisure time away from the home, and they usually choose to be with male friends who have a definite interest in farming. A favourite pastime is discussion of the minutiae of farm affairs.

The whole family is organized around the running of the farm and it seems reasonable to advance the hypothesis that when both husband and wife work in and around the home, the form of the work relationship will exert a strong influence upon the form of other aspects of the conjugal role-relationship. Evidence from five non-farm couples in Leadgill lends support to this hypothesis. In these five instances, husband and wife share the running of the

Table 2 Conjugal Roles and Social Networks of Farm and Non-Farm Couples

Conjugal role-relationship		Interconnectedness of social networks		
		Close-knit	Medium-knit	Loose-knit
Segregated	Farm	27	3	0
	Non-farm	15	7	4
Intermediate	Farm	3	0	1
	Non-farm	10	0	6
Joint	Farm	0	1	0
	Non-farm	8	7	14

Total number of farm couples = 35, non-farm couples = 71.

business and organize their work activities so that they are to some extent interchangeable. There is a similar interchangeability in the extra-occupational activities of these couples. Nevertheless it must be emphasized that this new hypothesis is only tentatively advanced and requires rigorous testing. It should be also noted that this hypothesis may be complementary to Bott's hypothesis. Among farm couples, for example, there is not a single case of segregated conjugal role-relationship occurring with a loose-knit network, nor is there any case of a joint conjugal role-relationship occurring with a close-knit network among the business couples cited.

Other non-farm families in which home and workplace are clearly separated do not show any distinctive pattern of marital or network interconnectedness. Nor does the fact that a wife goes out to work (six cases) seem to produce any specific pattern of conjugal role-relationship.

Geographic mobility

Bott found that geographic mobility tended to correlate with a loose-knit network structure. Leadgill couples were categorized into *dalesfolk* (both spouses born and bred in the area), *mixed* (one spouse only born and bred in the area), and *incomers* (neither spouse born and bred in the area). The conjugal role-relationships and network interconnectedness for couples in each of these three categories are given in Table 3.

In Leadgill, married couples in which *both* husband and wife

Table 3 Conjugal Roles and Social Networks of Dalesfolk, Mixed Couples and Incomers

Conjugal role-relationship		Interconnectedness of social networks		
		Close-knit	Medium-knit	Loose-knit
Segregated	Dalesfolk	24	5	1
	Mixed	16	4	2
	Incomers	2	1	1
Intermediate	Dalesfolk	8	0	1
	Mixed	5	0	4
	Incomers	0	0	2
Joint	Dalesfolk	6	2	1
	Mixed	2	4	2
	Incomers	0	2	11

Total number of dalesfolk = 48, mixed = 39, incomers = 19.

were not born in the area showed a marked tendency to develop loose-knit networks. This was undoubtedly due in many cases to the fact that incomers were able to maintain contacts with kinfolk and friends outside the community, and were in some instances not able to establish close friendships with many dalesfolk. These same couples were also likely to have joint conjugal role-relationships. Unfortunately data are not available to demonstrate the types of social network and conjugal role-relationships which they had developed before migrating to the community, although such a longitudinal analysis could possibly throw important light on processes involved in the development of social networks. It is interesting to note that the two incoming couples with close-knit social networks and segregated conjugal role-relationships both belonged to farm families.

In instances where one spouse is a dalesfolk and the other an incomer there is a comparatively wide spread of both conjugal role segregation and network interconnectedness. The relatively high number with segregated conjugal role-relationships and close-knit networks can possibly be accounted for by the fact that twelve of these sixteen couples are from farm families.

When both spouses are dalesfolk they are much more likely to have a close-knit social network (twenty-three couples) than a medium-knit (four couples), or a loose-knit one (three couples).

The conjugal role-relationships of these couples, however, do not show such a clear pattern: there are only fourteen couples with marital role-segregation compared with seven with an intermediate, and nine with a joint conjugal role-relationship. Geographic mobility, therefore, seems to be an important variable related more to network connectedness than marital role-education, there were no instances of a segregated marital role-relationship.

Educational level

The Leadgill evidence with regard to educational level is fairly inconclusive. The overwhelming majority of spouses, especially dalesfolk, left school at the minimum leaving age. If both spouses had spent the minimum statutory time in formal education this seemed to have little influence either upon network interconnectedness, or upon conjugal roles. Amongst the few couples in which one or both had received some form of higher education, there were no instances of a segregated marital role-relationship. There is a high positive correlation between receipt of higher education and following a professional or business occupation, however, which may possibly account for this finding.

Stage of developmental cycle

The stage a family has reached in the developmental cycle appears to have no significant influence upon either conjugal relationships or network interconnectedness amongst farm families. Similarly when the effect of geographic mobility is controlled there is no significant influence in the case of non-farm families. Bott's married couples were all in the first part of the child-rearing stage of the family cycle (i.e. they had one or more children under ten years of age). Non-farm couples from Leadgill at the same stage provide an interesting comparison group (Table 4).

Differences between London data (Bott) and Leadgill data obviously cannot be explained in terms of differences in the stage of the developmental cycle.

Table 4 Conjugal Roles and Social Networks of Non-Farm Couples with Children under Ten Years of Age*

Conjugal role-relationship	Interconnectedness of social networks		
	Close-knit	Medium-knit	Loose-knit
Segregated	3 (1)	4 (0)	2 (0)
Intermediate	4 (0)	0 (9)	2 (0)
Joint	4 (0)	1 (0)	2 (5)

Total number of couples = 22 (15).

*Bott's figures in brackets for comparative purposes.

5. Cosmopolitan or local orientations

Finally, an analysis of the nine couples with a cosmopolitan orientation failed to reveal any single pattern of marital role relationships or network interconnectedness. There was not one case in which both a close-knit network and a segregated conjugal role relationship coincided, but the pattern of marital role-relationships (two segregated, two intermediate, five joint) and the degree of network interconnectedness (two close-knit, three medium-knit, four loose-knit) of these cosmopolitan couples did appear to be influenced to a certain extent by occupation and geographic mobility.

Summary and conclusion

This paper, unlike the work of Udry and Hall (1965) and of Aldous and Straus (1966), is not claimed as a test of the Bott hypothesis. Rather, the Leadgill data has been explored in order to see whether any useful suggestions can be made for future research. The general approach has been to examine a number of variables in addition to network connectedness and degree of conjugal role-segregation. These variables, occupation, geographic mobility, educational level, local and cosmopolitan orientation, and phase in the developmental cycle of the domestic group, were ones upon which at least some data were available, and also ones which at an intuitive level seemed relevant to the analysis.

In line with Bott's hypothesis it was found that a marked segregation of the sexes in activities involving network members was invariably accompanied by marital role-segregation. In other cases, however, network connectedness was not a good predictor of degree of conjugal role-segregation. Occupation appeared to be an important variable, and a tentative hypothesis was advanced that when husbands and wives both work in and around the home the form of the work relationship exerts a strong influence on the form of other aspects of the conjugal role-relationship. This hypothesis may or may not prove to be complementary to Bott's hypothesis. A second variable, geographic mobility, appears to be related more closely to network connectedness than to a degree of conjugal role-segregation, and on this ground alone merits attention in future research. The evidence with regard to educational level, cosmopolitan local orientations, and stage of the developmental cycle was fairly inconclusive, but more systematic investigation is probably warranted.

The difference between Bott's results, the Leadgill results, and the two sets of American results may arise from methodological differences in respect of the operational definition of the key variables, differences in sampling techniques – the 'sample' was not drawn so as to be representative of a general population in any of the studies, or genuine differences in the local social structure and styles of family life – i.e. the hypothesis may not hold in every community/neighbourhood context.

One general conclusion which clearly emerges is that there has not yet been any satisfactory test of the original Bott hypothesis. A second conclusion which can be drawn from the examination of the Leadgill data is that several variables other than degree of network connectedness and degree of conjugal role-segregation might profitably be taken into account in any rigorous attempt to test the Bott hypothesis. In other words a multivariate rather than a bivariate research design is desirable.

In a multivariate research design the set of dependent variables would concern the marital relationship. The independent variables would include connectedness of social networks, size and composition of social networks, selected aspects of occupation, degree of geographic mobility, stage of the developmental cycle, educational level, and cosmopolitan and local orientation, besides any additional variables which the researcher might consider relevant. The systematic measurement and analysis of the relationship between the variables outlined in the research design might also be accompanied by an investigation into the mechanisms and processes by which the variables are linked one to another. This is a challenging research problem.

References

ALDOUS, J., and STRAUS, M. A. (1966), 'Social networks and conjugal roles: a test of Bott's hypothesis', *Social Forces*, vol. 44, pp. 576–80.

BLOOD, R. O., and WOLFE, D. M. (1960), *Husbands and Wives*, Free Press.

BOTT, E. (1955), 'Urban families: conjugal roles and social networks', *Human Relations*, vol. 8, pp. 345–83.

BOTT, E. (1956), 'Urban families: the norms of conjugal roles', *Human Relations*, vol. 9, pp. 325–41.

BOTT, E. (1957), *Family and Social Network*, Tavistock.

DENNIS, N., HENRIQUES, F., and SLAUGHTER, C. (1956), *Coal is Our Life*, Eyre & Spottiswoode.

KEPHART, W. M. (1950), 'A quantitative analysis of intragroup relationships', *American Journal of Sociology*, vol. 55, pp. 544–9.

UDRY, J. R., and HALL, M. (1965), 'Marital role segregation and social networks in middle-class, middle-aged couples', *Journal of Marriage and the Family*, vol. 27, pp. 392–5.

18 W. G. Dyer

Role Theory and Patterns of Conjugal Role-Relationships

W. G. Dyer, 'Analysing marital adjustment using role theory',
Marriage and Family Living, vol. 24, 1962, pp. 371–5.

The forming of a new family constitutes a major change in the behavior patterns of the young man and young woman involved since they occupy now an entirely new status and role of husband and wife. Most of them are new to these roles and are inexperienced in adapting themselves to the demands of continually interacting with another personality. Role theory allows us more clearly to outline and understand the forms of adjustment that these persons in their new roles usually need to make relative to each other. Following are the major factors to be considered in marital adjustment using role analysis as the basic framework.[1]

Normative orientation

The way one behaves in his role in a social situation depends in large measure on his understanding of the cultural norms, or standards of behavior that direct and orient his thinking about the situation. The new husband and wife have learned over a period of years as a result of experience in their own and other families, and what they have read, seen or heard, what constitutes their basic attitudes about family life. Some of these understandings will be mutually agreeable since they have been reared in a common culture and these norms will be shared. Generally the couple will agree that the marriage should be monogamous, a ceremony should be performed before a legal official, and a number of other norms concerning marriage common in American culture. The indications are that the shared norms are becoming established around patterns of equality with some significant exceptions (Dyer, 1958).

1. For a more extensive treatment of these elements, see Newcomb (1950, chapters 8, 9, 13, 14 and 15).

However, the husband and wife through socialization and experience in non-shared social systems may be oriented to normative systems that may be conflicting or at least foreign to the new marriage partner. Nye and MacDougal (1960) suggest that each family builds its own sub-culture; thus, the new husband and wife, coming from different family sub-cultures are oriented to a certain set of different normative patterns. Since the new husband and wife are still an important, if not a central, part of their parents' family system there will still be some internal and external pressures to conform to the norms of their particular family of orientation. When we consider that the husband and wife may also be oriented to different religious, social, regional and political social systems or sub-cultures, it is apparent there is a great possibility that the new husband and wife may be directed by non-shared normative patterns. Since conflicts, disagreements or misunderstandings may arise out of behavior directed by these non-shared norms, adjustments of these disparate normative orientations is important in marital adjustment.

The situation of adjustment is further complicated when we consider that in addition to the possibility that the new husband and wife are oriented and directed by non-shared normative systems, they may also have certain personal, idiosyncratic beliefs and practices. These behaviors are not normative in the sense that they are not a part of a shared system of cultural or sub-cultural patterns. They represent the individual reactions and responses that have become more or less habitual with the person. Each person has his own individual components in the way he dresses, keeps house, reacts to tension, etc. Where these individual reactions irritate, conflict with or otherwise disturb the marital partner, some adjustment is necessary.

Position-role

Stemming from the norms held by the persons involved, each of the marriage partners comes into the new relationship with certain ideas as to how he or she should behave as a husband or wife. These perceptions of one's role in the new family are often not explicitly stated or understood by the person. Often he has only vague but rather strong feelings that he 'ought' to behave in a certain way. This involves usually two aspects: (a) an attitude about one's relative position or one's status in the new arrangement[2] and (b) an action element, or one's role – what one is supposed to do in the family.

The concept of role has been used in two ways: (a) to represent the sum total of the expected behaviors, normatively defined, for a given position, and (b) in the plural to indicate the several different behavioral demands of a position, each expected behavior being a role.[3]

In the first conception, the man assumes the position of husband and now has a generalized role composed of a number of functions. In the second conceptualization, the man in his position of husband has several roles, e.g. companion, breadwinner, handyman, etc.

The important aspect of either conceptualization is that the husband and wife in their new positions have a range of duties that are normatively defined for them. The central problem of roles stems from the condition that the new husband or wife are usually not experienced in these new roles and the definitions of these roles have often not been worked out between them but have been derived separately from the other social systems to which they were oriented before marriage.

One's role differs from one's norms or personal preferences as shown by this example: it may be agreed that it is part of the wife's role to prepare meals, but disagreements may occur as to what kind of meals should be prepared, how they are served, etc. In this case there is role agreement, but disparity comes either from behaviors that arise out of different sub-culture norms or different personal preferences. In a sense the role represents a general set of norms within which are also found a cluster of more specific normative and personal elements.

Position or status is never divorced from role and the major problems of position differences come as one performs his role in terms of his perception of his position. If a husband feels his position has higher status, he usually transfers these feelings into his role performance. If he is the higher status figure, then he often

2. Both Newcomb (1950, pp. 276–80) and Bates (1956) prefer the concept *position* to that of *status* in referring to one's place in a social system.

3. Newcomb uses role in the first sense and Bates uses the second conceptualization.

thinks he should make the final decisions, give the orders, demand favors, etc.

Role expectations

Not only does each marriage partner enter marriage with certain ideas as to how he should behave in his new position, but each has also certain expectations as to how the other person should behave in his (the other's) role. Role expectations, then, are the ways one person feels the other should behave (see Parsons, 1951, p.38). In terms of the new marriage relationship, the new husband has some ideas as to how he should behave as a husband (his role) and he also has some idea as to how his wife should behave in her role (his role expectations of his wife). Conversely the wife has some definition of her role and certain expectations of her husband's role.

One problem in the matter of role behavior is focused in the question of role definitions *v.* role performance. There is often a difference between what is agreed on as to what one should do and what one *actually* does. A husband and wife could both agree that it is part of the husband's role to plan and carry out the recreational activities of the growing boys in the family. In actuality the husband does not do this. It could be maintained that the husband's role is what he actually does in his position, but the expectations of the wife appear, at least at first in the marriage, to be derived from the definition of behavior that is agreed on between them.

In marriage each partner probably starts out with certain expectations as to how husbands or wives in general ought to behave and these generalized expectations are applied to the specific behavior of the other partner. Later, part of the expectations may be altered to include the specialized expectation of specific role elements derived out of their experience together. For example, at first a wife may expect her husband to be a general handyman around the house (derived from her generalized expectations) and is disappointed when he prefers to golf. Later an agreement may be reached that he must at least mow the lawn, wash the car and replace used light bulbs. If the husband does no 'handyman' type jobs at all he is violating a generalized expectation. If he fails to take out the garbage he is not meeting a specifically agreed on expectation.

It should be pointed out that each partner usually has not only expectations of *what* should be done by the other but also *how* the particular function should be carried out. The wife may not only expect her husband to share in the household tasks but to do it in a cooperative, pleasant manner. Her expectations can be violated should he not perform the task or if he does it in a surly unpleasant way.

A. R. Mangus (1957) in his article on mental health in the family, using a theoretical orientation very similar to the one used here, points out that expectations may also be centered around a conception of the marriage partner as a total personality. Each partner usually has not only expectations of what and how the other person should behave in his role, but also how the other person should be as a person. Conflicts may come when one's self-perception does not agree with the perception of the marriage partner. The husband may see himself as efficient, helpful, friendly while his wife sees him as stingy, suspicious and overbearing. If the wife expects her husband to be a certain kind of personality his behavior, manifesting symptoms of a contrary type, will elicit negative reactions from her. The problem is intensified when he cannot understand why she sees him this way because he sees himself so differently.

An important part of this analysis is to try to see expectations as attached to specific role functions rather than becoming generalized around the total person. If a wife sees her husband as a certain kind of person, this may distort her perceptions of him in all his role performances. Under these circumstances, adjustment in the sense to be described below may be difficult to achieve for it is uncertain that the change of role performance on the part of the husband will alter her perceptions of him as a total person, although it may be argued that alterations in role performance may be the most effective way for the wife to develop a new conception of her husband.

Sanctions

Sanctions are the rewards or punishments administered by one person to another to the degree the other person meets or fails to meet his role expectations. In the family situation, if the husband's performance in his role meets the wife's role expectations, she will generally apply positive sanctions or rewards such as praise, affection, good will, etc. If his role performance violates her expectations she will often apply negative sanctions – tears, quarreling or withdrawal of affection.

It is generally the case, that human interactions move along most smoothly if the following conditions exist: (a) if the parties interacting have a high level of agreement of norms and personal preferences; (b) if the parties involved agree as to the role definitions and role expectations of each other; (c) if the role performance of one is in agreement with role expectations of the other and positive sanctions are the end result of the interaction.

Marriage adjustment

Using the above conceptual scheme, we may now consider marriage adjustment:

Points of conflict

Conflicts in the marriage situation may arise at the following places in terms of the above schema:

1. If the norms and personal preferences of the husband are in conflict with those of the wife.

2. If the role performance of the husband does not agree with the role expectations of the wife.

3. If the role performance of the wife does not agree with the role expectations of the husband.

In each of the above cases dissatisfaction with the marriage relationship may occur with a resulting application of negative sanction. Negative sanctions may be directly or indirectly applied, or these feelings of dissatisfaction may be repressed or directed towards someone or something else. The frustration–aggression hypothesis could be applied here as each of these points of conflict could be sources of frustration (Dollard *et al.*, 1939).

Possible methods of adjustment

In each of the above conflict situations, there are certain kinds of adjustments available:

1. In conflict point 1, the couple needs to clarify to each other

their norms or personal preferences so that each knows exactly the point of view of the other. This of necessity involves mature and extensive communication. To the degree the disparity between norms is translated into role performance the following adjustments would be more applicable.

2. In conflict situations 2 and 3, the possibility of adjustment are the same:

(a) The husband (or wife) can change his role performance completely to meet the role expectations of his partner.

(b) The husband (or wife) can change his role expectations completely to coincide with the role performance of the partner.

(c) There can be a mutual adjustment, each partner altering some. The husband (or wife) can alter his role to a degree and the partner alters his role expectations to a similar degree so that role performance and role expectations are compatible. In each of the above cases the end result is an agreement between role performance and role expectations.

3. There is also another type of adjustment possible. In some cases the couple might recognize a disparity between role performance and role expectations or between norms and also acknowledge that change is difficult or impossible and could 'agree to disagree'. In such cases the one partner recognizes and respects the position of the other without accepting or adjusting to it. This pattern of 'agreeing to disagree' is not adjustment in the same sense as the others listed above. The 'adjustment' comes from both partners agreeing that a certain area is 'out of bounds' as far as the application of sanctions are concerned. There is not change in behavior but some change in expectations in that each now expects certain areas not to be raised as issues and that no sanctions will be applied over these 'out of bounds' issues. This type of adjustment may be possible in certain areas of married life but some areas may be too vital to the relationship not to have reached one of the other types of adjustment.

Some problems in adjustment

Public v. private adjustment

The above model emphasizes the actual outward, public behavior of the couple as the essence of adjustment. Complete adjustment would obtain only if the change in behavior were accompanied by a mental state of 'feeling good' about the change in behavior. If a husband changed his role performance to meet his wife's expectations publicly, adjustment would appear to occur, but privately he could resent 'giving in' to her and transfer this resentment into areas other than that around which the 'adjustment' took place.[4]

The need for feedback

An almost universal element in the process of change of social behavior is that of feedback – the receiving of information by one person from others about the effect of his behavior upon the others. It is difficult, if not impossible, for one partner to know exactly how he is violating the expectations of the other if the other does not respond with adequate feedback. Often feedback cues are given out by one partner, but the other may mis-read the cues, misinterpret them, or deny them if the feedback is not stated clearly in an atmosphere of acceptance when the climate is not 'defensive' (Gibb, 1959). This open communication of expectations and feedback about the degree the other has met, or failed to meet, these expectations is often extremely difficult for newly marrieds. There are fears that, 'if I give feedback to the other person I may lose the level of warmth and affection we now have', or fear that the other may retaliate. People are also inhibited from giving feedback by feelings of inadequacy as to how to proceed, lack of what might be an appropriate time, or feelings that one is not really sure he is 'right' about his own criticism of the partner.

Often one learns of the expectations of others and how he has

4. In testing similar phenomena, Kelman (1956) distinguishes between *compliance* (the adopting of a new behavior not because one believes in its content, but because he expects to gain specific rewards of approval and avoid specific punishments or disapproval); *identification* (the adopting of new behavior because it is associated with the desired relationship); and *internalization* (the adopting of a new behavior because one finds it useful for the solution of a problem or because it is congenial to his needs).

or has not met these expectations only via a trial-and-error method[5] or in a sudden outburst of feeling when the other feels 'I can't take it any longer'. Neither of these conditions of feedback maximize the opportunity for mutual sharing of data in an atmosphere of helpfulness where the feedback has the best opportunity of being perceived as being helpful to the total relationship.

Adjustment v. 'making-up'

Adjustment has been discussed above in terms of bringing into agreement the behavior of one person with the expectations of another accompanied by a feeling of acceptance of the modified behavior by the one who makes the adjustment. A phenomena recognized in many cases of marital discord is the subsequent process of 'making-up'. This is usually a process of repairing the feeling of unity and cohesion between the couple.

From an examination of a number of case studies it appears entirely possible for a couple to 'make-up' without achieving any adjustment in the sense described above. The violation of expectations often results in a feeling of discord and hostility between the couple. In a moment of mutual sympathy and regret for past actions, the couple may beg each others' forgiveness and 'kiss and make up'. This puts them back in a harmonious relationship with each other, but since no modification of either expectation or behavior has occurred, the disruption may occur again.

It is also possible for adjustment to occur without a resulting repairing of the emotional state of unity. It would seem that this would occur less frequently, particularly if there were also a private feeling of adjustment, since the result of the mutual agreement of expectation and behavior should be a response of positive sanction.

In terms of reinforcement learning theory it seems essential that a modification of either expectations or behavior on the part of one partner be rewarded by the other (Miller and Dollard, 1941). One not only needs to find out what one does wrong, but also

5. This 'trial-and-error' learning is similar to what has been called 'operant conditioning' – the subtle learning of subjects to respond to reinforcing stimuli, see Verplanch (1957, pp. 127–36).

what one does right. The continual giving of positive sanctions may be a necessary part of marital adjustment.

Role conflict and adjustment

In a previous paper, the author has outlined some of the conditions in role conflict (Dyer, 1960). Basic to the problem of role conflict is the paradoxical condition that in performing a role the same response brings *both* reward and punishment. A strongly religious wife who meets her husband's expectations by going skiing with him on Sunday may violate the expectations she and others may hold about her role as church member. The response of going skiing brings both reward and punishment – reward from husband and punishment from self through feelings of self-recrimination of having violated another role one has internalized.

A marital partner may also find himself in conflict because of differing expectations as to how his role should be carried out. The young wife may discover that her husband, mother and mother-in-law each have differing expectations as to how she should perform her wife's role. She finds that in adjusting to her husband's expectations she violates the expectations of significant others. It is apparent that this type of conflict is difficult to resolve, especially when each faction feels its expectations are legitimate. Sometimes it is possible to change people's expectations of the role. Sometimes one needs to perform the role in terms of his own considered definition of what is appropriate despite the demands of others. This latter action lessens one's inner conflicts but does not eliminate the external pressures.

Cautions

1. The above is a logical outline of adjustment possibilities from a particular frame of reference. It does not pretend to cover the social-psychological dynamics involved in the difficult process of attitude or behavior change. One should never presume that such adjustments are psychologically easy.

I have argued that all conflict is a result of one person's behavior not meeting another's expectations, or vice versa. The correction of such conflict is often more complex, for one's behavior and/or expectations may be related to one's 'personality', i.e. certain temperament factors, conceptions of self, important self–other needs, etc. The changing of one's role behavior or expectations may demand personal adjustments that are extremely difficult. One's level of maturity will also be an important factor determining the capability of one to make adjustments.

2. The above outline does not suggest which of the types of conflict is most frequent nor which of the types of adjustment is easiest. More research is needed in the area of marital adjustment using this schema. It is, however, a commonly held position that it is easier to change one's role expectations than to change another's behavior.

3. It should be noted that there are other methods available for the *reduction* of conflict in marital situations without actually adjusting in the sense defined above – that is, the marriage partners making some alteration of norms, roles or role expectations. This avenue generally is the alteration of the *situation* that may be fostering certain role behaviors or expectations. For example, if conflict occurs between a husband and wife because he spends too much time with a group of old cronies (his behavior thus violating her expectations), a change in residence may put so much distance between husband and friends that the situation is altered and the husband now spends time with his wife. However, since no adjustment was expected in this area it is always possible the husband may make a new set of 'cronies'.

The marital situation is often changed by such actions as moving, changing jobs, having a baby, family disasters, etc. The altered situation may actually eliminate the point of conflict or perhaps bring about a reappraisal of role or expectations leading to adjustment as discussed herein.

References

BATES, F. L. (1956), 'Position, role and status: reformulation of concepts', *Social Forces*, vol. 34, pp. 313–21.

DOLLARD, J., *et al.* (1939), *Frustration and Aggression*, Yale University Press.

DYER, W. G. (1958), 'The institutionalization of equalitarian family norms', *Marriage and Family Living*, vol. 20, pp. 53–8.

DYER, W. G. (1960), 'Looking at conflict', *Adult Leadership*,
September.

GIBB, J. R. (1959), *Factors Producing Defensive Behavior with Groups,
VI*, Final Technical Report, Office of Naval Research, Nonr-2285 (OI).

KELMAN, H. C. (1956), 'Three processes of acceptance of social
influence: compliance, identification and internalization', paper read at
the meeting of the American Psychological Association, Chicago,
Illinois, 30 August.

MANGUS, A. R. (1957), 'Family impacts on mental health', *Marriage
and Family Living*, vol. 19, pp. 256–62.

MILLER, N. E., and DOLLARD, J. (1941), *Learning and Imitation*,
Yale University Press.

NEWCOMB, T. M. (1950), *Social Psychology*, Dryden Press.

NYE, I., and MACDOUGAL, E. (1960), 'Do families have
sub-cultures?', *Sociology and Social Research*, vol. 44.

PARSONS, T. (1951), *The Social System*, Free Press.

VERPLANCH, W. S. (1957), 'The operant, from rat to man: some recent
experiments in human behavior', in E. L. Hartley and
R. E. Hartley (eds.), *Outside Reading in Psychology*, Crowell.

19 R. O. Blood and D. M. Wolfe

Resources and Family Task Performance

Excerpts from R. O. Blood and D. M. Wolfe, *Husbands and Wives: The Dynamics of Family Living*, Free Press and Collier-Macmillan, 1960, pp. 68–9, 57–68.

When any new group of people first come together, there is a period of tentative trial-and-error searching out of the pattern of who will do what. At first, no one knows how his own skills compare with those of other group members. If the tasks are strange, there is all the more necessity for various members of the group to try them out before it is eventually discovered who is best at each. As such discoveries are made, each person comes to perform those tasks for which he has the greatest skill and other resources. This process of eventual specialization results from what economists call 'the principle of least effort' – whoever can get results with the least effort tends to perform that task. He himself finds greatest satisfaction in doing so, and the others more and more defer to his competence. As a result, he plays an increasingly specialized role as time goes on.

In the case of the family, role differentiation has a head start – even for newly-weds. From early childhood the bride and groom have observed the standardized model of their own parents and of parents generally – the model of traditional role differentiation along sex lines. In the process of being brought up, there has usually been explicit training – especially for the girl – for the tasks that she will perform when she becomes a wife and mother in her own right. So by both informal and formal socialization, the husband and wife have been prepared to enter marriage with similar expectations about how they will divide up their duties.

Despite this preliminary preparation, there is still something in marriage of that initial tentativeness which characterizes all new groups. For one thing, the role expectations the partners bring to marriage are not likely to coincide in every respect. Some tasks crop up which both partners expected to be their own – the money and bills, for example. Other tasks may be mutually wished upon the partner – such as taking out the garbage. Discrepancies in role expectations produce a period of Alphonse-and-Gaston tugging and hauling before a settled pattern emerges.

Moreover, few modern young people come to marriage completely rehearsed in the tasks of keeping house. The less well trained the partners, the more they must engage in mutual experimentation. The proverbial hard-as-a-rock first buns may well lead to husbandly advice, collaboration in reading the recipe, or even a temporary change of cooks if he has been 'baching' it before marriage. Likewise, husbands who have never repaired a broken lamp cord before are apt to find someone looking over their shoulder, proffering assistance. [. . .][1]

Resources for getting things done

Nothing could be more pragmatic and non-ideological than the sheer availability of one partner to do the household tasks. This is precisely what seems to be the prime determinant of the division of labor.

If the dishes need washing and the lawn needs mowing, somebody must do it. As far as the needs of the family are concerned, what matters is not who does it but that someone does it. As long as the option is equally available to either partner, the work is usually done along traditional lines. But if circumstances arise which make it impossible for the customary performer to do his duty, the 'show must go on'. In this sense, every husband is a 'stand in' for his wife, and every wife for her husband. It is true that he may not have learned her lines very well or consciously prepared himself for this emergency. But when the emergency arises, he is under pressure to take over her roles lest the household functioning break down. Not every spouse rises to the occasion, but the moral pressure and the practical urgency are there. If he doesn't, he presumably must face the criticism of the incapacitated partner – and perhaps that of his own conscience as well.

As in the case of decision making, the moral norm which determines how families ought to differ from one another in their division of labor is appropriateness. Ordinarily, it is appropriate

1. The rest of the selection looks at some of the factors which influence the precise patterns of task performance which are adopted. [Ed.]

that the husband do the male tasks and the wife the feminine ones, because these tie in efficiently with masculine constitutions and feminine child-bearing. But in extraordinary circumstances, it is appropriate for the alternate partner to come to the rescue of his overburdened or unavailable spouse even if it means playing an unfamiliar role.

Time as a resource. Availability is partly a matter of space, partly of time. To be able to help out at home, an individual must be home. So, factors which keep the husband or wife away from home reduce his or her participation in household tasks. But even if both partners are home, they are not always equally available. The husband may be home in body but not in mind, his thoughts preoccupied with occupational responsibilities. Such a husband is not likely to be much use to his wife. Or the wife may be so heavily burdened with child-care responsibilities that she just plain runs out of time. Then the only way of getting the work done is to tap the husband's time.

Farm and city schedules. Differential availability seems to explain why farm wives do so much more housework than city wives. Superficially one might expect farm husbands to do more around the house because they don't have to leave home to go to work. Yet Table 1 shows farm husbands doing less of everything except the farm-relevant account keeping and shovelling a path to the barn. Not only do farm wives do more feminine tasks but they even do more of the other two masculine tasks. (The small differences shown in this table are compounded at the other end of the scale where only 44 per cent of the farmers do all the lawn mowing compared to 66 per cent of the city husbands, while the city husbands similarly edge out the farmers on exclusive home repairing, 73 per cent to 55 per cent.)

In the aggregate, these differences add up to a much larger percentage of farm wives who do more than half of the tasks all by themselves. Whereas only 39 per cent of the city wives handle this many tasks, 70 per cent of the farm wives are found at this hard-working end of the continuum.

The fact that farm wives perform more of both female and male tasks explains why there is a rural–urban difference in the amount

Table I Unilateral Performance of Specific Household Tasks, by Farm and City Wives (178 farm families, 731 city families)

Families where only wife performs task as a percentage*

Task	Repairs	Lawn	Walk	Bills	Groceries	Breakfast	Living room	Dishes
On farm	6	13	6	25	45	86	86	88
In city	3	7	7	30	36	66	65	70

*Reciprocal percentages of the 178 farm husbands and 731 city husbands help with these tasks at least occasionally.

of work done without a difference in the aggregate conformity to traditional norms. Although farm wives adhere more closely to the traditional pattern on feminine tasks, they more often invade the masculine sphere, producing low masculine stereotypy.

How can this rural diligence be explained? Since farm couples are comparatively unstereotyped on male tasks, the differential output can hardly be attributed to rural conservatism. Perhaps some people would say city wives are spoiled, but does that mean rural husbands are, too? Surely not.

The very confidence with which it can be said that the American farmer is no slouch provides a clue to the mystery. In many ways, farm work is like women's work – it's never done. Not only is there an endless amount of painting, fence mending and wood chipping that could be done on the typical farm, but it's always so near at hand that it provides the husband with counterclaims to any demands that might come from the wife. The typical city worker leaves his job behind when he punches the time clock at 5.00. While this allows him more leisure, it also leaves him morally defenseless when there are tasks to be done at home.

If this interpretation is correct, the farmer's perennial involvement in his work makes him relatively unavailable for household tasks, whereas the city husband's separation from his place of work makes him highly available for part-time 'employment' at home.[2]

Urban occupations. Urban husbands differ among themselves, however, in the extent to which they leave their jobs behind. Generalizations about separation of work-place and residence apply primarily to blue-collar workers since they seldom have reason to be preoccupied with business problems in their spare time. The boss, however, doesn't have it so easy. As an executive, he has problems to solve that plague him over the weekend and keep him awake nights. Even if he doesn't bring his paper work home in the proverbial briefcase, his mind will not easily forget. So, whether working late at the office, figuring in his study, or puzzling over a problem in his easy chair, the responsible executive is unavailable for housework. The more responsible he is, the less available he becomes – for the means to promotion is over-

2. For a more extended discussion of this question see Blood (1958).

time work, and the consequence of promotion is more overtime work.

In Detroit, the differences between entire occupational groups are minor, although the business and professional group does have the highest task performance by the wife (5·49)[3] and the low-blue-collar group the least (5·20). The big difference between city husbands is not between occupations as such but reflects the amount of involvement of the husband in his occupation.

Occupational preoccupation. Two measures of the husband's success in his occupation are available. The first is the amount of income he earns. Presumably the more time and energy a man invests in his job, the more he is financially rewarded.

Table 2 Household Task Performance, by Husband's Income

	Husband's income			
	Under $3000	$3000 –6999	$7000 –9999	$10,000+
Wife's mean task performance	5·11	5·27	5·65	6·21
Number of families	61	357	86	52

The evidence from Table 2 is unmistakable: high-income husbands do less work around the house. It is important to remember that this is not just because wealthy men hire gardeners to mow the lawn. Since this is the *relative* division of labor between husband and wife, for everything the successful man does less of, his wife does correspondingly more. She, too, of course, may have more servants and more labor-saving devices to cut down on her own household tasks. But the rise in her index of task performance

3. The couples interviewed were asked about performance of eight tasks: repairs around the house, lawn mowing, snow shovelling, keeping track of money and bills, grocery shopping, getting husband's breakfast, tidying the living room when visitors were expected and washing up in the evening. On each of these the couple was placed on a five-point scale from wife always (scored 5) to husband always (scored 1). The task performance scores given in brackets are the means of these aggregated individual task scores set, as are all other scores, on a ten-point scale. The first three tasks are considered to be traditional male tasks, the last four, traditional female tasks. [Ed.]

shows that the housework as a whole becomes increasingly her responsibility because her husband is so absorbed in his career.

Table 3 Household Task Performance, by Husband's Intergenerational Occupational Mobility

	Husband's intergenerational mobility		
	Downward	Stable	Upward
Wife's mean task performance	5·10	5·28	5·67
Number of families	162	176	207

A second measure of occupational success involves comparing the husband's occupation with that of his father before him. Those who now hold a better job have been 'upward mobile', in comparison to those who have stayed in the same occupational stratum or moved downward.[4]

The differences shown in Table 3 are not great but they substantiate the generalization that the more successful the husband is in his occupation, the less the wife can count on his help at home. Not that successful husbands disdain household tasks – they are just too busy being successful to have the time. [. . .]

Job-involved wives. So far, only the husband's involvement outside the home has been mentioned. But since many wives also work, both partners' employment influences their availability for household tasks.

Table 4 shows a striking difference between wives who are not employed (and therefore fully available for household tasks) and those whose jobs take them out of the home. When the wife is away most of the day (nearly all working wives in Detroit have full-time jobs), she faces the potential burden of two jobs: paid work plus housework. Under these circumstances, the husband feels obliged to help out more at home and takes over an appreciably larger share of the housework. The working wife still has a more strenuous life than the housewife, no doubt, but the husband may come to her rescue sufficiently to cushion the

4. Occupations were rated on the National Opinion Research Center's scale of occupational prestige. 'Stable' husbands were those who had not moved more than five percentile points from their father's rating.

Table 4 Household Task Performance and Adherence to Male and Female Roles, by Comparative Work Participation of Husband and Wife

| | Comparative work participation | | | | | |
| | Wife not employed | | | Wife employed | | |
	Husband overtime	Husband full-time	Husband none	Husband overtime	Husband full-time	Husband none
Wife's mean task performance	5·81	5·57	5·64	4·66	3·40	2·33
Adherence to female roles	6·20	6·12	6·33	4·88	4·32	1·33
Adherence to male roles	6·64	7·00	7·26	7·51	7·90	8·33
Minimum number of families*	198	218	28	50	58	3

*Each cell in the column above a particular number contains at least the number of families indicated, with minor variation upward wherever the number of 'not ascertained' cases diminishes. For example, in the first column above, the actual numbers on which the means are computed are 198, 206 and 204 (reading from top to bottom).

physical strain on her and to minimize resentment against him.

However, his ability to come to her aid depends on the extent to which he works himself. If he is home all the time, the three cases in Table 4 suggest that he can pretty much take over the housework even if he is unable to hold a regular job. But if he has two jobs himself (as many overtime husbands do), there will be less reason and less possibility for him to help out with the wife's second area of responsibility.

The comparative availability of the husband has the same effect when the wife is not working – but it makes less difference then. If the wife is home all the time, she can do her traditional tasks without much help from the husband. Even if he's home full-time (as when neither partner works), he is not likely to invade her sphere as long as she is capable of doing her own traditional work. Most non-working couples involve a husband who has retired but spends his time largely in pottering around rather than in doing half of the housework.

This suggests a limitation on the principle of comparative availability: *under conditions of strain*, tasks will be reallocated in the direction of the more available partner. From this point of view, the full-time housewife whose husband is employed full-time is the normal pattern. She has full-time to devote to the feminine tasks and he has his spare time in which to get around to the masculine tasks.

When the husband retires, there is no additional strain on the division of labor because the wife still has plenty of time to get her work done. Only if she takes a job does a stay-at-home husband come under pressure to change his role.

On the other hand, if the husband works evenings and weekends, it may be difficult for him to accomplish even the traditional male tasks – so the wife who is home all the time may find herself taking over his tasks.

For the husband to work overtime puts less strain on the traditional division of labor than for the wife to go outside the home to work. This is a simple question of the number of hours in the week. Husbands rarely put in as much as forty hours overtime but this is the usual outside investment of the wife who goes to work. The ability of the husband to respond to this major deficit in his wife's time budget may be seen by comparing the size of the changes in household participation according to the varying amounts of time the husband has available. Overtime husbands, with the least time to spare, still manage to squeeze out a major shift in task performance of 1·15 points in response to the radical alteration of the wife's daily schedule when she works. But husbands with a normal complement of spare time shift even more (2·17 points difference), while men retired from the labor market make the biggest shift of all (3·31 points).

To summarize: (a) the more the conventional division of labor is disrupted, the more tasks must be reallocated; and (b) tasks are re-assigned to the other partner in proportion to the amount of time he has available.

Comparison of two-income and one-income families by degree of stereotypy in the allocation of tasks shows that working-wife families depart appreciably from traditional roles.[5] However, this over-all difference holds primarily for families where the husband's income is less than $5000. At this low income level, 32 per cent of the two-income families but only 15 per cent of the one-income families have unstereotyped roles (less than half of the tasks done in the traditional manner).

Do higher income families have more resources with which to adapt to the strain of the wife going to work? Perhaps their financial position enables them to employ substitute task-performers under the supervision of the traditional partner and to mechanize the latter's work sufficiently to enable her to do her tasks in what little time is available. Apparently, then, it is especially at low-income levels that the wife's departure leaves no alternative but for the husband to pitch in and help out.

Actually, total role stereotypy is an ambiguous way of looking at changes which reflect the lessened availability of one partner. A decrease in the availability of one partner tends to reduce stereotypy in his role area but to increase it in the partner's area. This occurs in farm families where the husband's lessened availability results in the wife invading his role but doing her own tasks all the more onesidedly. The same is true when the wife goes to work – but in the reverse direction.

Table 4 shows that the extra pressure on husbands of working

5. The authors are indebted to Buse (1955) for preliminary analysis of this area.

wives caused them to help their wives out more with feminine tasks at the same time that they do more of their own tasks. The result is that two-income families are more stereotyped in the masculine area and less so in the feminine area. This dual shift occurs at both low and high income levels, though not quite symmetrically. Above $5000, the wife's working prompts the husband to do more of his own tasks, with the net result that high-income marriages move slightly in the traditional direction on total stereotypy. Lower-income husbands, however, not only increase their masculine work, but move even more substantially into the female area, producing a net shift away from general stereotypy.

It is incorrect, therefore, to say that two-income families are more companionable than one-income families in their division of labor. To be sure they share the bread-winning responsibility. They also share the feminine tasks. But they do not share the masculine tasks as much. The net result is greater equality in decision-making between husband and wife, and more participation by the husband in the total task of running the household – but not more collective participation in all task areas. Rather, the wife drops out of the husband's task areas as he moves into hers.[6]

Examination of the various tasks in relation to the wife's employment shows that husbands help out more with the working wife's home-centered tasks (getting the breakfast, doing the dishes, and picking up the living room) but the wife continues to do just as much of the grocery shopping. There her time shortage may be offset by the ease of shopping on the way home from work. On the other hand, the husband gets less of the working wife's help with his outdoor tasks (snow shovelling, lawn mowing), but there is no shift in household repairing. Perhaps the latter depends so much on technical skill that only the competent partner can do it. All the time in the world doesn't help if one lacks the know-how.

In keeping track of the money and bills, the distinction lies not between wives who are currently employed and those who are

6. This modifies Kligler's conclusion that working-wife families are consistently less bound by traditional lines separating husband–wife domains in the performance of traditional roles (1954).

home but between those who have *ever* worked and those who never have since marriage. Apparently participation in the world of work trains the wife in financial competence which is reflected in keeping the books (and making financial decisions) long after she quits working. Again, skill seems more important than time in this administrative task.

To summarize, husbands of working wives can expect to help out more in the home and get less help themselves outside the home – except where tasks are so technical in nature that the relative competence of the two partners matters more than their availability. The case of the working wife, therefore, requires further modification of the general thesis to say that families differ in their division of labor according to how easy it is for either partner to do it. Ease is a combination of time and skill. Another way of putting it would be to return to the concept of resources. Time is a resource for getting work done. So is skill. Hence, the division of labor is determined by the comparative resourcefulness of the two partners in accomplishing the necessary household tasks. [. . .]

Skill as a resource. Skill is more important than time in determining whether the husband or the wife will repair things and keep track of the finances. No other information on mechanical skill is available but book-keeping ability can be gauged in various ways. For instance, whichever partner has more education keeps track of the money and bills (even when controlled on the husband's occupational level).

Table 5 Wife's Financial Task Performance,
by Husband's Income

	Husband's income				
	Under $3000	$3000 –4999	$5000 –6999	$7000 –9999	$10,000+
Wife's mean financial task performance*	3·20	3·32	3·30	3·11	2·88
Number of families	70	181	198	88	57

*Keeping track of the money and bills.

Of even greater significance, however, is the husband's income. Once he gets above $7000 a year and especially when he gets over $10,000, he assumes the financial responsibility more often. Below $7000, most of the money goes for groceries and other subsistence items anyway. But when income exceeds this level, problems of investment and savings arise which swing insurance decisions to the husband. When money gets to be this plentiful and decisions about it correspondingly complicated, the successful husband's extra experience with money becomes doubly valuable.

References

BLOOD, R. O. (1958), 'The division of labour in city and farm families', *Marriage and Family Living*, vol. 20, pp. 170–74.

BUSE, D. (1955), 'An analysis of past and present employment of wives in relation to division of labor in the family', Detroit Area Study (mimeo), Ann Arbor.

KLIGLER, D. S. (1954), 'The effect of the employment of married women on husband and wife roles: a study in culture change', unpublished Ph.D. thesis, Yale University.

20 R. Rapoport and R. Rapoport

Family Roles and Work Roles

R. Rapoport and R. Rapoport, 'Work and family in contemporary
society', *American Sociological Review*, vol. 30, 1965, pp. 381–94.

In traditional societies, work and family structures tend to be
linked as parts of an integrated cultural whole sustained by a
complex web of social controls, so that the relations between work
and family life in any individual case are primarily a matter of
degree of conformity to a dominant cultural norm. In contemporary urban society, life patterns tend to be segmented and
norms are heterogeneous, but the relations between work and
family life are not unstructured, i.e. an infinite variety of
arrangements, subject only to the individual's wishes, does not
exist. Cultural, social-structural and personal regularities interact
to determine the ways in which work and family life affect one
another. Our concern here is to detect some of the regularities.
We propose to do so by studying a *process* whereby the structure
of interrelationship is established rather than by attempting to
sort out the permutations and combinations of structures characterizing work–family relations.

The process we have in mind is that of *task accomplishment*.
We are concerned specifically with the intrinsic stimuli presented
to individuals at critical role transitions in the life cycle. We
suggest that certain tasks are inherent in each such transition,
and that the pattern of dealing with them affects subsequent
structuring of work–family interrelations.[1]

1. Our psycho-social approach to critical role transitions has roots in both
social science and psychiatry, and like-minded efforts are currently being
made in Harvard's Laboratory of Community Psychiatry. For example, cf.
Caplan (1961, 1964). Based to some extent on the work of Lindemann
(1944) Caplan's work supports and is complementary to several basic social
science research programs. Recent published work in the family research
program includes the following: Rhona Rapoport (1963, 1964) and Rhona
Rapoport and Robert Rapoport (1964).

After considering some of the prevailing theoretical issues implicit or explicit in the relevant professional literature, we shall apply the task-accomplishment framework to *one* critical life-cycle role transition – the formation of the conjugal family unit through marriage – in *one* occupational group – professional technologists at the point of completing their university training.

Current issues of work–family interrelations

The relations between work and family life have seldom been studied explicitly, for specialists in family sociology, kinship, industrial sociology and occupational psychology have tended to treat each of these areas as a relatively closed sub-system. It is as though family structure, organization and functioning depended entirely on factors associated with the family and the individual personalities within it, while the organization and functioning of work groups could be explained exclusively in terms of the work situation.[2]

Those who have considered the relations between these two spheres of life have generally been concerned with one or more of the following theoretical points:

1. *Family and work have become increasingly differentiated* in our society, due to the specialization of work roles and the importance of universalistic norms in contemporary society.

2. *Work and family roles vary in their relative salience* in the lives of their incumbents. In general the professions require the strongest commitment of their incumbents and therefore poten-

2. Exceptions include Caplow (1954). Caplow is concerned on the one hand with the way in which a man's occupation locates his family in the social class system and, on the other hand, with the difficulties married women encounter in reconciling occupational and familial roles. Fitting together work and family life has long been seen as a 'problem' for women but not for men. Here we concentrate on situations in which only the husband is employed, but our conceptualization would encompass the entire range of situations. A comparable precursor from the family vantage point is Angell (1936). This book reflects a common tendency to see work–family interrelations as problematic when severe disturbance occurs in one sphere or the other. We concentrate on the processes of patterned interaction in 'normal' situations here, but our conceptualization applies as well to the more traumatic and unpredictable crises.

tially compete most with family roles for emotional involvement. Salience of work as a positive area of personal commitment tends to decline as one descends in the social class-hierarchy.

3. *Work and family modes of interaction tend to be isomorphic;* they affect each other in such a way as to induce similar structural patterns in both spheres. Heteromorphism also occurs frequently, however, particularly in occupations that lack salience or are highly threatening for their incumbents.

4. *The life-cycle stage affects relations between work and family life.* The situation at the beginning of marriage, for example, differs from what it is at the time of rearing small children, and at an early point in the work career, from what it is at retirement. Furthermore, whether a critical transition in one sphere (e.g. marriage) precedes, coincides with or follows a critical event in the other (e.g. graduation from college), it also affects relations between family life and work.

The differentiation of work from family roles has long been recognized as fundamental to the evolution of contemporary society. At the simplest levels of social organization, the division of labor that held for work closely paralleled that of the family. The primitive band, for instance, was both a food-producing and consumption unit, and its members tended to be kin. Curle describes the situation associated with the ideal-typical tribal society:

Among the most primitive peoples ... life is all of a piece. It is not split, as it is for a vast majority of the habitants of Western Europe and America, into what one does to earn a living – called work – and what one does during the rest of the time (1949, pp. 41–7).

Thus, activities in both spheres are subject to the same over-arching cultural beliefs and values, and the significance of an event or object in one sphere is comprehensible only with reference to the other sphere as well. Firth expresses this notion well with reference to the value of a cow in African tribal cultures:

The value of a cow in African culture cannot be reckoned by what its yield of milk, flesh, hide, horns, etc. will bring on the market, but to this must be added the non-economic values of their importance as displays of wealth, their part in initiating or marrying a son, their place in ritual sacrifice (1938).[3]

These tightly integrated and pervasive norms and values accompany a relatively rudimentary division of labor. Under these conditions (characterized by Durkheim as *solidarité mécanique*), everyone did pretty much what everyone else did. Major social segments based on the differentiation of productive economic roles developed only after a series of technological revolutions made possible large concentrations of people, storage of predictable food supplies, etc.

Because more diversified normative patterns tended to develop in various segments of society associated with this differentiation of occupational roles, family structure was necessarily affected. But the logic of modern industrial enterprise called for separation of familial considerations from those of the industrial undertaking. Weber, among others, called attention to this as one of the essential conditions for the formal rationality of capital accounting in any modern productive enterprise. He notes, among other factors, the importance of 'The most complete possible separation of the enterprise and its conditions of success or failure from the household or private budgetary unit and its property interests' (Weber, 1947). Smelser (1959) has analysed the actual process of differentiation in some detail, elucidating some of the changes in the English textile industry in the eighteenth and nineteenth centuries that led to enduring structural changes in relations between work and family life.[4] Initially weaving and associated tasks were performed by family members in the service of family subsistence. As textile production had increasingly to be geared to a cash market and to compete with similar operations elsewhere,

3. We do not mean to imply that cultural traits in the Western societies are not adumbrated with values and meanings from other spheres (e.g. in American society, the social and psychological significance of driving a large, late-model car) but that the *degree* of functional interdependence among the spheres tends to be less in Western than in tribal societies.

4. Goode (1964) notes that since the Second World War the leaders of countries wishing to facilitiate industrialization have introduced legal changes, well ahead of public opinion, to create family patterns more compatible with the demands of urban and industrial life (p. 2). Also see Goode (1963) for an analysis of world-wide patterns of change in family life under the impact of technological change.

problems of efficiency became more salient, which encouraged specialization of function and the selection of specialists according to competence rather than traditional kinship duties and obligations *vis-à-vis* the entrepreneur. Entrepreneurial success came increasingly to depend on assigning specific jobs to the most competent individuals available, regardless of senti-mental or familial connexions.

Throughout this over-all development, however, one kind of enterprise has succeeded partly because family members have special commitments and loyalties to one another. Under favor-able conditions some family firms have flourished throughout the industrial revolution and in various national–cultural settings. And among the executives of large corporations, work and family life are intermingled to a degree reminiscent of pre-industrial revolution times, not only in the great family firms of Europe (whose astonishing growth since the Second World War con-tradicts predictions based on the notion that family involvement in industrial management is disadvantageous), but in the U.S. as well. If Whyte's (1956) observations are accurate, advancement in a large firm often hinges on the way an individual's wife behaves and on her attitudes and values.[5] Industrial management is susceptible to the wife's influence, for she may influence her husband's orientation to problems of human relations, and his willingness to work late hours, to move his household, and so on, depends partly on her attitudes and aspirations.

These examples suggest that family–work differentiation has not proceeded to its ultimate, logical limit. Indeed, contemporary observations of work–family relations indicate that several countervailing trends or forces have interfered with complete segregation of work from family life. For one thing, more women are being formally educated than in the past, and more of them are entering the full range of occupational positions. Though wives are no longer as economically dependent on their husbands as formerly, they now more often share with them certain in-terests and role dilemmas. At the same time, in the complex urban setting, the force of corporate primary groups based on

5. cf. Litwak (1960) for the resiliency of extended family relations under the impact of occupational mobility, and Wilensky (1960) for an analysis of new trends of work–family relations.

extended kinship, neighborhood or age has diminished. One consequence has been an intensification of involvement in the nuclear family and its activities. Together, these trends have produced a new, more egalitarian kind of marital relationship. Women and men have access to similar educational, economic and associated opportunities. Diffusion of role definitions has not only permitted wives to take on many roles traditionally reserved for men, but also made it possible for men to perform and gain gratification from certain traditionally feminine activities. Zweig (1961) notes, in his observations on changing work–family relations among British workers, that even in this relatively conservative segment of British society men are increasingly engaged in hitherto unthinkable activities, like changing baby's diapers.[6] Indeed, one might say that a 'second revolution' in marital relations is going on, and that it is intimately associated with the attempt to work out new solutions to the issues of occupational and household role definitions. This second revolution is no longer focused, as the first one was, on the issue of giving women access to the traditional masculine occupational privileges, but on re-allocating familial and occupational roles on the basis of skills and interests, using sex-correlated elements where appropriate, but not necessarily according to conventional constraints.[7]

The relative *salience* of work and family life varies according to the type of work involved. At one extreme are the professions, whose historical model, that of the clergyman with his divine 'calling', is still preserved in the celibate Roman Catholic priesthood. The roles of artist, statesman, athlete and scientist, like those of doctor, lawyer and clergyman, illustrate the higher levels of commitment to work expected in the professions. Oeser and Hammond (1954), who gave systematic attention to the salience or 'potency' of work in the individual's life space, found in Australia that considerations of work had much greater weight

6. Some of the forthcoming reports by Marc Fried and his colleagues dissect the variations in family structure associated with this process in an urban working-class neighborhood. Cf., for example, Fried and Fitzgerald (no date).

7. Alice Rossi's (1964) position is based on a sophisticated view of the possibilities for reciprocal realignment in marital roles at different points in the life cycle. An articulate specimen of the phenomenon itself is Robert Varga (1965).

among middle-class than among working-class individuals. Numerous other findings and observations about the relation between attitude toward work and class position lead to similar conclusions.

The public image of professional work tends to assume that family requirements are inherently incompatible with those of work. For instance, when the former British cabinet minister, Maudling, was being considered in 1963 as a possible successor to Macmillan, it was said that he was too happily married to make a good Prime Minister.[8] The British railway engineer, Brunel, once said (for professionals generally), 'My work is my only true wife' (Rolt, 1961). This is not to say that active professional life is *necessarily* incompatible with a happy marriage, only that sources of potential conflict increase. New potentialities for deepening the complementary basis of the marriage also arise, as reflected in the Shavian image of the Webbs ('two typewriters beating as one'), or in the public image of the Franklin Roosevelts.

Thus, work assumes its maximal personal meaning for individuals when the occupational role is highly individualized, notably among the professions. Other high-status occupations, e.g. executives in large corporations, demand a similar primacy of commitment, with perhaps somewhat less scope for individualized participation than the 'free' professions, but with other incentives for a high degree of involvement. Where especially gratifying incentives do not exist, as in the lower-status occupations, work has less salience, or it may take on negative significance, with different kinds of repercussions on family life.

While relative salience is probably the single most important factor in the patterns individuals develop to integrate work with familial role demands, others exist that are less closely related to occupational prestige. Thus, the requirement that an individual frequently relocate his residence may pertain to a migrant laborer or to a space-age technologist; extensive traveling may be expected of a hobo, a salesman or a physician; job insecurity may threaten an unskilled laborer or a highly specialized technician whose speciality is becoming obsolescent; competitiveness may characterize a Madison Avenue advertising firm, a criminal gang or an academic department. All of these occupational charac-

8. *Observer*, June 1963.

teristics affect familial role-relationships, and we shall consider a few of them illustratively in the context of 'isomorphism' between work and family life.

A number of statements in the literature support the impression that a general tendency toward isomorphism, or similarity of behavior patterning, exists between the major life spheres. Oeser and Hammond state the proposition in a psychological framework: 'The breadwinner's pattern of relations in both regions (work and family) is likely to have much the same form because in both cases his behavior will depend upon his beliefs and expectations about his "self" and others' (1954, p. 238). Inkeles (1964) argues from a social structural vantage point that individuals who are treated with dignity at work will tend to treat their families with dignity, i.e. isomorphically. Raymond Smith (1956) has evidence indicating that the structured instabilities of West Indian family life constitute a response to the instabilities of the male occupational situation. Robert Rapoport and Laumann (in press) interpret their finding that conjugal decision-making among the more science-oriented technologists is organized on a 'joint' basis more often than it is among the 'hardware' types partly in terms of the diffusion of universalistic norms associated with the life of science. Miller and Swanson (1958) concentrating on socialization, observe that entrepreneurially employed individuals encourage individualistic behavior in their child-rearing practices, and Aberle and Naegele (1952) observe in a middle-class suburb that fathers tend to evaluate their children's behavior in terms of the aggressiveness and competitiveness expected in the occupational world, despite their view that the two spheres should be kept quite distinct from one another.

On the other hand, tendencies toward heteromorphism have also been observed. For those in occupations that induce boredom or alienation C. Wright Mills characterized the situation as follows: 'Each day men sell little pieces of themselves in order to try to buy them back each night and weekend with the coin of fun' (Cotgrove and Parker, 1963, p. 16). Dubin (1956) suggests that the kind of compensatory tendency characteristic of the factory situation, in which mechanization has robbed the manual worker of the sense of ego-involvement that craftsmen formerly found in work, has led workers to develop an interest in domestic activities.

It is not only boring or alienating situations that stimulate heteromorphic complementarities, however. Dennis, Henriques and Slaughter (1956) describe an English coal-mining village in which the men are deeply involved in their work and have considerable autonomy on the job. The danger of the underground work encourages a propensity for mutual protection, taking the form of cooperation in crises, strong union organization and intense peer-group camaraderie during weekend 'pub crawls'. Miners expect their wives to feed them and look after them when they are out of the tense mine situation, but to be as undemanding as possible. Hence, the family structure emphasizes the subservience of the wife and the segregation of most of the spouses' activities, particularly in leisure hours, during which the men affirm their solidarity and seek release from the tensions of work.

The same tendency toward heteromorphism also occurs when the occupational role does not involve interpersonal relations reproduceable in other spheres – e.g., deep-sea divers, astronauts, racing-car drivers – and in other occupations, reproducing the occupational role at home is possible but grossly unconventional. The film *Cheaper by the Dozen* caricatured an industrial time-study man who organized his family according to his own prescriptions for the workplace. Presumably there are soldiers who organize their families like platoons, computer technicians who program their families as they do their machines, and boxers who use physical violence at home. The evidence suggests, however, that complementarity is often practiced, and the general human tendency is to segregate spheres of involvement and behave differently according to context.[9] And in situations where alienation from work is accompanied by a search for compensatory gratifications, the tendency toward heteromorphism is strengthened.

In general, the issues associated with isomorphism between work and family patterns are not satisfactorily conceptualized in the literature. A number of variables, properly separated for analytic handling, are dealt with as though similar issues of

9. Parsons and Bales have argued that the tendency is nearly universal for families to assign 'instrumental' activities to men and 'affective' activities to women. To the extent that the husband's role is confined to articulating the family with the outside world of work, in which the instrumental mode is dominant, and the wife's to managing behavior within the family, the tendency is toward heteromorphic complementarity.

psycho-dynamics and social-system functioning were involved, but individualism–collectivism, stability–instability, dignity–degradation, involvement–alienation, the fit between values and behavior, and other polarities are probably differently arrayed under different circumstances. For example, alienation from work might be associated in one situation with an increase in domesticity while in another it might be associated with withdrawal or discord in marital relations and increased peer-group activities. Intervening variables, such as cultural norms for marital roles, competitiveness in the work situation, and so on must be taken into account to improve the utility of the isomorphism concept.[10]

Finally, *life cycle stage* must be considered in generalizing about work–family relations. When two university students, both majoring in electrical engineering, marry while at college, role differentiation in their early marriage stage is likely to be minimal. Following the birth of their first child, the role differentiation is likely to increase, particularly if the husband is establishing himself in a new job or a course of graduate studies critical for his career (Robert Rapoport, Laumann and Ferdinand, in press). The salience of the work for the man in this stage is very high, while his wife's involvement is likely to be diverted into familial roles, at least temporarily. But this degree of salience is not lifelong, in most cases. At retirement, for example, the man must detach himself from the specific occupational involvements that hitherto engaged him and reapportion his involvements and interests.[11]

Another life-cycle phenomenon to consider is the fact that each sphere, work and family, has its own sequence of stages, and that critical role transitions may be scheduled as between the two spheres. To some extent timing the critical transition points is within the control of individuals, though traditionally, in Western society, it has been considered appropriate to deal with one's early, identity-establishing occupational transitions before

10. Marc Fried (in press) distinguishes between 'role-determined' and 'goal-determined' behavior patternings, a distinction useful in understanding the process of change and emergence of new structures where different segments of life are subjected to different kinds of influence.

11. For a good statement of the general developmental framework, see Rodgers (1964).

marriage. Until recently, professionals who deferred occupational entry longest married later than other occupational groups (Robert Rapoport, 1964). This supports the theory that the critical issues around identity (which, for many men and women, are closely tied up with occupation) naturally precede critical issues associated with psycho-social intimacy (Erikson, 1959). A similar view has been supported in several more overtly moral arguments. To show that marriage of college students should be discouraged, for example, early marriage has been said to interfere with studies, to exploit the wife, to reflect an immature choice that will produce later incompatibility, and so on. Research on the recent increase in marriages among college students, however, has indicated that the early marriers tend to be more mature, to be better academic performers, and to display fewer indications of marital disruption, than the students who were single or married after graduating from college (Robert Rapoport, Laumann and Ferdinand, in press).[12] The outcome of such marriages probably depends on the partners' ability to handle the situations confronting them at this point in their respective life cycles, rather than on the order in which they schedule the events. Obviously, more complex notions of identity and intimacy are necessary than those derived from a simple assignment of one or another institution to one or another psychological crisis. The framework we present here is one approach to the solution of such problems.

The task framework

The central question here has to do with the principles that govern choice among the many possible arrangements for dealing with the issues of the salience of work, isomorphism of work–family relations, scheduling transitions in the life cycle, and the form and degree of integration between work and family life generally. We believe that it is useful to concentrate on 'critical' points of major role transition, when the structural elements of both personality and social system are in a somewhat 'fluid' state and new structures are in the process of being established. These structures,

12. Medalia points to some of the problems that prevent general recognition of positive elements in the situation. The picture may differ somewhat for secondary schools. Cf. Burchinal (1960) and Moss (1964).

according to our view, are the resultants not simply of traditional socio-cultural prescriptions or of personal needs, but of the complex interplay among these in a given field of forces. The field of forces varies among different individuals at different points in their lives. We propose the variable 'task accomplishment' to encompass the resultant effect of elements on all levels that individuals mobilize to deal with new situations. We conceive each status-transition situation as presenting a specific complex of *tasks*, from which the work–family structure emerges.

The changes attendant on critical status transitions – marriage, death, adolescence, and so on – have long been emphasized in both sociological and psychological theory. In his classical work, Van Gennep (1960) highlighted the very wide prevalence of 'rites of passage', or ceremonies that help individuals pass over a threshold, leaving one form of social participation to enter a new one. The social relevance of these rituals has recently been elaborated further by Gluckman (1962) and other British anthropologists. The personal functions of the ritual activity associated with these transitions may be considered both restitutive – as in Freud's notion of the 'work of mourning' – and defensive against the anxiety engendered by leaving the familiar and security-giving conditions of the preceding stage and facing the threats and challenges of new situations (cf. Menzies, 1960).

Earlier writers in the field of family research saw marriage as an important transition, but they aimed to relate antecedent factors to subsequent marital success or failure.[13] Our interest is in understanding marriage as a transition process, a process more or less by-passed in earlier analysis.[14] By seeking to understand the relation between critical task accomplishment and outcome, we stress the couple's adaptability in shaping whatever resources

13. e.g. the classic work of Burgess and Wallin (1953).

14. Some of the recent work of Reuben Hill and his colleagues reflects an orientation similar in many respects to ours. For their use of the task concept see, for example, Duvall and Hill (1945), and Duvall (1962). The work of Erikson (1959), Lindemann (1944) and Caplan (1961, 1964) has been most directly relevant to ours. The concept of fluidity and the potentialities at this point for intervention are examined by Gerald Caplan (1960). Personality growth potentials in such experiences have been emphasized by psychologists like Robert White, Robert J. Havighurst, Nevitt Sanford and Abraham Maslow.

they brought to the marriage in their new situation (in contrast to an orientation emphasizing the determinacy of prior factors). Couples enter marriage with certain advantages or handicaps and cope with the tasks of making the transition with varying degrees of effectiveness or creativity. In the end, their success is determined by their skill in coping with these tasks, rather than being immutably set by the factors constituting obstacles for them at the point of transition.

Despite the fact that previously defined conventional patterns for coping with the major life-cycle transitions are no longer adequate in a heterogeneous and rapidly changing society, we expect to find that individuals combine personal and social structural elements to form *patterns* of task accomplishment.[15] In the quest for these emergent patterns of behavior, our central question is: Under what conditions is task accomplishment maximally functional? That is, when is it consistent with the individual's established personality needs, with the needs and expectations of others whose roles are reciprocal with his in this particular sphere of behavior, and with requirements in other spheres of life?

Factors allowing or inhibiting a maximally functional resolution include personality, early experience and socio-cultural elements, as well as a situational factor presenting, on the one hand, intrinsic tasks to be faced and adapted to, and, on the other hand, uncertainties due to the absence of adequate behavioral models. The lack of prior models is stressful, but it also provides new opportunities for creativity. The potentials are further enhanced by the fact that at critical role transitions not only do new situations arise, but new persons – wives, colleagues, etc. – enter in reciprocal roles, and these people are likely to be working at new forms of adaptation too. The adaptive solutions to tasks presented at these times may either confirm prior patterns, further crystallizing them in the personalities and behavior of the individuals concerned, or encourage growth and development.

15. The term 'task' may seem to imply some notion of hard work and an unpleasant or chorelike quality. This is not what is meant. The process of task accomplishment may be automatic, pleasurable or painful, depending on the situations and persons involved. By 'task' we mean only that issues must be joined and the necessary energy expended to shift orientation and behavior patterns as the expectations encountered in the new status require.

But in either case we assume that the period of heightened susceptibility is relatively brief; new patterns are crystallized within a few weeks after the critical transition period of intensive involvements.[16]

Simultaneous status transitions: graduation and marriage

When two critical transitions in the life cycle must be accomplished simultaneously, as, for example, when an individual marries at about the same time that he graduates from college, each behavioral structure is in a condition of maximum fluidity; at this point they have the greatest mutual influence. To investigate this influence, we studied couples who were undergoing these transitions simultaneously, and our preliminary findings illustrate the postulated utility of the task framework. In other words, we have studied the process of work–family interaction when a transition point in the occupational sphere – graduation – coincides with a transition in the family sphere – marriage – for a specific type of occupation, namely the professional engineer.

Occupations vary tremendously in the degree to which choices made have enduring, and to some extent irrevocable, consequences. Some occupations are entered casually with little intention on the part of incumbents to form a life-long commitment, while others involve the expectation of life-long commitment once the occupation is entered. Some are entered early, some later, after various stages of prior experience or preparation. Some involve an expected progression of stages of advancement toward a remote peak position, while others are relatively undifferentiated, the individual expecting simply to 'hold a job' until death or retirement.[17] The professional career, with its preparatory stages prior to formal entry, its high degree of expected commitment, and its anticipated sequence of stages of advancement, bears the greatest structural and psychological resemblance to the family, and for this reason we chose in the first instance to examine professional engineers.

16. Psychiatrists interested in preventive intervention at points of maximal fluidity have judged that the period of effective flux, or 'crisis', tends to be about two months: see Lindemann (1944) and Caplan (1960).

17. We owe thanks to David Riesman for some of these ideas, generated in informal discussion, and to Everett C. Hughes (1958).

Table 1 Critical Transition Tasks for Early Career and Family

	Phase 1 Career: training	Family: engagement*
Personal tasks	1. Accomplishing the tasks set by the curriculum at a satisfactory level of proficiency. 2. Paying the financial costs of training. 3. Deferring gratifications that require an income and a full occupational role, for whatever time the training period takes.	1. Accepting the emotional responsibilities of marriage. 2. Accepting the material responsibilities of marriage. 3. Developing a pattern of gratification compatible with the partner's expectations and needs.
Interpersonal tasks	1 Accepting the teacher's authority. 2. Working out satisfactory arrangements to meet other obligations (e.g. to parents). 3. Competing with peers in the same training situation.	1. Establishing an identity as a couple. 2. Developing a mutually satisfactory sexual adjustment for the engagement period. 3. Developing a mutually satisfactory orientation to family planning. 4. Establishing a mutually satisfactory mode of communication. 5. Establishing satisfactory relations with others. 6. Developing a mutually satisfactory work pattern. 7. Developing a mutually satisfactory leisure pattern.

	8. Developing a mutually satisfactory plan for the wedding and early marriage.
	9. Establishing a mutually satisfactory decision-making pattern.

	Phase II *Career: choice of career line*	*Family: honeymoon*
Personal tasks	1. Gathering information about available alternatives.	1. Learning to participate in an intimate sexual relationship.
	2. Deciding among actual offers.	2. Learning to live in close association with the spouse.
Interpersonal tasks	1. Undergoing job interviews in such a manner as to satisfy the prospective employers that one is technically competent.	1. Developing mutually satisfactory sexual relations.
	2. Undergoing interviews in such a manner as to satisfy prospective employers that one is personally acceptable.	2. Developing a mutually satisfactory shared experience as a basis for the later marital relationship

*Rhona Rapoport (1964); Rhona Rapoport and Robert Rapoport (1964).

Table 1 continued

	Phase III	
	Career: early establishment	Family: early marriage
Personal tasks	1. Developing a rhythm of life geared to the world of work.	1. Helping to establish the home base.
	2. Adapting one's performance to the multiple criteria for good job performance, to which the skills learned in the training phase must be accommodated.	2. Accommodating daily living patterns to the marital situation.
		3. Developing further sexual competence.
		4. Developing an appropriate commitment to the marriage.
	3. Broadening the range of tasks dealt with in the course of one's work to suit the expectations of the work role.	5. Developing a self-concept congruent with one's marital role.
	4. Developing gratifying leisure activities.	
	5. Developing a self-image consistent with new status.	
Interpersonal tasks	1. Accommodating oneself to relations with peers on the job.	1. Cooperating with spouse to set up the home base.
	2. Accommodating oneself to the authority structure of the job.	2. Developing a mutually satisfactory network of external relations.
	3. Developing commitment to work and loyalty to the organization and to one's professional reference groups.	3. Developing an internal organization for managing domestic routines.
		4. Developing mutual esteem and a positive orientation to the marriage.

Our restriction to a single stage in the life cycle and to a single occupational type simplifies our analysis as well as providing symmetry, but another restriction reduces symmetry in the interest of concentrating on the more prevalent situation. Our sample consists of couples in which the husband was entering a professional career, while the women are distributed randomly in this regard.

From exploratory interviews in depth with a dozen couples undergoing the twin transitions, we have developed an initial formulation of tasks inherent in these status transitions. For convenience of presentation we have listed them together in parallel fashion, but they do not necessarily coincide in this timing and sequence in all situations (see Table 1). In each sphere, we distinguish personal tasks, or those involving an individual's personality, from interpersonal tasks that involve his marital partner or his colleagues at work. The three phases are more clearly indicated in our data on the marriage transition (where marriage, honeymoon and establishment of a neo-local residence are institutionalized) than for the career, where there are wider ranges of variation.

In each of these phases, the patterns set up in one sphere must be accommodated in some degree to the requirements of the other sphere. Thus, during the early marriage phase, family-building tasks must proceed in the context of some effort to establish or maintain an economic base for the family. For a majority, this means the husband's job, though it may also involve the wife. Relatively few couples have no need to work at all. Similarly, in the early career-establishment phase, married individuals must to some degree accommodate the demands of the work situation to domestic life. Patterns of accommodating work to family needs and developing a family life in the context of a career are the resultants of the task-accomplishment process with which we are now concerned.

A survey of 1954 graduates of three technical universities indicates that the wife's religion is related to career-line choices.[18]

18. This survey, reported in Robert Rapoport and Laumann (in press) was conducted by mailing career questionnaires to all 1954 graduates of three technical universities representing a spectrum of technological types, in the northeastern region of the U.S. The case presented here was drawn from a sample of recent graduates of the same institutions.

The graduate's own religion is not significantly correlated with mobility, but those with Catholic or Jewish wives were less likely to move about geographically. Graduates with Catholic wives had less intense a general professional orientation, even on a local basis; within the profession such individuals are found more frequently in the lower technical or managerial jobs. The lower-level career type is associated with a conventional family structure in which the division of labor is based on highly differentiated sex roles rather than on the more 'joint' organization of shared activities and decision-making characteristic of graduates who express a stronger commitment to professional values and a greater tendency to seek science-oriented (research or academic) positions.

The following specimen case from our intensive interview series involves the socio-cultural features just described, but the outcome deviates from the modal one in our sample. Not only does it illustrate relations among patterns of career, marital and individual functioning, but it shows how the 'task' framework permits us to explain a wider range of variant patterns.

Task accomplishment as an independent variable in a variant case

Rosalie was the only child in an urban Jewish family possessing considerable wealth and many cultural interests. Relations within her family of orientation, however, were somewhat strained, and one of her own goals was to achieve a warm and happy family life. Elmer, on the other hand, grew up in a large, very warm and tight-knit small-town Protestant family and, from childhood, was a 'typical' American boy in his interests. He was athletic, loved to tinker with automobiles, considered being a mechanic but in view of his aptitude responded to the scholarships that enabled him to attend a technical university.

During Elmer's career in the university, he 'shopped around' in various courses and programs, but his grades and summer job experiences in his first two years confirmed his basically 'hardware' orientation to technological studies. He performed at an 'average' level of academic accomplishment, a level made relatively easy for him by his natural aptitudes. The reason he gave for not doing better was that he didn't feel that the commitment required to get top grades was worth it in terms of his other values: an easier pace of life and maintenance of social relationships including dating relationships. He was confident that he would do well as an engineer without taxing himself unduly during his university years, that he was learning enough to be conversant with the relevant fields, and that he could qualify for a wide range of technical jobs in his field, increasing his specialized knowledge on his own when he found out what a specific job required. At the university, Elmer's professors were aware that he was meeting the requirements of the program relatively easily, but not making the extra effort needed for outstanding performance. He got on well with his peers and belonged to a fraternity. Here again, others felt that he took life relatively easily, doing enough to get through comfortably but not placing himself under undue strain. His summer job experiences confirmed his technical skills, and he knew by the end of the second summer that he could already perform many of the role requirements of professional engineers, but that his problem would be to find a career line that would do more than provide a source of income. He did not seek more challenging professional interests, but rather greater personal meaning in his extra-professional activities. After he became engaged to Rosalie, who was a student in a neighboring university, he began to participate in the more cosmopolitan and humanistic world of her interests.

Rosalie, a student of social work, was intensely preoccupied with the need to find socially significant meaning in her life and activities. She was dedicated to various welfare interests and to such causes as the civil liberties movement. While she did not value the accumulation of money as a goal in itself, she had wide-ranging interests and would eventually require a fairly high living standard. Unlike the modal Jewish wife in our survey, however, she was familistic without being 'local'. She was willing to go anywhere so long as there was a chance for her to do good works.

During their engagement, Elmer and Rosalie discussed various issues of family life and actually rehearsed possible future joint involvements when Elmer took summer jobs associated with social work agencies. He applied some of his technical skills to automobile maintenance and various odd jobs, while she worked at apprentice social-work tasks. He experienced gratification not only from the technical application of his skills, but from doing something worthwhile, and jointly with Rosalie. He began to think of career possibilities that would cultivate the rewards he experienced in this type of situation. Thus, these summer experiences, followed through in his junior and senior years at the university, gave Elmer and Rosalie a basis for working out a possible pattern of life together and at the same time allowed him to reconsider his own career plans, the issues of which were becoming acute as his graduation approached. During their engagement, they frequently visited each other's families and worked out satisfactory relations all around, resolving such issues as religious participation and so on.

By the time of graduation, when the critical issues of job choice were at hand, Rosalie and Elmer had worked out together the following plan. He would take a job in the airplane company that had given him scholarships throughout his educational career. Although he was not under pressure to repay this as a debt, he did feel a moral obligation he wished to discharge, 'all other things being equal'. The fact that they had a plant nearby would allow her to finish her training and together they could continue to consolidate their position as a family and to visit both families of orientation. His prospective job was neither too abstract for his training nor too 'purely hardware' to interest him. He was sure that the job would satisfy many of his technical requirements, which he had spelled out quite explicitly to himself and explored in detail with company representatives and through company visits, as well as his financial requirements. He was less certain, however, that it would satisfy his growing interest in doing something worthwhile for humanity and in working with people over problems with which they personally were concerned.

In discussing future phases of their work-family development, Elmer and Rosalie planned to consider mutually acceptable alternatives. They felt that they would be less interested in living locally, as time went on, but would go wherever the best situation, that is, a satisfactory job for Elmer, was available; welfare work was more or less universally available for her. From Elmer's point of view, however, the enthusiasm that she had generated for good causes made him more interested in finding something in which they could both participate. He mentioned as one alternative a career in teaching. Perhaps they would put in a period with the Peace Corps.

Their wedding took place in his home town and church. Afterwards, their honeymoon was assisted financially by her parents. Their physical intimacy, which was satisfactory for both, seemed to be cemented by the idealistic goals that they re-emphasized as binding them together and overriding their differences in background. On the job he was popular with colleagues and considered intelligent and competent by his employers. Though only average at the university, his performance was more than adequate in the industrial setting, and he was considered stable professional material for an orderly advance through technical and perhaps managerial promotion within the firm.

Elmer missed a feeling of fulfillment in this kind of work, however, and as he had half expected prior to entering the job, he began actively to entertain the idea of changing his career line. At our last contact with them, they had decided to make joint application to the Peace Corps.

Following this experience, he resolved to enter teaching, probably in secondary-school science. He and Rosalie were planning a family life in which both would work, and in which the pursuit of their interests and values would prevail over attachments to locality and extended family contacts.

In Phase I, both Elmer and Rosalie were involved in career as well as engagement tasks. Each accomplished satisfactorily the tasks set by the curriculum; neither had difficulties with the financial task. They both pursued their career training without pressure and attained much personal gratification from their courtship; they accepted university requirements and competed with their peers while maintaining good interpersonal relations, and both sustained satisfactory relations with their families. During their engagement, each developed a responsible economic orientation and an appropriate pattern, in terms of each other's norms, of gratification in an intense emotional relationship. Their family-planning and communications patterns were mutually satisfactory, and they established satisfactory relations with others, including their parental families; they planned successfully for the wedding and its immediate aftermath.

In his relations with Rosalie at this time, Elmer's values and personality underwent considerable development. His previously covert conflict between a conventional technical career and a more humanistic one became overt. In choosing his first job, he had a number of attractive options; he chose to remain with the firm that had financed his training. Although this did not satisfy his humanistic goals it did offer the characteristics he desired in a technical job.

In the job he performed satisfactorily but was personally dissatisfied because his work activities did not further his humanistic goals. As his wife entered the critical transition of graduation, a new family–work decision was precipitated, involving the resolution of conflicts between work and family life as well as his intrapersonal conflict.

This case indicates how the task-accomplishment framework supplements the traditional predictive analysis, relating antecedent variables like religion, social class, personality and value orientations to the outcome. We would hold that even if it were possible to introduce a wide range of other independent variables with known effects the task-accomplishment framework would still provide an important set of intervening variables, showing how the antecedent variables are interrelated in the specific situation of transition. For example, even if we could measure the personality dispositions of Elmer and Rosalie, to show that she was less committed to her parental family and values than the modal Jewish wife in our culture and that he was more sensitive to human problems than the modal engineer, several outcomes would still be possible. For example, Rosalie and Elmer could have been expected to settle close to his family, under which circumstances Rosalie might have used his family as a substitute basis for realizing the culturally valued familial ties that had been unsatisfactory in her own particularly family background. Elmer might then have derived sufficient gratification of his humanistic interests through her work, through his leisure activities, or through management or personnel work. Other possibilities include those actually mentioned, e.g. the Peace Corps or teaching, new lines of endeavor that were of interest to both.

By closely analysing their patterns of coping with status transitions, we have learned just how this couple dealt with their divergent backgrounds and values so as to find mutually acceptable solutions. The patterns of task accomplishment themselves helped to determine the outcome. For example, their efforts to share each other's interests as much as possible led to his taking a summer job in her sphere of interest rather than in the usual line of engineering summer jobs, an experience that contributed to a change in his conception of his capacities and career alternatives.

Conclusion

At critical transition points in work and family role systems, patterns of task accomplishment in one sphere affect those in the other. While the inter-system influence is probably maximal when individuals are undergoing transitions in both simultaneously, all points of status transition necessarily involve a process of readjustment, potentially affecting not only the specific behavioral spheres, but others linked to it.

When transitions occur simultaneously in two spheres, conflicts and stresses are not necessarily multiplied. The concurrence of the challenges presented by the two sets of tasks may, under some circumstances, have mutually beneficial consequences, and coping with one set of challenges does not necessarily detract from performance on others. Mobilization of latent types and levels of involvement, perhaps hitherto impossible for the individual in question, may improve his capacity to make choices and to commit himself to a challenging performance level, rather than making him perform one set of tasks at the expense of the other. Task accomplishment in conformity to normative patterns for the group to which the individual belongs does not necessarily entail good psychological functioning, nor does task accomplishment in a variant pattern necessarily entail stressful consequences.

The problem of apportioning ego involvements, or 'sub-identities' (Kahn and French, 1962), is a vital one in contemporary society. On the one hand, a great variety of possible patterns are available, due to rapid social change and to the complexity of urban life. On the other hand, the traditional emphasis is so much on achievement, productivity, competence and similar values that men find it difficult to look elsewhere for self-fulfillment. But with the increase in shared activities, the family can play a new role in relation to the world of work. Family and work are no longer subject to a single over-arching set of role prescriptions in an integrated cultural whole, nor are family functions as residual as they are when work is either over-valued or alienative, as it was in the era following the industrial revolution. Individuals now have a wider range of possibilities to consider in choosing both work and spouse, and greater freedom in organizing family life in relation to job requirements. Social prescriptions set broad limits of acceptability but family structure, both internally and in relation to work, is increasingly determined by the individuals' personality needs, their interpersonal 'fit' and, as a derivative of these dimensions, their capacity to cope with the tasks specific to each phase of family life. Similarly, the career options open to individuals, particularly in the high-demand professions, are numerous enough to permit each person to develop a pattern of work participation according to his personality needs, his relations with others, and his capacity to cope with the tasks of career development at each phase. Fitting participation patterns in work and family together, like coping with the tasks posed within each sphere, is partly a matter of an individual style that emerges as the individuals meet each successive situation, rather than the outcome of conformity to or deviance from a pre-existing normative pattern.

References

ABERLE, D. F., and NAEGELE, K. D. (1952), 'Middle-class fathers' occupational role and attitudes toward children', *American Journal of Orthopsychiatry*, vol. 22, pp. 366–78.

ANGELL, R. (1936), *The Family Encounters the Depression*, Scribner.

BURCHINAL, L. G. (1960), 'Research on young marriages: implications for family life education', *Family Life Coordinator*, vol. 8, pp. 6–24.

BURGESS, E., and WALLIN, P. (1953), *Engagement and Marriage*, Lippincott.

CAPLAN, G. (1960), 'Patterns of parental response to the crisis of premature birth: a preliminary approach to modifying mental health outcome', *Psychiatry*, vol. 23, pp. 365–74.

CAPLAN, G. (1961), *An Approach to Community Mental Health*, Grune & Stratton.

CAPLAN, G. (1964), *Principles of Preventive Psychiatry*, Basic Books.

CAPLOW, T. (1954), 'Occupation and family', in *The Sociology of Work*, University of Minnesota Press.

COTGROVE, S., and PARKER, S. (1963), 'Work and non-work', *New Society*, vol. 1, pp. 18–19.

CURLE, A. (1949), 'Incentives to work: an anthropological appraisal', *Human Relations*, vol. 2, pp. 41–7.

DENNIS, N., HENRIQUES, F., and SLAUGHTER, C. (1956), *Coal is Our Life*, Eyre & Spottiswoode.

DUBIN, R. (1956), 'Industrial workers' worlds', *Social Problems*, vol. 3, pp. 131–42.

DUVALL, E. (1962), *Family Development*, Lippincott.

DUVALL, E., and HILL, R. (1945), *When You Marry*, Heath.

ERIKSON, E. (1959), *Identity and the Life Cycle*, International Universities Press.

FIRTH, R. (1938), *Human Types*, Nelson.

FRIED, M. (in press), 'Social problems and psychopathology', G.A.P. Symposium no. 10.

FRIED, M., and FITZGERALD, E. (no date), 'Structure in marital role relationships: role interaction and social class variations', Research Document no. 26, Center for Community Studies, Boston.

GLUCKMAN, M. (ed.) (1962), *Essays on the Ritual of Social Relations*, Manchester University Press.

GOODE, W. J. (1963), *World Revolution and Family Patterns*, Free Press.

GOODE, W. J. (1964), *The Family*, Prentice-Hall.

HUGHES, E. C. (1958), *Men and their Work*, Free Press.

INKELES, A. (1964), Paper delivered before the Society for Applied Anthropology, San Juan, Puerto Rico, Spring.

KAHN, R. L., and FRENCH, R. P. (1962), 'A programmatic approach to studying the industrial environment and mental health', *Journal of Social Issues*, vol. 17, pp. 1–47.

LINDEMANN, E. (1944), 'Symptomatology and management of acute grief', *American Journal of Psychiatry*, vol. 101, pp. 141–8.

LITWAK, E. (1960), 'Occupational mobility and extended family cohesion', *American Sociological Review*, vol. 25, pp. 9–21.

MEDALIA, N. (n.d.), 'Explaining the increase in college student marriage: some observations on an institutionalization crisis', unpublished paper.

MENZIES, I. (1960), 'A case study in the functioning of social systems as a defense against anxiety', *Human Relations*, vol. 13, pp. 95–122. [Reprinted as Tavistock Pamphlet no. 3, 1961.]

MILLER, D., and SWANSON, G. (1958), *The Changing American Parent*, Wiley.

MOSS, J. (1964), 'Teenage marriage: cross-national trends and sociological factors in the decision of when to marry', *Acta Sociologica*, vol. 8, pp. 98–117.

OESER, O. A., and HAMMOND, S. B. (eds.) (1954), *Social Structure and Personality in a City*, Routledge & Kegan Paul.

RAPOPORT, RHONA (1963), 'Normal crisis, family structure and mental health', *Family Process*, vol. 2, pp. 68–80.

RAPOPORT, RHONA (1964), 'The transition from engagement to marriage', *Acta Sociologica*, vol. 8, pp. 36–55.

RAPOPORT, RHONA, and RAPOPORT, ROBERT (1964), 'New light on the honeymoon', *Human Relations*, vol. 17, pp. 33–56.

RAPOPORT, ROBERT (1964), 'The male's occupation in relation to his decision to marry', *Acta Sociologica*, vol. 8, pp. 68–82.

RAPOPORT, ROBERT, and LAUMANN, E. O. (in press), 'Technologists in mid-career: factors affecting patterns of ten-year out engineers and scientists from three universities', in Robert Rapoport (ed.), *The Impact of Space Efforts on Communities and Selected Groups*, American Academy of Arts and Sciences, Committee on Space.

RAPOPORT, Robert, LAUMANN, E. O., and FERDINAND, T. (in press), 'The power of choice: critical career decisions of senior technologists, 1964', in Robert Rapoport (ed.), *The Impact of Space Efforts on Communities and Selected Groups*, American Academy of Arts and Sciences, Committee on Space.

RODGERS, R. H. (1964), 'Toward a theory of family development', *Journal of Marriage and the Family*, vol. 26, pp. 262–70.

ROLT, L. T. C. (1961), *Isambard Kingdom Brunel*, Longmans; Penguin Books, 1970.

ROSSI, A. (1964), 'A good woman is hard to find', *Transaction*, vol. 2.

SMELSER, N. (1959), *Social Change in the Industrial Revolution*, Routledge & Kegan Paul.

SMITH, R. (1956), *The Negro Family in British Guiana*, Routledge & Kegan Paul.

VAN GENNEP, A. (1960), *The Rites of Passage*, University of Chicago Press.

VARGA, R. (1965), 'Dilemmas of a househusband', *Saturday Review of Literature*, 2 January, p. 100.

WEBER, M. (1947), *The Theory of Social and Economic Organization*, trans. A. M. Henderson and T. Parsons, Hodge.

WHYTE, W. H. (1956), *The Organization Man*, Simon & Schuster; Penguin Books, 1960.

WILENSKY, H. (1960), 'Work, career and social integration', *International Social Science Journal*, vol. 12, pp. 543–60.

ZWEIG, F. (1961), *The Worker in an Affluent Society*, Heinemann.

Part Five Marital Dissolution

This selection from the work of Goode (Reading 21) shows something of the current state of research on this topic. A large number of correlations have been established between individual background variables and above average probabilities of divorce, though we still lack any very satisfactory explanation of many of these correlations. We have made very little progress, however, even at assessing the relative importance of the large number of factors which have been suggested as causing this average level to vary between societies or over time. This largely remains a topic for future research. Professor Goode offers us here an analytical framework within which such analysis could perhaps be conducted.

21 W. J. Goode

A Sociological Perspective on Marital Dissolution

Excerpts from W. J. Goode, 'Family disorganisation', in R. K. Merton and R. A. Nisbet (eds.), *Contemporary Social Problems*, Harcourt, Brace & World, 2nd edn, 1966, pp. 493–522.

Divorce as a part of the family system

The Western reader tends to view divorce as a misfortune or a tragedy, and high divorce rates as evidence that the family system is not working well. This attitude is part of our religious heritage, which was strong enough to make divorce a rare event until the early part of the present century, although various sects in the Protestant Reformation asserted the right to divorce as early as the sixteenth century, and Milton's famous plea for this right was written in the seventeenth century[1]. Our Western bias in favor of romantic love views marriage as based on love, so that divorce means failure.

All marriage systems require that at least two people, with their individual desires, needs and values, live together, and all systems create some tensions and unhappiness. In this basic sense, then, marriage 'causes' divorce, annulment, separation or desertion. But though a social pattern must be able to survive even when many individuals in it are unsatisfied, it will also contain various mechanisms for keeping interpersonal hostilities within certain limits. Some family systems prevent the development of severe marital strains, but offer few solutions if they do develop. Two main patterns of prevention are discernible. One is to *lower the expectations* about what the individual may expect from marriage. For example, the Chinese praised family life as the most important institution, but taught their children that they were not to expect romance or happiness from it. At best, they might achieve contentment or peace.

A second pattern, widespread in pre-industrial societies and also found among the Chinese, is to value the kinship network

1. *The Doctrine and Discipline of Divorce* was first published in 1643.

more than the relation between husband and wife. Elders direct the affairs of the family, arrange the marriages of the young, and intervene in quarrels between husband and wife. The success of the marriage is rated not so much by the intimate emotional harmony of husband and wife as by the contribution of the couple to the lineage or extended kin. Consequently, tensions between husband and wife would be less likely to build up to an unbearable level.

In addition, there are some social patterns in all groups by which marital tensions may be *avoided*. One pattern is considering certain disagreements trivial. For example, individuals in the United States are told that disagreement on the relative value of bowling and bridge is not important. Another pattern is suppressing some irritations. As individuals become adult, they are increasingly forced to control their anger, unless the problem is serious. Still another is training children and adolescents to expect similar things in marriage, so that what one spouse does is in harmony with the demands of the other.

Societies vary in their definitions of what is a *bearable* level of dissension between husband and wife, as well as in their *solutions* for a difficult marriage. It seems likely that public opinion in the United States during the nineteenth century considered bearable a degree of disharmony which modern couples would not tolerate. People took for granted that spouses who no longer loved one another and who found life together distasteful should at least live together in public amity for the sake of their children and of their standing in the community.

As to what should be done about an unsatisfying marriage, even Western countries vary considerably. Spain, Ireland, Italy and Brazil permit only legal separations, which are common in the last two of these four countries. In Chile, marriages are mostly dissolved by annulments (Jacobson, 1959, p. 97). In societies with extended kinship networks, but without divorce as an alternative, husband and wife may continue their daily tasks but confine their contacts to a minimum. In a polygynous society, a man may refuse to spend any time with one of his wives if their relationship is an unhappy one. Under the family systems of Manchu China and Tokugawa Japan, a man could take an additional wife or bring a concubine into his house. In China, a dissatisfied husband might be unable to afford a concubine, but might instead stay away from his home for long periods of time with distant relatives or on business trips – thus, a form of separation.

These devices to avoid trouble, to divert dissension, to train individuals to put up with difficulties or to seek alternative relationships to ease the burden of marriage, show that societies generally do not value divorce highly. In no society, with the possible exception of the Crow, has divorce been treated as an ideal mode of marital behavior. The reasons for this are easily seen. Divorce grows out of dissension but creates additional conflict between both sides of the family lines. Prior marriage agreements are broken, and prior harmonious relationships among in-laws are disrupted. There are problems of custody, child support and remarriage, as will be analysed in more detail later on.

In no society, however, are the mechanisms for avoiding or reducing marital conflict enough to make all couples able to tolerate their marriage. Divorce is, then, one of the safety valves for the inevitable tensions of married life. At present we cannot say why a particular society adopts the pattern of divorce rather than that of separation, or of living together but enlarging the household to take in additional wives, but divorce is clearly a widespread solution for the problems of marital living. Moreover, the alternative solutions that various societies offer are only a variation on the pattern of divorce.

Divorce differs from these variations principally in that it permits remarriage to both partners. In societies without divorce, ordinarily only the man can enter a new union, even if it is not entirely a legal one. Thus, in India, a man might take an additional wife or, in China or Japan, a concubine, but no such possibility was open to the woman who was dissatisfied with her marriage. In a polygynous society, a man might marry additional wives in order to have a tolerable marital life, but the woman whom he disliked was not permitted additional husbands. In Western nations where separation is permitted, but not divorce, the attitudes opposing a wife's entering into an unsanctioned public union are very strong, but the husband is usually permitted to have a mistress outside his household.

It is not correct to speak of divorce as a more extreme solution than some of the other patterns already described. Whether divorce creates more unhappiness, for example, than the introduction of a concubine into the household, is unknown. Whether it is more extreme to divorce or to bear the misery of an unhappy marriage is not measurable, and in any event is partly a matter of personal or social evaluation. [. . .]

Countries with high divorce rates

The United States has the highest divorce rate among Western nations. Nevertheless, various countries in the past have had higher rates than the United States; e.g. Israel (1935–44), Egypt (1935–54), Japan (1887–1919), Algeria (1887–1940). It is perhaps useful to look at some of these briefly in order to understand better the relationship between divorce and the family system. In the following table (Table 1) various divorce rates are presented for comparison.

Westerners are likely to think of Japan as having a stable society. It is therefore instructive to consider that in 1887 there were 320 divorces per 1000 marriages and that this level of marital instability continued until the late 1890s, when certain changes in the marriage law were made. Indeed, not until the 1920s did Japan's divorce rate begin to fall below that of the United States, the present rate being considerably lower. Yet there is no evidence to suggest that the higher degree of marital instability in the past has, in any way, undermined the Japanese social structure. [. . .]

Changes in divorce rates as indices of other social changes

Such changes in the rate of divorce in various countries need not indicate that these societies are becoming disorganized. They do provide an index of change within the family system and an index of change in the larger social structure. Clearly, the industrialization under way in most countries does not imply an increase in divorce rates. In Japan, the divorce rate has been dropping for well over half a century, and the recorded drop in the Arab-Algerian rate suggests that other Arab countries may eventually experience a decline as well. By contrast, divorce rates have risen in every western European country where divorce is possible and

Table 1 Divorces per 1000 Marriages in Selected Countries, 1890–1963

Country	Year 1890	1900	1910	1920	1930	1940	1950	1963
U.S.	55·6	75·3	87·4	133·3	173·9	165·3	231·7	258 (1960)
Germany		17·6	29·9	40·7	72·4	125·7	145·8	80 (1962)
England & Wales			12·4	8·0	11·1	16·5	86·1	81 (1962)
Australia		13·6		20·4	41·2	41·6	97·3	91
France	24·3	26·1	46·3	49·4	68·6	80·3	106·9	96 (1962)
Sweden		12·9	18·4	30·5	50·6	65·1	147·7	165 (1961)
Iran						194	211	173 (1960)
Egypt					269 (1935)	273	273	238 (1962)
Japan	335	184	131	100	98	76	100	87 (1961)
Algeria	370 (1897)	352	288	396	286	292	+*	161 (1955)

Sources:

All figures calculated from governmental sources and from *United Nations Demographic Yearbook*, 15th Issue, United Nations, 1963.

*1950 Algerian figures are not used, because in that year over 200,000 marriages from previous years were registered civilly, for the first time, thus reducing the true level of divorce rates. How much this under-registration in previous years inflated the divorce rate is not known. Decennial years are used in the table, but in a few cases the true year is one year off.

A better measure of divorce frequency is the number of divorces per 1000 *existing* marriages, but the latter figure is not often available. The above rate compares marriages in a given year, with divorces occurring to marriages from *previous* years. However, changes from one year to another, or differences among countries, may be seen just as clearly by this procedure.

at a faster *rate* than the increase in the United States. For example the divorce rate in England a generation ago was about 6 per cent and is now 30 per cent that of the United States. In the industrializing areas of sub-Saharan Africa and in Communist China, divorce rates are rising. As noted earlier, the Indian Marriage Act of 1955 extends the privilege of divorce to the entire Indian population, so that the divorce rate is also rising there.

Both of these opposite developments are the result of a change in all these family systems toward an emphasis on the independent conjugal family unit. This new type of system has a relatively high divorce rate, but the rate may be lower than in the system which it replaces. Let us look at this conjugal system briefly.

Under the fully developed conjugal pattern, as in the United States, people have greater freedom of action and the right to choose their own mates. Under industrialization, people can begin their marriages on the basis of the jobs to be had in the new occupations, in factories or offices; they no longer require land in order to make a living. They depend less upon their older relatives, feel fewer obligations to take care of their elders, and, of course, receive less aid from them. Correlatively, the social controls on both sides are less exacting and effective.

This type of family system, characteristic of the West for several generations, therefore requires that husband and wife obtain most of their emotional solace within the small family unit made up of husband, wife and children; the extended kin network no longer serves as a buffer against the outside world. The conjugal family unit carries a heavier emotional burden when it exists independently than when it is a small unit within a larger kin fabric. As a consequence, this unit is relatively fragile. When husband or wife fails to find emotional satisfaction within this unit, there are few other sources of satisfaction and few other bases for common living. The specialization of service in an industrialized economy permits the man to purchase many domestic services if he has no wife, and the woman is increasingly able to support herself, even if she has no property and no husband. For these reasons, the independent conjugal family is not highly stable. On the other hand, where the union was fragile because of the elders, as in Japan, or dependent on the whim of the man, as in Arab countries, the new independence of the young couple, their emotional ties with one another, and the increased bargaining power of the woman may mean somewhat greater stability of the family unit.

A large change in the divorce rate betokens a 'breakdown' of the older system, but the fundamental functions of the family – the reproduction, social placement, maintenance and socialization of the child, and social controls over members of the family – may be as well served as they once were. In addition, the freedom and mobility of this newer system seem to fit better the needs of an industrializing economy. If these systems were truly becoming disorganized, illegitimacy rates would rise. However, in Western countries the data show a slight decline (as also in Japan). Moreover, the percentage of men and women who are willing to take the gamble of marriage has not dropped at all, and there is even a slight rise in some countries. In spite of the many changes ocurring in the family systems and the larger social structures and the changes in the personal fortunes of individuals who do marry, the blanket term 'disorganization' seems not to be applicable.

Fluctuations and trends in United States divorce rates

Divorce rates in the United States have fluctuated a good deal over the past century, but have shown a consistent trend upward. Table 2 presents this trend. [...]

Examination of the long-term trend in United States divorce rates poses the question, 'What are the changes in social structure that have taken place in the last one hundred years, and that have had an effect on the family system and thus on the divorce rate?'

Perhaps the most striking changes have occurred in the general *values* and *norms* relating to divorce. Certainly there has been no acceptance of a philosophy that divorce is good, a thing to be desired, but divorce is no longer viewed as a shameful episode that one must hide from others, or as a sufficient reason for casting a person out of respectable social circles. It is an experience to be regretted, one which commands some sympathy, but it is not viewed as a violation of public decency. Whether the individual sinned or was sinned against, his divorce is generally understood as one possible solution for his family difficulties.

Table 2 Number of United States Divorces per 1000 Existing Marriages, 1860–1956*

Year	Number
1860	1·2
1880	2·2
1900	4·0
1920	7·7
1940	8·7
1956	9·3
1960	258 divorces per 1000 marriage ceremonies†

Sources:
*Jacobson (1959, p. 90). The data from 1920 on contain annulments, and all these data are partly estimated, since not all states are included in the divorce registration system. The earlier rates are, of course, even more open to question than the later.

†Bureau of the Census (1964, p. 64).

No public opinion surveys of this change of attitudes during the last half of the nineteenth century were made, but newspaper debates, the novelist's increasing use of divorce as a solution for bad marriages, and congressional debates in various states where new divorce legislation was being considered, all throw some light on the growing toleration of divorce.[2] It must not be supposed that public opinion, even a hundred years ago, was unequivocally set against divorce. Churches and their leaders fulminated against divorce, and most public figures drew freely on Biblical sources to denounce it, but strong opponents of the indissolubility of marriage did not cease their attacks. The border and frontier states, with their shifting and rootless populations, seemed not to have had rigid views against divorce, and Connecticut on the seaboard had liberal laws (Barnett, 1939, p. 36). The growing feminist movement sought freedom for women, especially from the disabilities which existing family laws imposed; and though feminist leaders could not muster compelling theological arguments, they were able to best their opponents on humanitarian grounds (Barnett, 1939, pp. 40 ff.).

It is not possible to state the 'causes' of this basic change in

2. A good compilation of this material, concentrating on the novel, may be found in Barnett (1939 especially chapters 3 to 5).

attitude. It is merely one facet of a broader set of changes in Western society, called 'secularization': patterns that were once weighed by strong moral norms come to be evaluated by instrumental norms. Instead of asking, 'Is this moral?' the individual is more likely to ask, 'Is this a more useful or better procedure for my needs?' Sometimes the term 'individualism' is applied to this change, for instead of asking whether one's church or one's community approves divorce, the individual rather asks, 'Is it the right thing for *me* to do?'

However, a change in values alone does not necessarily lead to a great change in action patterns; other elements are always involved. Certainly, one important change has been in the types of *social pressures* from kinfolk and friends when there is marital discord. A hundred years ago, these pressures were essentially unidirectional. The individual was told by everyone to adjust, to bear the burden, and to accept his fate. He was told that for the sake of the children it was necessary to remain with his spouse, and he recognized that a divorce would mean losing his standing in his social circle. Although, in contemporary society, friends and kin do give advice to people who are involved in marital difficulties, and though it is safe to say that in the initial stages, at least, the advice is to stay together, especially when there are children, these pressures are not nearly so strong as they once were. They relax even more when those within the social circle recognize that the marriage cannot be mended.

A substantial change has also taken place in the *alternatives* which the husband or wife faces when considering a divorce. Formerly a man found it very difficult to get along from day to day unless he had a wife. This was especially true on the farm, where many activities were defined as female activities, but it was true in urban areas as well. Women had almost no opportunities for employment outside of domestic work. Few women were technically trained, and even when a woman's family had money, a return to her family was always viewed as a shameful alternative to continuing her marriage. These alternatives have radically changed. The man can get along quite well without a wife, for he can purchase most of the services which a wife would perform. Women's alternatives have, of course, expanded even more. Many more women are trained to handle jobs that pay substantial salaries. Finally, and most central in this change, is the fact that since being divorced is no longer a stigma, and since there are many people who have been either widowed or divorced, the person in marital difficulty can hope for another marriage as an alternative.

We should also consider some deeper factors that have influenced the continued rise in the divorce rate. The egalitarian ethos, which has spread throughout much of the Western culture complex during the past hundred and fifty years, has argued consistently for equality of rights for women. Men have fought a rearguard action, winning this battle and losing that one, but in general retreating. This change has a philosophical basis, but it is also rooted in the demands of an industrialized system, which offers each person the opportunity to develop his skills as fully as possible and to utilize them in the economy. An industrial economy apparently requires the services of women as well as men, and only to a limited extent are these services defined by sex roles.

Men typically exaggerate when they assert that women have achieved equal rights. It seems fair to say that women demand a greater range of *rights* than men are willing to concede, just as men are willing to impose a few more *obligations* than women are willing to accept. In a period of great change of sex roles, there is necessarily considerable tension in the day-to-day interaction of husbands and wives. Love is likely to be the crystallizing element in the decision to marry, both in fact and ideal, and the assumption that married life has personal happiness as its aim has come to be widely accepted. Combined with these two factors, the existence of tensions in sex roles means that there are bound to be more conflicts between husbands and wives now than a hundred years ago; and that when such conflicts do arise, individuals feel that the *primary* aim of marriage has not been achieved. Since the only common enterprise is now the family itself, when this fails to yield the expected personal satisfactions, it cannot be surprising that the likelihood of divorce is greater than a century ago.

These pressures and patterns are not at all peculiar to the United States. The general rise in the divorce rate in Europe is not caused by the insidious influence of 'bad' American customs, like Coca-Cola and chewing gum. Rather, the United States is in the vanguard of a process which is becoming worldwide. The European countries follow behind simply because they are going through similar phases at a later date. The same processes have been taking place in Communist China, Japan and parts of Africa.[3] [...]

Divorce and desertion in different segments of the United States population

[...] A recent summary of various research studies, sample surveys and census data has clearly demonstrated an inverse relationship between socio-economic rank and divorce rate (Goode, 1965, chapters 4 and 5).[4] Table 3, taken from this summary and calculated from national data, shows this relationship. [...]

What do such correlations mean? Husbands and wives do not ordinarily quarrel about their respective social or economic

Table 3 Proneness to Divorce by Urban Occupation, United States, April 1949

Occupation	Index of proneness to divorce
Professional, semi-professional	67·7
Proprietors, managers, officials	68·6
Clerical, sales	71·8
Craftsmen, foremen	86·6
Operators (semi-skilled)	94·5
Service workers	254·7
Laborers (except farm and mine)	180·3

Source: Goode (1956, p. 46). Of course a wide range of occupations is included under 'service', such as night watchmen and hairdressers. Properly speaking, this survey used the category, 'Other marital status' (other than single or married). The survey from which these data were calculated is found in *Current Population Reports, Labor Force*, Series 3-R50, no. 22, 19 April 1950, table 5. If different occupational categories are used, a somewhat different ranking may be obtained, but the basic relationship between socio-economic position and divorce remains the same.

3. For these data see Goode (1963). For China, see especially C. K. Yang (1959) and O. Yang (1946). See also Dore (1958) and Phillips (1953).
4. See also Goode (1962) and Hillman (1962).

positions, or their education. It is rather that socio-economic factors are among the social influences playing on the family, and thus indirectly affect many decisions within the family. For example, in our society most individuals come to want a wide range of material things that their limited incomes deny them. Individuals are not reared to accept *normative* limits on their economic goals, although of course many people realistically accept the limits of *fact*; that is to say, although they know they cannot afford a fine car, a house or fur coat, they do not feel they have no right to these goods. As a consequence, most families feel that their income is insufficient. The responsibility for satisfying these desires rests primarily with the husband, and any failure is his failure. At the same time, almost every study of job satisfaction shows that men in jobs with greater responsibility and prestige enjoy those jobs more than men in lower-ranking jobs enjoy theirs. Thus, both job satisfaction and economic reward point to a similar possibility: that there is more socio-economic dissatisfaction in the lower strata, and thus possibly more marital tension from this source. Just as personality problems can be displaced onto economic factors within a marriage, so too may economic strains be displaced onto non-economic relationships such as sex and marital adjustment.

Other factors varying by socio-economic position also affect divorce rates. Upper and lower social strata contrast in these relevant ways:

1. More of the income in the upper strata is alloted to long-term investment expenditures, such as houses, insurance, annuities, and so on, while more income in the lower strata is allocated to consumer goods such as cars and television sets. One consequence is that the husband in the upper strata cannot simply 'walk out' on his obligations.

2. The difference between the potential earnings of the lower-class wife and her husband is smaller than between those of the wife and husband in the upper strata. Consequently, the wife's potential loss is much greater in the upper strata.

3. The network of both kin and friends is larger and more tightly knit among the upper strata than among the lower strata, so that the consequences of divorce are likely to be greater. It is easier

for the lower-class husband simply to abandon his marital duties, either by separation or desertion. He cannot be so easily traced, and often loses little if he obtains an equal job in another city where he is unknown. Men are now more easily traceable than formerly, through social security, F.B.I., Veterans Administration, and other bureaucratic records, but a differential between upper and lower levels nevertheless remains.

We now see that even if tensions from economic factors were the same at all economic levels, the objective complexities and difficulties ensuing from divorce are greater for upper-strata marriages, so that these are more likely to stay together. [...]

The meaning of differences in social background

[...] In this section, an assessment is made of some specific background traits of couples who marry. These experiences cannot be called 'causes' of divorce, except in the sense that they help to generate (or lower) the tensions that may finally erupt in annulment, desertion or divorce. [...]

To the extent that certain characteristics of social position and background experiences increase or decrease the likelihood of marital dissolution, it may almost be said that divorce 'begins' before the first quarrel, or before the couple even meet. It is not possible to review here all of the factors which have been related to eventual marital breakup, but those which seem to be based on good evidence can be presented, together with their sociological meaning. These may be summarized in Table 4:

Table 4 Background Characteristics Associated with a Greater or Lesser Proneness to Divorce

Greater proneness to divorce	Lesser proneness
Urban background	Rural background
Marriage at very young ages (fifteen–nineteen years)	Marriage at average age (males, twenty-three; females, twenty)
Short acquaintanceship before marriage	Acquaintanceship of two years or more prior to marriage
Short engagement, or none	Engagement of six months or more

Table 4 continued

Greater proneness to divorce	Lesser proneness
Couples whose parents had unhappy marriages	Couples with happily married parents
Non-attendance at church, or mixed faith	Regular church attendance, Catholics, and adherence to the same church
Disapproval by kin and friends of the marriage	Approval of kin and friends
General dissimilarity in background	Similarity ('homogamy') of background
Different definitions of husband and wife as to their mutual role obligations	Agreement of wife and husband as to the role obligations

These findings are in conformity with common sense, but they also deserve sociological annotation. First, the evidence on which they are based varies considerably, for some are derived from national samples or censuses of individuals, analysed by marital status, and other characteristics, for example, the finding that the divorce rate of women fifteen to nineteen years of age is about 50 per cent higher than that for women in higher age categories (Glick, 1957, p. 154). Other studies have taken small samples of people who are still married and have measured their *marital adjustment*, sometimes comparing a happily married sample with a sample of couples whose marriages ended in divorce (Locke, 1951).[5] The important sociological factors contributing to these and similar findings may be placed under four main headings:

1. The likelihood that an individual from a particular background has a stronger set of *values* against divorce.

2. Various types of *social pressures* against divorce.

3. The way the processes of mate selection sort out the marriage partners.

5. Goode's (1956) study often compares divorced couples with the married population.

4. The ease of marital adjustment between people of similar social backgrounds.

Although a specific factor may play some part in more than one of these sets of processes, the general categories will help to clarify exposition somewhat.

There is a greater tolerance of divorce in the United States today than there was a century ago, but many groups still oppose it strongly and view it as a nearly inconceivable alternative to even a bad marriage. Catholics are strongly against divorce, but many Protestant sects also oppose it. Rural populations are more strongly against divorce than urban areas. It seems likely that those with less education are less tolerant of divorce (but more tolerant of other marital deviations) than those with more education. In general, people from a 'conventional' background and circle feel more strongly opposed to divorce than those with a less conventional background.

These differences may not lessen the *possibility* of conflict, but they do lessen the likelihood that individuals strongly opposed to divorce will accept that solution for their marital difficulties. However, these differences in opposition to divorce have lessened in the United States. For example, rural–urban social differences are gradually being erased, because the country as a whole is becoming more concentrated in large urban agglomerations and the remaining rural areas have increasingly taken on urban characteristics.

Values in opposition to divorce work in reinforcing ways. The individual who has such values is less likely to think of divorce in the first place.[6] He is also more likely to be involved in *circles* that are opposed to divorce and press him toward reconciliation or some other adjustment to the conflict. For example, the individual who regularly attends church is also part of a social circle whose general advice and pressure are against divorce. When kinfolk and friends approve a marriage, they are likely to advise the couple to adjust and not to take their conflict seriously.

6. Marriage demands a certain amount of repression from the partners, who must in a sense 'not see' all of each other's faults, or all the ramifications of a quarrel. Cf. Waller and Hill (1952, pp. 516–17). An important phase in the dissolution process occurs when one or both spouses first consider divorce seriously as a possibility.

Since a divorce within any social network threatens to some extent the ties which bind it together, the members of the network have a personal stake in attempting to prevent the divorce of any couple.

Some of these background factors, especially the approval of kin or friends, also help an individual to find a congenial companion, and to adjust to that person even before marriage. We should, therefore, think of the approval of kin and friends as having a double aspect. On the one hand it represents a kind of *prediction* that the engaged couple seem fitted for one another. Such circles know one or both of the individuals and judge whether they will fit together. On the other hand, the approval actually helps to bind them together, since their approval makes the interaction between the engaged or the married couple easier and more pleasant. Similarly, the length of acquaintance and the length of engagement may be viewed as an *index* of their adjustment to one another, but it is also a *period* of shared experience, during which adjustment can further take place. If a man and woman know one another for a long period of time, it is likely first of all that they have already, or acquire, common and mutually congenial characteristics. Next, if they stay together during a long period of time, their interaction has likely been productive or pleasant. Finally, a long period of acquaintanceship or engagement gives an opportunity either to become better adjusted or to break the tie. It is not surprising then that both of these background characteristics are associated with stability in marriage.

The length of the engagement is in part, however, a reflection of still other factors. Often, for example, marriages which take place without any engagement at all are really forced marriages, and marriages based upon premarital conception are more likely to end in divorce. Next, short engagements seem to be much more characteristic of lower-strata families, and we have already seen that the divorce rate is higher in such strata. Thus, a short engagement may be either a cause or an effect. Finally, it seems likely that the length of engagement has a different social meaning in different strata. A very short engagement in a middle- or upper-class stratum is more likely to be a deviant union in some respects than it would be in the lower strata. It at least suggests that there may be background characteristics of the two couples that are incompatible.

Throughout this and earlier discussions, the theme has been developed that the disorganization of a marriage is much more likely to occur if the couple have very different social characteristics. In nearly all the world's marriage systems, whether marriages are arranged by elders or by the young couples themselves, the process of mate selection results in marriages between men and women who are similar to each other in a wide range of social characteristics, but especially with respect to family prestige and wealth.[7] Elders have an interest in establishing a stable marriage, since they invest some of their own time and wealth in it, and common sense has long recognized that a young couple will be more compatible if they are alike in important ways. The elders are also interested in maintaining the prestige and financial standing of their own family, and so will attempt to find a mate who is the *equal* of the young representative of their own family. When marriage choice is formally free, the informal associations and acquaintanceships of young people are nevertheless restricted, so that even if they marry someone whom they fall in love with, they can fall in love with only the people they meet, and these tend to be generally of the same class level and social background.

The more than a hundred studies of homogamy have shown that the likelihood of husband and wife sharing almost any characteristic is greater than chance expectation, whether this characteristic is a physical one, such as height or color of eyes, or an economic factor such as occupational background. Not all of these are of great importance in marital adjustment, but a smaller problem of adjustment exists when the couple can count on finding in each other quite similar attitudes, habits and tastes. This general range of elements relates also to the factors already mentioned. It is probable, for example, that those who are alike in many respects will share a similar and approving social circle. The selection process itself will often break up the relationship between people of very different backgrounds.

7. For a summary of research on homogamy, see Burgess and Locke (1953, pp. 369–72) and Cavan (1953, p. 377).

Social homogamy and complementarity of needs

One line of psychological research suggests that, though marital stability is higher among socially homogamous marriages, two individuals may be more contented in marriage if certain of their psychological characteristics are *not* alike (see Winch, 1963, chapter 18; and 1958). The theory of complementary needs is not an explanation of divorce, but merely says: 'in mate selection each individual seeks, within his or her field of eligibles, for that person who gives the greatest promise of providing him or her with maximum need gratification' (Winch, 1963, p. 404). These needs have been developed from an earlier classification worked out by Henry A. Murray and include such characteristics as: autonomy – to be unattached; independence – to avoid or escape from domination and constraint; deference – to admire and praise a person; nurturance – to give sympathy and aid to a weak, helpless, ill, or dejected person or animal; recognition – to excite the admiration and approval of others; succorance – to be helped by a sympathetic person, to be nursed, loved, protected, indulged. (See Murray *et al.*, 1938, chapter 3; Winch, 1963, pp. 408–9.) Three general traits are also postulated: anxiety, emotionality and vicariousness ('the gratification of a need derived from the perception that another person is deriving gratification').

The above list includes only part of the full classification of thirteen needs. Although some modification of this list may be necessary in the future, it includes many of the individual's basic personality needs. Once the young people in a given circle of eligibles having similar social characteristics begin to pair off in marriage – 'what Jane sees in Tom' is not only his future earning capacity or his handsomeness. What she feels is an attraction based upon the fact that some of her needs are gratified when she is with Tom. For example, if she likes to take care of people and Tom in turn likes to be taken care of, it is much more likely that they will get along well, and feel drawn to one another, than if both share the same need in the same quantity.

However, the theory can be pushed beyond the mere matter of choice of mate. One possible direction of inquiry, for example, should be a study of the extent to which people *mis*perceive others' ability to gratify given needs, especially in our own courtship system, which puts a premium on a 'smooth line' and teaches all of us to fit ourselves to the apparent wishes of the other. The dating situation creates a socially *structured* misperception on both sides. Long acquaintanceship and engagements are conducive to marital stability, in part because the chances of such misconceptions are diminished over time.

The theory of complementary needs also throws light on adjustment and conflict in marriage. Individuals may fit well along one dimension, but not along another. For example, Jane may like to take care of Tom and Tom like to be taken care of by Jane – that is, her need for nurturance complements his need for succorance. However, Jane's deference need may be frustrated by the fact that Tom has no great need to excite the admiration and approval of others. It may happen, then, that the attraction and the later marriage are based upon *some* complementary needs, but there may be *other* needs which are not well met. How the later situation of marriage changes the relative weight of satisfaction of some needs as against some dissatisfactions is a matter for further study.

From this point of view, the stable marriage is likely to be one in which a range of the wife's and husband's needs are mutually gratified. An unhappy marriage leading to divorce may well be one in which some few needs are met, but others are frustrated or ignored, so that the union means a continued unhappiness for either or both persons. How far the adjustment of husband and wife to the reality of their situation is generally sufficient to tolerate this failure of need gratification is a question yet to be answered.

References

BARNETT, J. H. (1939), *Divorce and the American Divorce Novel, 1858–1937*, University of Pennsylvania, privately printed.

BUREAU OF THE CENSUS, *Statistical Abstract of the United States: 1964*, Washington, D.C.

BURGESS, E. W., and LOCKE, H. J. (1953), *The Family*, 2nd edn, American Book Co.

CAVAN, R. S. (1953), *The American Family*, Crowell.

DORE, R. P. (1958), *City Life in Japan*, University of California Press.

GLICK, P. C. (1957), *American Families*, Wiley.

GOODE, W. J. (1956), *After Divorce*, Free Press.

GOODE, W. J. (1962), 'Marital satisfaction and instability: a cross-cultural class analysis of divorce rates', *International Social Science Journal*, vol. 14 (3), pp. 507–26.

GOODE, W. J, (1963), *World Revolution and Family Patterns*, Free Press.

GOODE, W. J. (1965), *Women in Divorce*, Free Press.

HILLMAN, K. G. (1962), 'Marital instability and its relation to education, income and occupation: an analysis based on census data', in R. F. Winch, R. McGinnis and H. R. Barringer (eds.), *Selected Studies in Marriage and the Family*, rev. edn, Holt, Rinehart & Wilson.

JACOBSON, P. H .(1959), *American Marriage and Divorce*, Holt, Rinehart & Winston.

LOCKE, H. J. (1951), *Predicting Adjustment in Marriage*, Holt, Rinehart & Winston.

MURRAY, H. A., *et al.* (1938), *Explorations in Personality*, Oxford University Press.

PHILLIPS, A. (ed.) (1953), *Survey of African Marriage and Family Life*, Oxford University Press.

WALLER, W., and HILL, R. (1952), *The Family*, Dryden.

WINCH, R. F. (1958), *Mate-Selection*, Harper & Row.

WINCH, R. F. (1963), *The Modern Family*, 3rd edn, Holt, Rinehart & Winston.

YANG, C. K. (1959), *The Chinese Family in the Communist Revolution*, Harvard University Press.

YANG, O. (1946), *Chinese Family and Society*, Yale University Press.

Part Six
Parents and their Small Children

A mass of research has established that there are major differences in socialization practices between different socio-economic groups. These differences have been described not only in the area of child-rearing techniques, but also in methods of discipline, in the ways in which affection is manifested, in the kinds of use to which toys are put, in the ways mothers talk to their children, and in parental ambitions for them. A number of different explanatory variables have been proposed, but common to most recent research has been the notion that these variables do not operate directly, but rather lead to the development of value differences which are the immediate spur and support for behaviour. Kohn has been one of the most original writers in this area, and in Reading 22 he elaborates this general perspective and suggests that the values he is discussing are a logical extension of variations in the father's occupational role. It will be obvious to the reader that major problems of verification remain to be solved in this area, but the general perspective seems sound enough.

22 M. L. Kohn

Social Class and Parent–Child Relationships

M. L. Kohn, 'Social class and parent–child relationships:
an interpretation', *American Journal of Sociology*, vol. 68, 1963,
pp. 471–80.

This essay is an attempt to interpret, from a sociological perspective, the effects of social class upon parent–child relationships.
Many past discussions of the problem seem somehow to lack this
perspective, even though the problem is one of profound
importance for sociology. Because most investigators have
approached the problem from an interest in psychodynamics,
rather than social structure, they have largely limited their
attention to a few specific techniques used by mothers in the
rearing of infants and very young children. They have discovered,
inter alia, that social class has a decided bearing on which techniques parents use. But, since they have come at the problem from
this perspective, their interest in social class has not gone beyond
its effects for this very limited aspect of parent–child relationships.

The present analysis conceives the problem of social class and
parent–child relationships as an instance of the more general
problem of the effects of social structure upon behavior. It starts
with the assumption that social class has proved to be so useful a
concept because it refers to more than simply educational level,
or occupation, or any of the large number of correlated variables.
It is so useful because it captures the reality that the intricate
interplay of all these variables creates different basic conditions of
life at different levels of the social order. Members of different
social classes, by virtue of enjoying (or suffering) different conditions of life, come to see the world differently – to develop
different conceptions of social reality, different aspirations and
hopes and fears, different conceptions of the desirable.

The last is particularly important for present purposes, for from
people's conceptions of the desirable – and particularly from their

conceptions of what characteristics are desirable in children – one can discern their objectives in child-rearing. Thus, conceptions of the desirable – that is, values[1] – become the key concept for this analysis, the bridge between position in the larger social structure and the behavior of the individual. The intent of the analysis is to trace the effects of social class position on parental values and the effects of values on behavior.

Since this approach differs from analyses focused on social class differences in the use of particular child-rearing techniques, it will be necessary to re-examine earlier formulations from the present perspective. Then three questions will be discussed, bringing into consideration the limited available data that are relevant: What differences are there in the values held by parents of different social classes? What is there about the conditions of life distinctive of these classes that might explain the differences in their values? What consequences do these differences in values have for parents' relationships with their children?

Social class

Social classes will be defined as aggregates of individuals who occupy broadly similar positions in the scale of prestige (Williams, 1951, p. 89). In dealing with the research literature, we shall treat occupational position (or occupational position as weighted somewhat by education) as a serviceable index of social class for urban American society. And we shall adopt the model of social stratification implicit in most research, that of four relatively discrete classes: a 'lower class' of unskilled manual workers, a 'working class' of manual workers in semi-skilled and skilled occupations, a 'middle class' of white-collar workers and professionals, and an 'élite', differentiated from the middle class not so much in terms of occupation as of wealth and lineage.

Almost all the empirical evidence, including that from our own research, stems from broad comparisons of the middle and working class. Thus we shall have little to say about the extremes of the

1. 'A value is a conception, explicit or implicit, distinctive of an individual or characteristic of a group, of the desirable which influences the selection from available modes, means, and ends of action' (Kluckhohn, 1951, p. 395). See also the discussion of values in Williams (1951, chapter 11) and his discussion of social class and culture (p. 101).

class distribution. Furthermore, we shall have to act as if the middle and working classes were each homogeneous. They are not, even in terms of status considerations alone. There is evidence, for example, that within each broad social class, variations in parents' values quite regularly parallel gradations of social status. Moreover, the classes are heterogeneous with respect to other factors that affect parents' values, such as religion and ethnicity. But even when all such considerations are taken into account, the empirical evidence clearly shows that being on one side or the other of the line that divides manual from non-manual workers has profound consequences for how one rears one's children.[2]

Stability and change

Any analysis of the effects of social class upon parent–child relationships should start with Urie Bronfenbrenner's analytic review of the studies that had been conducted in this country during the twenty-five years up to 1958 (Bronfenbrenner, 1958). From the seemingly contradictory findings of a number of studies, Bronfenbrenner discerned not chaos but orderly change: there have been changes in the child-training techniques employed by middle-class parents in the past quarter-century; similar changes have been taking place in the working class, but working-class parents have consistently lagged behind by a few years; thus, while middle-class parents of twenty-five years ago were more 'restrictive' than were working-class parents, today the middle-class parents are more 'permissive'; and the gap between the classes seems to be narrowing.

It must be noted that these conclusions are limited by the questions Bronfenbrenner's predecessors asked in their research. The studies deal largely with a few particular techniques of child-rearing, especially those involved in caring for infants and very young children, and say very little about parents' over-all relationships with their children, particularly as the children grow

2. These, and other assertions of fact not referred to published sources, are based on research my colleagues and I have conducted. For the design of this research and the principal substantive findings see Kohn (1959a and b) and Kohn and Carroll (1960). I should like to express my appreciation to my principal collaborators in this research, John A. Clausen and Eleanor E. Carroll.

older. There is clear evidence that the past quarter-century has seen change, even faddism, with respect to the use of breast feeding or bottle feeding, scheduling or not scheduling, spanking or isolating. But when we generalize from these specifics to talk of a change from 'restrictive' to 'permissive' practices – or, worse yet, of a change from 'restrictive' to 'permissive' parent–child relationships – we impute to them a far greater importance than they probably have, either to parents or to children.[3]

There is no evidence that recent faddism in child-training techniques is symptomatic of profound changes in the relations of parents to children in either social class. In fact, as Bronfenbrenner notes, what little evidence we do have points in the opposite direction: the over-all quality of parent–child relationships does not seem to have changed substantially in either class (1958, pp. 420–22 and 425). In all probability, parents have changed techniques in service of much the same values, and the changes have been quite specific. These changes must be explained, but the enduring characteristics are probably even more important.

Why the changes? Bronfenbrenner's interpretation is ingenuously simple. He notes that the changes in techniques employed by middle-class parents have closely paralleled those advocated by presumed experts, and he concludes that middle-class parents have changed their practices *because* they are responsive to changes in what the experts tell them is right and proper. Working-class parents, being less educated and thus less directly responsive to the media of communication, followed behind only later.[4]

Bronfenbrenner is almost undoubtedly right in asserting that middle-class parents have followed the drift of presumably expert opinion. But why have they done so? It is not sufficient to assume that the explanation lies in their greater degree of education. This might explain why middle-class parents are substantially more likely than are working-class parents to *read* books and articles

3. Furthermore, these concepts employ *a priori* judgements about which the various investigators have disagreed radically. See, e.g. Sears, Maccoby and Levin (1957, pp. 444–7) and Littman, Moore and Pierce-Jones (1957, esp. p. 703).

4. Bronfenbrenner gives clearest expression to this interpretation, but it has been adopted by others, too. See, e.g. White (1957).

on child-rearing, as we know they do.[5] But they need not *follow* the experts' advice. We know from various studies of the mass media that people generally search for confirmation of their existing beliefs and practices and tend to ignore what contradicts them.

From all the evidence at our disposal, it looks as if middle-class parents not only read what the experts have to say but also search out a wide variety of other sources of information and advice: they are far more likely than are working-class parents to discuss child-rearing with friends and neighbors, to consult physicians on these matters, to attend Parent–Teacher Association meetings, to discuss the child's behavior with his teacher. Middle-class parents seem to regard child-rearing as more problematic than do working-class parents. This can hardly be a matter of education alone. It must be rooted more deeply in the conditions of life of the two social classes.

Everything about working-class parents' lives – their comparative lack of education, the nature of their jobs, their greater attachment to the extended family – conduces to their retaining familiar methods.[6] Furthermore, even should they be receptive to change, they are less likely than are middle-class parents to find the experts' writings appropriate to their wants, for the experts predicate their advice on middle-class values. Everything about middle-class parents' lives, on the other hand, conduces to their looking for new methods to achieve their goals. They look to the experts, to other sources of relevant information, and to each other not for new values but for more serviceable techniques.[7]

5. This was noted by John E. Anderson (1936) in the first major study of social class and family relationships ever conducted, and has repeatedly been confirmed.

6. The differences between middle- and working-class conditions of life will be discussed more fully later in this paper.

7. Certainly middle-class parents do not get their values from the experts. In our research, we compared the values of parents who say they read Spock, Gesell or other books on child-rearing, to those who read only magazine and newspaper articles, and those who say they read nothing at all on the subject. In the middle class, these three groups have substantially the same values. In the working class, the story is different. Few working-class parents claim to read books or even articles on child-rearing. Those few who do have values much more akin to those of the middle class. But these are atypical working-class parents who are very anxious to attain middle-

And within the limits of our present scanty knowledge about means–end relationships in child-rearing, the experts have provided practical and useful advice. It is not that educated parents slavishly follow the experts but that the experts have provided what the parents have sought.

To look at the question this way is to put it in a quite different perspective: the focus becomes not specific techniques nor changes in the use of specific techniques but parental values.

Values of middle- and working-class parents

Of the entire range of values one might examine, it seems particularly strategic to focus on parents' conceptions of what characteristics would be most desirable for boys or girls the age of their own children. From this one can hope to discern the parents' goals in rearing their children. It must be assumed, however, that a parent will choose one characteristic as more desirable than another only if he considers it to be both important, in the sense that failure to develop this characteristic would affect the child adversely, and problematic, in the sense that it is neither to be taken for granted that the child will develop that characteristic nor impossible for him to do so. In interpreting parents' value choices, we must keep in mind that their choices reflect not simply their goals but the goals whose achievement they regard as problematic.

Few studies, even in recent years, have directly investigated the relationship of social class to parental values. Fortunately, however, the results of these few are in essential agreement. The earliest study was Evelyn Millis Duvall's (1946) pioneering inquiry. Duvall characterized working-class (and lower-middle-class) parental values as 'traditional' – they want their children to be neat and clean, to obey and respect adults, to please adults. In contrast to this emphasis on how the child comports himself, middle-class parental values are more 'developmental' – they want their children to be eager to learn, to love and confide in the parents, to be happy, to share and cooperate, to be healthy and well.

Duvall's traditional–developmental dichotomy does not des-

---

class status. One suspects that for them the experts provide a sort of handbook to the middle class; even for them, it is unlikely that the values come out of Spock and Gesell.

cribe the difference between middle- and working-class parental values quite exactly, but it does point to the essence of the difference: working-class parents want the child to conform to externally imposed standards, while middle-class parents are far more attentive to his internal dynamics.

The few relevant findings of subsequent studies are entirely consistent with this basic point, especially in the repeated indications that working-class parents put far greater stress on obedience to parental commands than do middle-class parents.[8] Our own research, conducted in 1956–7, provides the evidence most directly comparable to Duvall's (Kohn, 1959a). We, too, found that working-class parents value obedience, neatness and cleanliness more highly than do middle-class parents, and that middle-class parents in turn value curiosity, happiness, consideration and – most importantly – self-control more highly than do working-class parents. We further found that there are characteristic clusters of value choice in the two social classes: working-class parental values center on conformity to external proscriptions, middle-class parental values on *self*-direction. To working-class parents, it is the overt act that matters: the child should not transgress externally imposed rules; to middle-class parents, it is the child's motives and feelings that matter: the child should govern himself.

In fairness, it should be noted that middle- and working-class parents share many core values. Both, for example, value honesty very highly – although, characteristically, 'honesty' has rather different connotations in the two social classes, implying 'trustworthiness' for the working class and 'truthfulness' for the middle class. The common theme, of course, is that parents of both social classes value a decent respect for the rights of others; middle- and working-class values are but variations on this common theme. The reason for emphasizing the variations rather than the common theme is that they seem to have far-ranging consequences for parents' relationships with their children and thus ought to be taken seriously.

It would be good if there were more evidence about parental

8. Alex Inkeles has shown that this is true not only for the United States but for a number of other industrialized societies as well (1960, pp. 20–21 and table 9).

values – data from other studies in other locales, and especially, data derived from more than one mode of inquiry. But, what evidence we do have is consistent, so that there is at least some basis for believing it is reliable. Furthermore, there is evidence that the value choices made by parents in these inquiries are not simply a reflection of their assessments of their own children's deficiencies or excellences. Thus, we may take the findings of these studies as providing a limited, but probably valid, picture of the parents' generalized conceptions of what behavior would be desirable in their pre-adolescent children.

Explaining class differences in parental values

That middle-class parents are more likely to espouse some values and working-class parents other values must be a function of differences in their conditions of life. In the present state of our knowledge, it is difficult to disentangle the interacting variables with a sufficient degree of exactness to ascertain which conditions of life are crucial to the differences in values. Nevertheless, it is necessary to examine the principal components of class differences in life conditions to see what each may contribute.

The logical place to begin is with occupational differences, for these are certainly pre-eminently important, not only in defining social classes in urban, industrialized society, but also in determining much else about people's life conditions.[9] There are at least three respects in which middle-class occupations typically differ from working-class occupations, above and beyond their obvious status-linked differences in security, stability of income and general social prestige. One is that middle-class occupations deal more with the manipulation of interpersonal relations, ideas and symbols, while working-class occupations deal more with the manipulation of things. The second is that middle-class occupations are more subject to self-direction, while working-class occupations are more subject to standardization and direct supervision. The third is that getting ahead in middle-class occupations is more dependent upon one's own actions, while in working-class occupations it is more dependent upon collective action, particularly in unionized industries. From these differ-

9. For a thoughtful discussion of the influence of occupational role on parental values see Aberle and Naegele (1952).

ences, one can sketch differences in the characteristics that make for getting along, and getting ahead, in middle- and working-class occupations. Middle-class occupations require a greater degree of self-direction; working-class occupations, in larger measure, require that one follow explicit rules set down by someone in authority.

Obviously, these differences parallel the differences we have found between the two social classes in the characteristics valued by parents for children. At minimum, one can conclude that there is a congruence between occupational requirements and parental values. It is, moreover, a reasonable supposition, although not a necessary conclusion, that middle- and working-class parents value different characteristics in children *because* of these differences in their occupational circumstances. This supposition does not necessarily assume that parents consciously train their children to meet future occupational requirements; it may simply be that their own occupational experiences have significantly affected parents' conceptions of what is desirable behavior, on or off the job, for adults or for children.[10]

These differences in occupational circumstances are probably basic to the differences we have found between middle- and working-class parental values, but taken alone they do not sufficiently explain them. Parents need not accord pre-eminent importance to occupational requirements in their judgements of what is most desirable. For a sufficient explanation of class differences in values, it is necessary to recognize that other differences

10. Two objections might be raised here. (a) Occupational experiences may not be important for a mother's values, however crucial they are for her husband's, if she has had little or no work experience. But even those mothers who have had little or no occupational experience know something of occupational life from their husbands and others, and live in a culture in which occupation and career permeate all of life. (b) Parental values may be built not so much out of their own experiences as out of their expectations of the child's future experiences. This might seem particularly plausible in explaining working-class values, for their high valuation of such stereotypically *middle-class* characteristics as obedience, neatness and cleanliness might imply that they are training their children for a middle-class life they expect the children to achieve. Few working-class parents, however, do expect (or even want) their children to go on to college and the middle-class jobs for which a college education is required. This is shown in Hyman (1953), and confirmed in unpublished data from our own research.

in middle- and working-class conditions of life reinforce the differences in occupational circumstances at every turn.

Educational differences, for example, above and beyond their importance as determinants of occupation, probably contribute independently to the differences in middle- and working-class parental values. At minimum, middle-class parents' greater attention to the child's internal dynamics is facilitated by their learned ability to deal with the subjective and the ideational. Furthermore, differences in levels and stability of income undoubtedly contribute to class differences in parental values. That middle-class parents still have somewhat higher levels of income, and much greater stability of income, makes them able to take for granted the respectability that is still problematic for working-class parents. They can afford to concentrate, instead, on motives and feelings – which, in the circumstances of their lives, are more important.

These considerations suggest that the differences between middle- and working-class parental values are probably a function of the entire complex of differences in life conditions characteristic of the two social classes. Consider, for example, the working-class situation. With the end of mass immigration, there has emerged a stable working class, largely derived from the manpower of rural areas, uninterested in mobility into the middle class, but very much interested in security, respectability and the enjoyment of a decent standard of living (see, e.g. Miller and Riessman, 1961). This working class has come to enjoy a standard of living formerly reserved for the middle class, but has not chosen a middle-class style of life. In effect, the working class has striven for, and partially achieved, an American dream distinctly different from the dream of success and achievement. In an affluent society, it is possible for the worker to be the traditionalist – politically, economically and, most relevant here, in his values for his children.[11] Working-class parents want their children to conform to external authority because the parents themselves are willing to accord respect to authority, in return for security and respectability. Their conservatism in child-rearing is part of a more general conservatism and traditionalism.

11. Relevant here is Seymour Martin Lipset's somewhat disillusioned 'Democracy and working-class authoritarianism' (1959).

Middle-class parental values are a product of a quite different set of conditions. Much of what the working-class values, they can take for granted. Instead, they can – and must – instil in their children a degree of self-direction that would be less appropriate to the conditions of life of the working class.[12] Certainly, there is substantial truth in the characterization of the middle-class way of life as one of great conformity. What must be noted here, however, is that *relative to* the working class, middle-class conditions of life require a more substantial degree of independence of action. Furthermore, the higher levels of education enjoyed by the middle class make possible a degree of internal scrutiny difficult to achieve without the skills in dealing with the abstract that college training sometimes provides. Finally, the economic security of most middle-class occupations, the level of income they provide, the status they confer, allow one to focus his attention on the subjective and the ideational. Middle-class conditions of life both allow and demand a greater degree of self-direction than do those of the working class.

Consequences of class differences in parents' values

What consequences do the differences between middle- and working-class parents' values have for the ways they raise their children?

Much of the research on techniques of infant-and child-training is of little relevance here. For example, with regard to parents'

12. It has been argued that as larger and larger proportions of the middle class have become imbedded in a bureaucratic way of life – in distinction to the entrepreneurial way of life of a bygone day – it has become more appropriate to raise children to be accommodative than to be self-reliant. But this point of view is a misreading of the conditions of life faced by the middle-class inhabitants of the bureaucratic world. Their jobs require at least as great a degree of self-reliance as do entrepreneurial enterprises. We tend to forget, nowadays, just how little the small- or medium-sized entrepreneur controlled the conditions of his own existence and just how much he was subjected to the petty authority of those on whose pleasure depended the survival of his enterprise. And we fail to recognize the degree to which monolithic-seeming bureaucracies allow free play for – in fact, require – individual enterprise of new sorts: in the creation of ideas, the building of empires, the competition for advancement.

At any rate, our data show no substantial differences between the values of parents from bureaucratic and entrepreneurial occupational worlds, in either social class. But see Miller and Swanson (1958).

preferred techniques for disciplining children, a question of major interest to many investigators, Bronfenbrenner summarizes past studies as follows: 'In matters of discipline, working-class parents are consistently more likely to employ physical punishment, while middle-class families rely more on reasoning, isolation, appeals to guilt and other methods involving the threat of loss of love' (1958, p. 424). This, if still true,[13] is consistent with middle-class parents' greater attentiveness to the child's internal dynamics, working-class parents' greater concern about the overt act. For present purposes, however, the crucial question is not *which* disciplinary method parents prefer, but when and why they use one or another method of discipline.

The most directly relevant available data are on the conditions under which middle- and working-class parents use physical punishment. Working-class parents are apt to resort to physical punishment when the direct and immediate consequences of their children's disobedient acts are most extreme, and to refrain from punishing when this might provoke an even greater disturbance (Kohn, 1959b). Thus, they will punish a child for wild play when the furniture is damaged or the noise level becomes intolerable, but ignore the same actions when the direct and immediate consequences are not so extreme. Middle-class parents, on the other hand, seem to punish or refrain from punishing on the basis of their interpretation of the child's intent in acting as he does. Thus, they will punish a furious outburst when the context is such that they interpret it to be a loss of self-control, but will ignore an equally extreme outburst when the context is such that they interpret it to be merely an emotional release.

It is understandable that working-class parents react to the consequences rather than to the intent of their children's actions: the important thing is that the child not transgress externally imposed rules. Correspondingly, if middle-class parents are instead concerned about the child's motives and feelings, they can and must look beyond the overt act to why the child acts as he does. It would seem that middle- and working-class values direct parents to see their children's misbehavior in quite different ways, so that misbehavior which prompts middle-class parents to action does not seem as important to working-class parents, and vice

13. Later studies, including our own, do not show this difference.

versa.[14] Obviously, parents' values are not the only things that enter into their use of physical punishment. But unless one assumes a complete lack of goal-directedness in parental behavior, he would have to grant that parents' values direct their attention to some facets of their own and their children's behavior, and divert it from other facets.

The consequences of class differences in parental values extend far beyond differences in disciplinary practices. From a knowledge of their values for their children, one would expect middle-class parents to feel a greater obligation to be *supportive* of the children, if only because of their sensitivity to the children's internal dynamics. Working-class values, with their emphasis upon conformity to external rules, should lead to greater emphasis upon the parents' obligation to impose constraints.[15] And this, according to Bronfenbrenner, is precisely what has been shown in those few studies that have concerned themselves with the over-all relationship of parents to child: 'Over the entire twenty-five-year period studied, parent–child relationships in the middle-class are consistently reported as more acceptant and equalitarian, while those in the working-class are oriented toward maintaining order and obedience' (1958, p. 425).

This conclusion is based primarily on studies of *mother*–child relationships in middle- and working-class families. Class differences in parental values have further ramifications for the father's role.[16] Mothers in each class would have their husbands play a role facilitative of the child's development of the characteristics valued in that class: middle-class mothers want their husbands to be supportive of the children (especially of sons), with their responsibility for imposing constraints being of decidedly secondary

14. This is not to say that the methods used by parents of either social class are necessarily the most efficacious for achievement of their goals.

15. The justification for treating support and constraint as the two major dimensions of parent–child relationships lies in the theoretical argument of Parsons and Bales (1955, esp. p. 45) and the empirical argument of Schaefer (1959).

16. From the very limited evidence available at the time of his review, Bronfenbrenner tentatively concluded: 'though the middle-class father typically has a warmer relationship with the child, he is also likely to have more authority and status in family affairs' (1958, p. 422). The discussion here is based largely on subsequent research, especially Kohn and Carroll (1960).

importance; working-class mothers look to their husbands to be considerably more directive – support is accorded far less importance and constraint far more. Most middle-class fathers agree with their wives and play a role close to what their wives would have them play. Many working-class fathers, on the other hand, do not. It is not that they see the constraining role as less important than do their wives, but that many of them see no reason why they should have to shoulder the responsibility. From their point of view, the important thing is that the child be taught what limits he must not transgress. It does not much matter who does the teaching, and since mother has primary responsibility for child care, the job should be hers.

The net consequence is a quite different division of parental responsibilities in the two social classes. In middle-class families, mother's and father's roles usually are not sharply differentiated. What differentiation exists is largely a matter of each parent taking special responsibility for being supportive of children of the parent's own sex. In working-class families, mother's and father's roles are more sharply differentiated, with mother almost always being the more supportive parent. In some working-class families, mother specializes in support, father in constraint; in others, perhaps in most, mother raises the children, father provides the wherewithal.[17]

Thus, the differences in middle- and working-class parents' values have wide ramifications for their relationships with their children and with each other. Of course, many class differences in parent–child relationships are not directly attributable to differences in values; undoubtedly the very differences in their conditions of life that make for differences in parental values reinforce, at every juncture, parents' characteristic ways of relating to their children. But one could not account for these consistent differ-

17. Fragmentary data suggest sharp class differences in the husband–wife relationship that complement the differences in the division of parental responsibilities discussed above. For example, virtually no working-class wife reports that she and her husband ever go out on an evening or weekend without the children. And few working-class fathers do much to relieve their wives of the burden of caring for the children all the time. By and large, working-class fathers seem to lead a largely separate social life from that of their wives; the wife has full-time responsibility for the children, while the husband is free to go his own way.

ences in parent–child relationships in the two social classes without reference to the differences in parents' avowed values.

Conclusion

This paper serves to show how complex and demanding are the problems of interpreting the effects of social structure on behavior. Our inquiries habitually stop at the point of demonstrating that social position correlates with something, when we should want to pursue the question, 'Why?' What are the processes by which position in social structure molds behavior? The present analysis has dealt with this question in one specific form: why does social class matter for parents' relationships with their children? There is every reason to believe that the problems encountered in trying to deal with that question would recur in any analysis of the effects of social structure on behavior.

In this analysis, the concept of 'values' has been used as the principal bridge from social position to behavior. The analysis has endeavored to show that middle-class parental values differ from those of working-class parents; that these differences are rooted in basic differences between middle- and working-class conditions of life; and that the differences between middle- and working-class parental values have important consequences for their relationships with their children. The interpretive model, in essence, is: social class – conditions of life – values – behavior.

The specifics of the present characterization of parental values may prove to be inexact; the discussion of the ways in which social-class position affects values is undoubtedly partial; and the tracing of the consequences of differences in values for differences in parent–child relationships is certainly tentative and incomplete. I trust, however, that the perspective will prove to be valid and that this formulation will stimulate other investigators to deal more directly with the processes whereby social structure affects behavior.

References

ABERLE, D. F., and NAEGELE, K. D. (1952), 'Middle-class fathers' occupational role and attitudes toward children', *American Journal of Orthopsychiatry*, vol. 22, pp. 366–78.
ANDERSON, J. E. (1936), *The Young Child in the Home: A Survey of Three Thousand American Families*, Appleton-Century-Crofts.

BRONFENBRENNER, U. (1958), 'Socialization and social class through time and space', in E. E. Maccoby, T. M. Newcomb and E. L. Hartley (eds.), *Readings in Social Psychology*, Holt, Rinehart & Winston.

DUVALL, E. M. (1946), 'Conceptions of parenthood', *American Journal of Sociology*, vol. 52, pp. 193–203.

HYMAN, H. H. (1953), 'The value system of different classes: a social-psychological contribution to the analysis of stratification', in R. Bendix and S. M. Lipset (eds.), *Class, Status and Power: A Reader in Social Stratification*, Free Press.

INKELES, A. (1960), 'Industrial man: the relation of status to experience, perception and value', *American Journal of Sociology*, vol. 66, pp. 1–31.

KLUCKHOHN, C. (1951), 'Values and value orientations', in T. Parsons and E. A. Shils (eds.), *Toward a General Theory of Action*, Harvard University Press.

KOHN, M. L. (1959a), 'Social class and parental values', *American Journal of Sociology*, vol. 64, pp. 337–51.

KOHN, M. L. (1959b), 'Social class and the exercise of parental authority', *American Sociological Review*, vol. 24, pp. 352–66.

KOHN, M. L., and CARROLL, E. E. (1960), 'Social class and the allocation of parental responsibilities', *Sociometry*, vol. 23, pp. 372–92.

LIPSET, S. M. (1959), 'Democracy and working-class authoritarianism', *American Sociological Review*, vol. 24, pp. 482–501.

LITTMAN, R. A., MOORE, R. C. A., and PIERCE-JONES, J. (1957), 'Social class differences in child rearing: a third community for comparison with Chicago and Newton', *American Sociological Review*, vol. 22, pp. 694–704.

MILLER, D. R., and SWANSON, G. E. (1958), *The Changing American Parent: A Study in the Detroit Area*, Wiley.

MILLER, S. M., and RIESSMAN, F. (1961), 'The working class sub-culture: a new view', *Social Problems*, vol. 9, pp. 86–97.

PARSONS, T., and BALES, R. F. (1955), *Family, Socialization and Interaction Process*, Free Press.

SCHAEFER, E. S. (1959), 'A circumplex model for maternal behavior', *Journal of Abnormal and Social Psychology*, vol. 59, pp. 226–34.

SEARS, R. R., MACCOBY, E. E., and LEVIN, H. (1957), *Patterns of Child-Rearing*, Row, Peterson.

WHITE, M. S. (1957), 'Social class, child-rearing practices and child behavior', *American Sociological Review*, vol. 22, pp. 704–12.

WILLIAMS, R. M., Jr (1951), *American Society: A Sociological Interpretation*, Knopf.

Further Reading

General

H. T. CHRISTENSEN, *Handbook of Marriage and the Family*, Rand McNally, 1964. Review papers on all major topics. Dense, encyclopedic; mainly for reference. Chapter 1 is a useful review of the development of the sociology of the family and of the difficulties of the field.

C. C. HARRIS, *The Family*, Allen & Unwin, 1969. Probably the best short textbook, with stimulating comments on most topics; not always easy.

M. ZELDITCH, 'Family, marriage and kinship', in R. E. L. Faris (ed.), *Handbook of Modern Sociology*, Rand McNally, 1964. A useful introductory summary of the state of the field.

Diversity and social change

There is a mass of community-focused studies which contain much useful data and many insights. Theoretically and methodologically they are mainly less sound. Among the best are:

N. DENNIS, F. HENRIQUES and C. SLAUGHTER, *Coal is our Life*, Eyre & Spottiswoode, 1957.

C. ROSSER and C. C. HARRIS, *The Family and Social Change*, Routledge & Kegan Paul, 1965.

M. YOUNG and P. WILLMOTT, *Family and Kinship in East London*, Routledge & Kegan Paul, 1957; Penguin Books, 1962.

Other useful works are:

J. KLEIN, *Samples from English Cultures*, Routledge & Kegan Paul, 1965. Klein summarizes usefully and analytically a mass of data.

W. J. GOODE, *World Revolution and Family Patterns*, Free Press, 1963.

T. P. R. LASLETT (ed.), *The Comparative History of Family and Household*, Cambridge University Press, in press.

M. A. NIMKOFF and R. MIDDLETON, 'Types of family and types of economy', *American Sociological Review*, vol. 25, 1960, pp. 215–25. Reprinted in R. F. Winch and L. W. Goodman, *Selected Studies in Marriage and the Family*, Holt, Rinehart & Winston, 1968.

T. PARSONS, 'The social structure of the family', in R. N. Anshen (ed.), *The Family: Its Function and Destiny*, Harper & Row, 1959, pp. 241–74. An elaboration of the arguments of Reading 2.

D. A. SWEETSER, 'The effect of industrialization on intergenerational solidarity', *Rural Sociology*, vol. 31, 1966, pp. 156–70. Reprinted in R. F. Winch and L. W. Goodman, *Selected Studies in Marriage and the Family*, Holt, Rinehart & Winston, 1968. A paper interesting for its hypotheses on the relative impact of industrialization on male side and female side kinship relationships.

Relationships with kin

B. N. ADAMS, 'Interaction theory and the social network', *Sociometry*, vol. 30, 1967, pp. 64–78. A rather different approach to kinship and friendship from that presented in Reading 12.

R. FIRTH et al., *Families and their Relatives*, Routledge & Kegan Paul, 1970.

R. FIRTH, *Two Studies of Kinship in London*, Athlone Press, 1956. A splendid short analysis of the British kinship system as seen by a social anthropologist, and two case studies in the best anthropological tradition.

E. LITWAK, 'Geographic mobility and extended family cohesion', *American Sociological Review*, vol. 25, 1960, pp. 385–94.

E. LITWAK, 'Occupational mobility and extended family cohesion', *American Sociological Review*, vol. 25, 1960, pp. 9–21. Reproduced in the Bobbs-Merrill reprint series. Both Litwak's papers are influential. Personally, I find his theoretical arguments much more persuasive than his empirical material.

H. RODMAN, 'Talcott Parsons' view of the changing American family', in H. Rodman, *Marriage, Family and Society: A Reader*, Random House, 1965. A balanced view of Parsons's position.

M. B. SUSSMAN, 'Relationships of adult children with their parents', in E. Shanas and G. F. Streib, *Social Structure and the Family: Generational Relations*, Prentice-Hall, 1965, pp. 62–92. Reprinted in M. B. Sussman, *Sourcebook in Marriage and the Family*, Houghton Mifflin, 3rd edn, 1968. The most comprehensive survey of data on kinship relationships in Western industrial societies. A number of other papers in Shanas and Streib's volume are also well worth reading, notably those by Back, Litwak and Townsend.

Most of the community studies also have useful data and ideas on this topic.

Mate selection

P. M. BLAU and O. D. DUNCAN, *The American Occupational Structure*, Wiley, 1967. Pages 346–60 show excellently a way forward for research on homogamy.

W. J. GOODE, 'The theoretical importance of love', *American Sociological Review*, vol. 24, 1959, pp. 38–47. Reprinted in R. F. Winch and L. W. Goodman, *Selected Studies in Marriage and the Family*, Holt, Rinehart & Winston, 1968; and reproduced in the Bobbs-Merrill reprint series. Goode examines factors affecting the freedom of choice in mate selection.

A. D. HOLLINGSHEAD, 'Cultural factors in the selection of marriage mates', *American Sociological Review*, vol. 16, 1950, pp. 619–27. Reprinted in R. F. Winch and L. W. Goodman, *Selected Studies in Marriage and the Family*, Holt, Rinehart & Winston, 1968; and in M. B. Sussman, *Sourcebook in Marriage and the Family*, Houghton Mifflin, 3rd edn, 1968. A classic.

A. C. KERCKHOFF and F. D. BEAN, 'Role-related factors in person perception among engaged couples', *Sociometry*, vol. 30, 1967, pp. 176–86. Difficult; shows well the contribution and the limitations of social psychological theories in this area.

A. C. KERCKHOFF and K. E. DAVIS, 'Value consensus and need complementarity in mate selection', *American Sociological Review*, vol. 27, 1962, pp. 295–303.

R. F. WINCH, *The Modern Family*, Holt, Rinehart & Winston, 1963, chapters 10 and 18. An excellent summary of Winch's original position.

Conjugal roles

J. BERNARD, 'The adjustment of married mates', in H. T. Christensen, *Handbook of Marriage and the Family*, Rand McNally, 1964. A thought-provoking theoretical perspective on the topic of marital adjustment.

R. O. BLOOD and D. M. WOLFE, *Husbands and Wives*, Free Press, 1960. Chapters 2, 3, 6 and 7 are particularly worthwhile.

E. BOTT, *Family and Social Network*, Tavistock, 1957. A second edition of this book, in press, contains Bott's reply to her critics.

B. FARBER, *Family: Organization and Interaction*, Chandler, 1964. Chapter 8 has a difficult but stimulating discussion of role conflicts in marriage.

P. G. HERBST, 'The measurement of family relationships', *Human Relations*, vol. 5, 1952, pp. 3–35.

J. PLATT, 'Some problems in measuring the jointness of conjugal role-relationships', *Sociology*, vol. 3, 1969, pp. 287–97. Both Herbst's and Platt's papers show up some of the difficulties of conducting empirical research in this field.

A.-M. ROCHEBLAVE-SPENLÉ, *Les rôles masculins et féminins*, Presses Universitaires de France, 1964. Part 2 is a fascinating though wholly descriptive analysis which shows up the marked international differences in cultural expectations of conjugal role behaviour.

Marital dissolution

G. LEVINGER, 'Marital cohesiveness and dissolution: an integrative review', *Journal of Marriage and the Family*, vol. 27, 1965, pp. 19–28. Reprinted in R. F. Winch and L. W. Goodman, *Selected Studies in Marriage and the Family*, Holt, Rinehart & Winston, 1968; and in M. B. Sussman, *Sourcebook in Marriage and the Family*, Houghton Mifflin, 3rd edn, 1968. Levinger summarizes a mass of data around a useful conceptual framework.

G. ROWNTREE and N. CARRIER, 'The resort to divorce in England and Wales, 1858–1957', *Population Studies*, vol. 11, 1958, pp. 188–233. An interesting attempt to disentangle empirically the legal and other social factors in changes in divorce rates.

Parent-child relationships

J. KLEIN, *Samples from English Cultures*, vol. 2, Routledge & Kegan Paul, 1965, especially pp. 475–526. A useful review of literature on this topic, with many ideas not assembled elsewhere.

D. G. McKINLEY, *Social Class and Family Life*, Free Press and Collier-Macmillan, 1964. A slightly different approach to the occupation/child-rearing link.

J. and E. NEWSON, *Four Years Old in an Urban Community*, Allen & Unwin, 1968, Penguin Books, 1970.

J. and E. NEWSON, *Patterns of Infant Care in an Urban Community*, Allen & Unwin, 1963, Penguin Books, 1965.
The Newsons' books are full of data, but weak on explanatory analysis.

L. I. PEARLIN and M. L. KOHN, 'Social class, occupation and parental values: a cross-national study', *American Sociological Review*, vol. 31, 1966, pp. 466–79. One of a number of papers where Kohn and associates produce empirical data on this topic.

Acknowledgements

Permission to reprint the Readings in this volume is acknowledged from the following sources:

Reading 1   Harvard University Press, Conrad M. Arensberg and Solon T. Kimball
Reading 2   Routledge & Kegan Paul Ltd and Free Press
Reading 3   Harper & Row Inc.
Reading 4   Routledge & Kegan Paul Ltd and Humanities Press Inc.
Reading 5   Routledge & Kegan Paul Ltd, Humanities Press Inc. and Josephine Klein
Reading 6   Cambridge University Press
Reading 7   National Council on Family Relations, Marvin B. Sussman and Lee G. Burchinal
Reading 8   McGraw-Hill Book Co.
Reading 9   Routledge & Kegan Paul Ltd and Humanities Press Inc.
Reading 10   Markham Publishing Co. and Bert N. Adams
Reading 11   Routledge & Kegan Paul Ltd, Humanities Press Inc. and Colin Bell
Reading 12   American Sociological Association and Eugene Litwak
Reading 13   University of North Carolina Press
Reading 14   American Sociological Association
Reading 15   National Council on Family Relations and Robert F. Winch
Reading 16   Plenum Publishing Co. Ltd and Elizabeth Bott
Reading 17   Plenum Publishing Co. Ltd
Reading 18   National Council on Family Relations
Reading 19   Free Press and Robert O. Blood, Jr
Reading 20   American Sociological Association, R. Rapoport and R. Rapoport
Reading 21   Harcourt Brace Jovanovich Inc. and W. J. Goode
Reading 22   University of Chicago Press and M. L. Kohn

Author Index

Subject Index

Marriage
and divorce, 44, 301
early, results of, 282, 313
rates, 44–5, 48
stability of, *see* Divorce
as transition, 32–3, 247, 259–60,
283, 285–94
Married
children, *see* Fathers, Mothers,
Parents
women, *see* Employment
Matchmaking, 32–7
Mate selection,
filtering process in, 205, 208, *see
also* Complementary needs,
Conjugal roles, Homogamy,
Kinship, Matchmaking,
Propinquity
Mothers
and children, 321–37
children's attitudes to, 66
and married daughters, 51, 66–9,
144–8, *see also* Parents

Neighbours
and conjugal roles, 220–22,
224–30, 238–46, 276–7
and family, 98, 149–53, 157–8,
160–62
see also Crises, Geographical
mobility
Networks *see* Social networks
Norms, 10–11, 12, 15, 87–8, 115,
121, 122, 127–9, 134–8, 182–4,
197–8, 225–9, 247–8, 259–61,
see also Divorce, Homogamy,
Socialization
Nuclear family
functions of, 56–61, 156–62, *see
also* Isolated nuclear family

Occupation
and child-rearing, 279, 330–32
and conjugal roles, 70–77, 216,
230–32, 240–41, 245, 263–70,
272–96
and divorce, 311–13
and homogamy, 179–84
and religion, 289–90, *see also*
Employment
Occupational system
and family structure, 51–6, 123–5,
149–50, 153–5, 306
and neighbourhoods, 149–53, 222,

see also Class, Employment,
Work
Orphans, 88

Parents
as information channels, 130
and married children
affect, 66–9, 110–11, 127, 131–3,
135–8, 143
assistance to, 51, 88–94, 97–8,
101–3, 107–9, 110, 143–8
contact, 39, 66–9, 97, 109–10,
120–21, 126–7, 129, 131–4
co-residence, 31, 50, 66–9, 82–6,
90–94, 120
as corporate economic unit, 36–9,
51, 79–80, 91, 120
gift/service exchange, 40–42,
97, 101–3, 107–9, 110, 113, 121,
126–7, 131–3
in rural Ireland, 31, 36–9, 94, *see
also* Fathers *and* Mothers
Personality
and conjugal roles, 222
and divorce, 308–9
in family structure, 10–11, 13,
57–61
in mate selection, 200–214
in status transitions, 282–96
Political system
and kinship, 123–4
Power, marital
in farm families, 21, 27–30, 41
and kinship, 139
in 'traditional working class',
67–9, 74–7
Poverty *see* Economic uncertainty
Primary groups *see* Friends, Kin,
Kinship, Neighbours, Nuclear
family
Propinquity
of kin, 68–9, 105, 121
in mate selection
and homogamy, 187–90
intervening opportunities, 193–4
inverse distance, 194–6
textbook treatment, 187–90

Religion
and divorce, 301, 315, 414
and homogamy, 165, 175–85
and occupational choice, 289–90
Remarriage, 39, 44–5, 88, 303

Role
  conflict, 256
  theory
    and complementary needs, 204–13
    and conjugal roles, 216, 247–57,
      272–96

Secondary relationships
  and divorce, 64–5
Separation, 301, 302, 303
Servants
  residence of, 81
Sex
  and complementary needs, 208–12
  and kinship, 66–9, 132–3, 144
  and task performance, 20–24,
    30–31, 70–77
Sexual
  morality, 8, 43
  relationships, 71, 77
Siblings
  affect, 127, 129, 131–3, 135–8
  aid exchange, 107–8, 121, 127,
    131–3
  contact, 109–10, 120–21, 127, 129,
    131–3
  co-residence, 51, 82–90
  as intermediaries, 145
  rivalry, 127
  in rural Ireland, 39–42
  and socialization, 59
Socialization
  and conjugal roles, 247, 259
  as family function, 7, 57–9
  in farm families, 22, 24–6, 30
  as neighbourhood function, 158
  and values, 321–37, see also Class
Social mobility
  and conjugal roles, 231, 265
  and homogamy, 179–84
  and kinship, 15–16, 100–101, 112,
    133–9, 142–8, 149–50

Social networks
  concept, 219–21, 227, 234–7
  factors affecting, 224–31, 239, see
    also Class, Conjugal roles,
    Geographical mobility
Social welfare
  organizations and family, 78–9,
    88–9, 90–94, 160–62
Sociology of family
  development of, 8–13
Spouse
  adjustment to, 247–57, 259–60,
    288, 293
  attitudes to, 66–8
  economic interdependence, 276
  in farm families, 20–24, 30–31
  and divorce, 65, 306, see also
    Conjugal roles
Status see Class, Kinship

Task performance
  age differentiation in, 20–21,
    24–30, 30–31
  conjugal
    allocation of, 249–50, 259–60
    in farm families, 20–24, 30–31
    and skill, 259–60, 269–71
    and time, 261, 263, 265–9
    in U.S.A., 52–6, 261–71, 335–6
    sexual differentiation in, 20–24,
      30–31, 259, 335–6
  by social network, 225
  see also Child-rearing,
    Socialization

Urbanization see Industrialization

Values see Norms

West room, 36
Widowhood
  and kinship, 37, 84–6, 89, 91
Work
  and family, 272–96, see also
    Employment and Occupation